The House in the Hollow

Allie Cresswell

Contents

Allie Cresswell

1

Yorkshire

November 1811

Our journey here, to this wild, rugged and faraway place took many days, travelling with unseemly speed in a closed, unmarked carriage and attended by strangers. We stopped only to change the blowing, sweat-lathered horses and take hurried sustenance at filthy wayside inns. Mother insisted we retain our veils, even while we ate. She is practiced in subterfuge, at concealing, beneath a façade of respectability, the deplorable truth.

The cold was bitter; no quantity of rugs or blankets could keep my limbs from trembling. To be sure, the weather was appalling. Sheets of rain like relentless curtains of ice-shards assaulted the carriage. It seeped in through the thickly-shrouded windows and ran down the interior, soaking the thin seat-cushion. But the incubus of shock and grief equalled the weather's onslaught. I could not still my body's shaking.

My mother, beside me on the seat, offered no word of comfort or of mitigation. She sat like a figure carved from stone, her eyes fixed on the opposite seat. She was as thickly swathed as I, in shawls and wraps, but she did not tremble. Her face, like her intention, her resolution, was iron. She will do this to spite me, and if, in doing it, she spites herself, she does not care.

At night, on the hard, malodorous mattresses we were forced to share, her body emanated no heat and I concluded she has no corporeal warmth, no blood in her veins, no heart to pump it. She is cold, cold, cold. In any case I cannot bear to touch her, or for her to touch me. I hate her.

What little I could see of the country—beyond the ordure-slicked stable yards of the inns—was grim and dour beyond expression. Nothing could be further from the bucolic pastures and gentle hills that surround Ecklington, where I have spent all my life, up to this violent and unexpected removal. The sky, as we travelled, was a charcoal shroud of laden cloud or a deluge of steely, remorseless rain. The days seemed hardly to get light at all. There were smudged hills, dark canvasses of moor, mean-streeted towns of mud and shadow. The people were grey and stooped and spoke a dialect of broken teeth and hacking expectoration.

Then we came here. From a landscape of wind-scoured heath that seemed to go on for eternity until it melded with the storm-torn sky, we plunged down what felt like a sheer ravine. Mother and I were thrown forwards. Her jewel-case, which she had stowed beneath the seat, slid from its place and hit the backs of my ankles with such velocity that I cried out. She gripped the edge of the opposite seat and threw me a look of withering contempt. Trees on either side scratched the sides of our carriage, like skeletal hands of clawing ghosts. I could hear the horses' hooves scrabbling to keep a purchase on the precipitous slope, their snorts of remonstrance and the answering yell of the coachman as he hauled on their lines. We lurched sharply one way and then the other, thrown against the carriage doors and against each other, jostled like flotsam on a flood. Then, mercifully, the slope levelled, we righted ourselves and the coach skidded to a halt.

The groom got down and opened the carriage door, but with difficulty; the wind would have snatched it from his hand. The door of a building so drear and ugly—all shadows and blackness and forbidding façades—opened and Mother hurried inside. I followed, the door closed and I heard the carriage pull away.

'Our luggage,' I called out, but hopelessly.

'It's all right miss,' said a voice that was familiar to me. 'They'll bring it in the back. It's more sheltered there.'

She carried a candle—the only illumination in the room—and held it aloft in such a way that it highlighted her features unnaturally. She was all bony brow and shadowed eyes and hollowed cheek. But I knew her.

'Annie?' I said in wonderment.

My pleasure at seeing her—a benign face from the kinder past, a friendly figure—was obliterated by my sense of disappointment; that she should be party to this obscene deception.

'Come upstairs,' she said. 'It's late. I have a room ready for you.'

2

Yorkshire

February 1812

We sit and wait, Mother and I, for the culmination of her spite. It will not be long now.

As dreadful as the events were that brought us to this place, and as tortuous as the journey was, at least they were—in a macabre, warped way—a preparation. This house, and the marooned, godless chasm of Yorkshire limestone where it sits, is a fitting finale for both.

We are as far removed from society—indeed, from civilisation—as hell is from heaven. We are as remote from anything life has ever exposed me to, from anything I have been prepared for, as the moon is from the earth. The house squats in a deep combe[i] of rock and impenetrable trees. The combe is gouged from a limitless swathe of moor, and beyond the moor I cannot see. It feels like a barren plateau beneath a disk of sky, a flat plain as the sailors of old believed the whole earth to be, with edges that crumbled down into fathomless space.

Mother and I might be the two last remaining creatures on earth. She sits on one side of the fireplace sewing something. I cannot tell what, and perhaps it has no form, no function other than as an activity for her hands. It is just a place for her eyes to look so that she does not have to look at me. I sit opposite her and stare at a book, for much the same reason. When we speak at all it is to discuss the weather, but our vocabulary for this is proving inadequate—it is cold, it is wet, it is windy—the ways of expressing the multiplicity of miserable elements are finite. Other than that we make polite enquiry; did we sleep well? Would we like tea? Will we eat mutton today? Then our discourse falters for there is nothing else we can possibly say—no subject on earth—that will not have us at one another's throats.

One day I broke the code and said to her, 'Mother, are you absolutely set on this course? Is this really what is going to happen?'

She lifted her eyes from her amorphous needlework and regarded me with a look of such coldness that it sent a chill to my bones. 'It is not my fault,' she said. 'You chose to disoblige me by your wilful behaviour, making matters worse by contriving schemes to delay the *only* resolution that would have served, didn't you?'

'You are very cruel,' was all I could reply.

I sat and stared into the fire, aware that my righteous anger looked like petulance but, in the end, unable to prevent myself from flinging out, 'And as to the contrivance of schemes, I had a good teacher in you.'

She put her head on one side and lifted one eyebrow, ignoring my jibe. 'This is the result of your own disobedience, Jocelyn,' she said with a shrug, 'and your flagrant disregard of what was due to me, and to your father.'

3

Robert Talbot was my step-father, but since I knew no other I always called him Father. His forebears had styled themselves privateers, though others called them pirates. Their assets, comprising a small flotilla of leaky ships crewed by ne'er-do-wells, had preyed on Spanish and Dutch vessels plying a trade between Europe and the Americas. By far the likeliest outcome of these endeavours was death, whether from cannon fire, drowning, or fever-induced delirium on a mosquito-infested island. I gather that several generations of Talbots had indeed succumbed to one or other of these fates before being able to multiply themselves to any significant degree. Fortunately, seeking a longer, more settled and more prolific existence, an enterprising descendant had regularised the business by allying it to the East India Company and by investing a large proportion of the family's ill-gotten gains into that concern. Thus, by the middle of the eighteenth century, the Talbots had become merchants in a respectable, and certainly a very successful way.

My father garnered what learning he could from school before being taken by his father to India when little more than a boy. There, despite being not much more than a child, he joined his older brothers and sundry Talbot cousins to fight under the flag of the East India Company, protecting Madras from the forces of Hyder Ali in the second Mysore war.[ii] Father and son survived the war itself and the hard-living and disease that followed, but the rest of their clan did not. One by one they fell, at the hands of cut-throats, maddened by fever, lost in swamps or putrid with infection. Undeterred, the two surviving men set about establishing and reinforcing their holdings in Bengal. My father used to speak of this at length. He was proud of what they achieved. He spoke of it particularly to my brother, even then feeding his enthusiasm for the business he would one day be required to take up.

The Talbots built warehouses in Madras to house goods ready to ship back to Europe and on to the Americas. They also engaged in trade with China; opium, in exchange for tea. Whatever came from the Indian continent in the holds of their ships found a ready market: silks, spices, dyes, fine cloth and intricately wrought artworks. The return voyages were fully laden with the necessaries of life for the small but growing ex-patriot community, and with passengers seeking to make or improve their fortunes on exotic shores.

I do not know if it was my father or my grandfather who decided that they should return to England. I know the Act of 1786 regulated the powers of the Company to such a degree that it was felt their former unhindered powers to generate wealth were at an end. Even so, I rather think my father came home against his inclination. In India he was respected, on equal standing with the other traders and merchants. In England he was nobody, lacking the rank, name or ancestry that were so important to one's place in society. Who can guess his thoughts and feelings as he watched the jostling quayside of India get smaller as he sailed away? It must have been like bidding goodbye to himself. His father succumbed to fever on the voyage home and was buried at sea. Robert Talbot stepped ashore in Liverpool as the sole remaining branch of his family tree.

He did not step ashore alone though. His father had taken the care of two Indian boys under his wing and it was now left to my father to provide the education and situation in English life that his father had promised them. The two lads—aged at that time perhaps twelve and fourteen—were undaunted by England. Its climate did not dismay them, the mud and noise and stench of the docks did not appal them. They brushed off the rude stares of passers-by and returned sneers with wide smiles, the whiteness of their teeth startling in the caramel brownness of their faces. They were enthusiastic about everything, interested, irrepressibly eager for all that life in England could offer them. Accordingly my father enrolled them in school as the Eagerly brothers. Onkar became Oscar and Vidur became Victor.

My father always looked much older than his years, his skin prematurely aged. He must have been bronzed by the sun. He had left England as a boy and endured the hardships of war and camp-living. He had assimilated much of the culture of India and of the British in India, which, being based on military control and mercantile activity, did not always replicate the niceties of manner and speech of native Englishmen. He spoke Bengali like a native. None of these things were calculated to ease his passage into society, yet he was very eager to effect that transition and, in his naivety, saw no impediment to it. He was wealthy; his licence to export saltpetre—a constituent of gunpowder—to His Majesty's army in the Americas had generated untold thousands in profit[iii].

My father's early experiences had made him into a bluff, self-reliant fellow with a more-than-usual degree of self-assurance. In the beginning he mistakenly believed that his genial nature and general air of confidence would break down the reserve of men with bluer blood and more renowned family trees than his. Alas, he had no notion of society's strict codes of precedent, no idea that a self-made man—no matter how charming or how rich—could not stand on equal terms with baronets and earls. His personal qualities could not compensate for his lack of education and his rough-and-ready manners. A good address, fine clothing and a beautifully liveried carriage did not, he found, the gentleman make.

He suffered a good many disappointments before this lesson was driven home. To his annoyance he was denied membership in various clubs; no existing member would agree to nominate him. Invitations to shoot, hunt or dance at country estates passed him by in spite of him making clear he was very ready to accept them. I am sure his very eagerness counted against him; gentlemen are not supposed to pester like puppies. They are supposed to be restrained, imperturbable. He hosted lavish dinners but found them patronised by rascals and hangers-on, and by women whose reputations debarred them from more respectable entertainments. These occasions became notorious and earned my father a name for loose living, and decreased still further the likelihood of him being welcomed into polite society.

At last he was taken in hand by an impecunious viscount. In return for ready cash to wager on horses and at cards, plentiful dinners, cases of claret and sundry other expenses, the young nobleman inducted Robert Talbot into the ways of a gentleman.

A rigorous period of personal reinvention followed as my father's demeanour, conversation and table manners all came under strict review. I want to imagine him railing against the idiocy of it all—the right fork, the napkin held just so, the bows and flourishes and the correctly tied stock—but I fear the truth was that he applied himself to it like a physician's leech. He was given books to read and sent to galleries to view art and sculpture, and tutored in the kind of opinion that was fashionable on such topics. He was taught to ride like a gentleman, to hunt, shoot and dance. He and the viscount travelled abroad, that Robert Talbot might reinvent himself in Rome, Florence and Paris. They toured cathedrals religiously, mused in galleries and lounged in piazzas. They sojourned in Baden-Baden, Vichy and Montecatini Terme until they were a-swill with their therapeutic waters. Once the viscount felt my father could pass muster in polite English society they returned home and applied themselves to the domestic tour; Derbyshire, the lakes and the south west counties—but not Yorkshire, interestingly. Little by little they permeated the outer membrane, that invisible but very real boundary that surrounds English society.

There was always a brooding tension in my father, a sense of discomfort and irritation like one gets, for example, when wearing shoes that are too small. He had a searing temper that sometimes blazed forth like an incendiary. I put it down to this: that he squashed himself into a mould that was too constricted for him and made himself into something that he utterly despised. As rich as he was, as elegantly as he lived, as successful as he was, in the end, at breaking down the barriers to even the highest echelons of society, the yoke of his humble beginnings always chafed his shoulders. The higher he rose the more it seemed to press down on him. His desire for gentility forced him to deny the man he really was. It made him into a hypocrite. I often heard him harangue men in private of whom, in public, he was flatteringly complimentary. He cultured the acquaintance of men he scorned.

Whilst behaving for all the world as a man of leisure—sauntering around town, sitting in coffee houses, riding his horse in the royal parks—he was in actuality much occupied with his business. He established an office in the city, bought and fitted out warehouses to receive his shipments and established a network of carriers to distribute his goods across the country. He needed ships, many more ships, and these were put under construction although with difficulty, because prickly relations between Britain and France meant His Majesty's Navy required the endeavours of every shipwright worth his salt. Papa's efforts compounded his success and yet it did not do to show any pride in it. This must have been a further source of irritation; a stone in the shoe that pinched. A real gentleman was nonchalant about his wealth; he took it for granted as something he had always had, like the nose on his face. To celebrate it was unthinkable. Almost as unthinkable as the idea of losing it, or of never having had it in the first place.

Discreetly then, uncelebrated, Robert Talbot's coffers overflowed.

At last, whether in respect of his efforts or his coffers, or the patronage of Lord Petrel, my father came to be tolerated by men with rolling acres and ancient family seats. They admitted him into their society, but cautiously. He felt their scrutiny as he wallowed near them in the baths and danced with their daughters at balls. Their wives watched him narrowly as he sipped his tea, waiting for the spill or slurp that would confirm their reservations; that he was no gentleman at all. Father carried doggedly on, swallowing his gall at being seated low at table, begrudgingly giving way to baronets with barely a penny to their names. Then, with his foot over the threshold, it was time to choose a wife.

My mother's family could trace its lineage back four hundred years. They were not ennobled but they were established; her father and his father before him and so on back to time immemorial had been country squires. They had a house in town and one in the country, parklands and woods and tenanted farms. Their second and third sons were rectors or captains in the militia; commendable, thoroughly respectable, gentleman-like occupations. Their daughters married well. But over the last hundred years or so the family's fortune had eroded. Taxes, too many sons for whom commissions or livings must be bought, unwise investments and general profligacy had brought them to a state of near penury. These were the circumstances of my mother's family when my father was introduced to them and it did not take great insight to recognise that the two parties could do each other a great deal of good.

The family had three unmarried daughters at home but my father's eye was caught by their oldest girl, Hester, who was a young widow. She had been married at a young age to a staid, studious gentleman much older than herself who had mercifully died, leaving her with me, a baby daughter. She had married for expediency once and it was to be supposed that she would do so again. Clearly, she understood her duty. My mother was elegant and accomplished if rather haughty. Not to put too fine a point on it, she was a snob; perhaps my father surmised that, of all the girls, she would equal his own desire for elevated status and pursue it tirelessly. Well, I can say that, for all the ways she failed him as a wife, in *that* way she fulfilled her purpose.

Father did not deceive himself that he was the man her people would ideally have chosen and I doubt they made many bones about it. No amount of embroidered waistcoats, no lace cuff, be it ever so frothy, no elegance of figure or erudition of speech could eradicate the fact that his family connections were of dubious—not to say infamous—repute. But he was wealthy, and their family estate was crumbling around their ears. They had other children for whom spouses and incomes must be secured. My father's wealth would undoubtedly ease their difficulties and this was a powerful inducement to consider him in a favourable light. Summoning every axiom of etiquette Lord Petrel had ever imparted, my father set about courting my mother, intimating meanwhile to her father that he required nothing by way of a dowry. In fact, he as good as spelt out, he was happy for the flow of money to be all the other way. It *would* flow, copiously, but he thought it a thoroughly good exchange for the hand of a lady of such personal attraction and familial credentials. It was a bargain, something my father was quite used to making. No doubt he found her charming. She was certainly beautiful. It was not a *hard* bargain as far as he was concerned.

For my mother though, it was a bitter pill, and the aftertaste of it soured her ever afterwards. To marry against ones inclination once might be thought sufficient. But no. She was called upon to sacrifice herself a second time. The chalice came to her and her lip curled in distaste at the contents. Despite rigorous schooling, her new husband was not then— and never would be—a *real* gentleman in the way her father and brothers were gentlemen. He had no breeding. He had no crest. He had no seat. Whatever the tutelage of Lord Petrel had achieved, however expensive my father's clothes or fine his horses, in her eyes these things could only ever be a veneer beneath which he was a hobbledehoy. She was critically conscious that her peers would look askance at her, not for marrying money, but for marrying beneath her. It was a disagreeable prospect, but necessary. Her family required it, and her daughter needed a home. Perhaps she reassured herself by acknowledging that my father was not brutish even if he was somewhat rough around the edges, and he seemed most eager to improve. He would no doubt be very grateful. If she were to confer on him the great honour of her hand and her family connexion she could expect him to be generous in return. Like him, she knew the marriage would be a bargain. Her pride would not allow her to recognise that she was essentially a beggar and could not therefore be a chooser. She thought far more of her great condescension in accepting his hand than of the considerable cost he would outlay to secure it.

In good faith of the considerable cost, my father bought a tumble down property called Ecklington Grange, located in Oxfordshire, half a day's ride from London. He had it demolished, and plans drawn up for a modern replacement in the Palladian style. My mother's taste and opinion were solicited down to the last detail of décor and furnishing.

They married, and my mother held her head up very high. Indeed, in the years to come, the more she felt the little snubs, the more conscious she was of whispers behind fans and patronising glances, the higher she held it.

In time she presented my father with an heir, my brother George.

All of this is what she means, I suppose, when she says that she has done her duty.

4

Yorkshire

March 1812

The day came, and the thing was delivered.

With what anguish and pain and terrible labour it was brought forth I will not relate; I have blanked it from my mind. I know that these old walls reverberated with screams. I should think the trees and rocks without shook with them, that they melded with the groan and creak of the moor itself and rose up to meet the cries of curlew and buzzard and the moan of the ceaseless wind above. If God heard however, he did not answer the importunate prayers they carried.

When it was done they brought the thing to me but I would not look at it. Now it is in the attic with a wet nurse. It cries, too, but not with the woe that brought it forth. Its little whimper is feeble, it scarcely moves the air.

The next day my mother left this house. I suppose she considers *her* duty done, and now leaves me to do what she conceives is mine.

5

Yorkshire

September 1812

Can this really be my fate? Can they really intend that I should be left here, in this remote, wind-blasted place, for ever, until I die? Am I never to return to Ecklington at all?

The summer has gone by—a summer of squelch and mizzle, of dull, wet, dripping green, of mould and ooze. I have waited, my ears tuned to the sounds of the basin, penetrating the silence that is not silent at all, but a cacophony. Water-rush is a constant, maddening trickle; day and night it never stops. Rain sops from trees; drip, drip, drip. It is torture. The canopy is full of frantic birds and the restless agitation of wind. Across the moor wind howls like wolves. Somewhere within all that I have tried to discern the rumble of wheels on the driveway that will herald a coach, my brother George or my father; rescue. Quite hopeless. Even had they come the bowl's orchestra would have drowned out the sound of them. It is like a gaoler, whistling tunelessly, adding to my penance from the other side of the bars.

This place is like an amphitheatre and every tiny sound is multiplied and amplified. One bird becomes twenty, twenty thousand, a flurry of feathers, sharp beaks and beady eyes. The croak and cackle of rooks—or crows, I do not know which they are—on the rooftops is raucous, gloating. They are laughing at me. Their noise is unbearable—a torture in itself.

To turn the screw on my anguish the child cries in the night—thin and feeble but at just that pitch which is like a hot needle in a sensitive tooth. It fills my head until I think my brain will burst. I am addled by conflicting feelings; every nerve strains towards her except that I fear if I lay hands on her I might shake her and not stop. Worse, I might love her, and then where would I be? How, then, would I keep the flame of my hatred alight? My fear lashes me to the mast of my resolve. At night I pull the covers over my head. Even there, the splash and gurgle of water down mossy runnels and between the rocks becomes the rush and roar of an ocean swell. I fear it will overwhelm me. The wind—that harrying, relentless, madness-making companion that I cannot escape—is strident, a demented clamour that jangles as much within my head as it does without. It blows me around the garden, torturing me out of shape, pulling my dress this way, my hair that, catching me up and tossing me back down again. I want to add my voice; to scream, and cry and bellow. I want to shake the earth into silence with the sound of my own insanity, but when I open my mouth it seems no sound will come out. Whatever little vibration I can produce is a mere hum, the smallest reverberation in the cataclysm of sound around me.

Suddenly it is dark, and I am lost.

Annie Orphan—housekeeper, and my sole attendant—puts her hands upon me and guides me back into the house from the darkness of the terrace where I have been standing, in a storm, screaming.

6

Yorkshire

January, 1813

I think I was ill, at the end of last year. I remember little about it except being seated in a chair by the fire, wrapped in a thick blanket. At times I fancied I was in a nightmare, the vividly real kind from which you cannot wake. And then on other occasions the reality was as bizarre, as phantasmagorical as dreams but without the relief that it would end. The weeks passed in a hybrid of sleep and wakefulness, a lustreless stupor.

I am always so cold. The cold is within my bones, I cannot get away from it.

As hot as Annie Orphan makes my tea, when I put the cup to my lips it is tepid and imparts no warmth to me. She puts warming pans in my bed before I get into it at night, and builds the fire up very high, so high that she will not leave me alone with it, but sits in the chair in case a coal should fall.

'It's not the room that's cold, nor the bed,' I try to explain. 'It is me.'

'You need to eat more,' she says. 'There is no flesh on your bones.'

I have no appetite. Everything tastes like ashes.

'You should see the child,' she urges.

'No. No,' I moan, and turn my head away from her. I cannot.

She makes no reply, but takes my hand and rubs it gently. Annie always smells nice; of herbs and flowers and soothing balm. We are both comparatively young women—neither of us yet thirty years of age—but she seems imbued with wisdom and maturity that are beyond me. Something of her healing seeps into me and, when I am able to, I turn again and meet her eyes. They are older now, and wiser, but a shadow of self-doubt remains, the reflection of the little orphan girl—no more than a scrap of skin and bone—who came to Ecklington.

Sometimes, in the night, I think I can hear her speaking, perhaps praying. Her voice is very troubled, verged by tears.

'My fault,' I make out, and, 'Oh! What have I done?'

In the morning, she is gone, and the words I thought I heard are melded into fragments of dreams.

7

Annie Orphan 1800

Annie and Sally Orphan were not related beyond whatever kinship is engendered by being born to mothers too wretched to care for them, and so given away. It just happened that they came together into the employment and patronage of Mrs Talbot, but their coming together, from the same place at the same time, connected them ever afterwards. They were at that time aged approximately eleven or twelve. An approximation was all that could be made; nobody, least of all the girls themselves, knew the precise when and where of their births, but anyone could surmise that they had been miserable occasions for all concerned. Their early years in the damp and drear compounds of the workhouse were scarcely more comfortable but their being taken notice of by Mrs Talbot, and chosen by her to take up service in her household, was a decided and unarguable opportunity if they could but prove themselves worthy of it.

The orphanage was one of Mrs Talbot's enthusiasms, like harp-playing and embroidery, none of which lasted long. She moved on from it to other worthy causes in the same way that the harp was supplanted by the spinet and embroidery by charcoal pencils. By that time however, Annie and Sally were established in the household, a lasting legacy of a brief if well-meant philanthropic fervour.

Both girls were set to work as scullery maids, the lowest order of household servant. If they did well they could hope to advance to duties in the household. If not, they would be relegated to the dairy or even the fields. Annie, the quieter of the two, was over-awed by the sheer size and magnificence of the Talbots' country house at first, and cowed by the other servants. She ran in terror from the wrath of the cook. The heat and shouting and clash of saucepans as the hour for dinner service drew near were, in her child's mind, an all-too vivid recreation of perdition. The raucous laughter of the other kitchen wenches made her cringe. She picked at her food, suspicious of its abundance and wholesomeness. She wept often; silently, in corners. As doleful as her accommodations in the orphanage had been, and as hard-handedly as the attendants there had treated her, she cried for them.

Sally, in contrast, adapted immediately to her new situation. From the moment she arrived at Ecklington Grange she seemed to assume a sort of right to be there. She flounced into the servants' hall more like a mistress than a maid, stretched her filthy bare feet out to the huge fire and helped herself to a slice of cake from the table, which had been spread for the servants' tea. Before the day was out she was on first name terms with the other maids and had got the measure of the other servants. She had her ears boxed for impersonating the limping gait of Mr Talbot's valet, a punishment that made her laugh uproariously, to his extreme annoyance.

That night, in their truckle bed beneath the eaves, while Annie cried into her pillow, Sally stretched herself out between the clean, coarse sheets, luxuriating in the new-scrubbed pinkness of her body and the glossiness of her fresh-washed hair.

'I don't know what you're blubbing for,' she said, giving Annie a poke.

'We've fallen on our feet here. I never seen such hams and cheeses as there is in the larder, and there's a boy bakes fresh bread every day. Fresh bread! Think of that!' She heaved a contented sigh. 'No more maggots.'

Annie continued to whimper, although more quietly.

'We might've been sent to the mill,' Sally observed. 'If we were boys we'd've been down the pit. This will be better than either. You don't know when you're well off, you don't.'

But Annie seemed unable to appreciate her good fortune. Every day was a trial spent by turns terrified, lost and lonely. The work was arduous, demanding strength she did not have, her stature being small and her frame puny. She was required to carry coals to keep the kitchen stove hot, and buckets of greasy water to the sluice. Floors had to be scrubbed; it was agony to kneel on the cold stone floors on her bony knees. She had her hands in water all day long, hot water that scalded and cold that made her fingers blue. Her skin cracked and bled. By the end of each day she was white and wilting, barely able to lift her spoon to her lips, a situation taken advantage of by Sally, who sat next to her at table and stole the food from her plate.

The house was large; the servants' quarters alone a bewildering labyrinth of corridors and antechambers. The house being newly built, the doors were all fresh painted in the same shade of green, the larder indistinguishable from the cold-store, the boot-room from the linen-room. Each was labelled in flowing script, but Annie could not read. She spent many hours wandering, looking for the laundry or the pantry, the stillroom or the sluice. One day she was sent for eggs from the poultry yard that lay on the far side of the kitchen garden. She took a wrong turn and ended up on the smoothly sloping lawns of the formal garden, in full sight of every window in the house. Naturally, her appearance there, where she had no right to be, where scullery maids were barely even acknowledged to exist, was an abomination. A gardener, hoeing the immaculately neat borders as unobtrusively as possible, gave her an appalled look before pointing urgently at a gap in the hedge. But before she could escape, a footman burst from a pair of French windows and bore down on her with shouts of such horrified indignation that she wished the ground would swallow her whole. She earned a reprimand for that misadventure and was sent to bed without her supper.

Mrs Butterwick, the housekeeper, who had herself endured an awkward interview with Mrs Talbot on the subject of keeping the maids out of sight, watched Annie scamper along the servants' corridor *away* from the stairs that would take her up to the attics and shook her head. Annie's first few weeks at Ecklington Grange did not augur well. Not for the first time, Mrs Butterwick considered sending her back to the orphanage.

Her inclination to send Sally back was even stronger. Sally treated life at the Grange as a sort of holiday; an opportunity to eat and drink and enjoy herself. She had soon explored every nook and cranny of the house and the estate buildings and made herself thoroughly mistress of them. She knew where the cat had stashed her kittens in the stables, where the autumn fruits were stored; her breath was sweet with apple and pear. She thought nothing of going to the dairy to sip cream from the churn. She found a sunny spot behind the smoke-house—where she had no business on earth to be—where she would sit smothering her laughter, as the yards rang with the cries of others, calling her name, running in panic hither and thither in case she had fallen into the midden or locked herself in the ice house. Her plump figure and glossy curls grew healthier with every passing week. Even as young as she was, she drew lascivious glances from the male servants. Mrs Butterwick shuddered to think what trouble would ensue once the child became a woman. But Sally was a bright, appealing girl who lightened the mood below stairs considerably—if sometimes inappropriately. Her burbling laugh could always be heard. The other servants liked her but despaired of her, often required to make good the deficiencies of her work. Sally could not be relied upon to get up on time, to have a starched apron or clean hands. Her hair could not be contained in any cap. Her face could not be taught to disguise the thoughts that teemed behind it—ribald, unseemly thoughts of mischief and disrespect. Woe betide anyone who caught her eye at these moments; she was infectious and her mischief got others in trouble. Annie often—unfairly—took the brunt because the two girls, although so different, were inextricably linked in the other servants' minds. When Sally was not in cook's reach for a cuff across the ear, Annie was often found to do quite as well.

Mrs Butterwick allowed her heart to soften a little, as, from the corner of her eye, she watched Annie creep *back* along the corridor towards the precipitous attic stairway. She sighed and softly closed the door of her private sitting room. She consulted the clock on the mantelpiece and poured herself a small glass of Madeira. She supposed Mrs Talbot's heart was in the right place. What hope would those two girls have had without her intervention? It was early days. Perhaps the two orphans would settle down in time. After the staff had supped she would send Sally upstairs with some bread and cold meat or a slice of pie for Annie. No, she would not send Sally. *She* would be sure to consume Annie's supper. Someone else would have to be sent.

8

Yorkshire

February 1813

We are enduring a hard winter. Very wet. There are many days together when I cannot go out at all. The rain is a biblical deluge, pouring from the skies, an inundation of judgement like Noah's flood. It is a wonder that the bowl does not fill, that water does not surge over the sills and drown us in punishment of our sins. The sky barely gets light. The cloud—low and lowering—is an iron lid on our soggy cauldron.

My thoughts and my moods are grim and bleak. Dark, like the days.

I wrote—again—to George, directing my letter care of the bankers for I know if I send it to Grosvenor Square or to Ecklington Grange Mama will intercept it. I can only think that he has returned to India. I pray he has not enlisted, although why I should have a care for him when he was so careless of me I do not know. I beg him to reply, to *explain*.

I know I should be more active. When I look in the mirror I do not like what I see. I am too thin, I think. My skin has not a good hue and although my hair has ever been fine and only a mousey shade of brown, it used to shine. Now it looks dull. I crave fresh air and exercise but to go out and get a soaking would be counter-productive to health. Sometimes, when the oppression of the house has been too much to endure, I have summoned the carriage and been driven out, up through the tunnel of driveway and out onto the moor. A grey ribbon of roadway leads into the village but I direct the carriage away from there, across the grassy tracks that criss-cross the moor. There is nothing at all to be seen, just a grey curtain of mizzle over the greyer tufts of heather, outcrops of rock and shadows of bog. The grass, beneath the wheels of the coach, oozes sepia water. The carriage seems claustrophobic and I do not stay out long. The coachman is soaked when we return from these ill-conceived outings, the water literally cascading off his greatcoat and dripping from his hat.

Mrs Foley, the vicar's wife, called today. I suppose it was kind of her. I know her from Oxfordshire—her papa was Rector of the parish that encompassed Ecklington—so we have been acquainted these many years, but we have never been friends. Her husband's taking the living here in Yorkshire—such an out-of-the-way place—seems to be more than a coincidence. Have they been sent to watch me and to send back reports to Mother? Or did Mrs Foley come from spite, to grind the axe she holds against me? It is hard to know. More charitably I suppose it is possible that they were sent to be a comfort, as familiar faces in this barren wilderness. If that is the case I fear I must report she is failing in her task. She brings no comfort. She perches in judgement—gathering her skirts lest they be contaminated, and retaining her gloves—her expression disapproving and vinegarish. She brings out her Bible and reads passages to me that are meant to convict me of my sin. She would have me in sackcloth and ashes.

We did not converse of Ecklington; that territory is too dangerous for us to tread. Instead I enquired after her cousin, who I knew as Lieutenant Willow but who is now promoted to Captain. She told me that he was in Portugal with Wellesley at the end of last year[iv], but more than that she could not say. She did not meet my eye when she spoke, and I knew she could say more, but chose not to.

I wonder if he is injured, or married, but I cannot ask her. No. She is the last person of whom I could make that enquiry.

As she left she offered to take our letters, which she usually does at the conclusion of these visits. It is kind of her, I suppose.

9

Yorkshire

March 1813

It is a year since my mother left me here, in exile. The chalice of my wrath against her is still very full. As to this house and my situation within it, I think perhaps I am beginning to see it with a kind of perspective.

I am punished, but not physically. I am imprisoned, but not by bars or chains. My being here is more insidious than literal captivity; typical of my mother. My punishment is so dignified, so *respectable*. What coercion brought me to it, what demonic covenant I was forced into is irrelevant in the world's inexorable blindness. I am put away. I am banished from the sight of society, that I do not offend the respectable eye. To that eye I am fallen so far that I have simply disappeared from view, cast so far into the wilderness that I am beyond the edge of oblivion. I am shamed, because I have offended morality. Quite simply, I am not fit to be seen.

How ironic, then, that here in my den of disgrace everything is so very dignified. My food is tastefully arranged on fine porcelain, served by a liveried footman named Burleigh. He is a magnificent specimen of a man—easily six and a half feet tall, his face beautiful, dark-skinned, as though sculpted from rosewood. He treats me with the utmost decorum, as though I am not fallen at all, but the highest born of ladies. He pours wine into a crystal glass and places burnished silver cutlery either side of my plate; soup spoon, fish knife, marrow scoop, fruit fork. He shakes out crisp napery that I may lay it on my lap, and fills a crystal finger bowl with warm water. Neither of us makes a sound. Not he, as he arranges dishes or lifts the covers. Not I as I cut and chew and swallow. The longcase clock ticks the minutes away with an air of shame for disturbing the silence we have so painstakingly wrought between us.

How comfortable is my punishment! I sleep on a well-stuffed mattress between laundered linen sheets. Mrs Orphan—I must call her so now, as she is housekeeper here, and housekeepers are always 'Mrs' although they never have husbands who are extant—brings me tea in the morning and lays out my clothes, as I have no maid, but I *have* clothes—I am by no means in rags. My chamber is well furnished; a curtained bed with heavy quilts, thick rugs on the oaken floor. I have an upholstered chair by the fire, a washstand, a press. The casement is draughty and the fire smokes but then they *all* do here.

I complained about it once. 'Oh Annie,' I cried out, as a cloud of acrid smoke billowed from the flue and carried smuts over my breakfast tray. 'This is intolerable. What can be done? *Something* must be done.'

She turned a mortified face to me. 'I'm sorry,' she said, tears springing into her eyes. 'I'm so sorry.' She lifted her apron up and bawled into it, broken-hearted, though it was but a silly little thing.

I felt ashamed afterwards. Mrs Orphan leaves nothing undone that might add to my comfort and it was wrong of me to blame her for the poor flues. I imagine she feels sorry for me. Perhaps, also, she feels remorse for her part in my mother's stratagem. She looks at me sometimes with such speaking eyes. On other occasions she will not meet my eye at all. What a profound soul she is, a repository for wisdom beyond her years or her experience. Whatever her fund of insight however, she keeps it to herself. I believe she is one of those people who speaks little but does much. Her character is expressed in her work. This room, in the old part of the house, is the one that she had prepared for me when I arrived. I can see, as I look about it, that great care has been taken in its furnishing and appointments. I did not appreciate it at the time. I did not even observe it. Now I am used to it and, even though the ones in the newer east wing are more spacious I have not chosen to remove myself from it. I like its situation: it is some distance from the attic stair.

I conjecture that the idea of my incarceration is that I will just go mad; that my mind will descend into bedlam. It is already dull. I am stupefied. I have lost the capacity for thought. I have no conversation, no stimulation. Day follows day.

Since there is no other stimulation I am beginning to know the house quite well. It is antiquated, but I suppose it cannot help that; the lintel over the door is dated 1620. I find it has been in the Talbot family since the beginning although my father never mentioned its existence that I can recall. I can't think why his ancestors might have chosen this spot to build unless—as now—they had something to hide. The original house was square, built solidly of the scar-stone that surrounds us, with little in the way of comfort. At some point before my arrival—but not, I think, in anticipation of it; there wouldn't have been time between my mother's conception of her vindictive plan and her execution of it—an east wing had been added, with attic accommodation above.

I believe the kitchen was improved but I have not been there. The downstairs rooms were clad with panelling and a grand oak staircase put in to replace the stone one that had stood there before. I am told that only a few days before I got here there was a consignment of furniture and books, paintings for the walls, window hangings. Annie Orphan had been sent from Ecklington to oversee it all so it was ready when we came.

I rise in the mornings, dress and eat breakfast. I order the dinner, walk in the grounds, read, drink tea. Occasionally I ride out with Burleigh as my escort. We plod over the moors in aimless exercise. In the evenings I sew or write in my journal. It is all so very *civilised*, here in my pit of ignominy!

This morning the bowl around the house was filled with mist. When Mrs Orphan opened the shutters the world outside was white and thick with moisture. I could not see the trees across the lawn. No breath of wind disturbed the veil and no birds sang. On days like this the house is eerie; everything is muffled. The fires are more reluctant than ever to draw. Smoke hovers above the grate in a ghostly billow, as though the mist outside is trying to invade, and the air smells acrid. The only solution is to open the casements in the hope of creating a draught, but then the upholstery gets damp and the wood panelling becomes bloomed with an odd, dull residue that has to be polished away with beeswax.

The morning mist cleared by midday. It didn't blow away but dissipated, saturating back into the grass and trees, sponging into the old stones of the house. When I walked on the terrace this afternoon the slabs were slick. Everything dripped. The moist chill penetrated my wrap and beaded my hair.

Now it is evening and rain hurls itself against the windows. I have a candle to illuminate my book. Today is my birthday. I am six and twenty.

10

Yorkshire

April 1813

There is a garden, and these last few days the weather has favoured us with warmth and very little rain. Believe me, this is not a frequent occurrence. The plants and shrubs in the garden have responded to this respite and I think perhaps that I have too, a little.

I am taking an interest. I am looking about me and since the only human creatures I can see are the servants, I am looking at them.

A man who lives in the gatehouse hoes the flower beds and trims the shrubs. The same man sees to the kitchen garden and the poultry and shoots game for the table. He is a tall, broad-set man, very well-muscled, but not much of a talker. He has eyes of the palest blue I have ever seen. His wife, Sally, is supposed to help with the laundry and the heavy work but she is lazy—she has always been lazy. Like Annie Orphan, I know her from before. It seems to me that whatever Sally does, Mrs Orphan must do over while Sally plays with her children—she has three—or dawdles around the rooms with a duster that is never used, or—and this is what she likes best—sits on the low garden wall swinging her legs and smiling, watching her husband as he works.

Mrs Orphan seems to enjoy the garden too, and is in it as soon as her many household duties are done. She busies herself in the kitchen garden and the orchard. I must say she is indefatigable in her efforts to make the place as efficient and productive as possible, to provide for my needs.

Burleigh, when not serving my meals, polishes the silver and brings in ladders to collect the dust and cobwebs that accumulate in the ceiling corners. He also drives the carriage and grooms the horses. I see him in his shirt sleeves, leading them to and fro, or polishing the tack, quite a different manner of man to the sentinel, silent attendant in the dining room.

The wet nurse walks about with the baby over her shoulder but she knows better than to do so anywhere near me.

Between them all there seems to be a pleasant, business-like relationship. I see no angst, no sense that they feel they are being punished for my troubles. Perhaps, for servants, it is different. I wonder if Mrs Orphan considers her position here as exile. Does she resent me for her embroilment in my predicament? I suppose she wishes she could have stayed at Ecklington. It is a great house, more comfortable than this. Being housekeeper there would be something to be proud of; this place is negligible in comparison. What has *she* done to deserve this? Or Burleigh? Or Sally? Well, as to Sally, I can guess. But she seems not to care. She carries her disgrace quite cheerfully, it seems to me.

How do they regard being the instruments of society's censure? Are they my gaolers? If I asked Burleigh to put the horses to and drive me to Ecklington, would he do it? *May* I leave, if I wish?

Do I wish?

Could I hold my head up and ignore the snubs, the pointing fingers, the whispers? I have no doubt that I am quite the scandal, the subject of gossip behind fans. It is certain that no respectable house would admit me. No family of quality would own acquaintance with me. Only here can I be sure of courtesy and care. Only here do they know the truth and so, perhaps, this is the best place for me to be.

This epiphany changes a great deal. My resentment abates. I watch the servants from the corner of a kinder, more appreciative eye as I sit near the fountain with a book or some embroidery. They are all profitably occupied with laundry, beating carpets, hoeing vegetables, husbanding the poultry and the pig. I envy their industry. When I eat the scones or the cake that comes with my tea, or the vegetables from my dinner plate, I wonder what it would be like to be able to produce such things. Of course I am a lady, or was brought up as one. I can speak French and stitch samplers. I can dance the Allemande and Cotillion without putting a foot out of place. But what use are those accomplishments to me here? I have no partners, no polite company, only these servants. In my abject isolation I have known myself to linger in the hall near the door that heads the stairs down to the kitchens. I like to catch their voices as they talk, to hear the clash of pans, the thud of the poker as they stoke the fire. Their voices are real and prosaic. I am drawn to them.

The first swallows have returned. Something about their exuberance, and their great feat of survival energises me in a way I have not experienced for some long while. I heard them in the eaves as I dressed this morning and could hardly wait to get breakfast done and my domestic duties despatched so I could go outside. The day was almost warm. I stepped off the terrace and onto the lawn. My boots were immediately wet with dew. I walked across the lawn leaving a silver trail in my wake. The daffodils are all spent now but masses of primroses carpet the shady area under the trees. Their scent is very sweet.

The swallows swooped overhead and I lifted my face to the circle of sky that is visible to me above the cove. Thin white clouds crossed the blue like clippers on a brisk day. The swallows skimmed the treetops and circled the bowl with their characteristic lift and drop, lift and drop, zigzagging, tumbling, performing acrobatics in the sky. It made me dizzy to watch them, with my head tilted back and my eyes narrowed against the sun. Their freedom and exhilaration were contagious. I strode out, past the fountain and up a little pathway that leads between the trees. The way is steep and soon I was too warm, but I climbed on, feeling energised because spring is with us.

I had the idea that I would test the walls of my captivity. *Is* it all in my mind? Or will I, in fact, step out from our bowl and find myself teetering on the precipice of the world?

I decided I would walk out along the moorland pathways unencumbered by Burleigh or the carriage. Those short-cropped tracks are easy to follow, quite safe. There would be curlews over the moor; how delightful to hear their ecstatic, lilting cry! The ground would glitter with rivulets and pools. It was possible that some of the ewes would have lambed. Seized with this idea I climbed in earnest up the winding path that twists between the trunks of old greenwood and newer coniferous trees. The ground beneath my feet was spongy with pine needles and moss. In the depths of the trees I could hear the chatter of blackbirds, a robin's trill, the coo of doves. At a distance, human voices—laughter, chanting, a game of some kind—told me that the wet nurse had brought the child outside, that Sally's children were playing in the gardens. I turned from the sound and continued on my way. The track is steep, occasionally crossed by little watercourses. I think the man from the gatehouse comes this way; it is well trodden, and comes out onto the drive just inside the gates, where the gatehouse sits, where he and Sally raise their brood.

I had just emerged at this point, breathing heavily, hot, with twigs caught in my shawl and one foot rather wet where I had mis-stepped over a stream, when I came upon Mrs Orphan. She had a basket over her arm. Clearly she had been to the gatehouse to deliver or collect something. But she had gone via the driveway; a longer route, but easier.

She seemed very startled by my appearance—alone—and, I suppose, by the clear light of intent she read in my eye. 'Ma'am,' she said, clutching her shawl to her throat.

'I am taking a walk,' I told her, stating the obvious.

'Indeed ma'am. It is a pleasant day,' she replied, looking about her.

'And you?' I enquired. I did not mean it as a challenge. I am mistress but it could be that my authority is what you might call titular—just a show.

'I have been to the gatehouse,' Mrs Orphan said. She lifted a white cloth from her basket to show me a dozen or so eggs nestling beneath. 'Sally has more pullets than she needs and two of our hens are broody. They will hatch these.'

'You should not delay,' I said. 'The eggs will cool.'

'Yes ma'am,' Mrs Orphan agreed, but she made no move to go on her way and we both remained, just inside the gates. I wondered if she would tell me that I must go back down to the house. If she did, I was resolved to refuse. Nominal or not, I am mistress. The moment stretched out between us. 'Where do you walk to, ma'am?' she asked at last.

'Oh,' I gestured vaguely at the gates. 'It is such a glorious day.'

She gave a little nod. 'You will call on Mrs Foley perhaps? Shall I send Mr Burleigh with the carriage to bring you home?'

'No.' I shook my head. 'I shall not go into the village. I shall walk on the moor.'

'Oh ma'am,' Mrs Orphan said with a frown, 'you should let me send Mr Burleigh to accompany you. Or I could...' she glanced down at her basket.

I hesitated. A walk with Mrs Orphan would be an excellent opportunity to see what she knew of my situation here, I thought; how it is explained at home, its likely duration. But then I recalled my purpose—to test, to defy. 'No,' I said again. 'You must get the eggs beneath the hens. In any case, I need no escort. I shall be quite all right. The path is smooth; I shall not turn my ankle. And the weather is fair. Go back to the house Mrs Orphan. I shall return in time for tea.'

I stepped past her then. What could she do? She could not physically restrain me. I left her standing in the shadow of the overhanging trees and passed between the gateposts and out onto the road. I found my legs were shaking and my heart beat very fast. I was powerfully reminded of the first occasion when I had defied authority. Mrs Orphan had witnessed that, too.

11

When Annie and Sally Orphan came to Ecklington Grange I was just fifteen years old. My adoption into the Talbot household and family was quite complete; I retained neither memory of nor any kind of tie with my paternal relations, if I had any. I had been excellently educated by my adoptive father, who employed governesses, singing teachers, art masters and instructors in deportment for my benefit and occupation. He provided every advantage that deep pockets and a sense of what was proper for a young lady of my station could procure. I accepted all he gave me but with more of compliance than of delight. I was by nature an obedient, reserved little girl and at that point in my life hardly knew what kind of woman I would grow into. I was then—and have continued to be, since—a sensitive soul. I feel things deeply and am critically aware of the feelings of others, conscious of the currents that flow beneath the surface of things but—as time has proved—not always understanding them.

I learned early to keep these qualities to myself. Whatever the thoughts and feelings that occupied my mind and heart, no clue of them should be read upon my face. I had to be careful. Tensions between my parents were such that an unguarded expression or careless word could be catastrophic. My father, as I have already described him, was abraded by the accident of birth that placed him on a lower rung than men who—in his view—had less merit. My mother felt herself constantly engaged in a battle to maintain a place in society; she took any little lapse my father or I might make as a personal slight. She was a stickler for propriety; she disliked emotional outbursts and fits of spleen.

Added to this delicate balance of sensibilities was the frequent presence in our home of Oscar and Victor Eagerly, who spent all their school vacations with us. Mother did not like them. Both were growing into fine young men. They were anglicised in their speech and manners and out-performed all their peers in their lessons but no amount of elocution or academic prowess could disguise their Indian appearance. Beside their English school friends they were startlingly dark-skinned, their hair jet black, their eyes dark and luxuriantly fringed with thick, black lashes. They were handsome, and I believe I had a girlish crush on both of them at one time or another, but they treated me with the utmost deference and did not presume upon the almost familial association that their connection with our family afforded. My father, indeed, welcomed them almost as brothers and saw no reason why they should not be introduced to his business and sporting associates. My mother had a different view. It was one thing, she said, to take pity on two orphan boys and give them a decent education and a start in some profession. It was quite another to present them as equals to our acquaintances; it set up expectations on both sides that could not possibly be met.

Lord Petrel, my father's particular friend, was a further cause for acrimony between my parents. He seemed to bring out the worst in both of them. When he was with us—which was very often—my father consumed an excess of wine and was urged to stay up late playing billiards for money which, incidentally, he usually lost. Lord Petrel encouraged my father to invite parties of gentlemen to Ecklington who were ribald and dissipated. This would drive my mother to distraction; she would be additionally spiky, especially alive to my father's shortcomings but obsequious to the viscount who, in her eyes, could do no wrong. I disliked Lord Petrel on this account—that he brought dissension and rancour to the house—but also on account of something malign about his presence. He seemed to me to be forbiddingly tall and broad. He exuded authority, speaking loudly and generally dominating any room he occupied. When I was a child I found these qualities daunting. I disliked it when he took particular notice of me—he would pinch my cheek and pull my hair, apparently thinking it great sport. As I grew older I added a distrust of his character to the scales of my enmity; I discerned him to be wily and lascivious.

Thankfully, I did not often encounter the viscount and was shielded by my governess from the worst of the mischiefs he wrought. I spent a good deal of time with her or alone. In London my parents had a large circle of acquaintance but at that time I rarely accompanied them to town so I did not encounter other girls of my age. Perhaps my parents thought to save me the kinds of snubs and slights they endured on a regular basis from noble and landed families of ancient lineage; the same cold, sneering behaviours that made my father chafe against the restraints of decorum and my mother intensify still further her icy hubris. In fact, what their protection created was a daughter who was shy and lacking in confidence. How could I know—having encountered no others—whether I was a pretty girl, an accomplished girl, a clever girl?

Then, I thought myself a tame, vapid creature of the type that is rarely moved to passion. I did not have fits of temper, never threw hysterics, never swooned. I wanted to be dutiful, to please my mama and papa in all things. I certainly saw the expediency of these things when he unleashed his temper or she a tirade of vitriol. Now I think that my nature was of a more complex type that had simply not been worked out. Like a barrel of gunpowder, I needed only the right spark to ignite me.

If there was a fissure in my smooth, imperturbable demeanour it was brought forth by my brother. George made his appearance a year subsequent to the marriage of my parents, when I was five years of age. I recall looking down on him in his cradle and something stirring within me. I neither cooed nor cried. I did not clap my hands. I knew that either of those responses would have earned me a reprimand. Something like, 'Do not be sentimental, Jocelyn. He is not a puppy or a doll.' I set myself to his care—discreetly, in a way that looked like a duty rather than a pleasure. Many a time, in the night, I would get out of bed and go into the nursery to ensure that he slept soundly and was adequately covered. I would make enough noise to waken the wet nurse set to watch over him, but not enough to wake the baby himself. As he grew—sturdy and strong in the mould of his papa—I would patiently entertain him. I did not fuss over him or fondle him, but I was vigilant. When, like all boys of good family, he was sent to school at eight years of age, I missed him.

When he came back from school he was no longer my George, although I loved him still. He was rumbustious, sneering of all things feminine, caring only for riding and sports, his head full of his friends and quite empty of any Latin declensions. I was jealous and heart-broken, but my sense of his betrayal *then* was nothing to what I would suffer later. I think now my heart never quite healed from the little wound he inflicted on me as a child so it was vulnerable to the much greater one he dealt me as an adult. They say, don't they, 'Once bitten, twice shy.' I cannot allow myself to be hurt that way again.

But on the day I am now recalling, the agony of soul that waited around the corner was unsuspected by me. It was Eastertime and, my governess having gone to visit her family, I was at liberty. I was in my brother's chambers ready to over-see the renewal of the bed linens and the polishing of the floor, since he was expected home for the Easter holidays. Since the previous autumn George had been attending Stonybeck, a new school, one more likely to make the declensions stick—and, with them, the French vocabulary, the algebra, the dates of the English Kings and Queens and all the other information that George often failed to retain in his memory. I had thought when he came home for Christmas that he was not as carefree as he had been. Stonybeck's regime seemed irksome to him. I feared he was unhappy and so wished to make his homecoming especially pleasant for him. There was no necessity at all for me to undertake this task but I wanted very much to do something that would contribute towards his comfort and sense of welcome. Probably I should not have yielded to my compulsion. I know my being there surprised Annie and Sally Orphan very much. They had been sent to undertake these tasks along with Mary-Jane, a parlour maid charged with their supervision. Other than her personal attendant, a lady never expected to encounter a maid other than by accident and all maids knew it was their duty to be silent and invisible, so they all stopped short in the doorway on discovering me present in the room. Their chatter ceased abruptly. Sally almost dropped the stack of freshly ironed sheets she carried and Annie's two pails clattered and clashed together alarmingly. They all bobbed what curtseys their encumbrances allowed, Mary-Jane's being merely the weight of responsibility for her two apprentices.

'Begging your pardon, miss,' Mary-Jane stammered into the shocked silence of the room. 'Mrs Butterwick left word we've to get the little master's room ready.'

'Quite so,' I said. 'I heard mama give her the direction this morning. I am pleased that you have brought clean sheets. Please continue.' I took a step back and indicated that they should carry on with the work in hand.

Sally, who I suspect had merely been given the sheets to carry, made so bold as to say, 'That's what I thought, miss. Nothing like a nice clean bed to get into, is there?' as though the idea of clean bed linen had been all her own. She pushed past Annie and Mary-Jane and placed the bundle of linen on a coffer. 'We'll strip off these ones and Annie shall carry them down to the laundry, when she's laid the fire.'

Mary-Jane's mouth flapped at Sally's audacity. I wanted to smile but kept my face very straight.

'Very good,' said I. 'I shall see to the arrangement of Master George's books and toys. I expect they are dusty.'

'Oh, but miss,' Mary-Jane put in, appalled at the idea that I should put my hand to such menial work, 'let us see to that. Sally! Fetch a duster at once, if you have not already got one in your apron pocket, which you *should* have.'

'I gave mine to Annie,' Sally retorted archly, and, I could tell, quite untruthfully.

Annie still held the heavy coal scuttle in one hand and a bucket of kindling in the other. She was very slight to the point of thinness—she still is very slender—and I wondered why, when Sally and Mary-Jane were both so much more robust, she had been given the heaviest work to do. Her work dress fell from her narrow shoulders to her ankle, unsculpted by bosom or hip. Her hair, what I could see of it from beneath her cap, was fine and lifeless. Her eyes seemed too big for her face, grey and dull with what I think now must have been shock or trauma or perhaps just lack of sleep. The skin of her face was very white, bloodless. I don't know how to describe it now and certainly, then, I was only partly aware of it, but something within me saw and understood Annie Orphan. Call it empathy or instinct or just common fellow-feeling, but I read in her demeanour all that she had suffered and suffered still.

She threw Mary-Jane a panicked look.

Mary-Jane, who clearly had no duster about her either, said, 'Go and *get* one, and quick about it.'

Sally crossed the room boldly and twitched the heavy curtains. 'Oh look,' she cried, quite as though casual conversation was allowed, 'you can see the woods from here.'

Annie put down her burdens and scurried off down the landing in the direction of the servants' stair.

Sally cast a weather eye over the window casement and yelled, 'And bring a pail of water back with you, Annie! These windows need cleaning.' Her voice reverberated around the room and echoed down the long corridor.

Mary-Jane was a stocky, lumpen girl, not at all well favoured. Her round face went vermillion at Sally's behaviour. She hissed, 'Sally! Keep your voice down! How many times have you been told?' She turned a despairing face to me. To save her blushes I had moved to the window and stood looking out over the gardens to the woods beyond. 'I'm so sorry, miss,' Mary-Jane said, mortified. 'Sally and Annie are only scullery maids. They didn't ought to have been sent, only Edna's had a tooth drawn and her face is swelled like a bladder, and Madge has got the ague.'

'Yes, I know about that,' I said, not turning my gaze from the gardens. From the corner of my eye I watched Sally begin to strip the sheets from the bed. I clasped my hands together firmly. I did not like her touching George's things.

'These look clean mind,' Sally said. 'Never been slept in, if you ask me.'

'Nobody *is* asking you,' Mary-Jane muttered, adding, 'Keep your opinions to yourself,' before saying more loudly, 'They are damp. We can't have Master George sleeping in damp sheets.'

'Mrs Brixie will have a fit if she's asked to wash sheets what's already clean,' Sally said. 'Why don't we just hang them by the fire for an hour or two?'

I saw Mary-Jane grab Sally's arm and dig her fingernails into it. 'Keep your mouth *shut,'* she mouthed. 'I'll finish the bed,' she said aloud. 'You sweep the floor before we polish it.'

'No point doing that until Annie's done the fire,' Sally declared, pulling her arm from Mary-Jane's grasp. 'Look what you've done to my arm! You've nearly drawn blood, you have!'

Just then Annie returned, carrying a duster and bucket of water. I was struck again how woebegone she looked in comparison to the others. In her haste the water had slopped up the side of the pail and her skirts were wet.

Mary-Jane, frustrated in her inability to exercise authority over Sally, turned on Annie instead. 'About time too,' she almost snarled, 'and look at the *state* of you! You shouldn't be above stairs looking like that.'

Annie hovered, unsure whether to stay or go, but at last placed the pail of water by the window and tentatively held out the duster to me. With a shriek, Mary-Jane snatched it from her. 'You hussy,' she cried, 'how *dare* you insult Miss Talbot!' She slapped Annie so hard across the cheek that the girl stumbled and almost fell into the fireplace.

I gasped, 'Mary-Jane!'

The maid went very red, and then suddenly, very white. She threw looks like daggers at Sally, who had her face buried in one of the pillows trying to stifle gales of laughter. Annie knelt on the hearthrug and began to sweep out the fire but her cheek was aflame from Mary-Jane's slap and she could not suppress the occasional snivel. I wanted to comfort her but of course that was out of the question.

It was obvious to me that my presence in the room was making matters more fraught than they would otherwise have been. 'I shall go and gather some flowers from the hot-house and return in a while,' I said. 'You do what Mrs Butterwick has directed and I will arrange Master George's things when you are done. Thank you Mary-Jane.' I picked my way across the floor, avoiding the tumbled sheets, the coal scuttle and the kindling bucket. But at the door I hesitated. I could only imagine what further punishment Mary-Jane might inflict, how Sally would allow Annie to do all the work. The unfairness of this galled me but, more than that, my urge to remove Annie from their spite was overwhelming. 'You. Annie, is it?' I said. The girl gave a stiff little nod. 'You come with me,' I said. 'You can carry my basket and secateurs.'

I made my way down the main staircase of the house, across the hall, through a drawing room and along a high-ceilinged gallery, coming at last into the glass conservatory. Annie, after some hesitation, scampered after me, keeping close behind, her eyes fixed on the floor and the hem of my skirts. Before we were halfway down the stairs I knew I had made a mistake. Scullery maids were not allowed in the principal areas of the house where they might encounter a member of the family or a house guest. Annie wore wet skirts and a soiled apron. She had a smudge of soot on one cheek, the other was livid from Mary-Jane's slap. But having taken her under my wing I would not abandon her. I set my shoulders back and lifted my chin, taking courage from the fact that I knew Mama and Papa were from home and Mrs Butterwick likewise. We passed two footmen. They wore disapproving expressions, but neither of them attempted to intervene. The butler, however, could not be expected to allow such an aberration to go unchallenged. He stepped forward to say, 'Begging your pardon miss. Is there something *I* can assist you with?'

'Oh, no thank you, Swale,' I replied, as haughtily as possible and raising my eyes to his.

Swale was a very august personage indeed, much to be feared by the likes of Annie and perhaps also a little by me. He gave a tight little cough that intimated the matter was by no means dealt with. Annie, no doubt quailing to think of what repercussions might follow, shrank even further into herself and cowered closer to me. Strangely, her fear increased my resolution. He made a second attempt. 'Perhaps Mrs Butterwick could assist you, miss? Annie has duties below stairs.'

'Annie is helping me with something,' I said in a voice that was quiet but very firm. And then, wishing to placate his ire, 'I shall not keep her very long.'

'Very good, miss,' Mr Swale replied, but in a tone that suggested it was not very good at all.

The conservatory stretched along a large proportion of the southern façade of the house. As soon as I brought her into it I realised that Annie would never have imagined, let alone seen, so many flowers. How could she? She was a workhouse girl. She stood blinking with wonder on the threshold, amazed at the intensity of the light, the enveloping warmth and the beauty all around her.

I indicated the basket and a pair of short-nosed scissors that I kept tucked behind a wicker sofa. 'You carry those,' I said. 'Let us see what lovely blooms we can find to welcome George home.' I wandered amongst the ranks of flowers, touching one and smelling another, apparently lost in my thoughts but really wishing to give Annie a moment to appreciate the beauties of the conservatory. It was very fine—easily the most impressive room at Ecklington—and one where I spent a good deal of my time. Annie stared in wonderment at the vast expanse of black and white tiled floor, the gleaming windows, the distant sparkle of water in a fountain further along the room.

Presently I said, 'You haven't been in here before? Your duties haven't brought you here?' The house was always clean—free of dust, the rooms aired, cushions shaken out—although I rarely saw a maid at work. I knew the footmen were responsible for the dining room, the silver and crystal, and also for the replenishment of candles. They I had seen, solemn, in white gloves, their eyes fixed on their tasks as they went about them. But the maids got up very early and did their work before my parents and I rose from our beds.

Clearly Annie was not one of those trusted—yet—to take care of the family possessions. She shook her head but couldn't bring herself to speak. Now I know that her duties would have been confined to the below-stairs regions. She would pound laundry, empty slops and scour pans, scrub vegetables and mop floors. I would discover—because I decided to interest myself in her—that since her misadventure on the lawn she had not been permitted to go to the poultry yard or the dairy. At that time though, she was unable or unwilling to tell me anything of her life at Ecklington. She remained silent but not with any sullenness of disposition. I think she was just too over-awed.

I waited for a few moments before saying, 'Come then. Bring the basket. Do you know how to operate the secateurs? They are like scissors, but stronger. Here. Let me show you.'

Very much to Annie's discomfort, I put the secateurs into her hand. It was small. Her fingers were thin and bony but I noticed that her nails were clean and not bitten. I guided her towards one of the blooms.

'We cut here, like this, close to the main stem. A straight, neat cut. We need a long stalk or the flowers won't look right in the vase. There. That's good. Now lay the flower in the basket. Master George likes bright colours. And these have a delightful scent, do they not?'

Annie nodded dumbly and we moved along the row, me pointing out which flowers I wanted and Annie snipping the stalks. I asked questions that required one word answers, affirmative or negative, and at last Annie managed to croak out the occasional 'Yes, miss,' and 'No, miss,' as appropriate.

Our meandering through the plants brought us to a small arbour surrounded by tall, frondulant greenery that hid us from view. It was no accident, either that we came to that place or that it existed. I had gradually moved pots and troughs to create a place that was private and screened. I liked to read there, or just admire the view, and enjoy my moment of privacy. I sat down on an elaborate iron seat and beckoned Annie to do likewise. She baulked and took a step backward, 'Oh no, miss,' she said. 'I didn't ought to.'

'You *oughtn't* to,' I corrected gently, 'but I am inviting you to join me and it would be rude of you to refuse. In any case, no one will find us here.'

'Mrs Butterwick …' Annie began.

'Oh yes, I know Swale will have sent for her. But I happen to know that she has gone to call upon Sir Diggory's housekeeper this morning, so Mrs Butterwick will not be found, and I do not think Swale will risk being countermanded again. Did you not think I was very brave, to stand up to him?' Indeed, I had astounded myself with my bravery.

Annie nodded. 'Very brave.'

I sat back and surveyed the scene before me—a wide expanse of closely cropped lawn leading down to an ornamental lake—while I considered Annie's situation and what I might do to help her. I could tell she was very unhappy; unhappy enough to be almost ill, I thought. She was so very pale, the skin beneath her eyes bruised with tiredness or tears or both. She was skeletally thin. If Mary-Jane had shown no compunction about cuffing her in front of *me,* what other, crueller treatment did she get when she was entirely unprotected? I had no doubt that physical punishments were common amongst the servant classes. They were not *un*common amongst what Annie would call the 'quality'. My mother had raised her hand to me on several occasions. I'd had a governess who was very quick with the cane. I could not protect Annie from what was, after all, normal life for those of her station. It was unthinkable that I could befriend her in any way that would not be awkward for both of us. But, I thought, perhaps I could encourage her to stand up for herself. I could not materially improve her situation but perhaps I could help her accustom herself to it.

'On the whole,' I observed when my considerations were concluded, 'I have determined that it is best to do what is expected of me. I cannot change my situation; I can only make of it the best I can. It does no good to cower or cry, for nothing is gained and much may be lost. Do you think you might follow my example? Who knows? We may make a success of what does not seem at first to be very auspicious, if we are diligent.'

I paused, while Annie weighed my words. It must have been very hard for Annie to make any sensible comparison between my situation and her own. What hardships did *I* have to bear, I suppose she wondered. What cuffs, what slaps, what jibes and sneers? She raised bewildered, questioning eyes to mine.

'But occasionally,' I went on, turning my eyes back to the panorama beyond the windows, 'I find I need to assert myself, just a little. I cannot allow myself to be bullied by Swale for, after all, I am the master's daughter and he is the butler. If I may presume to advise you, Annie, I would suggest that you make a stand likewise.'

Annie was clearly astonished to be encouraged to stand up to Mr Swale. 'Oh miss,' she stammered, 'I wouldn't dare to … Mr Swale, he is so very …'

'Oh do not misunderstand me,' I interrupted. 'You certainly should *not* set yourself against Swale, or Mrs Butterwick or any of your superiors. But you must not allow that girl Sally to use you as a scapegoat, or Mary-Jane to take out her angst on you.'

I suspect she only partly comprehended. In hindsight the words 'scapegoat' and 'angst' were ill-chosen. But I think she gathered the gist of my advice. She shook her head sadly and a tear slid down her cheek. Her feelings were quite clear: no, no. She did not think she could stand up for herself.

'Do not give up before you have even begun,' I said gently. I looked around me for inspiration and found it—a small seedling I had transplanted into its own pot the day before. 'Little by little you will grow, like that plant there.' I pointed to the green shoot. 'How daunting it must seem to that little seedling, to push its way through the black earth and into the light. How tall and forbidding must these other plants look! But they started just as he did. So long as he tries his best every day, and drinks his water and takes in the sun, he will flourish. One day he will be the equal of these.'

'Do you think so, miss?' Annie made bold to ask.

I allowed myself a small smile. 'There! You have taken your first step. Yes, I think so Annie. I believe in him and ... I believe in you.'

Across the lake, where Ecklington's carriageway emerged from an avenue of trees, a plume of dust announced the return of Mama in the carriage. I stood up. 'The maids must have finished in George's room by now. I will take the flowers up and arrange them. Good morning, Annie.'

'Good morning, miss,' said Annie.

I remember being very anxious that Annie should suffer no ill-treatment as a result of being singled out by me. Almost as soon as Mama returned and had removed her wrap and hat, I told her what had occurred in George's chamber.

'I do not think that girl from the workhouse is thriving,' I said. 'She seems very timid and I fear the others pick on her. If we are not careful we will find we need the services of the apothecary.'

The apothecary's wife was a member of the benevolent society that just then was the beneficiary of Mama's charitable endeavours. If the other ladies heard that a charity case at Ecklington had sickened it would reflect very poorly on Talbot patronage.

'Very well, I shall mention it to Mrs Butterwick,' Mama said. 'Now ring the bell for tea, Jocelyn. I have been to call upon Miss Brigstock. She is very dry company.'

Later, while Mama dressed for dinner, I carried the little plant up to the attic, where the servants were housed, and placed it in Annie's garret. I had never been in that part of the house before and was careful to choose a time when the servants would be busy elsewhere. The plainness of the décor and frugality of the furnishings shocked me, I must admit. Annie's room contained only a simple wooden bed that I guessed she shared with Sally. The mattress was thin, stuffed with straw, and the sheets were coarse, but clean enough. There was a deal[v] washstand and a little coffer for spare frocks and undergarments. A threadbare greyish towel hung on a hook behind the door. A small, grimy roof light was the only source of illumination. I doubted the plant would thrive. The room was probably ice cold in winter, stifling in summer, with no opening casement. I hoped it would at least try. I hoped Annie would do the same.

12

Yorkshire

April 1813 (continued)

Free of the house in the hollow and feeling an odd sense of triumph at having broken through whatever barrier had been designed to keep me within it, I walked for several hours on the moor. The day was very fine, bright and dry, with an energising wind that came across the upland bringing, as I had hoped, the tumultuous sounds of birds and new lambs and the buzz of bees amongst the heather, wild thyme and crowberry. Here and there, pushing through the peat-black soil, are outcrops of rock. I suppose it is the same as the rock of the hollow. I gathered my skirts around me and lowered myself onto one of these little crags. It was a silvery-grey, colonised by lichens and little clinging plants with tiny white flowers. For some reason the tenacity of these plants in the face of the inhospitable weather—sometimes parched and sometimes drenched and always buffeted by winds—moved me. I had been thinking of my first encounter with Annie Orphan as I walked. These little plants reminded me of her as she was then, a frightened child placed into a new situation, grappling for survival. The success of things she has made since that inauspicious beginning is all her own achievement. I do not claim any part of it. And yet, perhaps, I mused to myself, as the fresh, fragrant wind caught at my hair beneath my bonnet and snatched at the hem of my skirts, perhaps I did just a little to encourage and to help.

Presently I got up and continued on my way. The moor is a vast expanse—largely unnavigable—of black bogs and impenetrable undergrowth. Around its perimeter there is bracken. Just now it is fresh-emerging from the russet skeletons of last year but by summer it will be thigh-high. This gives way to huge, dense, woody swathes of small, tufted shrubs. It is almost impossible and in any case unsafe to walk there. The plants snatch at ankles and cling to clothing. Here and there are smooth, green, deceptive clearings but these are sucking swamps where the unwary sink up to their knees in stinking water. Lacing across, around and through the moor is the network of tracks I have already mentioned. They are used by carters and farmers and by those on foot to cross the heath. Sheep graze the tracks so the grass is short. There are no signposts. I suppose the local people know by long usage the route they must take from one place to another. But at one point there is a standing stone, very ancient and much weathered. It must at one time have been a milestone but whatever inscription was on it is long worn away. My drives and rides with Burleigh have brought me to it and I made for it today without much conscious thought. It is visible for miles in every direction for those who are keen-sighted but the wind today was brisk and made my eyes water and it was at such a distance at first that it appeared to me like a mirage—hazy and insubstantial, a dark smudge on the blur of moor and sky. I kept it in view as I walked, my mind occupied with the flowers and plants besides me and with my memories of little Annie Orphan and my life in Ecklington before my troubles came.

Perhaps half a mile from the stone I stopped to tie my boot-lace more securely and to find a handkerchief that I might dry my watering eyes. I looked about me. The grey stone wall that encircles the hollow where the house is hidden was lost from view. I could not see the low roofs of the village houses, or any smear of smoke that might come from one of their chimneys. The moor stretched out on every side, immense and barren. Here and there the sun glinted on water and I could see where rocky bluffs like the one I had sat on earlier thrust up through the green and greyish brown of the surrounding herbage.

It came to me that since my arrival here I have been floundering, wallowing, bemired in self-pity. I have been waiting for rescue or reprieve when, all the time, the key has been within my reach. What advice had I given Annie Orphan? *Physician, heal thyself* I thought. Accept what you cannot change and make the best of it. But do not allow yourself to be down-trodden.

But then I looked again at the endless tract of land that surrounded me. In every direction it stretched, unrelieved by church-spire or hovel, country house or farm. My eyes filled with water as I strained to see some end to it—to the moor itself or to my banishment. All of a sudden my little victory did seem very small indeed; small and pointless. The best? What 'best' can be made of this? There is only bleakness and exposure, the relentless wind and endless moorland and heartless arc of sky.

Oh how clever my judge and jury have been, to send me here! Exile indeed! In the face of the wilderness around me the house in the hollow seems almost like a refuge; the safest, most sheltering place to be.

I looked again towards the milestone. There seemed little point now in covering the last half mile. The sky, so blue earlier, had turned white and then grey. The wind was suddenly chill. I fixed my eyes on the stone again. It moved! It was black, or as close to black as made no difference from this distance, its native grey darkened by moss and lichen and damp, but something about its outline had seemed, just for a moment, to shift. I squinted and looked again. A trick of the light? My eyes watering once more? No, it was there again, a shimmer around the edges and from its shadow stepped a man.

The milestone is perhaps eight feet tall. In the winter, when the snow lies thick, six feet or more are still visible and I conjecture that anyone who is lost on the moor in a blizzard will be able to see it and make their way thither. Burleigh, who is tall, had seemed dwarfed by it. This man seemed a similar size in proportion and at first I thought it *was* Burleigh, sent in defiance of my orders to escort me home. But I saw no sign of horse or carriage and he could not have got to the stone without passing me first. I looked again. The stranger leaned on a stick, so it could not be Burleigh. He wore a greatcoat that reached well down below the tops of his boots and had a hat on his head, so I could make out nothing of his features, his hair or his dress. He could have been anything from twenty to fifty years of age. He did not seem to me to be of the farming class. And in any case, I reasoned, what farmer would have leisure to stand about on the moor? No, the stranger's clothing and stature were of a gentleman. This raised all kinds of questions in my mind. *Was* there, then, a gentleman's house in the vicinity? It could not be too far distant as the man, like me, was on foot. Was there a wife and daughters or a mother about the place with whom I could establish regular visits, musical evenings, the occasional dinner? My imagination took flight at the idea of genteel company. But then, if they were in the neighbourhood, why had they not already called upon me? There was no possible excuse for such tardiness unless they declined to know me. Ah! Of course. *That* was the explanation.

I felt suddenly very angry. I do not know what stopped me from marching across the turf to accuse the man of gross injustice. What did he know of me, or of my circumstances?

He had seen me. He stood facing squarely in my direction. Something about his stance, about the tilt of his head, about the way he seemed to stand very straight in spite of his dependence of his stick, suggested strongly to me that he was as surprised to see me as I was to see him. I was *not* known to him, then. He did not know of the disreputable single lady at the house in the hollow. Rumour had not reached him. Oh! A clean slate! My anger dissipated as quickly as it had come and I was joyous once more. I wanted to walk to meet him. Something made me quite certain that if I took a step in his direction, he would reciprocate. But I held back. We were not, after all, acquainted and the niceties of introduction were impossible. I could afford to do nothing that might endanger my reputation—laughable though such a notion might be.

I chastise myself now for hesitating. Why should I have allowed the contrived, artificial rules of society to hold me back? Who knows better than I that they are a veneer; mere lustre on metal that is base?

The wind had strengthened and just then a gust of it contrived to buffet my bonnet to such an extent that the strings untied and the thing was swept from my head. It bounced along the ground behind me and came to rest on a bilberry bush. I chased after it, snatched it up and tied it back in place. When I turned back towards the milestone, the gentleman had gone. My eyes swept the horizon. I could just make him out, walking quickly, with the aid of his stick, down one of the paths that led away from the stone in a direction tangential to mine. I ought perhaps to have felt reprieved; after all he could have been a rogue, a robber, a highwayman. But what I actually felt was grief and frustration so abject that the tears filling my eyes from the sting of the wind were augmented by an overflow of emotion.

I turned for home. The brightness and pleasure had gone from the day. The wind was at my back. It blew me back along the path almost like a scolding nanny and I was back at the gatehouse in a little less than an hour whereas the outward journey had taken me almost two. I was very weary when I came out of the tunnel of trees at the bottom of the drive and walked the last few yards across the gravel of the sweep to where Mrs Orphan was waiting for me beneath the portico.

I thought she would frown and chastise me but she only said, 'You have had a very long walk, ma'am. I will serve tea directly in the library. There is a fire lit. Let me take your shawl and bonnet.'

13

Yorkshire

June 1813

They have sent a nanny to replace the wet nurse. Their dispassionate efficiency appals me! Of course the child should be weaned. They know it and provide for it, in the same way that every three or four years they sent men to paint the window frames at Ecklington, or sweeps to see to the chimneys. I am just a matter of business to be dealt with, like a mad uncle or a dribbling, geriatric grandmother: I am their disobliging daughter who had to be shut away. I speculate that my family has no hand in it, that it is passed on to some lawyer to oversee. *They* will not sully their hands.

The nanny arrived on foot, coming down the steep incline of the driveway and emerging from the shadow of the trees like a malign witch in a children's fairy tale. She reminded me of the crows on the roof; black-clad, with a strange sheen of oiliness on her hair and small, acquisitive eyes. She stood before me in the drawing room where I received her, her small valise clutched in hands that are cracked and chapped from being scrubbed—probably with lye soap and boiling water. There is no softness about them, or anywhere about her. Her nose is sharp, her mouth a thin, straight and disapproving line. That she holds me in utter contempt she made absolutely plain. We eyed each other and it was all I could do to hold her gaze. They must pay her a great deal. I cannot imagine what else would induce her to look after a bastard child.

She barked out her requirements: wax candles, plentiful coals, her own accoutrements for the making of tea, an entirely free hand with her charge.

I agreed to it all and then Mrs Orphan showed her up to the attic. After a while the wet nurse descended, weeping.

Now the child cries and cries! The sound stabs me in my most vulnerable places. How much more, then, would the sight of her, the feel of her flesh, undo me?

The attic floor reverberates with the harsh, military tread of feet to and fro as the nanny arranges matters to her own convenience. She has had buckets of hot water sent up, roof-lights prised open that have been sealed shut. Now, while the weather is clement, that is all very well, but in the winter, when the wind peels the very slates from the roof, she will be sorry.

We have endured two days and nights of incessant crying. This morning Mrs Orphan turned to me as she laid out my clothes for the day.

'If you do not remove that woman from the house,' she said, 'I shall do it. She is cruel. Does your heart not break at the sound of the child's unhappiness?'

'Is it not always so?' I asked. I feigned disinterest but in fact I had found the sounds from above very distressing. They had all-but destroyed the protective wall I had erected around my heart.

'No, it is not always so,' Mrs Orphan almost snapped at me. 'Do you forget where I spent my infancy? *I* know what it is to be rejected by a mother, but even I was not treated with such callousness. '

Her words stung me to the quick. My eyes filled with tears. 'But *I* cannot …' I began.

'You could if you would,' she interrupted. I had never known her to be so severe with me. I would have remonstrated with her. How dare she? But I did not have to delve very deeply into my heart to know that she was right. 'If *you* cannot care for the child, *I* will do it,' she said, more softly, for she could tell that she had moved me.

'Below stairs?' I stammered out.

'Yes. We have enough of Sally's children around our ankles. One more will make no difference.'

'But what manner of child will she become?' I asked. 'How will she … what prospects will she have?' Even as I spoke the words their hypocrisy assaulted me. How could I ask such a question? If I would not raise her, teach her, own her, love her, who did I think was going to? How could I object if she grew up to be a kitchen maid, a cottar's wife, a humble seamstress, when I would offer her no alternative?

Mrs Orphan threw me a look loaded with meaning, and I did not need her to say aloud that it was late in the day for me to be asking these questions. 'She will be a child who is loved,' she mumbled, but quite intending me to hear her jibe.

We bundled the nanny from the house and into the carriage which Burleigh had waiting by the door. She left in protest, threatening dire consequences, spitting with rage, but she left. I do not know where Burleigh took her; it could not be far enough. He was away from the house for many hours.

Mrs Orphan took the child downstairs to the kitchen where Sally's children absorbed her into their throng. Her cot has been moved down from the attic and into one of the bedrooms in the east wing. Mrs Orphan takes her rest in the adjacent dressing room, and tends to the child when she wakes in the night.

There is no more crying.

Do not think I am deceived. I know what this means. The girl is nearer to me now and it is harder for me to pretend she does not exist. I struggle to keep the fire of my resentment alight, for she is a pretty thing with curly hair that reminds me of George's. My feelings do battle with each other.

Somewhere beneath the skirmish is a tiny kernel of triumph though—that we have countermanded their orders and foiled their scheme. By 'they' I mean my family: mother, father, brother; those who have chosen to hurl me to the dogs. By 'we' I mean the inmates here in the house. *They* sent that harridan but *we* would have none of her. The little suggestion of community this implies to me is delightful, like a warm wrap on a cool day—just exactly what I need.

14

Annie Orphan 1800

When Annie had been at the Grange for about a month she dried her eyes, squared her bony shoulders and applied herself to the task in hand. It was in part the confidence of Miss Talbot that gave her strength, although she did not encounter the young lady of the house again for a long time. She decided to carry on *as though* Miss Talbot were observing her, and to make her proud. She took courage from the little plant. Although transplanted from the balmy air and bright light of the conservatory to the chilly gloom of the attic, and from everything that had been familiar to it, it struggled upwards towards the grimy light that showed beyond the glass of the little skylight. How much more, she mused to herself, ought she to thrive when she had been shifted from the gloom to the light?

She made sure to be clean and tidy at all times; washing herself night and morning in cold water from the cistern it was one of her tasks to keep filled for the servants' ablutions. She kept her frock and apron clean, and tucked her hair into her cap so that it was neat. She schooled herself to keep her shoulders back and her head up, even when being chastised. When set a new task she did not shrink or allow her lip to tremble but set to, ready to get it wrong and to be reprimanded for making mistakes, but determined to learn from her errors and try again. When she had a few moments at liberty she did not spend them, as the other servants did, lounging at the refectory table in the servants' hall, or perched on the mounting block in the sunshine of the stable yard. She trod the passageways of the below-stairs regions, learning to recognise the scuff on the door that differentiated the pantry from the larder, the broken tile at the turn that would guide her to the sluice instead of the cellar. Slowly the long, uniform corridors and identical doorways ceased to befuddle her.

When Sally attempted to blame her for a broken dish she gathered up her courage and said, 'No, it slipped out of *your* hands Sally. Yours are all sudsy with soap, look. Mine are dry.' Her logic was unarguable, even to the cook, who could not always be relied upon to see things reasonably. Annie felt a strange thrill of pride in herself even though Sally managed to take her revenge afterwards by treading hard on her toe.

She did not know if it was the change in her own demeanour or the influence of Miss Talbot, but she sensed a change in the other servants. Cook was more ready to give proper direction as to her duties, which in turn meant that she made fewer mistakes. Mrs Butterwick took note when her hands were chapped and bleeding from scouring pans—as they often were—and gave her a pot of salve from the stillroom. Even Mr Swale told her she had 'worked hard' and been 'a good girl' after a particularly arduous day of scrubbing floors and hauling coals.

Sometimes she was spared scullery duty altogether and sent to learn simple mending from Miss Nugent, Mrs Talbot's maid. She proved adept at this; her fingers were nimble and her eyesight good. She showed a proper awe for the fine cambric and lace of Mrs Talbot's petticoats and the silk of her stockings although her own needle was confined to sheets and pillowcases. The sewing room was quiet, with windows on two sides so it was always light and often sunny. Everything in there was clean; the fresh-washed linen, the floor and worktable. It was a relief to come away from the perpetual grease and heat of the kitchen, the soot, the caked-on food residue and the mud.

Miss Nugent was in her mid-thirties. She had no personal beauty—her face was thin, her nose sharp and her chin pointed—but her eyes were kind and she had a soft voice. She liked to talk confidentially as she darned Mrs Talbot's stockings and sewed up rents in her petticoats but she was no gossip; her privileged situation demanded the utmost discretion. Nevertheless she dropped hints to Annie that helped her understand the little annoyances and rivalries amongst her fellow servants. Mary-Jane, for example, had only lately been promoted to parlour maid. 'Before you came she was in the scullery, like you,' Miss Nugent said. 'Amongst the parlour maids she is the lowest, but of course it gives her pleasure to assert her authority over you. If you show her just a little deference, I think it will satisfy her.' Edna and Madge, the other two parlour maids, were in competition for the eye of one of the grooms. 'Do not allow yourself to be used by either one of them,' Miss Nugent warned. 'They will have you running to the stables with *billets doux* and morsels they have purloined from the pantry. If you are caught *you* will be punished, not they. The joke of it is that the groom in question is doe-eyed over a girl in the village. Neither Edna nor Madge stand a chance with him.' The cook's bad temper was due in large part to her bunions, which pained her sorely. 'I will show you a jar in the stillroom that has salts infused with dried cat's claw and eucalyptus in it. If you dissolve some in a bowl of hot water and bring it to her after dinner, that she may soak her feet, I think Mrs Bray will look kindly upon you. I will show you the receipt, and for willow bark tea also.'

'I cannot read,' Annie said in a small voice.

'Can you not?' Miss Nugent seemed very interested in this, though not altogether surprised.

Annie shook her head. 'Sally has nearly all her letters and some numbers, I think.'

Miss Nugent nodded. 'It explains why you were always lost and she was not. All the rooms have numbers, or labels.'

'I saw they had writing, but I could make nothing of it. I have learned other ways to know one door from another.'

'You are to be commended for your ingenuity,' Miss Nugent said.

They sewed in silence for a while and then Miss Nugent said, 'To be a lady's maid is a very great thing indeed, Annie. Of all the levels of domestic service it is perhaps the most privileged, equal only to a gentleman's valet. A lady's maid has unprecedented access, you see. Very often, as I prepare Mrs Talbot for bed, Mr Talbot will be in his dressing room adjacent and the two will talk—oh!—quite unreservedly! I overhear such things! But naturally, my lips are sealed. When I attend to Mrs Talbot's most personal needs—washing her hair, bathing, arranging her toilette—we are quite alone. And it is not unusual for her to make enquiries as to matters below stairs. She has of late, for instance, been eager to hear news of *you*.'

'Of me?' Annie replied, startled.

'Yes indeed.'

But then Miss Nugent sealed her lips and said no more.

One quiet afternoon soon after this exchange Miss Nugent took Annie into the stillroom. It was a small chamber lined with shelves on which were arranged jars containing dried leaves, wizened roots and greyish-looking powders. Each jar was identical but labelled in a small, neat hand. Other shelves had bottles, similarly catalogued, with distillations of various types and many different colours, foul-smelling unguents and unidentifiable things suspended in viscous liquids. Bunches of herbs hung from a rack above their heads. On a work bench were spoons and scoops of different sizes, mixing bowls, a pestle and mortar and a sharp knife. Annie almost shrunk from it all. There was a strange atmosphere in the room. She sensed potency, almost sorcery.

'There is nothing to be afraid of,' Miss Nugent said, ushering her in and shutting the door. 'In time I hope to explain to you the uses of many of these remedies. When your courses begin …'

'My courses?'

Miss Nugent looked at her askance. 'No one has explained?'

Annie shook her head.

'Oh dear,' Miss Nugent said, almost to herself, 'we have more work to do than I thought.' To Annie she said, 'But you know where babies come from?'

'From sin and wickedness,' Annie parroted. It had been the mantra at the workhouse.

Miss Nugent stifled a smile. 'From a woman's body,' she said gently. 'They are put there by a man. If the two are not wed, there is sin, for *both,* although the woman in general pays the price of it. When a woman's body is ready to receive a child it shows her by regular bleeding. It lasts a few days and then goes away, to return every month until she is too old to receive children. Then it stops.'

'Why does she bleed?' Annie asked.

Miss Nugent considered for a moment. 'I think,' she said at last, 'that it is to remind a woman that to receive and bear a child will be like separating off a part of herself. Part of her essence will be lost to the man who impregnates her and also into the child that results. She will never be the same again. That is why she should not do it unless she is sanctified by the church.'

Annie's expression—awestruck and solemn—showed Miss Nugent that the child had comprehended the import of her words.

'It will come to you, Annie. It comes to us all,' the older woman said in a voice that was almost affectionate. 'But there is nothing to fear. I will show you what preparations to make. Sometimes there is a little pain.' She reached down one of the jars from the shelf and removed the seal. 'If you cannot read the designation, learn the smell and texture and the look of it.'

Annie peered over the lip. Small, woody shavings filled the jar. They were much like those she had seen in the cooperage workshop at the workhouse but smaller, finer, and with a pinkish hue. Miss Nugent held the jar out to her and she breathed in the aroma. 'Ideally you will know each remedy by smell alone,' Miss Nugent said. She used a spoon to measure out a small amount and wrapped it into a fine muslin square from a bag on a hook. 'Measure carefully. Too much can be harmful. Now tie the neck tightly with string, then infuse the bag in a pot of boiling water. Drink the tea and your cramps will ease. It will work on Mrs Bray's bunion pain also. Mrs Talbot finds it beneficial for the headache.' Miss Nugent put the jar back on the shelf but handed Annie the prepared infusion. 'Put this in your pocket. See where I have placed the jar, Annie—between the brown senna pods and the orange turmeric root? Now you will know where to find it.' She selected another jar. 'Here are the salts infused with cat's claw and eucalyptus. Cat's claw is a plant. We do not in actuality remove the claws from cats! Eucalyptus came originally from the Holy Land! Imagine that! Both these plants grow in the physic garden. That, too, I will show you in time.' She went on to show Annie how to make up a foot soak for the cook. 'Hot water, to dissolve the salts. But not too hot! You do not wish to scald Mrs Bray's feet! Oh dear me, no.'

Annie tried her new skills that very evening, carrying the bowl carefully to where Mrs Bray sat before the fire, her hair limp with sweat, steam and grease, her apron filthy, her shoes kicked off onto the hearthrug. Her face was a rictus of agony.

'Begging your pardon ma'am,' Annie faltered. 'Miss Nugent sends her compliments ma'am, and she showed me how to make …' She looked around her, suddenly aware that she might appear to be very precocious, afraid that she had overstepped, had undone what her diligence and hard work over the past weeks had achieved. Mary-Jane and Marg sat at the servants' table, both yawning and ready for bed, but their attention was caught by Annie's appearance.

'*Beggin' your pardon ma'am,*' Mary-Jane mimicked Annie's tremulous voice.

'What've you cooked up there, Annie Orphan?' Edna crowed. 'It smells 'orrible.'

Annie looked down at the cloudy water in the bowl. Odd shreds and particles floated on its surface. It looked like the thin soup she had been given for supper at the workhouse. It did smell very pungent, not wholly unpleasant but certainly not appetising.

'It isn't to drink or eat,' she tried to explain.

'Thank heavens for that,' Edna re-joined. She rubbed her eyes. 'It's making my eyes sting. What's in it?'

Sally had been in the scullery scrubbing the last of the saucepans but had watched Annie take water from the pot that continually simmered on the stove, and stir in the salts and herbs. Now she came to the door to see what would transpire.

'Been closeted with Miss Nugent in the stillroom, haven't you Annie? Cooking up potions. She's got something in a teapot back here, looks like piss.'

'It's willow bark,' Annie said. 'Miss Nugent said ...'

'Sounds like witchery,' Mary-Jane said. 'I knew a wise woman killed off a whole family of gypsies with something she brewed up in the woods. I wouldn't touch it if I was you Mrs Bray.'

Annie remained where she stood. The bowl was becoming very heavy in her arms.

Mr Talbot's valet, who was across the room crouched over a copy of *The Times* that had been finished with upstairs, said, 'What ignorance. Willow bark is well known for its pain relieving properties. Miss Nugent makes it for Mr and Mrs Talbot. If *she* has instructed the wench in the receipt, there can be no harm in it.'

Mrs Bray, who had not spoken up to now, said impatiently, 'What's in the bowl, girl?'

'It is for ...' Annie cast her eyes down to where the cook's feet were propped on the fender. Even through the thick woollen stockings she could see the bulging toe joints, the criss-crossed toes and fallen arches.

'I see,' said the cook, and she sat forward in her chair, 'And do you think,' she spat out, 'that I will be taking off my stockings *here*? Before *him?* She threw a look of contempt across the room at the valet.

'If you did, ma'am, I should take no notice,' said the man, not looking up from his newspaper.

'Oh but pray, don't,' Mary-Jane said tartly. 'The reek is bad enough already.'

'From the stuff in the bowl, or Mrs Bray's feet?' Edna said with a snort of laughter.

'You'll see the back of my hand for your cheek, my girl,' snarled the cook.

'I don't come under you no more,' Mary-Jane taunted. 'Anyway, it's time I went and made up the fires in the bedrooms.' She walked from the room with her nose in the air making sure, however, to keep well out of the cook's arm-reach.

The cook turned her attention back to Annie who stood uncertainly before her, still holding the bowl. 'You should have asked permission before you helped yourself to my bowl,' she grumbled. 'And using up hot water that'll be needed for the master and mistress, I suppose.'

'Yes, Mrs Bray,' Annie almost whimpered.

Sally, her work done, sauntered over to the settle that stood on the other side of the fire and lifted her frock to unroll her stockings. 'If you don't want it Mrs Bray, I'll have it,' she said. 'My feet's killing me.'

The valet, who had declared no interest in the contents of Mrs Bray's stockings, was not immune to the contents of Sally's. Indeed the girl had very shapely legs and was not at all shy in displaying them. The valet gave a strangled cough as Sally hoiked her dress and petticoat to her knees and reached beneath to fumble with the fastenings.

'Sally Orphan!' Mrs Bray cried, 'you're brazen! You'll come to no good, mark my words! Get your pattens back on and go and throw out the slop water. I *know* you haven't done it. And bring in some fresh water while you're at it to top up the pot. You,' she gestured to Annie, 'take that bowl into my bookroom.' She indicated the little antechamber where she kept her receipts and her books of accounts. Annie hurried before her to place the bowl on the floor before fetching a towel and the pot of willow bark tea. By the time she got back the cook had removed her stockings and had her feet in the bowl. 'Ooo,' she crooned, 'this is lovely. You're a good girl, Annie.'

Making up the foot-soak for cook became a regular task for Annie, and Mrs Bray's demeanour was much improved by it.

Sally's irritation and resentment only increased however. 'You can do no wrong, now,' she grumbled one night as they got ready for bed. 'What a joke, when at first you could do nothing right! What's got into you?'

Annie stripped down to her shift and dipped a rag into the basin of cold water she had brought into the room. She thought about Miss Talbot's words in the conservatory. 'I've just decided to make the best of it,' she said. She wiped her face and neck, under her arms and between her legs. She scrutinised the rag carefully after this last operation, as she had done every day, since her talk with Miss Nugent. 'Sally, do you know about courses?'

'Oh yes,' Sally said, through a yawn. She climbed into bed without washing herself. 'There was a spaniel on heat at the stables. The stable lad showed me. It was shut up because the boy dogs was fighting over it. Then he let one in and I watched … Johnny got himself all in a lather over it.'

'Is Johnny the boy-dog?'

'No! Oh you're such a ninny, Annie. Johnny's the stable lad. You should've seen his face! Like that plum sauce we made for the roast duck! And as for the rest of him ..! All swelled up something awful he was!'

Annie dried herself with a rough towel. 'So Johnny told you about the sin, and about the being wed that makes it all right, and about the piece of yourself that comes away?'

Sally waved an impatient arm. 'Not about all of that. He said when I start to bleed like the spaniel I should go and tell him, and he'll do the rest.'

Annie blew out the candle and climbed into bed beside Sally. Sally's breathing was deep and regular; she was almost asleep already. 'Sally,' Annie said into the darkness. 'I think you should talk to Miss Nugent about the courses. I don't think Johnny will explain things exactly right.'

But Sally did not reply.

15

July 1813

It is many weeks since I saw the man on the moor, but he has exercised my thoughts. Who can he have been? Where does he reside? I survey the congregation at church closely from beneath my veil. Once we are inside our closed pew I can see only Mr Foley at the pulpit and I can assure you he does not reward close scrutiny, balding as he is, with grizzled whiskers on flabby cheeks and a bulbous, purple nose.

I have made it my custom to arrive at the very last minute, as the bell tolls its last few clangs, so that the whole parish is collected in the pews as I make my way to ours. Similarly, once the final chord of the concluding hymn is sung, I grasp my prayer book and stand up. Mr Foley hardly has a chance to get to the doors before I am out of our pew and following him up the aisle. I let my eyes range over the other congregants, right and left. Do any of the other worshippers look like people of quality? Or like servants from a respectable house? But no. They look like farmers' wives and ploughmen and blacksmiths and dairymaids. They spill out of the church behind me and gather in little

74

clusters to greet each other and gossip by the lych-gate, but I climb quickly into my waiting carriage once I have assured myself that there is no one there who might answer the memory I have of the gentleman on the moor.

Mrs Foley has been absent for some weeks on 'family business'—that is all her husband would say when I made enquiry—so I have not had even the limited relief of her visits and have not been able to make enquiry about the stranger by the mile post. Of course I have not called at the parsonage, knowing her to be from home.

My utter lack of society has seemed very oppressive to me since I saw the stranger. He offered me, however briefly, the possibility of company and—I can scarcely comprehend it, much less express it—come sense of amity. He looked, not lost, not lonely but ... alone, as I am alone.

I have had Burleigh drive me many miles in the carriage along the grey road that circumnavigates the upland tract. We passed cottages and farms, a mill and a smithy but I saw no park gates, no lodge house, no wall or fence that might denote a private estate or any house of noteworthy size. I have ridden, with Burleigh, again and again as far as the milepost, but it has always been deserted.

I have made casual enquiry of Mrs Orphan. Is there, I wondered, another parish church that serves villages and farms across the moor? She shook her head and said she did not know. I remembered aloud how Mrs Butterwick, the housekeeper at Ecklington, used often to call upon Sir Diggory's housekeeper. 'Do you have acquaintance with other housekeepers in the vicinity?' I asked.

'No ma'am,' she replied.

She bobbed a curtsey and would have left me but I said, without raising my head, 'The child. She thrives?'

'Yes ma'am. She *walks*,' Mrs Orphan burst out with vicarious pride, as though walking was a skill given only to very superior beings.

I nodded. 'Thank you, Mrs Orphan,' I said.

The servants are kept very busy. The vegetable garden is productive with crops that must be pickled and preserved, dried and made into jam. There is pork to be smoked, or salted and brined and stored in the icehouse. Their distraction has made it easy for me to slip away. Not that I *do* slip, in any clandestine way; there seems to be no need for it. But it has pleased me not to give them notice of my intention and not to make explanation for my absence. It feels pleasing to gather to myself this little garment of autonomy.

I have used their preoccupation with domestic chores to make an exhaustive exploration of the woodland that surrounds the house. The territory is steep and in places quite perilous, with screes of stone, slippery, moss-covered boulders and fallen branches. One day I got caught up in some brambles and it took me an hour to extricate myself, the lace of my petticoats, my stockings and at one point my hair becoming impossibly ensnared. It really did occur to me that I might have to take off all my clothes in order to escape! I came home very scratched. My hands in particular were badly lacerated and became infected to the point that Mrs Orphan had to make up a salve. Thankfully she is skilled in the stillroom and had the correct herbs and roots to hand. She clucked like a hen as she cleaned the grazes and applied the remedy and then bound them up, but she did not ask me directly how I had injured myself and I offered no explanation. I am less and less inclined to believe that she and the others are here to watch me in any restrictive way. They seem to share, rather than to govern, my confinement. No, I do not feel watched, I feel watched over, which is different.

My misadventure meant that I have not been able to sew or write for some days as my fingers were swollen and wrapped in strips of linen while they healed. In compensation for my usual pastimes, and because it has seemed unwise to walk out again for the time being, I have lost myself in my memories. Now that my hands are well again, I set my recollections down.

16

Our nearest neighbour at Ecklington was Sir Diggory Binsley. Sir Diggory was a man of advanced years, or so it seemed to me then. He must have been close to fifty. I never saw him without a wig— thickly powdered but always askew, an elaborately embroidered waistcoat— usually stained with snuff or gravy, and a thick matting of dog hair on his breeches. He was a country gentleman who enjoyed country pursuits of all kinds; he hunted, shot and fished. As regards society I think he rarely went up to town in search of any. He only had to stay with him at Binsley House such company as would increase his enjoyment of his sport, preferably gentlemen who were single and single-minded in pursuit of fox, fish and fowl. Whatever their marital status they must be the kinds of gentlemen who were not over-particular as to the cleanliness of things, an orderly household or the niceties of domestic comfort. None of these things could be relied upon at Sir Diggory's residence, where the upholstery was a hundred years old, faded and threadbare, the air pungent with damp tweed and wet dog, the floors muddy and the ash in the fire-grates ten inches thick.

Sir Diggory had no wife but he did have a sister-in-law, the widow of his younger brother. She was a formidable woman with two daughters out[vi] and two sons at Oxford. She had been threatening for some time to make an extended visit at Binsley House, a prospect resisted by Sir Diggory with all his might, who—quite rightly—felt that such a sojourn would try his cordial relations with his relative and test the mettle of his hospitality, which was notoriously shambolic. But Mrs Binsley was not to be put off and in April some two years after my encounter with Annie, it was known that she had taken up residence. My mother and I called upon her without delay.

By this time I was seventeen years old and my governess had been dispensed with. My education was done and I had made that transition from girl to young lady. I was expected to entertain myself with the ladylike pursuits I had spent the past ten or eleven years fostering: drawing, music and needlework, reading, riding and pouring tea. I had yet to go to town however, and still existed in a social circle that was narrow in the extreme, confined to the grounds of Ecklington Grange, church on Sundays and whatever acquaintance my mother had in the neighbourhood. She liked me to join her when she made her calls and to receive those who called on us so I was not surprised to be taken to Binsley House when news of Mrs Binsley's arrival there came to us at Ecklington.

We were ushered very quickly through the hall but not so quickly that I was not able to note the generally down-at-heel nature of the place. Dog-rugs were strewn before the inglenook fire. A settle whose legs showed evidence of gnawing and scratching was pushed beneath a narrow window thick with grime. A suit of armour was so thickly draped around with spiders' webs that it looked as though the old knight within had taken up lace-making. We were shown into a small sitting room that was clean and tidy enough although its drapery left much to be desired.

Mrs Binsley was very dignified, making no sign that she would welcome any but the most formal acquaintance with us. The only flicker of interest she showed in us was when Mama mentioned our particular intimacy with Lord Petrel. *Then* Mrs Binsley's eyes lit up, but since the viscount was—unusually—not at Ecklington just then and could not be produced, the light soon dimmed.

Her daughters made no appearance, which disappointed me. On our departure I glanced down a gloomy passageway to see sconces dripping with tallow and an array of stags' heads and antlers, all very dusty indeed.

From the coolness of Mrs Binsley's reception, Mother anticipated the mandatory return call but no more.

'It's a pity for you,' she sighed in the carriage on our way back to Ecklington Grange. 'The elder boy will inherit Sir Diggory's title and estates; he would be an excellent match for you, Jocelyn, if the Binsleys would but consider it. However, I fear they will look higher.'

To say that I was very startled at this observation would be understating the fact. I was barely out of the schoolroom. I had given no consideration whatsoever to my future. Matrimony, so far as it related to me, had never entered my head.

'The younger boy might expect the living at Binsley if he were to take Orders,' my mother went on.

This surprised me also. The living at Binsley was currently held by the rector, Mr Willow, who had two daughters at home and two more away at school. It was understood however, that Oscar Eagerly, who had by this time been ordained and was his curate, would in due course be given the preferment. Mr Willow was a stiff and upright gentleman, rather long-suffering on account of his garrulous wife, but he had always been kind to me. Mr Eagerly was very gentle and unassuming. He never presumed upon Papa's patronage and was especially deferential towards Mama. I suppose he knew that she did not like him. He was active amongst the poor of the parish. At first I believe people had been rather startled by his exotic appearance but he had soon overcome this and was by this time very well regarded. He took the early services and read the lesson in a soft voice but with an earnest tone, as though he meant to communicate something very particular through it. There were many young gentlemen who took Orders without much in the way of vocation but Mr Eagerly was not one of them; no one could doubt the sincerity of his belief. My own conviction was that when the time came he would make a better rector than Mr Willow, but I did not like to think that either of them could be easily supplanted.

'Or the parliamentary seat if he were to prefer politics,' Mama went on, oblivious to my wonderment. 'Either way, he will be amply provided for. Mrs Binsley was very tight-lipped on the subject, was she not? But I gather he is closer to you in age.' She heaved a heavy sigh. 'But what is the use in speculating? The Binsleys will be too proud to allow the connexion; they will look higher than a merchant's daughter for their boys regardless of how wealthy she will be.'

I found my mother's reference to my father as 'a merchant' almost more shocking than all that had gone before. It revealed to me the true nature of her opinion of him.

It was a great surprise to my mother, therefore, to find an embossed invitation on her breakfast tray some two or three days later.

She sat on a chaise-longue in an envelope of sunshine that slanted in through her bedroom windows. She wore a voluminous white, lace-trimmed wrap and a heavily fringed silk shawl. Her hair, as yet undressed, fell onto her shoulders. She eyed the envelope on the tray but poured herself another cup of chocolate and took a bite of her toast, delaying the moment when she must reach forward to pick it up. Nugent, her maid, tidied the room and passed in and out of the dressing room assembling Mother's wardrobe for the day. I perched on a footstool and fondled the ears of a pug.

Mama seemed almost pleased with the world; not a condition very usual with her. I was not sure I trusted it. A small smile played around her lips as she ate her toast and surveyed the room. She looked at me with something like complacency, her eyes travelling from the arrangement of my hair to my gown. Whereas normally I would expect some remark—some criticism—about the state of my nails or my choice of garment, on that day there was none. I cast around me to identify the source of her contentment. I knew my father was in excellent spirits; war with France looked likely and he had redoubled his shipments of saltpetre to be ready to meet demand. However Mama took scant interest in Papa's business dealings, so I did not think it could be that. Later that day they were to travel up to town. Papa had business to attend to and Mama very much wished to visit her dress-maker. In the evening they were to dine with Lady Pembroke—quite a coup. *That* must be the reason, I concluded.

Mama said to Nugent, 'I shall wear the blue silk to Lady Pembroke's. Be sure to pack my sapphires.'

'Yes ma'am,' Nugent replied. 'The fur mantle, ma'am, or the velvet cape? The evenings are still chilly.'

Mama pondered. 'The fur,' she said at last.

She looked at the envelope again and then snatched it up and broke the seal. She glanced over the beautiful copperplate script.

'Oh!' she cried. 'We are invited to dine at Binsley tomorrow.' She scanned the script again, '"In celebration of the arrival of Mr Edward Binsley and Master Gabriel Binsley from Oxford," she read aloud. 'Well! I do not know whether to be surprised or relieved. Mrs Binsley must have wrought great changes in Sir Diggory's household. It is hardly fit to host a gypsy to dinner! Such shoddy housekeeping! But whatever alterations she has brought about, they will not concern us, thank heavens. *We* are to dine at Lady Pembroke's. We can plead a prior engagement and save ourselves the ordeal. Your father would not wish to dine at Binsley in any case; he cannot abide Sir Diggory's superior attitude. I apprehend Mrs Binsley is cut from the same cloth. I shall not lament a missed opportunity to be looked down upon.' She looked as though she was about to toss the card aside when I drew her attention to a postscript written on its reverse. 'Hmm,' she said when she had made herself mistress of its message—something I had already achieved, from my seat opposite to her. 'The pleasure of *your* company is particularly requested, Jocelyn,' she sniffed. 'There is to be music and the young people are "avid for dancing." What do you think of that?'

I had already had a few moments to assimilate the note and my feelings in response to it. It had been my custom since the departure of my governess to join the family for dinner when they entertained but I had never dined out before. On the whole, the prospect of dancing rather appealed. I *could* dance; I had been well schooled in it. An informal dance, as opposed to a ball, would be an ideal testing ground for my skills. I could not think who else in the neighbourhood might have been invited to Binsley. A set required a minimum of four couples and preferably more. The neighbourhood could not command superior company; the Binsleys were the best of us. The rector's daughters, I speculated, and Mr Eagerly perhaps, with his brother, who was staying with him just then. But, with me, that would make one too many.

My thoughts were interrupted by my mother. 'It is but a hypothetical question, Jocelyn. Of course you cannot attend. You have no chaperone.'

A soft tap on the door gave me the opportunity to overcome my disappointment. Nugent opened it and there was a whispered conference before she closed the door softly and announced, 'Ma'am, the rector's wife is below.'

'Good heavens!' my mother cried, looking at the elegant timepiece on the mantel. 'It is too early to be making calls! What *is* the woman about? Oh, but I suppose I must receive her. Jocelyn, *you* must entertain Mrs Willow while I get dressed.'

My mother descended to the small drawing room some three quarters of an hour later, too late to prevent Mrs Willow from breathlessly explaining to me the purpose of her call.

Mrs Willow was a pleasant, motherly woman, rather rotund and very loquacious. 'Oh!' she gasped, 'I met with Sir Diggory's housekeeper quite by chance on the lane. She told me about tomorrow evening's entertainment. Such goings on! You can imagine the mayhem! Some rooms, she told me, have not seen a duster for twenty years! Not but what I think that is a matter for shame, but let that go by, *I* shall not stand in judgement … I had not at that moment even seen our invitation, for the rector always peruses the post … But she told me it was certainly the case that we were invited and I hurried home to find that it was so. Maud and Caroline are wild with excitement. They are looking out their frocks and ribbons as we speak. Music and dancing! Oh! What more can any young lady wish for? Now the housekeeper intimated to me that you were to be one of the party, but when I said as much to the rector he said that your mama and papa were to be from home. 'Oh!' I said to myself, (and also to the rector, but he took no notice of me so I might as well have been speaking to myself), 'Let that not be the cause of Miss Jocelyn missing out, for the chance to dance is rare enough. She shall go along with our girls, and I shall take particular care of her. Let me make haste to the Grange at once.' And so here I am, my dear, although unconscionably early, I know. I am sure your mama is not dressed. I would not have been myself, only, you know, the rector does require us to gather for morning prayers, before he retires to his study with his coffee and newspaper for his private devotions, and so … But I did not wish your mama to have written to decline before knowing that I am entirely ready to stand in her stead. I hope that is not impertinent of me. I do not wish to presume. But, if you are willing to place yourself in my care, our carriage shall call for you at two and we shall all go together. Will that not be pleasant?'

By the time Mama had at last made her appearance I had accepted Mrs Willow's proposal, 'So long as Mama has no objection,' and all that remained was to pen the note to Binsley Park.

17

It seems to me now, looking back, that the dinner at Binsley House was the real beginning of my life. Up to that time I had been cloistered in the nursery with Nanny or in the schoolroom with my governess. My exercise had mainly kept me within the bounds of Ecklington Grange. I have not much recollection of where I resided before the Grange was rebuilt to Papa's exacting specifications and Mama's superlatively genteel pretentions. All my memories are of its impressive hall and comfortable rooms and its artworks—chosen mainly for tastefulness, but also just a little as a nod to the wealth that had purchased them. I recall very vividly its wide park and formal gardens. It is no wonder that the narrow combe of this hollow has felt so claustrophobic, at times. My life had been humdrum, the days passing in quiet occupation relieved by church on Sundays. But the dinner with the Binsley family in conjunction with my parents' absence shifted the ground beneath my feet. To be sure, the party broke up after a few weeks, but something remained afterwards. Something had been lit that could not be extinguished, and not just for me.

As I was dressed and submitted myself to the maid's ministrations with my hair and toilette, I was conscious of fluttering wings of nerves and, to calm myself, wondered what remedial works had been put in train at Binsley in order to prepare for the dinner. Once I had stepped into the rector's coach it did not take Mrs Willow long to regale me with the details. 'Oh my dear,' she began, almost before the door had been closed behind me and I had quite settled myself in the seat, 'I think I can say we are in for a very pleasant time of it. Sir Diggory's housekeeper has quite exhausted herself in her efforts, by all accounts. Such removal of furniture and polishing of floors as there has been at Binsley! I own I am wild with curiosity to see what changes have been wrought. I know for a fact that extra girls have been taken up from the village. One told me that she was sure the candelabra in the house have not seen a duster for fifty years! Sir Diggory is a very genteel man, but a decided bachelor, and set in his ways. The rector, who happened upon Sir Diggory in a copse, reports him to be thoroughly out of sorts, and regretting very much ever having yielded to Mrs Binsley's hints. There was enmity, you know, between Sir Diggory and his late brother, and so before his decease there was no question of the two families enjoying any kind of intercourse. But since that lamentable event I gather Mrs Binsley has been most pressing, for, of course, her elder son will inherit, unless Sir Diggory marries and begets himself an heir, which, I conjecture, is a remote possibility. Poor Sir Diggory will hardly know himself! The kitchen has been frenzied with broiling and roasting! Now Maud, do not look sour. It is but a short journey. I know you do not like to travel backwards but Miss Talbot must have your place.'

I offered to change places with Maud Willow but her mama would have none of it. Maud was the oldest of the rectory girls. She was tall, like her papa, and rather too thin to be comely, but by no means ugly. At the time I thought her rather dour and haughty but now I wonder if she was not shy, or of an anxious disposition. I put her vinegary demeanour on this occasion down to queasiness; it is never very agreeable to travel with one's back to the horses. I noticed that she had made considerable effort with her dress, which was pretty enough, and I made a point of saying so, but was rewarded only with a thin smile. Maud was two or three and twenty and no doubt thinking it was high time she was married. But to whom? Apart from Mr Eagerly there was no one in the vicinity who would suit, and since he had been in the parish some three of four years by this time without any attachment being formed between them, it seemed unlikely ever to occur. There was talk of her removing to the bishop's palace, to be companion to her grandmother and where she might attract the notice of some genteel clergyman. The other girl was Caroline. She had been home from school for about a year. She was more like her mama, plump and quite pretty, but rather silly, likely to shriek and giggle. Naturally I saw both girls at church, and when Mama and I returned Mrs Willow's calls Maud and Caroline were generally in attendance. Our similar ages and our geographical proximity might have dictated our friendship but it never had done. I had no friends.

'There are to be musicians,' Caroline took up her mother's stream of information. 'Maud and I have been practicing our dance steps in the drawing room. Maud has had to take the gentleman's part of course. Oh! Will it not be amusing if she cannot make the transition back to the lady's steps! She is sure to step on someone's toe for she is so clumsy.'

'*You* are too eager,' Maud objected. 'Always half a step in front. No wonder I tread on your feet.'

'Oh girls, do not squabble,' said Mrs Willow. 'Here are the park gates. We are almost there.'

We were travelling in the rector's carriage, a rather tatty conveyance with scuffed paintwork and very meagrely padded seats. The rector rode up ahead. He was accompanied by his nephew. I knew of this young man's existence—Mrs Willow spoke of him at length and with fulsome praise whenever the opportunity presented itself and, sometimes, when it did not—but had never met him. He was Lieutenant Barnaby Willow, on furlough from his regiment while it rested and re-equipped itself at its barracks in the midlands. He had met me on the steps of Ecklington with a broad, dazzling smile, and handed me into the carriage with deliberately preposterous gallantry. His clownishness had instantly quashed my nervousness at dining out for the first time, alone. As far as I had been able to gather in that very brief moment he had the tallness of the rector but not the stiffness. His hair was corn coloured and curly, his face very pleasant. He had bowed very low over my hand, and swept off his hat, and his blue eyes had been merry. Now, as we turned between the gates of Binsley House he sat sentinel astride his horse, and saluted in a half heroic, half mocking way, his eyebrows waggling comically as we passed. I could not help laughing.

'My nephew Barnaby is a great favourite with Caroline,' Mrs Willow said with a speaking look in her eye.

'Oh! Mama!' Caroline protested, but blushing.

'He is four years her senior,' Maud remarked, as if this were an insuperable impediment, 'and will soon take ship to France if the news reports are to be believed.'

Caroline's face fell, and she interested herself minutely in a flounce on her dress that did not sit quite as she wished.

'Mr Eagerly would be a better prospect,' Maud said, more gently. 'He will not go to war.'

'He is older than Barney,' Caroline pouted, 'and ...' she had the grace to look ashamed by the nature of her other objection, but spoke it anyway, 'he is Indian. I am sure he will prefer an Indian lady. In any case, he has never given me the slightest cause to think ...'

'Neither has Barnaby, has he?' Maud returned quickly, 'but since he carried you home that time when you had turned your ankle, he has been your idol. He cannot have been older than thirteen then, for you were not more than eight.'

'Girls,' their mama interrupted. 'These speculations are inappropriate. What would your papa say if he heard you? Look! We approach the door. Make yourselves ready to descend.'

Binsley Park was a squat grey mansion, very old indeed, swathed in creeper and surrounded by parkland kept more for the benefit of ruminants and game than the occupant of the house. There was a garden but it was unadorned by fountain, *parterre*, shrubbery or statuary. When I had called previously the grass had been uncut, more of a meadow than a lawn, but much work had been done in the interim. The grass was now trim, such flower beds as there were had been hoed, and urns of spring bulbs had been placed on the low stone wall that separated the garden from the gravelled drive.

We were met, not by Sir Diggory, but by his nieces and nephews. The introductions were effected on the broad step. There was much clamour of conversation; the usual enquiries after health, rather superfluous questions as to our journey and, on the part of Mr Edward Binsley, much repetition of our names, for as soon as he seemed to understand that Maud was not Caroline and I was not Maud, he seemed to forget again.

'Upon my word,' he said at last, 'such a host of pleasant young ladies! How can a fellow tell one from another when all are so dashed pretty?'

Caroline Willow tittered. Maud almost blushed. I felt a vague disappointment that he had not the presence of mind, let alone the good manners, to remember three ladies' names.

'Do not overpower them with your flattery, Edward,' Miss Catherine Binsley admonished.

All Sir Diggory's nieces and nephews were well-favoured, which surprised me, as Sir Diggory himself had no elegance of feature whatsoever. Apart from Mr Edward Binsley's inability to get our names right their manners were unexceptionable and their dress stylish. All in all a more pleasant family it would be hard to imagine. Mr Edward Binsley was of average height but well-proportioned, with dark hair tied neatly into a stock, dark brows and brown eyes. I estimated his age to be three or four and twenty; I think he was due to take his degree the following term. In the absence of Sir Diggory he took upon himself the role of host, speaking loudly, issuing instructions to the servants—'You there, take the rector's horse, why don't you?'—that they perhaps did not need. As he led us through the hall and down the passageway I had seen previously—wax candles now burning brightly in the burnished sconces, all trace of dirt removed from the startled stags—he spoke quite as though the place were already in his possession.

'Dinner will be served directly, only we want four more guests as yet. I hope you are not cold, ladies. We have lit the fire in the great room. If you are not quite warm I shall call for more coals. When the dancing begins however, I think we will have warm work, will we not?' I had not been many minutes in his company before I began to find his manner somewhat disagreeable. He was much too sure of himself, with an arrogance that, in a young man, sits ill. He called for refreshments, which arrived promptly on a silver tray. But no sooner had they arrived than they were sent away again and something else commanded in their stead. Mr Edward Binsley appeared to wish to give the servants trouble just to demonstrate that he could.

I wondered where Sir Diggory might be. It seemed presumptuous of his nephew to assume so completely the mantle of *patron* when his uncle was, I presumed, somewhere about the house.

Mr Gabriel was fairer than his brother, still a somewhat youthful iteration of the man he would become. He had a suggestion of fuzz upon his cheeks that he perhaps hoped would be taken for whiskers. I guessed his age to be not more than nineteen. I liked him better than his brother however. He had more of an air of genuine interest in the family from the rectory and in me, taking trouble to speak to each of us. He was more quietly spoken and unassuming. I had an inkling that he was of a sensitive, artistic bent. He interested Maud and Mrs Willow with the view from the long windows. Did they not think that avenue of trees very fine? What was their opinion as to follies? Were they not of his opinion, that a folly on that hilltop would draw the eye most excellently? Would it not make the most perfect subject for a landscape painting? Did they draw at all? Or paint? I was surprised to hear Maud Willow murmur that she *did* draw, and that yes, the view from the long window presented an interesting perspective.

The two Miss Binsleys were very like each other in looks, with dark hair like their elder brother's, fine almond-shaped eyes and noses in the

Grecian style. They were neither tall nor short, not slim or plump but of that pleasing proportion of figure that is generally thought just right. Perhaps Miss Catherine Binsley had more beauty of countenance while her sister had more of prettiness. Miss Binsley certainly had a superior manner—she knew her worth—but I warmed to the character of Miss Elinor, who was friendly towards me and showed her inclination to be intimate from the start. She led me to a sofa and invited me to sit beside her. I speculated that the sofa had been brought down from some disused room in the house, dusted off and covered over with a fringed shawl that its balder places might not be so apparent.

'You can have no notion of how pleased I am to meet you,' she began. 'I was sorry not to see you the other day when you called. I *would* have seen you but Mama is so insistent that Catherine and I practise our music in the mornings. Not but what that has been rather trying here, for the pianoforte was all out of tune and some notes would not sound at all. When we looked under the lid we found a family of mice had eaten half the hammers. Sir Diggory has had to send to London to have a repairer come. Do *you* play Miss Talbot?'

I said I did play a little, which is what I had been taught was the correct response to this enquiry.

Still there was no sign of Sir Diggory. I wondered aloud to Miss Elinor where he might be.

'Oh, he will be about the place somewhere. He has been out since breakfast but I suppose he is back by now for Mama was very strict about the dressing bell being rung in good time. Perhaps he is busy getting into his finery, if he has any. Oh lord! I imagine it will be full of moth! Nearly everything is, here. The bed hangings in my room literally disintegrated when I pulled them. Catherine says there are rats behind the wainscot.'

I ventured to say I doubted this, as Sir Diggory's dogs would surely be a deterrent to an infestation of rats.

'They are a deterrent to everything,' Miss Elinor declared. 'An undisturbed dinner, for one thing. They sit beneath the table and whine if you do not pass them morsels from your plate. Gabriel found one doing something unspeakable to his riding boot. They are quite incorrigible. Mama wants them banished from the house but Sir Diggory will have none of it. How do you think Mama looks? Is she not a very elegant woman, for her age? Now she is out of her weeds I think she looks quite charming. Lord Rossendale called on us twice when we were in town. It would not surprise me at all if Mama did not marry again.'

I wondered—but did not ask—how Miss Elinor would feel about such a great change.

Mrs Binsley sat in a large armchair by the fire. She certainly was a nice-looking woman, with a fine complexion and a good figure. Her *hauteur* from the other day had softened rather, I thought. She regarded us all complacently. I suppose there can be nothing more pleasing to a woman who is a mother than to see her children happy, all their requirements met, delightfully engaged in pleasant company with the prospect of a good dinner, music and dancing before them.

Miss Elinor was speaking to me again and now we had been joined by Mr Edward Binsley. 'The dullness of the country has quite appalled us,' she said. 'We wished to meet people. We had no notion the country would be so sedentary. I said to Sir Diggory, "Sir, are there really no balls, no Assemblies, no theatricals to be had?"'

'I was hoping for sport,' Mr Edward Binsley drawled. 'But my uncle says the season is quite finished except for deer, and there are none in this county.'

I had heard my father and Lord Petrel on this topic so felt able to murmur, 'In the north, sir, Scotland and the uplands of Derbyshire, I believe there is good deer-stalking.'

'Quite,' Edward said, looking down his nose at me.

'Uncle offered you fishing tackle Edward,' his sister pointed out.

'Oh yes,' he replied, 'but I have not the patience for it.'

'We hope to ride,' Elinor went on. 'Do *you* ride? I wonder if you have a gentle little mare that would do for me. Uncle says he has only his hunters here, all too feisty to be trusted to any rider but himself. He has no horses suitable for ladies.'

'Let them be sent for then,' cried Mrs Binsley from her place across the room. She turned to the rector, who had until that moment been examining a display of medieval weaponry in a glass-fronted case. 'Young people must be entertained, you know Rector, or they get into mischief. We must have excursions! There must be beauty spots hereabouts? There is nothing like exploring to keep young people entertained.'

'Well,' the rector said doubtfully, 'there is a tumbledown abbey. And a waterfall or two. I seem to recall some craggy rocks some three or four miles distant that are considered to be worth the journey.'

'How I would love to see them,' Miss Caroline sighed.

'You *have* seen them, many times,' her sister sneered.

'Oh, but not in such company as this,' Caroline persisted. 'May we be of the party, Mrs Binsley?'

'Caroline,' Mrs Willow began, in a warning tone.

But Edward Binsley cut across whatever admonition she was going to make by crying, 'Indeed yes. We shall all go. A regular picnic. I assume carriages can be found to accommodate us all, although I had much rather ride. Willow!' Addressing the lieutenant, 'What say you?'

Lieutenant Willow raised his glass and an ironical eyebrow. 'A craggy rock and a waterfall?' he repeated. 'Quite perfect. I came into the county with no other aspiration.' He stood quite close to me, between the arm of the sofa and the end of the fireplace.

'Splendid,' said Mr Edward Binsley. 'That's agreed, then. The girls can take their sketching materials. Willow and Gabriel and I can bathe. Where there are waterfalls there are generally deep pools.'

'Well …' Mr Gabriel looked doubtful.

'You will catch your deaths, bathing in April,' the rector said with a frown.

'Indeed, I am of your opinion on *that,*' Mrs Binsley said. 'Edward! What an idea!'

'The weather may not be clement at all,' Miss Binsley remarked. 'There is nothing more miserable than a picnic in the cold and wet.'

'Oh do not be a prophet of doom, Catherine,' Miss Elinor said. 'It has hardly rained at all since we got here.'

'If it is at all damp, Maud will have to be excused,' Mrs Willow said. 'Her constitution is not strong.'

'Oh, but Mama I should very much like to go,' Maud objected warmly, 'particularly if there is picturesque scenery.'

'Very well!' Edward Binsley said, with an irritated shake of the head. 'We will go on a dry, warm day but we will not bathe. We will scale the rocks instead.'

Lieutenant Willow caught my eye. 'Derring-do,' he said quietly enough for only me to be able to hear. 'Just what I came home on furlough for.'

Mrs Binsley's further remonstrance was cut short by the arrival of the remaining guests. Mr Eagerly stepped into the room followed by his brother and Mr and Miss Brigstock.

18

Mr Eagerly had eschewed his clerical garb for the occasion and wore a suit of clothes that was not at all new and in a style not seen for some time. It was thoroughly brushed however and fit him very well. His hair shone as though oiled and he smiled broadly, his teeth very white against the darkness of his face. He was known to all in the company, even the Binsleys, upon whom he had apparently called soon after their arrival. He shook hands with everyone in the room and if some were less ready to take his hand than he was to proffer it, that was to their discredit, in my opinion; it is hard to imagine a more genial and worthy man than Oscar Eagerly.

'I beg leave to present my brother, my younger brother Victor,' he said, addressing everyone but especially Mrs Binsley.

Victor Eagerly made his bow. I had not seen him in some time; their visits to Ecklington were rarer since they had attained their majority. He had grown tall—taller than his brother—but he looked thin to me. His eyes were bruised by tiredness but retained a light of humour behind round eye-glasses. His clothing, though clean, was old and shabby. I could see his cuffs were frayed and noticed a not-very-expert repair in the seam of his breeches. His boots, although highly polished, were sadly worn.

It was unfortunate that the curate and his brother should have entered the room with the Brigstocks. It would have been hard for anyone to compare favourably with this brother and sister, who were superlatively fashionable, the last word in elegance and éclat. But against *them* the brothers did look very shoddy indeed and I wondered if my father knew that whatever allowance he made them was not proving sufficient. The Brigstocks were but newly come to the neighbourhood and had made no friends, being exceptionally reserved. They had dined at Ecklington once. My mother had not liked Miss Brigstock, finding her, I think, to be her equal in hubris; Mama had described Miss Brigstock as 'insufferable.' Their family connexions were veiled. They had come from the continent where they had been since childhood. They were wealthy. They might have been émigrés but they were not French. They referred occasionally to their relations in a tone that implied them to be very eminent, but who these superior people were *exactly* had never been clearly explained. The Brigstocks were exceedingly handsome. Miss Brigstock was gorgeously dressed in figured silk, the cut of her gown high-waisted in the modern vogue. Her hair was piled high upon her head. She glittered with gems— at her throat, on her arms and fingers, and also on her slippers, her gloves and her reticule. Mr Brigstock was scarcely less ornamented. I assumed it to be the continental fashion. His coat was braided, his waistcoat embroidered with gold and he wore a diamond ring on his finger. A handsomer man it would be hard to imagine, with lustrous hair and chiselled features, dark, smouldering eyes and white, even teeth. Every lady in the room was struck by his beauty. I thought Miss Catherine Binsley especially taken. There was a flush on her cheek and a sparkle in her eye I had not discerned up to this moment.

The Brigstocks looked around the room at the gathered company, and at the dowdy window hangings and scored floorboards with an air that most of the company interpreted as unmitigated disdain. I rather thought it might be self-consciousness however, that they had miscalculated in their dress and personal ornamentation. I thought they must have been expecting a party of a much more elegant nature, in a far more stylish locale. Their disgust—or, as I read it, their embarrassment—was so apparent that no one knew how to counter it. Even Mrs Binsley sat in a stupor of affronted pride. Now, more than ever, was Sir Diggory's presence wanted, but still he remained curiously absent. General conversation had ceased after Mr Eagerly had introduced his brother. All looked to the Brigstocks to greet their hostess, to the rector to effect an introduction, to the butler to announce dinner. But none of these things occurred. The silence stretched out. Caroline Willow stifled a giggle, but not very effectively. Miss Elinor reached surreptitiously for my hand. The lieutenant threw me a look that seemed to reflect the sympathy that was my own dominant emotion at the Brigstocks' discomfort. I wanted to say something to ease it but it wasn't my place. At last—at long last—Miss Catherine Binsley conquered her over-charged feelings to welcome them to Binsley House.

'Sir. Ma'am,' she said, curtseying deeply, but looking up at Mr Brigstock from beneath her lashes, 'we are honoured to have you join us.'

The Brigstocks murmured something in response and the moment passed.

'Victor studies at Cambridge,' Mr Eagerly said suddenly, attempting to smooth the awkwardness. He turned to Edward and Gabriel Binsley. 'I believe you are Oxford men? I also took my degree at Oxford, but Victor was of the opinion that Cambridge offered better tutoring. He is to be a physician.'

'I take my degree in May,' Mr Victor said, 'and then I shall apprentice myself to Dr Whitworth in Wimpole Street.'

'Edward will also graduate in May,' Mrs Binsley replied. She had offered her hand to Mr Brigstock with much coldness and now dismissed him to her daughter. Mrs Willow gamely attempted to engage his sister in conversation. I heard her reprising the catalogue of works and improvements made at Binsley with which she had regaled me in the carriage. I could not imagine it would interest Miss Brigstock very much but *someone* had to engage her in conversation and I doubted I was equal to it. The rector found himself marooned by the drinks tray and took recourse to it several times. Mr Gabriel showed Maud Willow a selection of curiosities in a cabinet. Caroline Willow stood near her cousin Barnaby and simpered.

'But Edward will apprentice himself to no-one thereafter,' Miss Elinor said dryly, 'other than perhaps a master of horse, for he has a yearning to be a jockey. Of course Mama will not hear of it.'

'A fellow must do something,' Lieutenant Willow remarked, raising an ironical eyebrow at me. He remained close beside me. He had taken but one glass of Madeira. His air was one of wry amusement and I must say I rather shared it. As my first outing into society the afternoon was providing much to wonder at.

'Indeed,' Mr Binsley replied, throwing his sister a look loaded with anger, 'it would be deuced boring if he did not!'

'I do not see Sir Diggory,' Mr Eagerly observed, thinking—quite rightly—that this line of discussion had better be diverted. 'I hope he is not unwell?'

'I hope not,' Mrs Binsley replied tartly. 'He is unconscionably late, however.'

At last the butler arrived to announce that dinner was served. There was some confusion as to precedent, since our host had still not manifested himself, but at last Mr Brigstock, looking as though he disliked the task extremely, offered his arm to Mrs Binsley. The rector, with a little unsteadiness, took Miss Brigstock. The rest of us made what shift we could. Lieutenant Willow stepped forward and offered me his arm, leaving poor Caroline to the mercies of Mr Eagerly. 'Do say you'll sit next to me,' the lieutenant said, 'and let us sit nowhere near the Brigstocks. They terrify me out of my wits.'

'I feel rather sorry for them,' I replied, but taking his arm none-the-less.

'Ah yes,' the lieutenant allowed, 'so do I. But not so sorry that I would relinquish my opportunity to become acquainted with *you*. I do not know how it can be, in all my many visits here, that I have never seen you.'

'I suppose your cousins have occupied all your attention,' I suggested, 'or that you have not attended church. I leave the grounds of Ecklington very seldom, but I do attend services.'

'Dear me,' said my companion, 'how penetrating you are. You state the case exactly.'

We progressed back along the passageway to the dining room finding, to everyone's surprise, that Sir Diggory was already seated and indeed was halfway through his soup.

'Upon my word, sir,' Mr Edward Binsley cried, 'we had all but given you up. I am happy to see you safely returned from your morning's exercise.'

Sir Diggory made some reply whose substance I could not hear but that concluded with the words 'dinner at four.'

'We came as soon as Cox announced,' Mrs Binsley said.

Sir Diggory suggested, through his soup, that the butler must have been tardy, an idea that made Cox bridle.

'Good day, Sir Diggory,' I said, in as clear and firm voice as I could muster in the tumult that accompanied our arrival in the dining room and the general confusion as we found our seats. 'My mama and papa send their best compliments to you and regret their prior engagement.'

Sir Diggory waved me away, I sat down and my soup was served. I think that from then on Sir Diggory uttered barely a word throughout the meal. Mrs Willow, at his right, was thankfully a woman who needed little in the way of reply to fuel her conversational diatribe, but even she was reduced in the end to making general observations that required none. Miss Brigstock, at Sir Diggory's other side, ate her dinner in stony silence. The other end of the table fared much better. Miss Binsley was at her sparkling best, next to Mr Brigstock. The rector occupied Mrs Binsley and the rest of us were much entertained in the arrangement of our forthcoming excursion. In between the general conversation Lieutenant Willow asked the kinds of questions calculated to draw a young lady out. Did I read? Ride? Had I travelled? In return I made enquiry of his family.

'I am the only surviving child of the rector's elder brother,' he told me. 'My aunt and uncle have quite brought me up and I am as fond of them as if they were my parents. I think of the rectory girls as sisters.' He said this with a deliberateness that implied to me that he meant something quite significant by it. 'You have a brother, I apprehend?'

'Oh yes, George.' I found myself telling Lieutenant Willow all about my brother, and in particular about my fears concerning his new school, until there was a change of course and I had to turn to my other neighbour.

I have not much more specific recollection of the dinner or the evening that followed it, other than that I had a thoroughly agreeable time. As we concluded dinner the musicians could be heard making their way to the great room. The ladies retired to the sitting room where Mrs Binsley had received Mama and me, leaving the gentlemen to drink their wine, but they were not long over this. Happily we were reassembled soon afterwards and the violinist struck up the first dance. Sir Diggory did not join us, but retired to his library as was his wont. Everybody thought this very singular behaviour and some did not scruple to say so but I did not wish to be critical of my host, no matter how bizarre his conduct, and kept my counsel.

I danced first with Lieutenant Willow and then with Mr Victor and afterwards with both the Binsleys. Miss Brigstock refused to stand up although Edward Binsley did request the pleasure in a tone that I, certainly, would not have dared to refuse. She was resolute however, and sat looking on the whole evening long with an eye very disdainful of the rest of us as we leapt and twirled and clapped our hands. A few times I saw her stifle a yawn behind her hand and I was sure she regretted very much having accepted the Binsleys' invitation. For myself, I felt most gratified to have been included, even when Mr Brigstock unbent himself sufficiently to dance with me. He partnered Miss Binsley and Miss Elinor also, but he did not deign to dance with either of the rectory girls, which I felt did not reflect well on him. Between the rest of us though, we had a merry time of it. The Binsleys, of course, led the way but where they showed us the example the rest of us were happy to follow.

Mr Eagerly was as energetic as anyone. 'You will not remember,' he said, as he led me down the set, 'but you and I used to do the galop down the long gallery at Ecklington. I hope you do not think it impertinent of me to mention it?'

'Not at all,' I said. 'You were patient with me, I recall. I am sorry we do not see you and your brother very often at Ecklington nowadays.'

'Ah,' he smiled. '"*now that I am become a man, I have put away childish things*"[xvii]

'I think your brother studies too hard,' I remarked.

'He has had to be very diligent,' Mr Eagerly agreed. 'It is sad—but too true—that people like us must prove ourselves. The world is prejudiced against the colour of our skin.'

'I like the colour of your skin,' I said, 'but surely the character of a person, beneath his skin, is what matters?'

'Ah, Miss Talbot,' the curate replied, pressing my hand, 'if only everyone were as wise as you.

When at last the rectory carriage brought me home, I was handed from the carriage into the care of Swale by Lieutenant Willow. He said, 'May I do myself the honour of calling upon you tomorrow, Miss Talbot?'

I was glad of the dim light, for I felt the blush rise to my cheek as I told him, yes, he could.

When I got within, and could hear the sound of the carriage wheels fading, Swale handed me my candle. I asked him if my maid had stayed up, and was informed that she had.

'Poor thing,' I said. 'I had not intended to keep her up so late. Goodnight, Swale.'

I made towards the stairs but Swale detained me.

'Miss,' he said. His voice was always sonorous but now it was even lower, confidential; almost a whisper. 'Lord Petrel is in the small drawing room.'

'Lord Petrel?' I felt a chill at my heart; I did not like Lord Petrel. Hitherto I had never found myself alone in his company but now I would have no choice. 'Was he expected?'

I stepped closer to Swale that we might confer as privately as possible.

'No miss. But he arrived with his man and seemed … disappointed to find the master and mistress from home. He felt sure there had been an understanding … He seemed to think there was an impediment to him returning to town tonight although I ventured to suggest that fresh horses could be provided from the stables. But he was insistent and so … I felt it right to allow him to stay. I hope I acted correctly, miss.'

'Indeed yes,' I said but, like Swale, I felt the difficulty. With mama and papa in town I was alone in the house. Not literally alone—there were a dozen or more servants—but I was unchaperoned. And although Lord Petrel was an old family friend, I was no longer a child. I wished that the rector or Mrs Willow, or the lieutenant had accompanied me into the hall, to relieve me of the onus of this awkward situation. Maud or Caroline could have remained here with me, or I could have been carried back to the rectory for the night. But they were long gone. I turned the matter over in my mind, my candle in hand. I knew that Swale, now retreated to a respectful distance, was quite as alive as I was to the delicacy of the situation Lord Petrel's unannounced arrival had placed us in.

The small drawing room was a room off the hall. We never used it as a family but it was a useful place for guests to wait before they were shown up to the large drawing room on the first floor, or into the library or my father's study. The door was ajar and I could see the candlelight spilling out onto the marble floor. It seemed to carry with it something of Lord Petrel's malign aura, as though he himself were encroaching nearer and nearer to where I stood. I heard the small chink as the lip of a decanter touched the rim of a glass and then a dry, artificial cough. The hairs on my arm stood on end. Nothing would induce me to enter the room where he was, this late at night, especially as he had been drinking my father's wine.

'Please offer Lord Petrel my apologies,' I said. 'I am very tired and am going to bed. I will see him in the morning. In the meantime, let a messenger be sent to Grosvenor Square as early as may be in the morning, so that my father knows that Lord Petrel is here. He may carry a word from Lord Petrel, if he cares to send one.'

Swale gave a small bow. 'Very good, miss.'

'Good night Swale,' I said, my voice quite loud enough to carry into the small drawing room. 'I trust to you to make the house secure. I shall ask my maid to remain with me.'

Swale nodded again, understanding very well what I was saying. I knew he would station a footman on the landing near my room.

I climbed the stairs. But my joy in the evening, in my new acquaintances, in the dancing and our plans for the next few weeks, had all but gone, overshadowed by the man in the small sitting room.

19

Annie Orphan 1802

'It is my opinion,' Miss Nugent said one day in the sunny sewing room, 'that you are not suited to work below-stairs. You are too slight and thin. You have not the strength for it.'

Annie and Sally had been at Ecklington Grange for two years and their age could be estimated at approximately fifteen years. Annie's spirit had not wavered in that time although, often, her frame had almost buckled beneath the weight of the arduous physical labour she was expected to carry out. Mrs Brixie, the washer woman who came up from the village, had identified Annie as a reliable worker and now expected her in the wash-house three days a week. Leaning over the vats of water, lifting the sodden sheets to the mangle, hanging them out and bringing them in as the rain came and went made Annie's back and arms feel as though they had been crushed to powder by the end of the day. The lye soap caused her hands to bleed. The hot-iron gave her burns on the backs of her hands and her arms.

Annie had grown a little but was still diminutive in stature. Her form had ripened to provide a neat swell of buttock and hip and small, rose-tipped moons of breasts. The courses had come. Her hair would never be pretty—it was a lustreless brown, very fine and straight—but her features were nicely arranged and all in proportion. Physically she would always be negligible, but her mind had expanded exponentially. She could read, now, and work figures. Mrs Bray depended upon Annie to calculate quantities for receipts and to list the bills from butcher, game-merchant and grocer. Miss Nugent had continued to train her in the stillroom and now it was just as likely to be Annie the girls came to with their cuts and burns and their monthly pains as Miss Nugent herself. Annie was bright, and she had learned to look ahead. If she saw Mrs Bray creaming butter and sugar she knew that eggs would be needed next, and would fetch them from the pantry without waiting to be asked, so that when the cook reached for them they were ready by her side. She was trusted to make sauces and soups while the other girls got on with the menial jobs of gutting fish and plucking fowl. She could be relied upon to know how many shirts had gone to the wash and how many awaited mending, when the icehouse needed ice or the range fresh coals. She had earned for herself the respect of the others servants. No one teased her now, or raised their hand to her.

Miss Nugent's remark, then, came as a blow. She could not deny that she lacked the physical capacity of the other kitchen wenches. After all the effort of taking herself in hand, it was a terrible disappointment.

She looked up from her work alarmed, her needle poised over the sheet she was hemming. 'You think I will be sent away?'

'Oh no, my dear,' Miss Nugent replied with a small smile. 'I think you would be better suited to work above stairs. I happen to know that Mrs Talbot is amenable to the idea. Do not deceive yourself, the work is hard and the hours just as long, if not longer. But a parlour maid is superior to a scullery maid; she requires a delicacy of touch and exceptional personal decorum. She must appreciate and respect the great trust that is placed in her. For, you know, a parlour maid looks after the master's treasures—the statuary in the gallery, the fine porcelain ornaments and the crystal vases. She brushes the fabrics of the furniture and window-hangings, which have been wrought by the finest craftsmen across the world. And, more than that, she is admitted to the family's private chambers. It is a position of great trust. Do you think yourself equal to it?'

Annie shook her head. It seemed a terrible responsibility.

'You show just the proper reticence,' Miss Nugent said. 'If you had assured me you were ready, I would have doubted my instinct, for that would have been most presumptuous. But your very misgiving shows me that you understand what a great thing it would be.'

'What will Mrs Butterwick say?' Annie asked. She would not go so far as to say she had made herself indispensable in the below-stairs regions, but she thought she might be missed. Certainly Sally had shown nowhere near her aptitude.

'Mrs Butterwick will do as Mrs Talbot instructs,' Miss Nugent replied. 'And, between you and me, I will go further, Annie. Miss Peake,' Miss Peake was Miss Talbot's maid, a woman past sixty with failing eyesight, 'Miss Peake will find it impossible to carry out her duties to Miss Talbot if her eyesight deteriorates much more. Look!' She indicated one of Miss Talbot's shawls that had been snagged on a bramble, and her fine cambric nightgown from which the lace trim had been torn. 'We are doing all the sewing that should be her lot for she can barely thread a needle! Should you do well in your promotion, I will offer to train you as a lady's maid.'

To be so close to Miss Talbot! Annie's heart and mind swelled with the idea of it.

But Miss Nugent broke in to her day-dream. '*That,* if it comes to pass at all, is some way in the future, Annie, and may not happen at all. Miss Talbot is of age, soon to be presented at court, if the mistress can arrange it. I know she is straining every sinew to make it so. Soon after that she will likely be engaged, for, as to dowry ... well!'

'I am sure she has good prospects,' Annie ventured. 'But, regarding my own future ..?'

'It is beyond *my* power to arrange but,' Miss Nugent gave a knowing smile as she bit off her thread, 'Mrs Talbot enquired, and I went so far as to suggest ... and so I should not be surprised if Mrs Butterwick summons you before the week is out.'

And so it proved to be.

While Annie had been diligent in trying to improve herself, Sally had been busy in finding out ways to avoid her fair share of the work. She could be counted on to be absent from the kitchen as the hour for serving dinner came near, and would frequently abandon pans and dishes to soak, rather than scrubbing at them with sand and soot until they were clean. She had got into a habit of sneaking over to the stables and the dairy, neither of which were places that a young woman chary of her reputation desired to be seen unless strictly on business for Mrs Bray. The maids in the dairy were very coarse and dissolute, likely to be found in the evenings stupid with cider and up to no good with the ploughman or pig swain. Sally had caught some of their manner, which was none to the good when it came to speaking back to Mrs Bray or engaging in haranguing matches with the other kitchen wenches. More than once Annie had been called upon to apply arnica to bruises or salves to split lips. Sally was known to be feisty. She was also flirtatious, finding it easy to get young men in her thrall. Two under-grooms came to a state of such enmity over her that one of them had to be dismissed. A gardener's boy fell and broke his leg in an attempt to climb onto the roof to access Sally's skylight, that he might watch her undress.

Sally had matured into a plump and dimpled beauty with large, firm breasts that strained the front of her pinafore, and a shapely behind. Her skin was creamy and very smooth, her hair a cascade of luxuriant curls, mahogany brown and lustrous. She had large brown eyes that sparkled with humour and mischief, a wide mouth with full lips and white, even teeth. She was coquettish rather than degenerate, managing to promise much with the pout of those moist lips and the flash of those alluring brown eyes, without delivering much more than a kiss or a quick fondle before slipping out of her admirer's arms, leaving him panting and inflamed. She thought this very good sport and her laughter could be heard burbling and trilling as she made her way back across the stable yard and through the gate that led to the glasshouses and kitchen gardens.

Annie and Sally still shared a room and a bed, but Mrs Butterwick had told Annie that she would be moved into different accommodations in another wing of the house once she started work as a parlour maid.

'It is high time,' Mrs Butterwick had said. 'You are a slip of a thing but I expect Sally Orphan takes up a good deal of the bed, does she not? *She* is grown into a big girl.'

Annie had admitted that it was so. 'Although,' she added, 'Sally is very warm, in the night time.'

'The parlour maids have a stove on their landing,' Mrs Butterwick said. 'It is to dry their aprons and dresses overnight. You *must* have a clean dress and apron, Annie, if you're to work in the house.'

'Yes Mrs Butterwick,' Annie had said.

'But the heat does permeate, I think, and so the rooms are warmer. Of course there is a pan, so there is hot water for washing. *You* do not need reminding about *that* though Annie. Your scrupulousness with hygiene is commendable.'

Now, as she washed herself, Annie told Sally of the new arrangements. 'You'll have the bed to yourself,' she said, 'for I am to move to the other landing.'

'That will be good,' Sally said, stripping off her frock and dropping it onto the floor. 'Lying next to you is like lying beside a corpse, you are so stiff and cold. I hope you'll take that thing with you.' She indicated the plant, which had survived, if it had not thrived. 'I think it's unhealthy, having a plant inside.'

'Yes, I will take it,' Annie said. She was proud of it, her gift from Miss Talbot. It reminded her of their conversation in the conservatory. The thought struck her that, now, she might be allowed to go in there again, even if it was only to clean the floor and the windows. How lovely it would be to work amongst the flowers and waving green leaves! What if she were to meet Miss Talbot in there! How proud she would be, to show how she had flourished. She bent to pick up Sally's dress and hang it on a hook. When she turned back Sally was already in bed, one arm outside the coverlet. It was bruised. 'What happened to your arm?'

Sally withdrew the other from where she had tucked it beneath the pillow. 'They're both as bad,' she said, holding them out. Annie could see the clear imprint of fingers and thumb on the plump flesh of Sally's arms between shoulder and elbow. 'Jackie Silver is getting hard to hold off,' she said. Silver was a man but lately come into the employ of Mr Talbot. He was of exotic extraction, wiry and swarthy, with black eyes and a moody demeanour. He was very good with horses however. Mr Talbot—or, more likely, Lord Petrel—had a desire to breed race horses and Jackie Silver had been recruited to oversee the acquisition and training of likely stock. He was much older than Sally—nearer thirty than twenty—and not at all like the under-grooms and stable lads with whom Sally had previously toyed, who were not much more than boys.

'I hope you do not put yourself in danger, Sally,' Annie said, shaking out her stockings and laying them carefully over the back of a little chair. 'Mr Silver does not seem to me like a man to be teased.'

'I can handle him' Sally laughed, tucking her arms back under the covers. 'And most times handling's all he wants, if you get my meaning.' She gave a naughty chortle.

Annie looked at her blankly. 'I don't think I do get your meaning, Sally,' she said.

'No.' Sally sighed. 'You wouldn't, so prim and proper as you are.'

Annie, stripped to her chemise, dipped her washrag into the basin of cold water and began her ablutions. 'I might be prim and proper,' she said at last. 'I would rather people think *that* of me than that they think I am a tease and a flirt.'

Indeed, now that she had so much to aspire to, she would be distraught if any ill-repute should sully her character.

Sally took the criticism in good part. 'Being a tease and a flirt is fun,' she said. 'You should see them—the men, I mean—reduced to jibbering and snivelling and pleading.' She mimicked the entreaties of her admirers; 'Oh Sally, just a little look, just a little touch and I won't say a word to no one, only I'm aching for you girl. Look at the state of me! I'm fit to burst if you don't open up.' She laughed in delighted remembrance of it but then was suddenly sober. 'There ain't much that you or me can do, at the beck and call of all and sundry as we are. Scrub that, carry this, pluck those … But when I see a man bending over hisself, all unmanly, well, it makes me feel like I *can* do something. And after all, being a flirt isn't as bad as being a doxy.'

'The one might lead to the other though,' Annie said, wiping herself with a towel, 'if you're not careful. Then you'll lose your place. Then you'll be right back where our mothers were.'

Sally gave a little shrug and stuck out an obdurate lip. 'Won't be my fault,' she said.

'It *will* be, if you let them. And even if you don't let them, if they *make* you do it, it will still be you who gets the blame.'

Sally heaved a heavy sigh. 'Hurry up and blow out the candle, Annie. I'll be glad when you've gone, I will.'

The following day Sally had her wish, and Annie began work as a parlour maid.

She learned quickly what was expected of her. She was to rise very early, before the sky was light, to empty out the night-soil from bedroom chamber pots before cleaning, laying and lighting the bedroom fires. She must work in silence, her tread light as air on the turkey rugs, careful not to clash the porcelain of the chamber pots against the rim of her bucket lest she woke the sleepers in the beds. She must work in near-darkness. She must know by instinct where the legs of ottomans protruded, where the family might have discarded their stockings and slippers before climbing in to bed, so that she did not stumble on them and disturb the family's slumbers. She learned to pick over the still-warm clinker in the grates with her bare hands and scoop ash with her palms because it was quieter than using the fire-irons. She knew by feel the texture of straw, kindling and coal, and how to blindly use them to compose a pyramid. The strike of the tinder was the loudest noise she made before gathering her things and slipping from the room.

Then she descended to the lower floors, to open curtains and windows that the rooms might be aired, to dust furniture and sweep out the fires. Glasses left behind by the family must be cleared away, dead flowers removed from the arrangements, cushions plumped, candle stubs replaced with new. All this must be done by the time the family had breakfasted, when they might take it into their heads to peruse books in the library, to write letters in the morning room, to await callers in the drawing room, or to do none of these things, to go out in the carriage, leaving empty rooms with brightly burning fires, preparations made for their comfort that would be wasted.

Whatever their movements, Annie made her way back to the bedrooms, to air the rooms and make the beds, to dust dressing tables and clean washstands and empty (again) the chamber pots. Only then could she descend to the servants' hall for her breakfast and a cup of weak tea.

This regime had been in place for about a month when the day of Sir Diggory's dinner came round. Although Miss Talbot was the only family member in residence, standards must be kept up, and Annie worked just as hard to make the rooms ready for one occupant as she would have done for three, or indeed an entire houseful. She spent her time after breakfast helping Miss Peake prepare Miss Talbot's gown for the dinner, and assisted the footmen to carry up the water for her bath. She managed to be in the gallery off the hall when Miss Talbot descended, polishing a bit of the floor beneath a console table, that she might glimpse her little mistress in her finery, and off to the ball. Miss Talbot looked so elegant, her dress falling just right, her hair arranged off her neck but with teasing tendrils about her ears. Annie gave a little thrill of pleasure as the door opened to admit the handsome young gentleman from the rectory. She liked the way he bowed low and offered his arm, and a tear or two dripped onto the floor where she knelt.

Mr Swale was a stickler for standards and allowed no deterioration in decorum because all the family members were from home. The servants had their dinner at the usual time and, because there was to be no dinner service upstairs, Mrs Bray set the kitchen girls to a thorough scouring and cleaning, a blacking of the stove and a scrubbing of the floors. Annie went to Miss Nugent to see if there was any sewing to be done. The rest of the day and the evening passed pleasantly.

Annie had been on the point of going up to Miss Talbot's room, to turn down the bed and replenish the coals, when a commotion in the hallway announced the unexpected arrival of Lord Petrel. Suddenly there was work to be done. Lord Petrel's usual room must be dusted, the sheets changed and the fire laid. Space must be made for his valet in the men's quarters. Lord Petrel required supper. Wearily, Mrs Bray tied her apron back on and Annie collected her bucket and duster and mounted the stairs.

20

Yorkshire

August 1813

The past weeks have been very fine here; quite the best summer weather
we have had since I came into the county. Long, warm, balmy days have
enticed me into the garden. The others have been busy picking and
podding, drying, pickling and bottling so the formal gardens—such as
they are—have necessarily been somewhat neglected. One day on
impulse I knelt and began to pull out weeds from the border. Once I had
begun I found the work compulsive; it released something that had been
pent up in me. I worked my way through the parterre until it was picked
clean. Then I dead-headed roses and gathered some flowers and greenery
to arrange in vases inside. I found the whole afternoon passed most
pleasantly. Afterwards, my back ached dreadfully and my hands were
very dirty, for I had worked without gloves and with only a small pair of
scissors that I had in my housewife[viii]. I called for hot water and bathed,
and as I lay in the water I thought of what I had achieved, what a
difference it had made to be *doing* something. I determined to supply
myself with better tools for another day for, having begun, I found I very

much wished to carry on, and did so the day afterwards and the day after that.

I do not know what Mrs Orphan made of my industry. Other than complimenting me on my arrangement of the flowers, she made no comment. Yet I always sense, with her, that behind her sealed lips, there are volumes of words.

I find that little by little, day by day I am becoming accustomed to my situation. I am still very angry at my mother, and bitterly disappointed in my brother. This situation was not of my choosing, no matter what skewed interpretation my mother might put upon it. It was foisted upon me; I am a victim as much—perhaps more—than the child. But in comparison to the other terrible alternative, is not this preferable? I am beginning to feel almost thankful, that it is *this* and not *that*.

When the weather has been too hot I have walked in the shade of the trees, sometimes climbing the path to the gatehouse but not often venturing out onto the moor where there are no trees and so no shade. I found that on one of these occasions I had missed a visit from Mrs Foley, who is back now from wherever she has been. Mrs Foley is a good woman, I suppose. I wish she could forgive me for whatever wrong she imagines I did to her. I presume my being here—the way things look—has only confirmed her earlier suspicions about me.

That day—the day I missed Mrs Foley—I had found a glade where, two or three trees having fallen in the winter storms, the sun had been able to penetrate the high canopy above and filter down to the ground. The grass was very green and lush there, fed by a rivulet that wound its way between scoured out banks and mossy stones down the incline of the hollow. The place was utterly peaceful, dappled with shade but not at all dark, the light a silver-greenish hue that made it seem part of the foliage all around and the rock beneath. In a way I cannot quite explain I felt that I, too, was permeated by that natural coolness. It seeped into me and drew me into itself so that I was melded with the limpid air, the verdant little dell, the running water and the rock beneath. The place was alive with birdsong, and I sat on a fallen log and watched a pair of small brown birds as they picked insects from the air and grubs from the soil, and offered them to their fledglings. I sat very still, and they did not seem disturbed by my presence. I forgot myself entirely for an hour or more, until a little dampness around my seat brought me to the consciousness that the day was cooling and the hour for tea had probably passed.

When I returned home and found that Mrs Foley had been there I was conscious of a surge of jealousy. I did not like to think that she had been here, in my house, touching my things, intruding.

'Did you show her into my sitting room?' I asked Mrs Orphan.

'No ma'am,' she said. 'She waited in the drawing room.'

'Good,' I said. 'That is good.'

I think there is something about this place, this house in the hollow, which is trickling into me. What I used to think of as a prison now feels more like a shelter, a refuge. I thought the house dour and comfortless at first but now I find it is not so. It is old and weathered, neglected and forgotten, and yet ... it stands. Time has pressed down on it. Weather has assaulted it. For long periods it has been left empty. But it is not broken down. In its resilience it is even beautiful, in a way. Whoever built it meant it to be more than just a dwelling. The mullions are intricately carved. The roof is adorned with finials and decorative curlicues. Even with the new wing there is a gracefulness about the balance of windows to door, the arrangement of chimney and gable. And yet it is a house that seems built—however beautifully—to be hidden. How curious! Its secrecy and mystery are almost part of its charm. I am reminded of faerie tales, hidden glens, languishing princesses in inaccessible towers—romantic nonsense, but not the less appealing for that.

Am I resigned, like this house, to a hidden life? I ask myself: because it *is* hidden, must it be hated? Might there not even be some beauty in it? Could it be that my cup of rage is almost drained?

If that is so there is a thorn I must grasp. It is there at the very heart of my anger and resentment, the cause—though indirect—of my shame and exile. I know it infects all the rest, as a thorn will, when left to fester. I must pull it free. But oh! What poison might be released if I do?

Writing in my journal has helped assuage my loneliness, resurrecting, as it has, the faces of those who were familiar to me. The dinner at Binsley House, the picnic that followed a few weeks later, the social intercourse that sprang up between Binsley and the rectory and Ecklington Grange—what a glorious few weeks it was! In comparison the years I spent in ducal castles and fashionable spas are dim and meaningless. I can almost feel again the sense I had then, at Ecklington and later, when I stayed at the rectory, of life beginning, of my life opening up to me. I recreate in my mind the happy scenes, and in some way I do not understand the joy of them superimposes itself on these grey walls. The rooms echo with the music and I almost believe that I see, in the periphery of my vision, shades of ghosts made flesh once more. They are as fragrant as a bouquet—a bouquet of memories.

I wrote those previous sentences last night, with the casements open to the still, perfumed air, the sound of birds still audible on the forested slopes around the house. I climbed the stairs weary, but conscious of dawning contentment, an acceptance of where life has brought me.

Oh! To tempt the malign power of the fates! Since then the house has been lashed by rain. The garden, hard-baked by weeks of sun, is now a lake. Plants and flowers bow their heads, bruised stems and battered petals are all that remain of the glorious summer colour. The sky boils above us, a canopy of moody grey that deposits rain as fine and relentless as mist.

But is it not often so—that neither pleasure nor pain are unalloyed? The sweet must necessarily be offset by the bitter, or how would we know it to be sweet?

So it was that spring, when the Binsleys, the Brigstocks and Lieutenant Willow came to light me up, and Lord Petrel cast me into his shade.

21

It was my habit to take my breakfast in my room, but as I knew Lord Petrel was in the house, and as I had left word that I would see him in the morning, I dressed and descended to the breakfast room quite early. I was sure that, by this time, the messenger to my parents would have been despatched, and comforted myself by thinking of him, riding hard, half way to London.

Lord Petrel was in the breakfast room when I arrived, sitting in the chair usually occupied by my father. He rose when I entered and made his bow.

'Good morning,' I said. 'I hope you slept well.'

There was a bed chamber in the house that was kept for Lord Petrel's use—he was such a frequent guest—into which he had gradually brought sundry items of clothing, spare boots, books and grooming requisites. My mother sometimes pretended to grumble that he might as well have taken up residence as he had made the place so much his own, but this was in jest, for she liked the allure that acquaintance with a viscount gave to our family and our house. Lord Petrel was one of those gentlemen who led an itinerant life, moving from one great house to another. He shot here, hunted there, attended race meets somewhere else. Where his own property was, or would be, I didn't know, precisely, other than that it was on the north Welsh coast. I imagined it to be some wretched, tumble-down place on a rocky promontory, miles from civilization and lashed by waves, but I suppose that is the image conjured by his name. Wherever it was, Lord Petrel showed no inclination whatsoever to spend any time there. Other people's hospitality was obviously far more appealing.

So my enquiry on entering the room was only a token; I knew the answer to it.

Lord Petrel chose to take it at face value however. 'One always sleeps soundly here,' he said, taking his place again when I had slipped into my own seat. 'So dashed quiet. Not like in town. And the pillows you have here are such as I never encounter anywhere else. I must ask your mama about them. There is a crack in the wash-stand, however. I mentioned it to Swale last time I was here, but nothing has been done. That was an inconvenience to my man. Shaving, you know …' He held forth in a similar vein whilst the footman brought me coffee and toast. I learned that he had woken early, as he usually did, and had enjoyed a turn about the grounds before breakfast. He had taken it upon himself to inspect the stables and, he told me, would have a word or two to say to my father about the management thereof. I ate my toast as he rambled on in his lugubrious, drawling tones.

For a man who purported to be such an active sportsman Lord Petrel was rather heavy-set. I guessed his age to be nearer forty than thirty. His face was round and although there was no suggestion of jowl at present it seemed very likely that before many years had passed the line of his jaw would sag. Good living had put its mark upon his skin, which was of a very high colour. His eyes were small and deep set in his fleshy face, his brows rather heavy. His mouth was full, but he was one of those people who speak without moving his mouth very much. He had dark hair that fell in a wave across his brow. I think it would not be fair to describe him as an ill-looking man, and he was always dressed very finely, in well-cut clothes of good quality, but he had an air of dissipation that detracted from the sum of his parts; I thought him to be greedy, over-fond of wine, and a parasite.

'I am very sorry you had a wasted journey here, Lord Petrel,' I said when his diatribe came to an end. 'I do not know when Mama and Papa will return. I suppose your business will take you back to town, to find them?'

'By no means,' he said, waving a dismissive arm at the notion. 'There is nothing of urgency there. A day or so, or even a week …' he cocked a speculative eyebrow, 'could be of no moment. When *do* you anticipate their return?'

'I'm afraid I cannot say. Mama did not mention a particular day.'

'Just so.' He sat back, seeming almost pleased by this. He motioned to the footman to bring him more coffee.

'Of course, I have sent word of your being here,' I said.

He nodded slowly. 'I gathered as much. I appended my own note, as you suggested. That was kind of you. I can reassure you that they will feel no compunction to hurry back on *my* account.'

My heart sank. Whatever urgency the message from Swale might have conveyed—that Lord Petrel had arrived unannounced, finding me at home alone, professing some business matter to be dealt with—his own missive had clearly defused. I decided to grasp the nettle. 'Lord Petrel,' I said, my voice level, and speaking very clearly, so as not to be misunderstood, 'you find me at something of a disadvantage. My parents are from home and I am here with only the protection of the servants. My mother had not anticipated the need to provide for guests while she was away and I fear the housekeeping may not be equipped to …'

But he cut me off. 'My dear Miss Talbot,' he exclaimed, 'do not discompose yourself to the smallest degree. As to the absence of your parents, that is a misunderstanding. I believed them to be at home when I did myself the honour of coming here. As to what you describe as 'protection' I count that as all the more reason why I should stay. Who better to be here than I, who have known you all your life, and been an intimate of your family for as long as anyone can remember? I stand quite as an uncle, I should say, or, rather, an elder brother, for there is not such a great discrepancy between our ages as all that!'

I disbelieved both of his claims. He was so frequently in my father's company that I could not conceive of him being unaware of the trip to town or the dinner at Lady Pembroke's. Indeed it surprised me more that Lord Petrel had not engineered himself onto the guest list. As to his age, that was laughable. He was certainly fifteen years older than me and probably more. His age was closer to my mother's than it was to mine. But he gave me no opportunity to voice my doubts.

'I think I hardly qualify as a 'guest' do I? How often has your papa told me to make myself quite at home? He is all generosity, both here and at his London house. As to housekeeping, I am sure Mrs Butterwick can find me a bit of mutton. If not, I shall provide my own sustenance. There are pheasant in the park, are there not?'

'There are, but it is not the season,' I said. My prevarication sounded hollow in my own ears and Lord Petrel laughed aloud at it. 'I shall not tell if you do not,' he said. 'Better that, than we go hungry, eh Miss Talbot?' He winked at me then, a leering, conspiratorial gesture I found disgusting.

But what could I say? Anyone with good manners would have seen the impropriety of remaining, and withdrawn. Clearly Lord Petrel's politeness did not extend to me, or he had reasons of his own for countermanding it. I could not throw him bodily from the house. I only prayed that my parents would return soon.

'Very well,' I said, rising from my seat and pulling my napkin from my lap. 'If you are quite sure you wish to remain, I shall speak to Mrs Butterwick and see what can be done. Good morning to you, Lord Petrel.'

I left the room with my head held very high, and went back upstairs with no very clear idea of where I would hide or how I would occupy myself. I only knew I did not wish to expose myself to Lord Petrel's company. I was but halfway up the stairs however, when I heard the sound of hooves on the sweep. It was much too soon for the messenger to have got to London and back again so for a wild, hopeful moment I thought Mama and Papa had returned. I hovered on the stairs as Swale approached the door. He opened it and there beneath the portico stood Lieutenant Willow and his cousin Caroline. I turned and scampered to the top of the stairs and into the drawing room, where the maid was still setting the room to rights. I could not conceive what she had found to occupy herself in there as the room had not been used for two days, but I sent her away and sat myself on a sofa, snatching up some sewing before dropping it again and smoothing my hair. Very quickly my guests were announced and came into the room.

'Good morning, Miss Talbot,' Lieutenant Willow said in a bright, genial voice. 'I hope we do not make our call upon you too early? We have been up for many hours, have we not Caroline? But we did not know what time ladies rose, or breakfasted, or what might be an appropriate time for our call. We were eager to make it however—*very* eager—and so here we are!'

Caroline gave his arm a playful nudge and made a grimace at his suggestion that *she* was not a lady. Her face was very flushed, mainly with the ride, I presumed, but also at pulling off the coup of preventing him from calling on me alone.

Lieutenant Willow gazed around the room; at the opulent furniture, heavy drapes and large mirror above the fireplace. 'My goodness!' he exclaimed, 'what a very splendid room.' He stepped further into it, his hands clasped behind his back, taking in other details: the ornate coving and heavy crystal chandelier, the silks, damasks and velvets that abounded. He heaved a long sigh and gave me a look that I thought had a light of resignation in it.

I laid my sewing aside and stood up, ready to show him anything that might particularly catch his eye, but Caroline said, 'This is where Mrs Talbot receives Mama. I have been in this room ever so many times, Barney.' I suppose she did not wish him to think of me in this room, without her being here also. Sure enough, she advanced across the carpet and indicated a small chair. 'I usually sit here. Can you picture me here, Barney, drinking tea with Mama and Mrs Talbot? I am sure,' she pouted, 'that if you *could,* you would think of me as a lady *then.*'

Lieutenant Willow barely glanced at the place she indicated, but made his way instead over to the large window. 'Certainly,' he said, 'but it is such a splendid day, and I can see there are grounds to explore. Shall we take a turn outside?'

'Oh, yes,' I said, but then remembered my duty. 'But I have offered you no refreshment. Let me ring for some tea.'

The lieutenant waved his hand. 'Later, perhaps. But it is too nice now to be sitting indoors and drinking tea. Let us walk first, if you please.'

'I am quite ready,' said Caroline, 'if Miss Talbot wishes to fetch her bonnet.'

I was quite as ready as she was, and went immediately to get my hat and a shawl. I almost bumped into Lord Petrel on the landing.

'You have visitors?' he asked. 'Pray, introduce me.'

It was impossible to refuse. I took him into the drawing room and made the introductions. 'Lord Petrel is a very old acquaintance of my father,' I said pointedly. 'He arrived last evening, while we were at Binsley House.'

'How awkward,' Lieutenant Willow said, comprehending immediately the delicacy of the situation. 'And you remained, did you sir? I believe the Rose and Crown is perfectly commodious.'

'Quite unnecessary,' Lord Petrel said, very haughtily. 'I am quite one of the family here, am I not, Jocelyn?'

His use of my name made me pale. Lieutenant Willow looked very surprised and threw me a questioning look; only someone on the most *intimate* terms would have taken such a liberty. Caroline, very much in awe of Lord Petrel, shrank behind her cousin.

Lord Petrel, oblivious to—or pleased with—the offence he had caused, allowed himself a self-satisfied smile. 'You are going walking, I apprehend? An excellent plan. I shall join you.' He swivelled on his heel as though to lead the way, and then noticed that I had not the appropriate apparel. 'Go and get your things, Jocelyn,' he said, as one would speak to a child, or a puppy. 'The weather is fine *now* but we cannot be sure it will last.'

Our walk around the grounds, which should have been such a pleasure, was an ordeal. As much as Lieutenant Willow tried to possess himself of my arm, my company, my conversation, Lord Petrel kept placing himself between us. He answered the questions that were directed at me and gave his own observations when mine had been sought. He pointed out the house's various appointments as though he himself were the architect. His behaviour was insufferable, and the minutes ticked away, the morning wasted itself, and I found myself getting angry. I wanted to consult Lieutenant Willow as to my predicament. It was increasingly evident to me that I needed to consult *someone*. I did not like Lord Petrel's manner, his interference, his possessive attitude. It was clear he was going to make a nuisance of himself. To be sure Lieutenant Willow was a very new acquaintance, and it was hardly right that I should throw myself on his counsel, but my situation was extraordinary and I did not know where else to turn. If only Caroline could have contrived to take Lord Petrel off for a few moments, it would have given me the time I needed to say something, but Caroline refused to so much as walk by his lordship's side, and we carried doggedly on, speaking platitudes and enduring Lord Petrel's arrogance.

We returned to the house at last to find a small party had arrived from Binsley—Mr Edward Binsley and his sister Miss Elinor—accompanied by Mr Brigstock. All were still mounted, so I gathered they had just arrived, but the gentlemen dismounted as we appeared around the corner of the house.

'Ah,' cried Mr Binsley, holding the reins of his horse, 'so you got the start on us Willow! We called at the rectory on our way past and were told that you'd set off two hours ago! We left my brother there. He was desirous of seeing Miss Willow's portfolio.'

'I wish him well of it,' Caroline said, with not-very-sisterly sarcasm. 'It is very thick. Maud is prolific with her pencil.'

'So is Gabriel, so they will have much to discuss,' Elinor said. She had remained on her horse and now leaned down to pat its neck. 'How do you like my horse, Miss Talbot? They came just this morning from a livery stable. I forget where, exactly. Somewhere close by. Uncle Diggory had them sent for us.'

'How delightful,' Lord Petrel said in a loud voice, imposing himself on the company. 'Welcome to Ecklington. I am Viscount Petrel, guardian to Miss Talbot in her parents' absence. Who do I have the honour of addressing?'

I stepped hurriedly forward—my anger, pent up all morning, almost at boiling point. I could barely contain it, but what option other than presenting my friends to Lord Petrel was available to me? The two things were day and night; the friends all brightness, Lord Petrel all dark. Who knows how caustic I might have been? Perhaps he saw my fulmination. I opened my mouth to make the introductions but he cut me off. 'Oh, but never mind about that now. We can effect introductions presently. Do you all come inside and take some refreshment. Jocelyn, my dear, why don't you go ahead and speak to Swale? Ask him to send a boy from the stables to take care of the horses.'

He went to help Elinor from her saddle, murmuring in a voice that was slick and unctuous, 'Do allow me, my dear,' and taking hold of her waist with both hands.

I found I had tears in my eyes as I mounted the steps and went in to the hall. Swale stood within. 'We have guests,' I managed to stammer out. 'Please serve tea and … whatever you think the gentlemen will like. I must just … excuse me … I will go and take off my bonnet.' I ran past him up the stairs and along the landing to my room where I burst into tears.

When I returned to the drawing room my guests were inside and there was a pleasant enough hum of conversation. Above all I could hear the drawl of Lord Petrel, holding court. I stepped into the room and felt my arm caught immediately. Lieutenant Willow was waiting just within. I was sure he had stationed himself there on purpose to waylay me.

'Miss Talbot,' he said in a low voice, guiding me back onto the landing. 'That man ...' he regarded me very closely, his eyes—blue, and very clear—taking in the stains of my tears. He had retained my hand in his, and pressed it as he spoke. His gesture communicated sympathy and strength.

'Oh, he's odious,' I burst out. 'I was horrified to find him here last evening. I wished you had not all gone, or I would gladly have come with you to the rectory and slept on the floor, rather than be here with him.'

Lieutenant's eyes widened. 'He did not attempt ...'

I shook my head. 'No. I kept my maid with me.'

'That was wise,' he said. 'I upbraid myself most severely that I did not accompany you properly into the house. I would have insisted on your coming back to the rectory with us the moment I understood the situation. As to your sleeping on the floor, I think my aunt could have found you a more comfortable resting place. However, with your permission, I will speak to her and we will rescue you from this before the day is done. You cannot contemplate ...'

'Oh! I *cannot*,' I said, anticipating all he implied; dinner alone with Lord Petrel, the long evening, and then another day of his oppressive insinuation. 'But he is my father's friend, and I do not wish to offend him.'

'He does not scruple to offend *you*,' Lieutenant Willow said stoutly. 'But do not worry. My aunt will manage things for you, one way or another.'

We went back into the drawing room and the lieutenant went to stand by Mr Binsley. I sat near Elinor Binsley and accepted a cup of tea from Mrs Butterwick who, in my absence, had been officiating at a sideboard where the tea things had been laid out. Swale had brought a tray with a sherry decanter and glasses. Lord Petrel, I noted, had already emptied his glass and held it out for more.

'Thank you Mrs Butterwick,' I said, as she passed me my cup.

Elinor Binsley seemed oblivious to the evidence of tears that must have shown on my face, or to my hand, which trembled as it held the saucer. Lord Petrel's imperious manner—standing on the hearthrug, declaiming loudly—did not seem to strike her as odd.

'The viscount,' she almost squeaked, smiling broadly. 'Wait until Mama hears! She will be livid! She took Catherine to Upton in the hope of finding *him,*' she nodded across the room towards Mr Brigstock. Upton Park was the name of the Brigstocks' house. 'Catherine is most taken with Mr Brigstock. She has spoken of no one else all morning. Did you not see how she behaved towards him last evening?'

'I thought I discerned a partiality,' I said. Mr Brigstock, probably hearing his name spoken, had turned his head towards us. 'You should lower your voice, Elinor,' I said in an undertone. 'I am sure he hears you.'

'He will not need *me* to inform him of Catherine's preference,' she said gaily, but more quietly. 'She made it clear enough, I thought. Well, he *is* handsome.' She sighed. 'We cannot get out of my uncle Diggory at all what the Brigstocks' situation is. Are they wealthy in their own right? He mentioned an Italian connexion. An aunt? Do you know anything of her? But other than that he could tell us nothing. Mama was quite angry with him, I don't mind telling you.'

'With Mr Brigstock?'

'With Sir Diggory! You are not listening, Miss Talbot!'

She was right. I was not really attending to her. My mind was too full of what it was to have acquaintance, to be called upon, and to have it all spoiled by Lord Petrel.

'His behaviour last night, for one thing,' Elinor went on. 'Whoever heard of such conduct? Not to socialise with his own guests? Mama was mortified. But if Mr Brigstock *is* rich enough … We girls will get something from papa, but not much, so money is a consideration. Mama wanted Catherine to wait until she has made enquiry. But Catherine would not. She put on her best morning gown and had her hair done ever so many times before they set out. How put out she will be to find that he was here with me! He came by the woods, he says, or he would have encountered the carriage on the lane. So Mama and Catherine will be stuck with Miss Brigstock. I thought her very cold, did not you? Look at Caroline Willow. What doe-eyes she turns on her cousin. He cannot but know that she is in love with him.'

'He told me he thinks of all the rectory girls as sisters,' I offered, still distracted. Lord Petrel had drawn the gentlemen's attention to the Adam fireplace, describing its composition and its ornamentations as though he had personally commissioned it.

'That's clear enough,' Elinor said. 'But she has not yet allowed herself to own it. No, she will never capture his heart in the way she wishes. And after all, perhaps that is for the best, for he is to go to war soon is he not? He must stand ready to repel Napoleon's invasionary forces.'

'I suppose so,' I faltered. I found I did not like that idea at all. I got up, ostensibly to return my cup to the sideboard but in fact to escape from the vision—violent and shocking—that had just come to me of Lieutenant Willow's golden hair all blood-soaked and matted, of his face disfigured, of his blue eyes dimmed.

I found Mr Brigstock at my side. 'Miss Talbot,' he said. His voice was low and measured and he stood very stiffly as he spoke. 'I am glad to have the opportunity of telling you how much I enjoyed the dancing last evening.'

His remark surprised me, for he had not given the impression of enjoying it very much. 'I enjoyed it very much too,' I replied. 'I will confess to you, Mr Brigstock, that I had been uneasy about the Binsleys' kind invitation. I was unacquainted with the family. I had only been to Binsley House once. I had never dined from home before, and to do so without my mama and papa ... But I need not have worried. I found everyone to be very agreeable, for the most part. I hope your sister is well.'

'She *is* well, thank you,' he replied tautly. I am sure my arrow about his sister had found its mark. 'I understand that she has company; apparently Mrs Binsley and Miss Binsley have called.'

'Miss Elinor mentioned it,' I said.

'I hope,' he said, 'that *you* will feel able to call on us at Upton Park. A dance, you know, is not always the best milieu to make new acquaintance. Conversation can only ever be very general.'

'General as to topic, yes, but generally very pleasant. *I* found it pleasant, but then I am unaccustomed to being in company. Do you prefer conversation to be particular, Mr Brigstock?' I asked.

A look passed over his face that perplexed me, a shadow of self-consciousness. He hesitated a moment before replying. 'Since you vouchsafe me a confession, Miss Talbot, I will make one in return. I am not a very sociable creature. Neither is my sister. As children, in Italy, we were expected to involve ourselves in company from an early age. It is the way, there. My family entertained a great deal, and were entertained in return, and Lydia and I were always included. Society in Italy is not as it is here in England. We were witness to things that no English child would ever be exposed to. Lydia, in particular … she was barely out of the schoolroom …' He threw a significant look across the room to where Lord Petrel now had Elinor Binsley deeply engaged in conversation on a low sofa pushed back into an alcove. He was sitting very close to her and, as we watched, extended a fat finger and brushed it across her wrist. She snatched her arm away but was powerless to escape; the way he sat on the sofa, crosswise, meant she was trapped. Mr Brigstock looked back at me and I met his eye. 'Some *gentlemen,*' he almost spat out the word, 'are predators,' he said. Then with a bow, he excused himself and crossed to where Edward Binsley, Lieutenant Willow and Caroline leaned over a map that they had spread on a table. He spoke a word, and immediately the map was folded and there was the movement of departure.

'Come, Elinor,' Mr Binsley said briskly. 'We must get back or Sir Diggory will have started dinner without us again.'

In the bustle of departure Lieutenant Willow pressed my hand once more and said a word or two as to the likely means of my being extracted from the clutches of Lord Petrel. As a result of his promise I went to my room immediately after the guests had ridden off down the drive and called my maid.

Accordingly, at three o'clock I was not surprised to hear the wheels of the rectory carriage on the gravel. I went downstairs where I met my maid with my portmanteau.

Lord Petrel emerged from the small drawing room. He had clearly continued to imbibe sherry, or something stronger, since the morning. His eye was bleary and his dress askew. 'And what is this?' he asked, as Swale admitted Lieutenant Willow and the rector. I could have wept with relief; the prospect of any evening with Lord Petrel had been awful enough but if he had been drinking …

'Mrs Willow solicits the company of Miss Talbot for a few days,' the rector said, in the same tone and with the same wrathful eye that he wore when he got to that part in the creed that lamented our sin against God and against our fellow men, the things we had done and the things we had left undone. It was very terrible. 'I must say, sir, I am surprised at your feeling no scruple at imposing yourself on the young lady.'

Lieutenant Willow motioned for the coachman to take charge of my belongings and then held out his arm to me with a courtly flourish. 'Miss Talbot,' he said, giving me a wide, warm and rather mischievous smile. 'Will you do me the great honour?'

'Imposing?' Lord Petrel blustered. 'I stand as her guardian, sir. I prevent any imposition.' He took a step towards me but stumbled and had to reach for the door jamb for support. 'Jocelyn, you shall not go off, shall you?' He looked almost dismayed, but his disappointment did not move me.

'Indeed Lord Petrel, I fear that I must,' I said, my head held high and my voice like ice. 'I think it is what Mama and Papa would wish, and since *you* would not withdraw, then *I* must do so.'

'Indeed it *is* what Mr and Mrs Talbot wish,' the rector pronounced, with great authority. 'I received a message from them half an hour since. They are distressed—inexpressibly distressed—to hear of your arrival during their absence. Business forbids them returning for a few days but they beg that your lordship will go to them in town. In the meantime, Miss

Talbot is to do us the honour of staying with us at the rectory.'

'Quite unnecessary,' Lord Petrel said, his face suffused with blood, his knuckles on the door white with rage. 'My standing is such with the family … You impugn my honour if you suppose … But if she must be so missish about it of course I will depart as soon as possible. Tomorrow.'

'Tomorrow will not be soon enough,' the rector said. 'Decorum, sheer common decency should have told you that you should not have stayed an hour once you had ascertained that the Talbots were from home. It was not gentlemanly of you, sir, to impose yourself on Miss Talbot. But even if you were to go this moment, which I apprehend, by your demeanour, will hardly be possible, I will not disappoint the ladies at the rectory. Good day to you sir.'

Lieutenant Willow led me down the steps and handed me into the carriage.

That night I slept in a narrow bed in a small room hastily vacated for me by Maud Willow. For a second night my slumber was banished by recollections of the day and the evening that had followed it. What fun it had been to dine informally with the rectory family, to play parlour games and to entertain ourselves with taking turns to play and sing at the pianoforte. How odd—but not unpleasant—to undress myself without the help of a maid, to manage my own toilette and to have Caroline Willow brush out my hair.

'You are very pretty, you know,' she had said to me, almost without a grudge, as she wrapped my tresses into papers. 'I saw how Mr Brigstock looked at you today. I do not think Miss Binsley has a chance with him.'

'We are all of us practically strangers,' I said. 'One cannot speculate about possible attachments after two meetings.'

'No,' she agreed. 'As to attachment, that might be true enough, but attraction can be instantaneous, can it not? It is there between Maud and Mr Gabriel. Of course I do not know what his usual manner is but *she* is more energised than I have ever known her. Good night, Miss Talbot.'

'I wish you would call me Jocelyn,' I said.

She seemed pleased. 'Very well,' she said. 'Good night, Jocelyn.'

When I had blown out my candle and laid myself down I thought over what she had said. Two days before I should have known nothing of attachment or attraction. But now, as I closed my eyes, I heard again the words Lieutenant Willow had spoken to me earlier. 'Whatever my aunt agrees to, I will rescue you from this if I have to climb the creeper and spirit you out through a window.' The giddy turmoil the remembrance stirred in me was unlike anything I had ever known and although I tried, I could get no sleep until long after the church clock had struck midnight.

22

Lord Petrel did not leave Ecklington Grange the following day. He lingered until the end of the week and then we heard—via a convoluted network of local informants that seemed to have Mrs Willow at its axis—he had suffered a fall rendering him incapable of travel. How glad I was not to have been marooned there with him, perhaps expected to nurse him! How doubly glad I was of the Willows' hospitality when it became apparent that my father's business in town would take longer than expected to settle. Unrest in India was disturbing his supplies of goods[ix]. All-out war with France was a certainty and demands for saltpetre were high. These were matters he wished to manage himself.

A full two weeks passed. I did not know if the Willows had anticipated a stay of such long duration when they had plucked me from the claws of Lord Petrel but of course, as he remained at Ecklington, they could not send me home. From time to time I sent to Mrs Butterwick and requested she have such things as a side of ham, a selection of pies and jars of preserves conveyed to the rectory but I think in this I erred as the rectory cook took umbrage.

'She thinks you quarrel with her cooking,' Maud explained to me one day. 'The ham was very nice, for we keep no pig here, you know, but as to pies and preserves, Mrs Johns objects to the idea that Mrs Bray's are superior.'

I was happy at the rectory, where life was delightfully informal, not at all like the studied decorum that Mama insisted on at Ecklington. I had company of my own age; all was laughter and amusement. Our new friends the Binsleys called upon us often, or we encountered them in our walks between the hedgerows of quiet country lanes. Often Mr Brigstock was of the party. He cast a sombre note, observing but never participating in the hi-jinks of the Binsley brothers and Lieutenant Willow as they wrestled each other in the meadow, raced their horses or played cricket on the village green. I wondered sometimes why he persisted in seeking our company when, having joined us, he kept himself apart, but I supposed he found Upton Park drear and certainly his sister was no very lively company. She showed her face on only one or two occasions, and only then from her carriage. She seemed disinclined for exercise of any kind. We spent the mornings walking or riding in the countryside, gathering elderflowers to make cordial and reconnoitring possible sites for our picnic, which we planned endlessly but never came to any fixed scheme. It was as charming as possible, the weather being extremely clement and the company so very agreeable.

Mrs Willow, though undoubtedly a garrulous woman of small intellect, was kind and motherly, very affectionate towards her daughters and also to me. I found I rather craved the comfort of physical embrace; Mama was not a tactile woman. Mrs Willow provided for us in the way of food and ensured we were provisioned with clean linen but apart from that she left us young people to a large degree to our own devices. She was busy about her duties in the morning, taking food to the poor and encouragement to the sick, and calling upon her acquaintance amongst the goodwives, widows and spinsters of the village. She gathered up gossip from them all with which she would regale us in the afternoons as we sat and sewed, drew or trimmed our bonnets as the dinner hour approached.

The rector could be stiff and humourless but he was outnumbered by the women in his household and I think had long since given up the battle against fits of giggles, crises of millinery, pouts and flouncing. He led us in prayers each morning and then retired to his library with a pot of coffee. We were to infer him to be occupied in prayer and meditation, religious reading and theological wrangling but I glimpsed him once through the French window and he was fast asleep with a novel on his lap. He would emerge again at one and take his walk, which was generally a long walk, returning in time for dinner.

Lieutenant Willow had surprising patience with his cousins and me, putting himself at our disposal most mornings. Caroline read more into this than he intended her to. He was jocular with her, kind and unceremonious—like a brother. I never saw him make a gesture, or heard him speak any word that could be construed as romantic, or demonstrate any partiality other than fraternal. Although she often tried to manage matters so that she was able to spend time alone with him he was usually successful in frustrating her efforts, inviting me to accompany them on a walk she had suggested or asking me to help him with his part in a duet she wanted him to try. Apart from the fact that I disliked coming between the cousins, and feared becoming the object of Caroline's resentment, I did not mind. Time spent with Lieutenant Willow was time pleasantly spent, as far as I was concerned. It surprised me very much that a friendship of only a fortnight could result in such intimacy and unreserve, but so it proved to be. I completely lost my shyness with him; he was amusing and agreeable and his dry wit made me laugh. He was considerate towards me, gallant in a light-hearted way that was by no means flirtatious. He was a natural gentleman, always ready to hand a lady over a stile or help her mount and dismount her mare.

Our conversation was wide-ranging, often light-hearted but occasionally more profound. We had both read a new translation of Dante's Divine Comedy[x], which we discussed at length. The lieutenant was a keen abolitionist, appalled by Bonaparte's reinstatement of slavery the previous year. This was a topic I had never heard discussed at home and

I was eager to know more of it. Maud Willow was a well-informed young woman and often participated in our debates, but Caroline only sighed at our seriousness, and tried to turn our attention to the cherry blossom. Did it not look just like confetti? she enquired. Could we not just imagine ourselves at a wedding, here beneath the cherry trees? Let Barney stand here beside her, and make believe they were being married. Lieutenant Willow only rolled his eyes and teased her for her silliness.

The accommodation at the rectory was insufficient to allow for more than the family to dine, but Mrs Willow was generous with her invitations to tea in the evenings. Mr Eagerly and his brother joined us on two or three occasions when the curate's pastoral duties and Dr Eagerly's studies allowed. The Binsleys came also. We played parlour games or cards and made very merry. Mr Brigstock came more rarely to these entertainments. His sister would decline Mrs Willow's invitations and I suppose he did not like to leave her alone in the evenings. I knew that he found the boisterous company trying. The rectory drawing room was not large; there was little he could do to escape the high spirits and shouting that the games provoked. For all Miss Binsley's evident preference for Mr Brigstock she seemed to have discerned nothing of his character or disposition, or perhaps she was just too selfish to deny herself the pleasure of the cards. Either way it fell to me to notice and effect some alternative entertainment for him. The evenings being mild, I might suggest a walk in the rectory garden. Once I took him into the rector's library where we examined some fine editions of Shakespeare. To be sure, Mr Brigstock was a lordly and uncompromising gentleman, tending to aloofness, but I had been vouchsafed a tiny glimpse into the truth of his character. I thought he was shy rather than proud, and I suspected his standoffishness to be a kind of defence. In any event I was not intimidated by him and found him quite conversable upon subjects that were neutral.

It was upon this occasion, as we turned the pages of the rector's books, that he said to me, 'The viscount remains at Ecklington, I hear.'

I nodded, and explained as much as I knew about Lord Petrel's injury, concluding, 'It seems he is incapable of travel.'

'He is capable of climbing into a carriage, and out of it again,' Mr Brigstock said, frowning. 'He did us the honour of calling upon us yesterday. I was from home. My sister did not receive him, naturally. She is particular about which callers she will receive and will certainly entertain no gentlemen callers when I am not present. He has been long acquainted with your family?'

'With my father,' I said. I did not wish to explain the precise nature of my father's relationship with Lord Petrel. 'They became acquainted when Papa returned from India.'

'I gather there is no Lady Petrel?'

I confirmed this to be the case.

'I wonder why?' Mr Brigstock mused, throwing me a fleeting, questioning look. 'He is not an ill-looking man, and many women would like to be a countess.'

'It might be some time before Lord Petrel becomes Earl,' I said. 'I think there is some scruple as to fortune. Lord Petrel is not a wealthy man.'

'That will be no impediment to *some*,' Mr Brigstock said with deceptive lightness.

There was the remnant of a small fire in the library. It threw out a comfortable heat but no light. We had only three or four candles to see by, but Mr Brigstock was turned at such an angle that I could not quite make out his expression. His features I could see well enough—dark, brooding eyes under heavy brows, finely sculpted cheekbones—but his gaze was on the volume in his hand and I could not penetrate it. I wondered how his thoughts were running. Could he be considering Lord Petrel as a possible suitor for his sister's hand? It seemed very unlikely to me, when I recalled his epithet in Ecklington's drawing room. But then again the Brigstocks, while being without apparent family connection, were noble to their fingertips. Miss Brigstock would certainly make a very good countess.

'Lord Petrel was not at Ecklington when you did us the honour of dining with us,' I observed. 'Your sister has not met him.'

The idea jolted Mr Brigstock from his seat with such violence that the book he held fell to the floor. 'I can assure you I do not wish her to,' he said most vehemently. 'He is *precisely* the type of gentleman I wish her to avoid. She has been taken in … taken advantage of … But I will say no more of that.'

He paced for a moment or two to expiate his choler. *Now* I could read his face and it was taut, his jaw clenched and his eye narrowed. It suddenly became manifest to me that the Brigstocks' precipitate departure from their native Italy and their arrival in the county—not clandestine but certainly unheralded–could well be the result of an unhappy liaison. It would certainly explain their air of intense reserve although Miss Brigstock did not seem to me to display the marks of heart-break. Indeed there were times—so icily composed was she, so stonily statuesque—when her possession of a heart was decidedly moot.

I knew it was none of my business to speculate on these things. I knew nothing of romance or of the world. What I did know was that I had upset Mr Brigstock. 'I have distressed you,' I said. 'I have hit a nerve. I am sorry.'

Mr Brigstock looked down at me where I remained on the sofa, and his anger evaporated. He sat himself beside me once more. 'You misunderstand me,' he said, resuming his usual measured tone. 'It is not Lydia I meant. It is you.' He lifted his hand from where it lay on his lap and I thought he would reach out and put it over mine, but he reached down to the floor instead to retrieve the book.

'Me?' I could hardly comprehend him. 'In relation to Lord Petrel?'

In the candlelight it was hard to see clearly but I think he almost blushed. 'I see you have no notion of such an arrangement,' he said. 'You have turned quite pale.' He went to a sideboard where a decanter and glasses were set, and poured me a glass of the rector's Madeira. I found I was very much in want of it and did not answer him until I had emptied the glass. 'The idea is abhorrent to me,' I said.

He favoured me with a smile—a rarity, with him. 'I am so glad,' he said. 'I did not like the man. I know his type. But I did not know what understanding there might be.'

'There is none that I know of,' I said, very decidedly.

It felt politic to change the subject. 'Do you think you will stay at Upton permanently?' I asked. Upton Park was only let to the Brigstocks. It was locally understood that their tenancy was initially for six months, but could be extended. Mrs Willow's sources suggested that the owner would be willing to sell.

'It suits us well for the time being,' he replied. 'It is retired—something we especially required. I think it likely, in the early autumn, that we might go away for a few weeks. Lydia wishes to explore the North Country.' He looked as though he might say more, but then thought better of it.

'You have family in the north?'

He shook his head. 'We have no family in England. Any that we might have had, at one time, we have long since lost connexion with. Our father married against his family's wishes and they threw him over.'

This seemed like another dangerous subject and I turned my attention back to the volume of sonnets.

23

The period of Lieutenant Willow's furlough had been set at two months. By early-June he was expected at his barracks, from whence it was certain that he would be deployed. From time to time he received communication from his commanding officer regarding regimental matters but it seemed he had nothing to do about them but read the communiqués and write a word in return by way of acknowledgement. Other than that his time was his own. It seemed surprising to me that a young man such as he would not wish to spend his furlough in town, with old school friends or brother officers also on leave of absence but he seemed to have no plans of that sort. He was happy to enjoy the domestic peace of the rectory and the company of the rectory family. I wondered that his imminent engagement with enemy forces did not weigh on his mind – if it *did* he gave no indication of it. I know Caroline worried about it a great deal, and Mrs Willow also. I must admit that, as I became more intimately acquainted with the lieutenant, I too began to feel a decided dread of the idea of him going off to fight but I did not analyse my sense of attachment to him.

I did not have cause to do so until one day when it had fallen out that the two of us became separated from the rest of the company. We were walking through pleasant woodlands that bordered the river demarcating the boundary of Sir Diggory's estate. Mr Binsley and Mr Brigstock had brought tackle and were trying their luck a quarter of a mile or so upstream. Mr Gabriel and Maud Willow had set up their easels. Miss Binsley had perched herself on a fallen tree trunk close to the anglers, determined to give her company and encouragement to Mr Brigstock whether he required it or not. That he did *not* was manifest to all of us except Miss Binsley. She had—to use a vulgar phrase—set her cap at him. He responded to her flirtation with consummate politeness but showed her no partiality she could misconstrue. Normally I would attempt to distract Miss Binsley in order to save Mr Brigstock from the embarrassment of her advances, but on that day I was powerless to turn Miss Binsley from her resolution. The rest of us sauntered along a path that wound between the trees. There was an abundance of bluebells there, an ultra-violet miasma beneath the trees that was quite breathtaking. Caroline and Miss Elinor fell upon them with a cry, wishing to gather armfuls to take home. I knew that the flowers would wilt and die before they could be got into vases.

'Oh! Do not pick them,' I cried. 'They look so lovely here, in their natural setting. Better to fetch your paint-boxes and commit their beauty to paper, than to ravage them.'

The girls were fixed in their intention however, so I walked on with the lieutenant. 'I cannot bear to watch them decimate that lovely glade,' I said. 'What they do not pick they will trample. I shall try to remember their beauty as it was before we intruded upon it.'

'Beauty in the remembrance is a great comfort,' the lieutenant said thoughtfully. 'Sometimes it is the only comfort we can be sure of.'

We both admired the scene around us. It was one of those truly lovely spring days. The sun was warm but not over-powering. A slight breeze moved the new-furled leaves of the trees in the canopy above us. Saplings at the water's edge swayed and shimmered in the light that reflected from the river and wild flowers nodded amongst the grasses. The woods were alive with birds, their song a concerto around and above us.

'Are you thinking of what will cheer you when you re-join your regiment?' I asked.

He nodded. 'I am gathering up a bouquet of pleasant reminiscences,' he said. 'I think, in battle, there will not be much of beauty.'

We walked in silence while I mastered my feelings. Then I said, 'Do you *know* what your situation will be?'

'We have had rigorous training,' he said, 'but I think nothing can really prepare one for battle. I expect a good deal of noise, dirt and confusion. I am only a lieutenant. My job will be to follow orders and keep the men I command in line. If I can do *that* I will be doing my duty and no man can aspire to more than that.'

'I am glad my brother George is too young to enlist,' I said.

'He may not be, before the war is done,' Lieutenant Willow said gently.

'I cannot bear to think of it.'

He threw me a look loaded with sympathy and understanding. Then he said, 'Let us not think of it. Let us think of happier things, as I shall do, when I am away from here. You have enjoyed your time at the rectory, have you not?'

'Oh very much,' I said, 'but I shall have to go home before too long. Mama and Papa will not be in town much longer, I do not think.'

'Do you miss them?'

His question caught me off guard. The truth was, I did *not* miss them. I did not know if I really even loved them. I was dutiful and respectful, but that was not love. I missed George. I *loved* George. He was the only creature who had touched my heart but even with him I had been forced to be measured about how my love might be displayed. The Talbots were not demonstrative. They were not cruel but they were cold. The affection I had seen exhibited at the rectory, even by the rector, far out-shone any fondness I had ever seen at home and it came to me then as I strolled along the river bank that I was desperate to be loved. My parents were so occupied with the appearance of things that they had neglected their engines of emotion, the inner substance of themselves, and they had failed to provide for mine. I felt it then, like an empty crater in my heart, a bowl, a fissure that ached to be filled.

My hesitation was enough answer for the lieutenant. He had been walking ahead of me along the narrow path but now he stopped so suddenly I almost bumped into him. 'I want to ask you …' he said, without turning round, so that it seemed as though the words were addressed to some third person who walked along with us, 'I wish to ask you if you will miss *me,* when I am gone. But I cannot. I *ought* not. It would not be fair.'

Then he did turn, and the light in his eye was like a blue flame, as intense and mesmerising as the bluebells had been.

'Not fair?' I croaked out.

He shook his head, and his golden curls tumbled across his forehead and fell into his eyes so that I wanted to lift my hand and brush them away. 'No. Because that would be looking forward to the future, which I dare not do. I cannot look forward at all. I hope you understand me, Miss Talbot. If I were at liberty, if I had my property, if I were not required by duty and honour to serve my country, *then* I could look forward and it would be fair of me to ask you to do so too. But, as it is, I cannot. And so it is not fair. I wish you to know though, that *I* have been very happy, this past fortnight. My bouquet of memories has been added to so substantially that I can hardly encompass it.'

The path had brought us close to the riverbank once more, a quiet, private spot where the water flowed smooth as silk and the willows leaned over to dip their trailing branches into its mirrored surface. Without my quite knowing how he had done so, he had taken my hand in his. I found I could not meet his gaze. I wore no gloves. My hand in his looked very small but he held it gently, as though it were a fragile bird. My heart was beating very fast. I comprehended his meaning, his intent—all he had meant but had not said—and admired his restraint. I knew I could not match it, neither his clarity nor his control. I feared that, as soon as I opened my mouth to speak, where he had implied, I would openly declare. Where he had held back, I would leap forward. How could I help myself from taking the love he offered me and using it to plug every gap in my poor, starved heart?

For a while I said nothing, but stared resolutely at our entwined hands. At last I mastered myself. 'I too have been very happy this last fortnight,' I said. 'But I must go back.' I meant really that I must go back to where the rest of the party was assembled, that I could not trust myself in that secluded glade with him, alone.

For once he misconstrued me. 'Back to live at the Grange, yes,' he said, 'but I hope you will not go back to your solitary life. Do not be like one of Caroline's bluebells. Do not fade and die because you have been discovered, and prized, and taken from the quiet seclusion of your native glade.'

Prized! The word set my soul on fire! But his image of me—limp and faded, abandoned—soon quenched it. I feared that was exactly what would happen. *He* would soon be gone, to who knew what future? He could be dashed from the deck in a storm, or shot to pieces by cannon, or ravaged by disease in some terrible, rat-infested camp. The Binsleys—certainly the two young men—would depart at the end of the following week. Mama had spoken of the desirability of a connection with the Binsleys but neither of the Binsley brothers had taken any particular interest in me. I doubted she would think acquaintance with the girls worth pursuing even if they remained in the county. I knew very well that she would not regard friendship with the family from the rectory—the kind of intimacy that had developed between us—with any approbation. Their hospitality to me had been useful to her; that was all. She would think them presumptuous to attempt to continue the degree of acquaintance we had enjoyed for the past two weeks. That left the

Brigstocks, and although they were our equals I knew Mama detested Miss Brigstock and could see no continuance of intercourse with them.

My idyll was almost over and I understood, now, why Lieutenant Willow denied himself sight of the future: it was bleak, filled with uncertainty.

'I do not know what Mama may permit,' I said in a flat voice, feeling very desolate.

He seemed to sense my despair. He gave my hand a little shake, as though to call me back to him. 'Your heart is full, and so is mine. Oh, what words would tumble out of it if I only set them free! But I *cannot* speak, Miss Talbot. You understand, don't you, that I cannot speak? I want you to understand what I would say if I *could* speak.' He dipped his head so that he could look into my eyes. His, like mine, swam with tears. 'Do speak a word. Just one word, so that I know you understand.' He spoke very quietly, with none of the humour that normally characterised his conversation. 'Let me,' he breathed, his mouth very close to mine, 'let me add that word to my bouquet of memories. You need not commit yourself. I ask you for nothing. It is *my* feelings alone … *my* hopes … the wishes of *my* heart … You are quite free. But tell me that you have understood me.'

I gave a little nod and a tear that had been trembling on my lashes fell onto the back of his hand. 'Yes,' I rasped out, and all of a sudden I knew that utter joy and abject sadness could exist, side by side.

When we returned to the rectory that afternoon I found a note waiting for me. My parents had returned to Ecklington and I was required to go home. With what sorrow did I pack my belongings and bid farewell to the little eaves room that had become so comfortable to me. How I fell upon the necks of Caroline and Maud and Mrs Willow!

'We will meet again very soon,' they all said. 'You must call, every day if you wish, and we will call upon you.'

'So long as Mrs Talbot permits,' the rector put in. He had cut short his walk so see me into the carriage that had been sent from the Grange to collect me. 'She may well not want a gaggle of silly girls cluttering up her drawing room.'

I knew he spoke the truth, and of all the emotions then vying for supremacy in my heart it was anger that predominated. It made me angry that my parents would discourage the Willows, such good, honest, honourable people that they were.

'And we have the picnic to look forward to,' Mrs Willow said. The date had just that afternoon been fixed for Wednesday of the following week, which would be the eighteenth of May. 'I must liaise with the housekeeper at Binsley, and with Mrs Butterwick, and with the Brigstocks' housekeeper in the matter of viands.'

I had the sudden idea that Ecklington should shoulder the burden of the provisions—I owed the Willows and the Binsleys hospitality, after all—and resolved to ask my mother about it as soon as I was home. The prospect cheered me, as I am sure Mrs Willow had intended it should. I shook hands with the rector, thanking him profusely for the generosity of his provision for me, and Lieutenant Willow handed me into the carriage. His smile had all his usual openness, warmth and cheer in it, but he pressed my hand most particularly.

24

It was odd to return to the studied elegance and decorum of Ecklington after the noisy, cluttered, somewhat rowdy atmosphere at the rectory. Swale seemed ridiculously wooden and po-faced as he opened the door to me and directed a footman to take charge of my little trunk. My footsteps on the marble floor echoed along the hallway and seemed to reverberate from the crystal droplets of the chandeliers in chimes of mockery. The house was preposterously large—so many rooms we barely ever used; so much furniture we never sat upon and pictures we never looked at. Everything was dust-free and immaculate; each figurine just so, the flowers in the vases so perfect that they looked artificial. Even the cascade from the fountain in the conservatory seemed prescribed. I longed for a melee of happy chatter, the cheerful strew of ribbons and lace on a work table, the sound of someone thumping out their scales on the little pianoforte in the rectory dining room.

I climbed the stairs and went into the drawing room. No indentation on the perfectly plump pillows of the sofa showed that anyone had sat there recently but I did discern a whiff of cigar smoke that would not normally have been there—Papa only ever smoked in the billiard room or in his study. I tried other rooms—Mama's sitting room, the music room and the library—but the house seemed deserted. I recalled with a jolt the times George and I had tried to play hide and seek at Ecklington, and given it up. You could wander for hours without finding the one you sought. The sudden recollection of George made me miss him and I realised that I had not despatched my weekly letters. I had been too busy enjoying myself.

At last I found Mama and Papa on the lawn drinking tea, and with them, of course, was Lord Petrel. He stood as I approached, or at least he would have stood had he not been hampered by one leg, which stuck out stiffly in front of him, thickly bandaged from the ankle to the knee. He had a cane, which he leant upon in his attempt to rise.

'Do forgive me, Miss Talbot,' he said, giving up the attempt and falling back into the wicker seat behind him. 'You see how I am placed.' Perhaps unconsciously he lifted a hand to the side of his face, which displayed a scratch or graze across it, almost healed now.

'Lord Petrel.' I curtseyed formally before kissing Mama and Papa—the lightest possible brush of my lips on their cheeks—and taking the fourth chair at the table. Mama offered me tea but I declined it.

'Lord Petrel injured himself,' Mama said unnecessarily. 'He was forced to remain at Ecklington for the duration.'

'It was quite right that you should go to the rectory,' Papa put in, but very mildly.

'I don't quite see it,' Mama retorted. It was clear that they had rehearsed this argument many times already.

'Neither do I,' Lord Petrel agreed. 'The rector was high-handed in the extreme. I *would* have gone however, if not for …' He indicated his injured leg. 'Travel, naturally, was out of the question.'

'Mr Brigstock was sorry not to have been at home when you called upon *him*,' I declared, giving Lord Petrel a very straight look. 'How did you hurt yourself?'

Lord Petrel's colour, always high, became higher. He plucked a handkerchief from a pocket and mopped his brow. 'My man spilt my shaving water,' he said when he had composed himself. 'I think I mentioned that the wash-stand is cracked? It was soapy and ...' he left the rest unsaid. Perhaps he did not wish me to imagine the incident— feet slithering beneath him, then an ungainly tumble, legs akimbo, into a puddle of soapy water—so I put my head on one side and stared into space for a moment, pantomiming just that, a wry smile on my lips. But in truth I didn't believe him. Far more likely that he had drunk too much of Papa's wine and stumbled. Indeed, I would not have put it past him to be feigning the injury altogether. A bandage, after all, proved nothing.

'You enjoyed yourself at the rectory?' Papa asked. 'I shall write the rector a note.' He turned to my mother, always the arbiter of etiquette. 'I suppose we ought to have them to dine?'

She gave a stiff little nod, her gesture saying more eloquently than any words: I suppose we will have to.

'I enjoyed myself very much,' I said, 'and, in point of fact Papa, on Wednesday next, there is to be a picnic. I wondered if we might provide the fayre. I should like to repay the Willows for their kindness. It would be just the same as inviting them to dine and the rector's daughters will enjoy it more.'

Papa pounced on the idea. 'Of course! Where is the picnic to be? Here?'

'No, it is to be at ... well, in truth I do not quite know. Some craggy place with waterfalls. The rector says it is a famous beauty-spot. It is hard by a derelict abbey.'

'It sounds disgustingly rustic,' Lord Petrel said with an artificial yawn. 'How boring.'

'Pockmorten,' my mother said. 'They must mean Pockmorten Abbey. In fact I believe it is very nice.'

'Pockmorten? That is five miles from here,' my father said. 'I had not anticipated a trek such as that for the servants. They will need both dog-carts and that is on the assumption that it does not rain. Much better have your little picnic here at Ecklington my dear. Then you can come indoors if it is inclement.'

'Thank you Papa,' I said, 'but I believe that the attraction of the entertainment is the drive there—or some will ride. The gentlemen, I suppose, will ride—and also the opportunity to explore. It is to be an excursion *and* a picnic. If you would rather not, Papa, if you think it will be too much trouble for Mrs Butterwick, I am sure Mrs Willow and Sir Diggory's housekeeper between them can ...'

'Oh no,' my father waved my words away. 'Whatever you like my dear. I am sure Mrs Butterwick will be equal to it.'

'Did you say gentlemen?' Lord Petrel enquired. 'Who, then, will be of the party? I had assumed you meant only the family from the rectory. Of course there is that nephew of theirs. An upstart puppy if ever there was one, leering and smirking as the rector took me to task. *He* is no gentleman.'

'Lieutenant Willow is perfectly gentlemanlike,' I said proudly and perhaps too hotly. 'Mr Edward Binsley and Mr Brigstock will be of the party—those same gentlemen you took it upon yourself to invite into Ecklington after the dinner at Sir Diggory's house. And perhaps the Eagerly brothers; I should like to include them. We see too little of them these days.'

Mama snorted, '*They* have been a drain on your Papa's resources for long enough. They must stand on their own feet at *some* point.'

'Of course they must,' Lord Petrel agreed, as though it were any business of his.

'*They* make every effort to do so,' I said pointedly, looking at Lord Petrel's bandaged leg. 'They are certainly too proud to ask for help, even if they need it, which, in my opinion, they do. Victor Eagerly's clothes are threadbare, Papa.'

My father shifted uneasily in his seat and threw a barbed look at my mother. 'Are they? Poor chap. I cannot allow him to struggle.'

'Why-ever not, Talbot?' Lord Petrel enquired. 'We all must, sometimes, you know. It is what makes men of us.'

I regarded Lord Petrel, sitting at his ease in a comfortable chair, his clothing of the best possible quality, the vastness of the Talbot resources absolutely at his disposal. His struggle did not seem very arduous. Indeed, it was hard to think of him being touched by anything to the least degree vexatious; he was the picture of satisfied complacency. He turned to me with an oily smile. 'But if they are in a slump, Jocelyn, best not to invite them to your little picnic. No need to expose their penury, eh?'

'Do not trouble yourself,' I sniped, 'with who I do or do not invite, for I would not presume to expose you to the *ennui* of it. Such a boring, *rustic* little affair will hardly interest you.'

'And that's telling *you,* old fellow,' my father said, waggling his eyebrows at his friend. 'Jocelyn, I think your time away has done you good. You have found some spirit.'

His praise pleased me, but I did not like the appraising look in Lord Petrel's eye. 'If I might be excused,' I said, getting up, 'I think I will go and speak to Mrs Butterwick now.'

My mother also stood up. 'I will come indoors,' she said. 'It grows chilly and soon it will be time to dress.' We walked together across the lawns. The long shadows of the cedars stretched out and we entered into their gloom.

Mama took my arm. 'Lady Pembroke thinks there will not be a ball[xi] this year,' she said. 'The situation with France, you know. So you will have to wait a year before your coming out. Shall you mind?'

'I had given it no thought,' I said truthfully, 'but I think it will not be necessary. I *am* out, am I not? Since I attended Sir Diggory's dinner …'

'Not at all,' she replied. 'A simple country dinner will not serve. You are to be presented, and we shall have a ball at the house in Grosvenor Square. You can aim very high, Jocelyn. You are a gentleman's daughter and your papa will be very generous.'

I knew that when she spoke of my father as a gentleman she did not mean Robert Talbot but her first husband, who had been a man of rank if an old, curmudgeonly one.

'I am a little confused,' I said, as we entered the house by way of the conservatory. 'Last time we had any conversation on the matter you described me as a merchant's daughter, and lamented that Papa's rank would be an impediment to a match even with the Binsleys.'

She stopped abruptly and turned to face me. '*Is* there such a prospect?' she asked me sharply.

I shook my head. 'No,' I said. 'They are both very nice, but there has been no partiality. Indeed, I rather think that Mr Gabriel has a fondness for Maud Willow.'

'Ha!' my mother half-shouted. '*That* will not do. I presume Mrs Binsley does not suspect it?'

I shrugged. 'I don't know. But where will be the impediment? Maud Willow is a gentleman's daughter. And I think the rector will not leave his girls unprovided for.'

'But nothing to what *you* will have,' Mama cried. 'Mr Gabriel Binsley is young—he has only been up at Oxford a year or two—but Miss Willow should know better than to set her sights so high. She was to have gone to Basingstoke, was she not? To see if she could not find herself an ecclesiastical husband?'

I had heard no mention of the scheme whilst I had been at the rectory and it felt wrong—disloyal and crass—to discuss the matrimonial strategy of a girl who had become my friend.

'I may well have spoken out of turn,' I mumbled. 'There has been nothing positively said. There is no understanding that I know of. But Mr and Mrs Willow, they have not discouraged the association.'

'I'll wager they have not,' my mother said.

By this time we were at the foot of the staircase. We went up together.

'Leave your talk with Mrs Butterwick to the morning,' Mama said. 'I have asked Peake to draw you a bath. It will be ready by now. I am sure you have not been able to bathe at the rectory, or to wash your hair. I bought you new things while I was in town. They will be in your room. Wear one of the new dresses for dinner, but come to me before you go down. There is much to talk about. I wish to hear all about your sojourn at the rectory.'

Before we parted I said, 'Lord Petrel. How long is he to stay, Mama?'

She could not quite meet my eye. 'Of course we cannot send him off until he is recovered,' she said. 'It was naughty of him to come here, Jocelyn, and I have told him so. *He* has some idea …but I have told him that you are too young and there is no possibility of such a thing. However, I think you will be wise to spend time with your new acquaintance, while the viscount remains with us. Gentlemen can be easily tempted …'

'I shall do nothing to tempt Lord Petrel,' I said hotly.

She looked at me narrowly, but then she took my hand and patted it. 'I believe you,' she said, reassured.

25

Annie Orphan 1803

The period of Miss Talbot's residency at the Rectory, coinciding with Mr and Mrs Talbot's being in town, should have been a time of furlough for the household staff. To be sure there were the kinds of jobs to be undertaken that could not be done when the family was in residence—curtains to be taken down and beaten, mattresses to be turned, chandeliers to be de-waxed and burnished back to brightness. But these could be done in a leisurely way and the staff looked forward to a period of comparative ease and relaxation. The rooms would not require daily dusting, coals need not be carried nor fires lit. There would be considerably less laundry. The girls in the dairy expected to make less butter and cheese and the gardeners looked forward to enjoying most of that year's asparagus crop.

Lord Petrel's presence in the house was therefore an unexpected and a most unwelcome inconvenience. Mr Swale's certainty that he would soon depart proved unfounded; he lingered, walking the grounds, riding his horse and spending hours in the stables consulting with Mr Talbot's new master of horse, Jackie Silver. His valet, Mr Goose, lounged in the servants' hall, distracting the maids and making a nuisance of himself.

Miss Talbot had been at the rectory some four or five days when Annie was awakened in the middle of the night by the sound of her door being opened and somebody stumbling through. The night was as dark as pitch. No moon showed through her little skylight and the lamp usually left burning low on the landing seemed to have gone out. There was a groan and a little whimper, and the intruder fell to the floor with such heaviness that the ewer on Annie's little washstand quaked and threatened to fall.

Annie fumbled for her tinder so that she could light her candle, mishandling it, almost knocking the candlestick over; it took her two or three attempts. Then she held the candle high and turned to the space near the open door. Sally lay on the rough wooden boards, insensible.

The left side of Sally's face was dark and swollen, the eye pulpy, the brow split and bleeding. Her lips were all misshapen and crusty with blood. Annie tried to turn her over and she let out a little groan.

Sally still wore her work frock, a practical dress made from good quality serge with buttons down the front. The yoke of the dress was torn, several buttons missing. Annie could see bruising at her throat and on her chest. She tentatively examined the remainder of Sally's body. More bruising to the arms, one stocking unfastened and down by her ankle, one shoe absent entirely. The knee of the bare leg was skinned and still oozed blood. The stocking on the other leg was filthy and torn, also bloody at the knee.

It was hard to imagine what had befallen Sally but sundry scenarios played through Annie's mind; she had fallen, been kicked by a horse or trampled by the dairy herd, she had been attacked. Any of these things was possible but what was certain was that Annie was not equal to treating injuries of such variety or of such severity. She could not even get Sally onto the bed without help. Miss Nugent, whose aid she would immediately have summoned, had accompanied Mrs Talbot to London. It was unthinkable that the help of a man should be sought. Annie crept down the servants' stair, her candle held high, balking at the shadows that seemed to lurk at every turn, jumping at every strange noise the night-time house emitted, to where Mrs Butterwick's accommodations were located.

Mrs Butterwick, in her nightcap and a long, loose dressing gown, took one look at Sally and then reeled off a list of things that Annie should fetch from the stillroom: extract of marigold[xii], an unguent made from Echinacea[xiii] and goose fat, willow bark[xiv], witch hazel[xv] and clean gauze. Annie descended the stairs again. When she returned Mrs Butterwick had rolled Sally onto her back and removed her dress and petticoat. She had re-lit the landing lamp and put a pan of water on the little stove to heat.

'You did right to wake me, Annie,' the housekeeper said, 'although I wish Miss Nugent had been here. She is more practiced than I. Now we must examine every inch of Sally to see where her injuries are. You begin at the head and I will start at her feet.'

Annie ran her hands carefully over Sally's skull, feeling for swellings or cuts. Sally's hair was badly matted and tangled with straw—she would be upset, Annie thought, to have it so. Sally's one vanity was her lovely, lustrous hair. Annie could feel no contusions however. She inserted a finger into Sally's mouth, feeling for loose teeth. One on the left felt spongy but otherwise all were firm. She leant closer and smelled Sally's breath. Cider.

'Is she intoxicated?' she asked Mrs Butterwick. 'Perhaps she drank too much cider, and fell? She may have hit her face …'

'I don't think so,' Mrs Butterwick said grimly. She had lifted Sally's wounded knees and now peered up beneath the material of her chemise. 'There is much swelling here, bleeding and bruising. I think she has been forced.'

'Forced?' Annie's mouth was dry.

'Yes. A man has forced her.'

Mrs Butterwick turned to Sally's hands. 'Her nails are broken. I think she tried to defend herself.' She felt gently up the length of Sally's arms. 'No bones broken though, and no fever that I can discern.'

Annie thought of Jackie Silver, but did not voice her thought.

'Her knees,' Annie said.

'Yes, she has crawled on them. There is gravel in them that will have to be got out.'

Between them they managed to lift Sally on to Annie's bed. It was unusual for Annie to see the housekeeper engage in any physical endeavour. Her habit was to direct and supervise and then to confirm that her orders had been carried out. She might sweep a hand over furniture that should have been dusted, pull back a sheet to ensure that a bed had been properly made. But now Annie found Mrs Butterwick quite capable of the lifting and shifting required to settle Sally comfortably, by no means shirking of what needed to be done.

They removed the rest of Sally's clothes and bathed her body, applying salves to her injuries and packing the place between her legs with some of the rags the girls used for their courses. Mrs Butterwick picked the gravel from Sally's knees and cleaned them with liniment. Sally winced and whimpered, but did not wake. Annie washed the dirt and crusted blood from Sally's eye and put a pad of clean material over it. She combed the worst of the straw from her hair. All the time she murmured reassurance although Sally made no sign of being able to hear. If anything the girl looked worse rather than better. Her jaw and cheek became blacker and more bloated as the night went by. She spoke no sensible word. Her good eye was glazed and unfocussed.

'I fear concussion,' Mrs Butterwick said, 'and her jaw may be broken, but I cannot tell.'

They worked in the light of a single candle. Its flame flickered in the draught as they moved about their task, throwing shadows across Sally's distended features, rendering them even more horrific. Annie's throat was clogged, tight with anxiety, and tears pressed the backs of her eyes. Beneath her concern lay a ventricle brimming with caustic anger at the man who had done this.

'Will she live, do you think?' Annie asked when they had covered Sally with a clean sheet and managed to dribble a little willow bark tea between her poor, swollen lips. They sat either side of the little bed. A greyish glow divided the square of skylight from the gloom of the rest of the room. Above them, in the eaves, the first sparrows began to stir.

'She will, if there are no injuries that we cannot see. If she is not awake and sensible by morning the surgeon must be called. She has been badly used, that's clear enough. But Sally's character speaks against her.'

'Because she is a flirt?'

Mrs Butterwick nodded. 'We must hope and pray there is no child. However it is come by, whether Sally be guilty or no, she will be dismissed.'

'And the man who did this to her? I believe it might have been Mr Silver. I know he has hurt her before. I saw the bruises on her arms. Surely he'll be sent packing?'

Mrs Butterwick pressed her lips together but did not reply.

Presently Annie dressed herself and went about her duties, creeping into Lord Petrel's chamber to light his fire. The room reeked of brandy and cigars, the air thick as a wet woollen blanket. When she had laid the fire and put a light to it Annie made her silent way across to the window, parted the shutters and pulled the casement open enough to admit some fresh air. Lord Petrel's room was on the east side of the house and although she had opened the shutters only a little the room was suddenly illuminated by a bloom of bluish morning light. The dawn call of a blackbird somewhere in the creeper that grew around the window was piercingly loud. She swivelled anxiously, to see if it had woken the man on the bed, but he slept on, oblivious. His lordship was sprawled across the counterpane, his head turned away from her. He had removed his coat but was still dressed in shirt and breeches, his stock untied, his stockings filthy. One boot was thrown across the room, the other was half off and half on, hanging askew from the side of the bed. He lay on his back with his mouth open, snoring. Annie felt herself fill with contempt. Drunk and snoring, and he a Lord!

The day progressed. Nothing was said in the kitchen about Sally's absence from her duties and Annie presumed that Mrs Butterwick had spoken a word to Mrs Brag.

While Annie ate her bread and butter and drank her tea Mrs Butterwick said, 'You need not trouble about the drawing room and library today, Annie. Edna and Marg will manage. You should return to your post upstairs.'

Sally lay as Annie had left her, immobile beneath the coarse sheet, her head to one side on the rough pillow, her hair pulled away from her face where it was injured. Her breathing was shallow but regular. From time to time she sighed, and passed her tongue over dry, cracked lips. Annie changed the dressings on Sally's eye and knees and swapped the rags between her legs for clean ones. She lifted Sally's head to a cup of water and Sally did seem able to swallow a few mouthfuls before dropping her head back onto the pillow with an anguished groan. Her eyes remained firmly closed—one, indeed, was sealed shut—but Annie knew that some consciousness had returned. Tears slid from the outer corners of Sally's eyes and ran into her hair as remembrance and understanding returned to the girl's addled mind.

'Don't try to speak,' Annie said in a half-whisper, although Sally had made no attempt to do so. 'You are safe now, and all will be well.' She only hoped it would be true. 'I will brew you some more willow bark tea, for the pain. I am sure you do hurt very badly, Sally.'

Sally made no reply but turned her head away.

Annie's way to the stillroom took her down the servants' staircase, past the concealed door that gave access to the principal bedrooms on the first floor. A furore was taking place. She could hear Lord Petrel's voice, loud and boorish, and the interjected remonstrance of his valet—scarcely less vehement. There was the clash and thud of things being dragged about the room. Annie hurried on her way, only hoping that the sounds denoted packing; that Lord Petrel and his man were making ready for their departure.

Her hope was soon quashed however. Lord Petrel's man appeared in the servants' hall, his arms full of soiled laundry, requesting a surgeon be sent for as his master had taken a fall and injured his leg. There had been a shaving accident also and his lordship required the immediate aid of someone practiced in the stillroom. 'He's bleeding like a stuck pig,' the man said, indicating the laundry. 'This shirt has blood on it,' he said, almost in an accusing tone. 'Is your laundry-woman equal to getting it off? His lordship's shirts are fine lawn.' He looked as though he was going to thrust the garments into Annie's arms.

'Annie's duties are no longer in the laundry,' Mrs Butterwick said. 'You must take those to Mrs Brixie. Annie will attend his lordship.' She turned to Annie, anticipating the girl's reluctance. 'Indeed, you *must* Annie,' she said. 'Take witch hazel and some strips of clean gauze with you. I must send someone for the surgeon.'

Annie quailed at the idea of attending Lord Petrel. 'More willow bark tea is needed … upstairs,' she said, hoping Mrs Butterwick would agree to see to the viscount herself.

'*I* will see to that in due course,' Mrs Butterwick said.

'I will go with you, child,' Mr Swale said, very unexpectedly. 'You will not be unchaperoned. Get what you need and I will await you outside his lordship's chamber.'

Lord Petrel's room was as disarranged as possible. The bed covers had been dragged onto the floor and the floor was wet. His lordship's trunk was open, disgorging shirts, gloves, stockings and undergarments. The bureau was littered with the general paraphernalia of a gentleman—his pocket watch and chain, a silver pencil, a small bone-handled knife. Lord Petrel himself sat on the floor with his back against the side of the bed. His hair was wet and glistening, presumably from his morning ablutions. His chin was soaped but only partway shaved. His cheek bled, but not as profusely as Annie had been led to believe. The wound was more of an abrasion than a cut and, to Annie's unpractised eye, not freshly inflicted. She knelt beside him but not so close that she had to touch him. In spite of the part-completed toilette he still reeked of brandy and cigars. He suffered her to clean the wound on his cheek, wincing through his teeth when the witch hazel stung. He did not meet her eye but she could tell he was waiting for her to make some remark about his injury—that it was already partly crusted, for example, that it did not look like a razor-cut but more like a scratch. Annie kept her counsel and dressed the wound with some gauze. His lordship wore only his nightshirt, which struck her as odd as he had not been undressed when she had been in the room earlier. There was nothing like so much blood on the nightshirt as there had been on the shirt his valet had carried to Mrs Brixie.

Lord Petrel's bare legs stuck out before him—the calves shapely but shockingly hairy. One of them was bruised and swollen about the shin, but not so badly, in Annie's opinion, that the services of the surgeon would be required. It was not her place to make comment however. She cleaned the shin also, while Mr Swale picked up his lordship's clothing and set the rest of the room to rights.

'My man is a shocking wastrel,' Lord Petrel said in a forcedly jocular manner once it was clear that Annie would raise no awkward questions. 'I have a good mind to dismiss him. *This,'* he indicated his face and injured leg, 'is all his doing.'

'Yes, my lord,' Mr Swale said, his voice very neutral. 'The surgeon has been sent for. In the meantime, I shall have your breakfast sent up here, shall I my lord?' Without waiting for a reply he said, 'Annie, as soon as you have finished, fetch some fresh bed linen for his lordship.'

'No need to trouble yourself further, Swale,' Lord Petrel said, dismissing the butler. 'Goose will see to matters here when he returns. You, girl,' he turned to Annie and held out one hand. 'I seem to have scuffed my knuckles also, if you would be so kind.'

Annie dabbed more witch hazel onto his lordship's hand, glad to see that Mr Swale remained. The more she saw and understood, the less she wished to be alone with Lord Petrel.

The surgeon who came to tend Lord Petrel's injuries was the regular man who served the district but he was accompanied by Victor Eagerly. 'This young man is known to the household I believe,' the surgeon said.

'He is to take his examinations very soon and has asked to accompany me in order to increase his experience of general practice. I assume your lordship has no objection?'

'Eagerly,' Lord Petrel said, his face a picture of disdain. 'I suppose I do not mind if he observes, but I will not have him examine me.'

Victor Eagerly gave a respectful bow. 'There is no requirement for that,' he said. 'Much can be ascertained from observation alone. I am thankful for your lordship's indulgence.'

The surgeon proceeded to examine Lord Petrel's injuries before advising him to take several days' rest while the bruising on his shin subsided. The news of his prescription caused dismay in the below stairs regions for by this time rumour from the stables had confirmed Annie's suspicions; feeling was very much against Ecklington's house guest. It was known that Sally had been in the vicinity of the stables the previous evening, with the dairy maids and some of the grooms. Lord Petrel, his valet and Jackie Silver had been there also. Lord Petrel had added brandy to their cups of cider and recollection of subsequent events was hazy. Mr Silver was not to be seen this morning, the door to his little chamber above the tack room firmly closed. Sally's patten had been discovered in the straw of one of the stalls.

While he was in the house Mrs Butterwick brought the surgeon and Dr Eagerly to Annie's chamber to attend Sally. By this time the girl was awake, though her swollen lips remained tightly sealed as to what had occurred to her. The surgeon examined her thoroughly and with none of the obsequiousness he had used with Lord Petrel. Dr Eagerly looked on frowningly at his mentor's brusque manner and unsympathetic mien. The surgeon pronounced the jaw to be bruised but not broken, the eye damaged but not blinded, the maidenhead certainly lost. His examination of Sally's private parts caused her terrible suffering. She clung to Annie's hand, shrieking and trembling, while the surgeon spread her knees to peer and probe into the torn folds of her brutalised flesh.

'You are as bad as them,' Sally almost spat at him.

Regardless of Sally's distress he stood back and indicated to Dr Eagerly that he should conduct his own examination, but this invitation was refused with a decided shake of the head. 'No, indeed sir,' Victor Eagerly murmured, 'I think the young lady has suffered enough.'

The surgeon shrugged, then rinsed his hands and buttoned up his shirt cuffs. Sally curled herself into a ball and turned her back on the room.

'*Them?*' Annie said, when Mrs Butterwick had escorted the men from the room. 'There was more than one?'

Sally began to cry; hard sobs that racked her body and made the flimsy bedframe shake. She cried fit to break her heart. Annie cried with her, and lay beside her that she might offer the comfort of her arms. Sally turned to her then, and lay her head on Annie's thin shoulder, crying all the more but nodding, yes, there had been more than one.

'Who, Sally?' Annie asked, when the worst of Sally's paroxysms were spent. 'Who was it?'

The weeping seemed to have expiated some of Sally's anguish. It had poured out beyond her ability to control it only a few moments before, but now she had a firm hold on it. 'I fell down the stairs,' she said mulishly.

Annie almost laughed. 'You fell down the stairs and lost your maidenhead? Sally! You have been molested! You have been brutally forced!'

Tears welled from Sally's eyes again and her lips—thickened and black with scabs—trembled. 'No, no,' she sobbed, and then, so quietly Annie almost didn't catch the words, 'I mustn't say.'

Annie raised herself up on her elbow. 'You mustn't say? But how else will they be punished?'

'*They* won't be punished,' Sally sneered, dashing the tears from her cheeks. 'Such as them never are. *You* told me that, Annie. The girl always gets the blame. And besides, I shall lose my guinea.' She disentangled herself from Annie's arms and settled herself back on the bed.

'Lose your ..?' Annie was dumb-founded. 'You did it for money, then? You agreed the price and they ..?' She got off the bed and smoothed the skirts of her dress. So Sally was a doxy, and, whatever injuries she had suffered, she had not been forced against her will.

Sally's attempt at stoicism crumbled. She shook her head. 'No. Afterwards, they said, if I didn't tell, they'd give me a guinea.'[xvi]

'But they *did* force you?' Annie knelt beside the bed and reached for Sally's hand. She did not know why, for the end result would be the same, but it mattered to her to know that Sally had not given herself for money.

Sally's head remained turned towards the wall, but she nodded and squeezed Annie's hand. 'I didn't like it,' she said in thin, bitter voice. 'They hurt me, Annie. Oh Annie, they hurt me, they did.'

Sally remained in Annie's room for the next few days and nights. The swelling subsided and the bruising turned from black to purple, then to green. Her knees scabbed over but long before that the rags between her legs had been clean and she had stopped using them.

One day, bringing a bowl of broth up to her patient Annie found Lord Petrel's man on the landing outside her room.

'What are you doing here?' she asked. 'This landing's for the parlour maids. No men are allowed.'

The man slouched away with his hands in his pockets. 'I must have missed my way,' he said, but carelessly. He began to whistle as he went back down the stairway.

Annie took the broth into her room. On the night-stand, beside a cup of water she had left there earlier for Sally, was a golden guinea.

26

Yorkshire

September 1813

It rained for a week. Rain here in Yorkshire takes so many forms that I feel sorry that there is only one word for it. I have known rainfall so heavy—each drop the size of a sloe—that to be hit by it is to feel assaulted by pebbles. I have seen it fall in continuous sheets like plates of glass, the individual drops melded into sheer panes that smash onto the terrace like dropped crystal. I have seen rain that does not fall at all, but hangs in the air, suspended vapour, and when you breathe it you feel you will drown. It comes in the lightest fairy-patter; the gentle plop onto leaves and plash into the fountain and plink into the tea it has caught me drinking. The garden comes alive with the music of it. The fall of it onto the leaves in the high canopy is as polite as an audience's applause. It can be brutal; a daily, relentless torture. It can be a relief, like forgiveness to the parched, praying soul. Sweet, cold, a bore, a blessing, solace, a scolding—rain in Yorkshire can be all of these things.

The rain that came to us after my epiphany in the little glade was of the persistent, drizzling type. It came without storm or wind, depriving me of the drama of a furious tempest above our ravine—the swirling, purple clouds that inspire me with awe and a thrilling sense of portent—but I did not mind. My work in the garden has made me jealous of it—I would not like to see the blooms bruised. Indeed the soil had been thirsty and if anything the plants and shrubs grew glossier and more healthful as they drank. No, it came without rancour and I found I could be patient with it, busy as I was with writing my memories down. Some days I needed candles so that I could see my book, and one afternoon I called for the fire to be lit, for an odd chill came upon me. I bore the rain without complaint. I did not rail, as I would once have done, at being confined within the house.

Despite the rain, Mrs Foley paid me a call. She drives herself about the parish in a little dog cart, taking food and succour to the poor and ill. In this she reminds me of her mother. At one time I thought Mrs Willow and Caroline were very much alike, but Caroline's good-tempered, easy manner has soured since her marriage, or perhaps from before that. Now she is dour and drained. Her zest for life and especially the flame of her romantic passion have been doused. I see no shadow in her of that laughing girl who gathered bluebells, of the starry-eyed dreamer who imagined cherry blossom to be confetti. Now she is a plain goodwife, fat rather than plump, dutiful about her husband's parish, devout in her religion and charitable towards me in a way that is superlatively self-righteous. I could tell her the truth, but pride and a fear that I will not be believed, prevents me. Although I condemn myself by my silence it pleases me to see her judge herself by misjudging me.

Mrs Foley drove down the drive in her dog cart, a large bonnet with a broad brim upon her head, a voluminous cape around her portly form. Her whole ensemble was beaded and running with rain but her face was set in that stoical expression it takes on when there is work to be done, regardless of how distasteful it might be. Burleigh ran out to take charge of her horse and Mrs Orphan showed her into the room where I was at work at my writing desk. I was momentarily annoyed by this. The room I use during the day is a small sitting room in the east wing. In the mornings it is sunny—when there is any sun—and the fire is less likely to smoke, perhaps because it is part of the new wing and the chimney has been better designed. It is a comparatively small room and so keeps warmer than the larger, grander drawing room and library. I think of it as my private place and I did not like Caroline Foley's intrusion into it. I was unhappy that she had caught me at my writing. Her eyes homed in on my book the moment she was shown in, and although I closed it quickly and stowed it in a drawer, for the rest of her visit her gaze kept on returning to the desk beneath the window.

She had her Bible with her but on this occasion she did not offer to read to me. We exchanged small talk, enquiring after each other's households, commiserating on the rain and the deleterious impact it would have on the harvest. Many of Mr Foley's parishioners are farmers and so this is a topic of great moment. If she had children I would ask after them, but she and Mr Foley have not been blessed with children. Maud has a multitude of sons and daughters and I do wish to know about them, but to ask would seem unnecessarily cruel and so I do not. Caroline asked if I was regular with my private devotions. Of course she believes me to be a sinner—she is worried for my eternal soul. No doubt she would have my knees raw from supplication, my eyes swollen from constant remorse. I nodded in a way I hoped would be pious enough to satisfy her.

'May I see …' she began.

'No.'

She always asks and I always refuse. What is the point labelling a thing a shameful secret if you repeatedly get it out and look at it?

'What news have you from the rectory?' I ask.

'None,' she replies.

So I asked about her cousin, Captain Willow, not out of spite or to retaliate, just to change the subject. 'Does he remain in Portugal?' I enquired.

'No,' she said, her face a mask that must have mirrored mine. She picked up her cup and took the smallest possible sip from it. 'He is back in England.'

'I am glad to hear it,' I said, very genuinely; indeed my heart gave a little skip of pleasure at the intelligence, 'but he is well?'

Mrs Foley placed her cup with extreme care back onto its saucer. She took so long about it, centring it with such precision, careful not to make the slightest noise, that I thought she had not heard my question.

At last she said, without looking up at me but keeping her eyes fixed on the Spode, 'He was injured at Burgos[xvii], then caught camp fever. We feared for his life. However, he has been spared, thanks be to God.'

'Thanks indeed,' I breathed.

I knew Barnaby Willow could be nothing to me now. Whatever troth he had pledged to me those many years before had been superseded by the events that had come since. I'd be the last woman to hold him to the promise he had implied but not made. I had been not much more than a child, he a young man on the point of departure for war—a reckless, hopelessly romantic combination! My fortnight at the rectory had made me careless of what was expected at Ecklington, of my mother's high ambitions and my father's visceral need for advancement. Captain Willow would think of me now as the world thought, as Caroline Foley thought. He did not know the choices that had been forced on me.

'I was thinking just now, before you came in, of our picnic at the waterfall,' I said to Mrs Foley.

Her head shot up at that and her eyes, again, strayed to my writing desk. 'Were you?'

'Yes,' I said, 'and of how, in a moment, everything can change.'

She opened her mouth but no sound came out. And then, the most extraordinary thing occurred. Her face—so inscrutable and fixed—crumbled. The muscles relaxed, her mouth drooped and a fat tear oozed from her eye. She opened her reticule in search of a handkerchief. Just for a moment I saw a glimpse of the Caroline Willow I had known—idealistic, hopeful, doe-eyed with love. The hard, matronly exterior she had cultivated in the intervening years cracked open enough for me to see that, within, she was still the girl with disappointed hopes, the broken-hearted lover I had seen as our picnic broke up.

'It was the end of all my dreams,' she said into her handkerchief, so indistinctly that I hardly heard her.

I wanted to say 'And of mine,' because I wanted to reach out to the old Caroline and draw her forth from the armour she wore, back into our friendship's sympathetic light. I did reach out a hand towards her, a gesture of commiseration I hoped she would not reject. But I realised that I could not honestly say that Lieutenant Willow's departure to war had been the end of all my dreams. My dream of him had hardly begun. His words to me had taken me by complete surprise, and although I had welcomed them into the dryness of my heart like the gardens around the house had welcomed the quenching rain, unlike them I had only that moment known I was thirsty.

So I did not speak the sympathetic word and Caroline dried her eyes and put her handkerchief away. She stood up and was again the reserved, dutiful vicar's wife. 'I must be on my way,' she said stiffly. 'Do you have anything for the post?' She nodded towards my desk. 'You were writing a letter as I came in, I believe?'

I shook my head. 'No, thank you, ma'am. I have nothing for the post today.'

She gave a curt nod. 'Very well. Good day, Miss Talbot.'

27

The day of our picnic was very fine. I had consulted with Mrs Butterwick about every aspect of the comestibles we were to provide and which conveyances had best be utilised. We had agreed which servants should be sent ahead—I had particularly urged that Annie should enjoy the day out—to set out the trestle tables, rugs, cushions, wind-breaks and parasols. We had thought long and hard about what 'necessary'[xviii] arrangements we might make for the ladies. She had been as helpful as possible, full of good ideas and thoughtful touches. The only issue we both feared was the weather but as Peake opened my shutters that morning I was delighted to see a clear blue sky, the trees barely moving, everything just as I had hoped.

I travelled in the barouche[xix] with Mama and Papa although I would much have preferred to ride with the Willows in their fusty old carriage; my parents seemed to relish the day with as much enthusiasm as a trip to have a tooth drawn. We called at Binsley House for Mrs Binsley. Her daughters were to travel in a hired gig that seated only two, in preference to Sir Diggory's brougham[xx] which they declared 'too stuffy'. The young

Binsley gentlemen rode. We arrived at Binsley House in good time and Papa stepped down to assist Mrs Binsley aboard and—somewhat reluctantly—to pay his respects to Sir Diggory who, naturally, had declined to join the party.

Mrs Binsley looked my father up and down with great narrowness, her eyebrows somewhat raised. Clearly she had not anticipated him to be so gentlemanlike. At last she nodded and allowed him to hand her into the carriage.

Mama and Mrs Binsley exchanged greetings. 'I have high expectations of a thoroughly agreeable day,' Mrs Binsley proclaimed.

'I hope you will not be disappointed,' Mama replied.

'As to my own enjoyment, that is nothing,' Mrs Binsley said. 'I am happy if *they* are happy. I am certain, as a mother, you feel the same. Miss Talbot,' she said, turning to me and not giving Mama an opportunity to reply, 'I understand that *you* have been the author of our entertainment today. I do congratulate you. I am sure neither Catherine nor Elinor could have pulled off such a coup. They would have left it all to the servants. It is a clever strategy, for then the servants can be blamed if things go awry.'

'I have had assistance from our housekeeper,' I said. 'But I shall not blame her if anything has been forgot.'

Mrs Binsley looked about her. 'But I do not see Lord Petrel,' she said. 'Is he not to join us?'

'He sends his sincere regrets,' I said. 'He is unable to do himself the honour.'

In point of fact Lord Petrel had continued to disparage the entire notion of the picnic. 'I set no store by such things,' he had said. 'What? To sit on the hard ground plagued by insects, and eat hot food that has gone cold, or cold food that has gone warm? I beg you will excuse me.' He had slouched off yawning after breakfast in the direction of the stables and I had been glad to see him go.

'Oh.' It was obvious that Mrs Binsley felt very differently. Her face fell quite markedly. 'Well, that *is* a great pity.'

I recalled Elinor Binsley's speculation about her mother's desire to remarry. She would not be much more than eight or so years Lord Petrel's senior, I speculated. Perhaps she had harboured hopes in that direction.

The Binsley girls were all excitement. I suppose, after their dinner, this was the occasion to which they had most looked forward, the country's compensation for its lack of galas, theatricals, assemblies and balls. The horse put between the shafts of their gig looked skittish to me—the groom struggled to hold his head while the girls got in and arranged their wraps, spare bonnets, drawing materials and parasols. I rather doubted Miss Binsley's ability to control the animal. She was very finely dressed for a young lady intent upon scrambling over the ruins of an abbey or exploring the boulders of the craggy hillside we had been promised, but I forbore to say so. Miss Elinor wore more practical attire.

Our *rendezvous* with the party from the rectory and with the Brigstocks was to be at a crossroads just beyond the gates of Upton Park. No one expected Miss Brigstock to attend the picnic—she had been all-but invisible since the day at the Binsleys'—but Miss Binsley confidently expected Mr Brigstock to be of the party, speaking very complacently and with too much familiarity of him as 'Brigstock'.

'I suppose Brigstock will ride his bay gelding,' she mused aloud to no one in particular, and, 'Brigstock declares he will certainly scale the rocky outcrops. He did a good deal of mountaineering in the Pyrenees.'

Her mama did nothing to correct her daughter's manner of speech and I wondered, briefly, if Miss Binsley had finally succeeded in getting Mr Brigstock to propose. I knew that in the few days since I had returned to Ecklington the Binsleys had been to Upton to dine, joined by the rectory family to drink tea in the evening. In one regard I had been disappointed not to have been included; I wished to think myself part of the happy intercourse that had blossomed so suddenly that spring. On the other hand I knew Mama and Papa would not have relished attending a dinner at Upton and would have been mortally offended by an invitation only to tea. '*We* are not the kind of lowly, supernumerary family to be fobbed off with a cup of tea and slice of cake,' I could almost hear her saying. 'Tea is all very well for the rector and the curate, but the Talbots are entitled to better.' Last of all there was the matter of Lord Petrel, who stubbornly remained at Ecklington even though his wound—if he had ever had one—had healed. He had taken Papa and their new master of horse off for a day or so to Newmarket but returned and showed no signs of quitting Ecklington in the near future. I knew that no consideration would have induced Mr Brigstock to invite Lord Petrel to dine and had concluded that this explained my being left out. For all I knew, then, the dinner at Upton had been the scene of Miss Binsley's triumph. She certainly looked very happy until the groom released the horse's head and the gig shot off at high speed.

I rode backwards in the barouche and whether it was that, or my sense of nervousness about the whole day—once I thought about it Mrs Binsley was right, a picnic might seem like a very informal, artless thing to pull off but had in fact been an ambitious undertaking—but something made my innards feel distinctly curdled. It would be the first time I had seen Lieutenant Willow since I had quit the rectory. I asked myself if I was nervous or excited, and concluded that I did not know. I was confused. Confused by the precipitateness with which he had— almost—declared himself, confused by the feelings his—near— declaration had provoked in me. I liked him a great deal, better than anyone I had ever met. But then the circle of my acquaintance was so very limited. He was handsomer than either of the Binsley brothers and friendlier than Mr Brigstock. He had not the earnestness of manner of— say—Mr Oscar Eagerly. His wry humour made me wonder if anything about him could be taken seriously. I was not sure about his handling of Caroline's infatuation. Was he kind to tolerate it? Or would it not have been kinder to put paid to it once and for all? There was nothing inscrutable about Lieutenant Willow; he was an open book. I was not sure that Mr Brigstock's reserve did not intrigue me more, and certainly it would be hard to imagine a man better favoured than the tenant of Upton Park. These thoughts occupied my mind as we drove the mile or so to Upton Green.

There is a little greensward hard by the crossroads at Upton and the rectory carriage was waiting there for us, the rector and Lieutenant Willow both mounted and standing ready. To my surprise the Brigstocks' barouche also waited just inside the Park's gates. Both Brigstocks were seated within. They, like us, were driven by liveried grooms.

Catherine Binsley's face fell when she apprehended that Mr Brigstock was not mounted, and to see that Miss Brigstock had deigned to favour us with her company. That Miss Binsley had some scheme afoot was obvious to me even if no one else divined it.

'Miss Brigstock,' she called, much too brightly, from her seat in the gig, 'how delighted I am to see you! Mr Brigstock, as pleasant as it must be to have your sister well enough to come out, I marvel at you not riding your gelding. *He* will be sorry to miss the exercise, will he not?'

'My horse's feelings are not my principal concern,' Mr Brigstock replied. He put his hand over his sister's where it lay in her lap. 'I am much more concerned with Lydia. *Her* comfort and enjoyment are my first consideration.'

'Indeed, you are a most devoted brother,' Miss Binsley said, her annoyance barely veiled. She turned away to adjust something on the seat beside her and I saw her sister make a gesture of sympathy and consolation.

At our arrival on the green Mr Gabriel had attached himself to the rectory party. There being a spare seat in their carriage he had tied his horse to the back of it and climbed in beside Maud. Lieutenant Willow dismounted and came to our carriage. 'I do myself the honour of bidding you good morning,' he said, addressing Mama and Papa. 'I have not been so fortunate as to have been introduced, but I am Barnaby Willow, nephew to the rector.' He straightened from his bow and lifted his open countenance and bright, eager smile up to us. His eyes—as blue as the sky above—shone with pleasure, and I could not help returning his smile with equal warmth. He did not address me however, but proceeded to exchange some remarks with my father: was he familiar with Pocklington Abbey? Had he visited the waterfalls? Was not the weather extremely propitious for our excursion?

The rector remained on his horse, which cropped the grass of the green. Mr Willow made no effort to greet us, showed no enthusiasm whatsoever for the occasion. He cast the only cloud of gloom on the occasion.

'My dear,' Mrs Willow called to him from the window of her carriage, 'will you not come and say a word to Mr Gabriel? Oh, *do* come and say good morning to him. He has decided to ride with us. Such gallant conduct! I am sure I never saw its like. What say you, my dear? Do you not think it handsome? Is that not very considerate of him, for I am sure he would rather ride alongside the other gentlemen.'

The rector made no move, but threw his wife a withering look that said, 'Why does he not do so, then?' as clearly as any words.

Miss Binsley managed to turn her horse with a little difficulty, Elinor emitting little shrieks of alarm every time he lunged and looked as though he might take flight.

At last she cried out in a voice that was high and unnatural, 'Catherine, I am not certain you are equal to managing this beast. The ostler did say he was hard to handle, you know.'

'I know,' Miss Binsley replied, but artificially. I got the impression that this dialogue had been rehearsed. 'But he was the only creature left for hire. He is very wilful.'

'Mr Brigstock,' Elinor fluted, 'could I trouble *you* for assistance? My sister cannot manage this hireling. If you would be so good as to take the ribbons, I will happily take your place in your barouche. I'd be honoured to keep Miss Brigstock company.'

Their scheme was so transparent that I almost laughed aloud at it. Lieutenant Willow caught my eye again and I saw one eyelid droop in the briefest possible wink, although he maintained his conversation with my father.

Mr Brigstock as good as rolled his eyes at Miss Binsley's obvious ruse to get him into her carriage. His sister paled at the prospect of losing his company, and clutched at his hand. There was some whispered conference between them that we needed no interpreter to understand; he felt honour-bound to assist and she was decidedly against his doing so. There was room in their carriage for both Miss Binsleys. The hired conveyance could have been returned to Binsley Park by one of the grooms but Miss Brigstock's strong reluctance to have anyone but her brother beside her precluded the suggestion. At last Mr Edward Binsley, who had been trotting his horse back and forth across the green, came forward and grasped the hireling's bridle.

'I'll hold his head,' he said irritably. 'Jasper's presence will steady him. Only let us be going. *That's* half the trouble, I think. The horses are eager to be off and, by God, so am I.'

At that he spurred his horse, taking the gig forward with such a jolt that Miss Binsley and Elinor were thrown backwards and both had to clutch their bonnets. The gig, the sisters and Edward Binsley disappeared down the lane in a cloud of dust. Lieutenant Willow remounted his horse and the rest of us followed.

Pocklington Abbey is located some half a mile off the road, through a derelict gateway and across a piece of common land. It has long been abandoned and is entirely ruined. The bare outline of its former precincts can be discerned; little more than the foundations of what must have been stout walls built of grey stone, very crumbling now and covered in lichen. It is impossible to make out the chapter house from the cloister, the refectory from the reredorter[xxi]. There are the tottering remnants of a tower or two, much overgrown with ivy and other creeping plants. The chapel has survived better than the rest with what was clearly the nave, the chancel and one transept still discernible amongst the fallen masonry and undergrowth. The whole site is pleasantly situated however, set amidst turf cropped short by a few meandering sheep, with a wild meadow behind and surrounded at a distance by leafy woodland.

This was our first site of exploration and we ranged over it pretty thoroughly, drinking the lemonade and eating the cake that I had arranged should be stowed in the barouche, served by the Ecklington grooms. The rector came unexpectedly into his own, explaining the architecture, history and religious practices of the place. With a ready audience asking interesting questions he began almost to enjoy himself. It was not quite by design, but rather convenient, that he was encouraged to draw the older members of the party away to closer inspection of some of the more obscure features of the ruin. Mr Gabriel Binsley and Miss Maud set up their easels immediately and began to sketch one of the towers. Miss Brigstock remained in her carriage and admired the abbey from its relative comfort but Mr Brigstock did descend, and strolled around the fallen lintels and tumble-down pillars. Miss Binsley was out of sorts. She perched herself on a fallen block and looked miserable. It looked to me that she had been crying, not because she was lovelorn and heart-broken but because she was frustrated and angry that her scheme had gone awry. She scowled and sulked and snapped at her sister until Elinor lost patience with her and walked away. This was Mr Brigstock's opportunity—Miss Binsley was alone and evidently most desirous of an approach—but he did not take it, and in the end Mrs Binsley had to lead her daughter away to a distance that she might mend her face and her manners.

Elinor looped her arm in mine. 'This is very pleasant,' she said as we walked across the grass. 'What a perfectly romantic spot. My sister had high hopes of it, but it seems it is not to be.'

'It is my opinion,' I said hesitantly, 'that Mr Brigstock's thoughts do not dwell on romance at present. He seems most preoccupied with his sister.'

'It is commendable,' Elinor remarked, 'although strange. She does not seem to be affectionate towards him, does she? She is a very odd creature, I think.'

I suspected—but could not divulge—something of Miss Brigstock's history. I conjectured some romantic entanglement that had gone sour, or a marriage arrangement that had been untenable to her or some similar crisis of an unhappy, personal nature that had compromised her emotionally and possibly morally. I said, 'I hope, when he is grown, that George will be as careful of me as Mr Brigstock is of his sister.'

'Oh yes, it's very nice,' said Elinor cynically.

'I thought it gallant of your brother Edward to step in,' I said, 'with the horse, I mean.'

'*Someone* had to,' Elinor said. 'It has been arranged that Gabriel is to drive the gig from here, and I must ride in the rectory vehicle.'

'That is a good solution,' I said.

'It is a *terrible* solution,' Elinor replied. 'I do not wish to ride in a closed carriage on such a lovely day. Gabriel does not wish to drive the nag from the livery stables. *He* wishes to sit beside Maud Willow. Catherine wishes she were dead, she says, and hates the very notion of a picnic.'

I felt my spirits sink: so many discontented people and the day had hardly begun.

'There is no help for it though,' I suggested, summoning courage. 'Your sister *will* be dead if she insists upon trying to manage the hireling by herself and clearly no consideration is going to persuade Mr Brigstock to abandon his sister. But look, I will give up my seat to you if you would prefer to ride in the Ecklington barouche. My parents are no very sparkling company but you will be with your Mama. Miss Binsley might agree to swap with Miss Willow. I will travel with Mrs Willow, Caroline and Miss Binsley in the closed carriage. Maud would like nothing better than to be driven by your brother Gabriel, I think.'

'You are wiser than you know,' Elinor said cryptically. 'But I am tired of trying to manage my family. They will do as they wish and I will do as I am told. I must go and ask Mrs Willow if she will give me a place in her carriage.'

I found myself alone in a grassy precinct of the ruins. Edward Binsley and Lieutenant Willow had scrambled atop one of the higher sections of masonry and were strutting along it, daring each other to leap off.

Caroline Willow, never far from her cousin, had attempted to follow but got her foot caught between two lose pieces of stone.

'I am quite stuck,' she called up, 'One of you gentlemen will have to rescue this damsel. Which of you shall it be?'

Mrs Binsley and her elder daughter strolled at a distance in the shade of the trees. Maud and Mr Gabriel sat at their easels. Somewhere behind the ruins I could hear the rector discoursing on the sacking of the abbey in 1536. I presumed my parents and Mrs Willow were the beneficiaries of his lecture and pitied Elinor who had no doubt been drawn in to it. I could see nothing at all of Mr Brigstock. The carriages were at a little distance behind me, on the common land we had crossed to access the abbey. The Upton grooms and those from Ecklington milled around the horses. Miss Brigstock sat in state beneath the shade of her parasol and I thought I had better go and bear her company.

I had almost reached the Upton carriage when I saw a rider turn in through the lop-sided gate posts and come towards where the carriages were assembled. Mr Eagerly and his brother had been invited to join us but had indicated they would be able to do so only for the second part of the excursion, at the beauty spot. I thought at first that one of them had decided to come early and raised my hand in greeting. The rider was too far away for me to be able to tell which of the brothers it was, but it was not many moments before I could make out that the rider was neither the curate nor his brother. Having made my gesture however, I felt I could do no other than meet the man. I passed Miss Brigstock's carriage by a few steps and in the next moment found myself before him.

His coat and boots were very dusty, and his horse lathered; it was obvious to me that he had travelled some distance. I summoned the groom to attend the man's horse, and offered him refreshment from the basket, which he accepted and drank down thirstily.

'I am indebted to you,' he said at last when he had handed the cup back to the groom. 'I have been riding hard these four hours.'

'And do you have much further to travel?' I asked, more from politeness than any desire to know his business.

'That I cannot tell you,' he said. 'I am in search of people by the name of Stockbridge. Do you know them?'

I said I did not. 'What condition of people are the Stockbridges?' I asked. 'If they are a farming family, or such as a smith or a miller, I would not be able to assist you. As to families of rank, I can say with a degree of certainty that there is none of that name.'

'They will be but lately come to the county,' the man said. 'I expect they live very privately. You do not know of any houses recently let?'

I could not say quite what it was, but some feeling, some odd sensitivity pressed on me from behind. Miss Brigstock's carriage was a few feet at the rear of where I stood. There came no sound from it, no creak of the chassis as she moved in her seat, no rustle of her dress, no in-drawn breath, but I knew, with some intuition I did not know I had, that she was intensely, critically affected by the rider and his enquiry. I could feel her tension in my marrow. It was palpable, like thunder in the air.

I do not know where I found such mendacity but I pretended to consider for a moment, putting my head on one side and performing a pantomime of thinking, wondering, deliberating, before at last saying, 'No. I am sorry I cannot think of any property hereabouts that has been recently let. But,' and here I pretended a salacious interest in tittle-tattle, 'you have piqued my interest. Why do you seek this family?'

The man gathered up his reins and prepared to resume his journey. 'It is a private matter,' he said as he turned his horse. 'They have been sought across Europe, I am told, to no avail. But I am not surprised they were not found *there* … You have heard the news?' He was speaking over his shoulder now, facing back towards the gates.

'No,' I shouted after him. 'What news?'

His voice came to me on the wind, a hollow sound, at odds with the chirping birds, the cheerful sigh of the breeze in the trees, the grinding of the horses' teeth as they cropped the turf. 'War is declared,' he said.

I stared after him for a few moments, watching him exit the gates and turn back upon the road. When I was sure he had gone I walked the few paces back to Miss Brigstock's carriage. Despite the heat of the day she wore a capacious shawl that covered her shoulders and fell in cascades across her bosom and onto her lap. I thought she must have been over-powered by heat but she sat beneath her parasol, her body rigid as though carved from stone, her face as smooth and bloodless as marble, and as white. The pallor of her face was ghostly. Her hands, where she gripped the handle of her parasol, were bone-white. Her eyes though, within that stony visage, were dark pools of angst, wide with shock; she stared ahead at the abbey but saw nothing at all of it. As I stood beside her carriage she turned them to me, but so slowly that it seemed they were frozen in their sockets. In them I read a dictionary of distress and fear, all her hubris and cold disdain melted away.

There was no point in pretending, in dismissing the rider as a meaningless interruption to our jaunt. I knew—and Miss Brigstock *knew* that I knew—all his words and his search portended for herself and her brother. 'What would you like me to do?' I asked her.

Her mouth moved but for a few seconds she could not find her voice. Finally she managed to croak out, 'If you could find Frederick, Miss Talbot …'

'Of course,' I said, turning at once to commence my search. But a guttural, inarticulate sound called me back to her.

'Do not say why he is needed. At least not until …'

I smiled my understanding. 'I understand,' I said. 'I shall be discreet.'

We had been at the abbey for over an hour and it was time, in any case, that we continued on our way. I made this my excuse to approach each group of our company. Caroline had been extracted from the ruins and now pretended an injury to her ankle that would require her to be carried by Lieutenant Willow.

'Not at all,' he said with patient good-humour. 'In cases like these the surgeon always recommends keeping the joint mobile. I will give you my arm, but you must be brave and walk as best you can.'

'You carried me once,' Caroline said with a sulky lip.

'Yes, but you were little, then.'

He escorted her past me, towards the waiting carriages, smiling as he went by and looking directly into my eyes. His eyes spoke much; that he was tolerant of Caroline but would rather have me on his arm, that our shared understanding of this private truth gave him pleasure, his determination that, before the day was many hours older, he *would* take my arm and far more willingly than he took Caroline's.

I smiled back, but sadly. The war was come and soon he would go away to face carnage on the battle field. I might never see him again.

Maud and Mr Gabriel began to tidy away their drawing apparatus, lamenting very much that they had made such poor progress on their sketches. I found the rector and his entourage examining some weathered, illegible gravestones behind the chapel.

'It is time to move on,' I told them. 'It is another hour's ride to the waterfalls and we are expected there at two for luncheon. Have you seen Mr Brigstock?'

They pointed him out to me. He was across the meadow, walking slowly and quite alone through the thigh-high grasses and wild flowers that grew in abundance. In spite of everything—the war and the threat to the Brigstocks—I felt a stab of selfishness. I had hardly explored at all. I would especially have liked to roam amongst the native species here. I could see trefoil, poppy, bee-orchid and fairy-flax. It interested me that Mr Brigstock had chosen the meadow, rather than the ruins, for his diversion. He saw me and raised his hand. I raised mine in answer, beckoning. He smiled and began to come towards me, removing his hat to wipe the sweat from his brow. His dark hair shone in the bright sunlight. His beauty struck me again but I saw now something I had not seen before. He seemed happy. His habitual reserve, his stiff, haughty air, had dissipated in the wild meadow. He strode, purposefully and strongly, through the grasses but he swung his arms, his shoulders were loose and easy. I wondered if his hour of solitude had accomplished this. His relentless devotion to his sister must be wearisome, I speculated; a burden, especially when—as I then knew—they were in such fear of discovery that they had found it prudent to change their name.

He continued to smile as he came towards me and I felt heartily sorry that I would have to break his moment of ease.

'Miss Talbot,' he called, as he came within earshot, 'I have been remiss. I do not think I have bid you good day. What splendid arrangements you have made for our entertainment. This meadow here,' he was near me now, and stopped, extending his arm to encompass the broad expanse behind him. 'What an utterly delightful spot.' He held out his arm to me. 'Will you walk with me a while?'

'I would have, with pleasure,' I said, 'but it is time for us to depart, and,' I lowered my voice although no one was near, 'there has been a man here, looking for … some people by the name of Stockbridge.'

Mr Brigstock's smile froze upon his face. It was just like watching a pool of water ice over. The smile faded from his lips, his eyes grew dull, the languid set of his shoulders stiffened.

'I will not pretend to know the cause,' I said, 'but the rider's enquiries have distressed your sister. She bids you go to her.'

He rammed his hat back on his head. 'Of course I will,' he said. 'But tell me, the rider?'

I shrugged. 'A journeyman of some kind, employed privately to locate a family who may have settled recently hereabouts. He said they had been sought throughout the continent, to no avail.'

'Yes,' Mr Brigstock said grimly, 'they *would* have been. A single fellow, you say?'

I nodded. 'Yes. I told him I could call to mind no one who might answer, and he went away.'

'In which direction?'

'Back the way we have come, towards Upton.'

We had begun to walk back towards the carriages where the rest of the party were reorganising themselves to accommodate the recalcitrant hired horse. Mr Brigstock walked so quickly I had to half run to keep up with him.

'There is nothing to be gained in our going home, then. Indeed, much might be lost by it,' he said, almost to himself. 'But preparations must be made ...'

'Mr Gabriel's horse is spare,' I told him. 'He is to drive the gig. One of your grooms could perhaps ...'

'Yes. Yes, that's a good idea,' Mr Brigstock said. 'By the time we return this afternoon things can have been made ready. We can travel overnight ...'

'You will leave, then, immediately?'

The anguish in my voice surprised me and it clearly caught Mr Brigstock's attention, even distracted as he must have been by other concerns. He stopped abruptly. We were still within the grounds of the abbey and could speak without fear of being overheard. 'I must get Lydia away,' he said. He wrenched his hat off his head and mashed it in his hands as he spoke to me. 'Oh, Miss Talbot, if I could only *tell* you ... But if she were found she would be forced to go back.'

'Back to Italy?'

He nodded.

'There is war, now,' I told him. 'That's the other thing the rider told me. There will be no sea-travel, unless under arms.'

My words seemed to relieve him a little, and I suppose it is an ill wind that blows *nobody* any good.

He crammed his hat back onto his head. 'Excuse me,' he said.

28

I had much to occupy my thoughts as we rode through the countryside to the wooded ravine where our picnic was to be served. In the end I rode in the rectory conveyance with Mrs Willow, Caroline and Elinor, Miss Binsley having claimed for herself my seat in the Ecklington barouche. Mr Gabriel drove Miss Maud in the hired gig and I think they were the only ones thoroughly pleased with the arrangement. Mr Brigstock had sent one of his grooms back to Upton on Mr Gabriel's horse, claiming the sudden recollection of a letter that must be posted without delay. He and his sister had brought their own personal attendants to Upton and I presumed that a word to one of these would put in train the packing and preparations necessary for their swift, secretive departure.

I felt very sorry for the Brigstocks, but I could not help also feeling that they had been less than honourable. They had come amongst us under false pretences, accepted and offered hospitality as though they had nothing to hide. That they must have their reasons and these reasons be extremely pressing I did not doubt, but it would have been better for them to have lived in complete seclusion rather than to engage in our local society. No wonder poor Miss Binsley had met with so little success! Mr Brigstock was not free to form an attachment with any young lady when he might be called upon to take flight at any moment. For myself, I did not feel quite so taken advantage of. In our private conversations Mr Brigstock had hinted at his sister's history. I suppose a worldlier girl than I might have guessed the rest.

Lieutenant Willow, the rector and Mr Binsley rode ahead of us and were at the picnic spot before the slower carriages drew up. By the time I arrived they had left their horses in the shade and scouted out the location, declaring everything excellently arranged. The Eagerly brothers had been earlier still and I gathered they had been of some assistance in choosing the location of the camp. My father greeted both of them with a display of affection unusual with him, shaking hands, slapping their backs, laughing loudly to disguise the rush of emotion I could plainly see had overwhelmed him. They reciprocated in kind and then turned to greet my mother with their usual deference. Then I saw Mr Eagerly's glance stray towards Miss Willow. I thought he might have drawn her to one side to look at the river, but she stayed close to Mr Gabriel and had eyes for nobody else. Mr Victor was his usual, genial self but he looked tired. I knew he had been studying hard for his examinations, something Mr Binsley could certainly not claim.

The gentlemen's enthusiasm and the sight of our picnic ground lifted my spirits. I was delighted to see that all my plans, and the careful arrangements of Mrs Butterwick, had been carried out to the letter. An awning had been put up to provide shade on a flat piece of ground a few yards from the tumbling river. A trestle table beneath was loaded with covered dishes. Thick rugs carpeted the ground thereabouts, with scattered cushions and three folding chairs, one each for Mrs Willow, Mrs Binsley and Mama. Annie Orphan, two footmen and another maid were busy about the table and our grooms soon went to assist the footmen in dispensing glasses of cool champagne and frothing ale as our guests arrived.

I stopped to say a word to Annie as I passed. 'You have done *very* well

Annie. Everything is just as I'd hoped.' I put as much gladness and delight into my voice as I could, but of course things were not as I had hoped. The rider, and the news of the war, and the changes to our company that these things would wreak, had put a shadow over my day.

Annie discerned no dissimulation on my part. She flushed with pleasure and bobbed a curtsey.

The site was well-chosen; a very nice, secluded glade, a mixture of packed earth and scrubby grass that sloped to a shingled beach. The canopy of trees above and around us was just enough to give shade and privacy without making the place gloomy. There was room for us to spread out, if we wished, with sundry large boulders for perching on, and good prospects for sketching across the river to the bucolic fields beyond. The river before us gave endless interest. The occasional bird swooped to feed and I saw the splash of a rising fish, leaping through the spume of the water as it surged around the scattered rocks that broke its flow. Already Edward Binsley was engaged in leaping from one to another in an attempt to cross to the other side—a pointless exercise and one that was sure to end in him getting very wet boots. To the left, downstream, well hidden in the densely-packed trees, I could just glimpse the sheeted enclosure which was the 'necessary'. Near it, primly seated on a fallen log, was Sally Orphan. I was surprised to see her, but not displeased. I knew she had been unwell of late, and was glad that Mrs Butterwick had thought to send her out for a day of fresh air to aid her recuperation. I could see that she had been scrubbed for the occasion, her unruly hair pushed into a mob-cap. She wore a clean frock and a pair of new patens. She stood ready to assist any lady who needed to use the necessary and to make good within the little pavilion after each visitation. The downstream positioning of this facility was an especially happy arrangement. To the right a path led away through saplings and from that direction we could hear the rush and tumble of the much-vaunted waterfalls. The craggy rocks would doubtless also lie in that direction and I was as eager as anyone to explore, but luncheon was ready to be served and we would all have to wait.

The rest of us were already seated and beginning to eat when Mr and

Miss Brigstock arrived. I imagine they had dallied while they discussed their departure later in the day. Mr Brigstock escorted his sister through the trees towards our camp with as much care as if she had been a china doll and indeed she did look very pale and fragile. The hand that held her parasol trembled. She retained her shawl, a long, beautifully embroidered, flowing thing that covered her completely from neck to hem. She smiled on us all in the beatific way that she had but I could see the edge of a hectic flush on her neck where her shawl fell open, and a pulse that throbbed in her temple. I would have thrown her a sympathetic look, a kindly smile, but she avoided my eye.

There was an immediate difficulty as to seats—she had not been expected and no folding chair had been provided—but thankfully Mrs Willow graciously resigned hers and Miss Brigstock perched herself upon it. She sipped her glass of champagne before placing it down on a flat stone and accepting the plate of cold meats and greenery handed to her by a gloved footman. I watched her narrowly as the meal progressed and saw that she ate next to nothing. Conversation among the rest of us was general but neither Brigstock contributed much to it. Mr Brigstock paced up and down the river's edge and ate from the plate he held in one hand. His sister looked around her a great deal, her eyes scanning the curtain of foliage that surrounded us as though she expected brigands to burst out of it at any moment and carry her off. She pretended to enjoy the scene as her head turned this way and that, murmuring, 'How pleasant. How delightful,' from time to time, but I could see that her words were specious; she was on edge, flighty, like a trapped bird.

Presently Gabriel Binsley, who had been sitting with Maud Willow on one of the substantial boulders, stood up and tapped his fork on the edge of his glass. 'If I may,' he said, blushing, coughing to clear his throat, 'If I may interrupt for a moment, I have something to say.'

No one who could see Maud's face, alight with happiness, needed to hear the remainder of Mr Gabriel's announcement to know that they were engaged. Of course it would have been better for Mr Gabriel to have sought the rector's permission before making the engagement known and I think perhaps Mrs Binsley might have appreciated the opportunity to veto her younger son's precipitate and possibly foolhardy plan. Certainly she looked less pleased than the Willows at the news, but I presume this was part of Mr Gabriel's scheme. Once the thing was announced, she could hardly oppose it. We all thought—but none of us said—that he was very young, at nineteen and with two more years at Oxford before him, to take such a step. Neither did we speculate aloud about Miss Willow's relief to have secured for herself—at last—a husband. A two year engagement would see her six or seven and twenty. No. We kept our reservations to ourselves and congratulated them heartily. Miss Binsley offered her felicitations and then walked away from the party with her chin very high, turning her back very decidedly on Mr Brigstock. Caroline shed a few tears on her sister's neck and turned her countenance to Lieutenant Willow, no doubt hoping that he would do as Mr Gabriel had done. For once he did not laugh off her silliness, or pet or placate her. He walked abruptly away, leaving her where she stood looking like a foolish child. His eyes were fixed on me. He strode over the stones and scattered cushions until he stood before me, his face serious and his gaze very direct. His look said everything his words could not and I looked back at him, startled and discomposed, until Mama called me to her side. Next time my eyes met Caroline's she returned my look very coldly and, from that day onwards, I have not enjoyed her friendship.

After we had eaten, the party set out to explore the vicinity. Miss Brigstock remained behind, rooted to her chair beneath the awning. Miss Binsley said that she would also stay. She took a novel from her bag and went to find a quiet spot to read. We walked up the path to view the falls, which were not as big as I had imagined but very splendid. The water fell from a rocky lip twenty feet or so above us. The rocks of the cliff were dark and mossy, very ancient. The sound of falling water echoed around the amphitheatre formed by the ravine. The sun did not penetrate there, so secluded and shadowed was it. It was a gothic, romantic scene that caused Maud and Mr Gabriel to get out their pencils straight away, but the rest of us did not wish to linger. Mrs Willow alone remained to chaperone the pair. We walked a quarter mile or so further along the path to where an ascent of the rock face was possible for those not hampered by skirts. Most of the young gentlemen made the attempt and soon disappeared from view over the summit. Mr Binsley called down to say that there was a deep pool just before the waters slid over the falls, and, to his mother's alarm, declared that they had all decided to bathe.

Those who did not climb—the rector and the curate and my papa—continued on the little path, intent upon further exploration of the riverbank. Mama decided she would return to the waterfalls and Mrs Binsley said she would do the same, leaving Elinor and me alone at the foot of the crag.

We listened in envy as, out of view, the gentlemen stripped off and swam in the icy waters. 'Don't you sometimes wish you had been born a boy?' Elinor said with a sigh, dusting off a ledge and sitting down on it. 'It seems to me that they have all the fun.'

The sound of the gentlemen bathing filtered down to us; gasps and shouts and vigorous splashing.

I thought about the imminent war. 'No,' I replied. 'To be sure, men do have a great deal more freedom than women. They can be independent, or choose a career to their liking, and it seems to me that society excuses in *them* much that it will not tolerate in a woman. But a man's duty can be very hard, Elinor. Sometimes he is asked to sacrifice everything.'

'Women must make sacrifices,' my friend said. 'We must marry where we do not love, sometimes, or languish at home while the ones we *do* love go out into the world to make their fortunes. We can ache with love for someone, but we may not declare it. We have to wait, demurely, and hope to be discovered.'

I turned to look at her. 'Do *you* love someone, Elinor?'

'Oh no,' she said. 'I am thinking of Catherine. She loves Mr Brigstock but he will have nothing to do with her.'

'Your sister hardly knows Mr Brigstock,' I said dryly.

'She has known him as long as Gabriel has known Maud Willow,' she retorted, 'and, come to that, as long as you have known Lieutenant Willow.'

'There is nothing between the lieutenant and me,' I countered.

'Not on your part, perhaps,' Elinor said, 'but we all saw how he looked at you just now. For two pins he'd have followed Gabriel's lead.'

'He is not free,' I said in a small voice. 'There is going to be a war.'

Elinor took my hand and looked at me with an earnest expression. 'All the more reason,' she urged, 'to take hold of happiness while you can. A few months, a few weeks, even a few days with the one you truly love is better than a lifetime of regret, isn't it?'

'It is too late,' I said. 'He has, at the very most, a few hours. But do not tell him, Elinor. Let him have every moment of happiness that he can.'

We spoke of other things, then, until we were disturbed by the sound of scrambling from above, and Mr Binsley descended the rock. 'I told you I would swim,' he crowed. His hair was wet and his shirt clung to his back. He carried his coat over his shoulder. 'Willow swims like a fish, I must say. He dove down to the bottom of the pool although the doctor advised against it. Brigstock is in there still. He is made of stone if he does not feel the cold, for it *is* glacial.

'I arranged for hot tea,' I said. I got up from where I had been resting. 'I will hurry back down the path and let the servants know it will soon be wanted.'

The path back to our encampment was longer than I had recalled it. The route was comparatively unfrequented and I missed my way. The path I thought I had been following petered out into grass and then I found myself at an impenetrable brake of brambles, surrounded by saplings. As I turned to retrace my steps I saw a glimpse of something pale through the trees and made out Caroline Willow, quite alone in a gloomy enclave of holly, alder and ash.

'Caroline,' I called out to her, 'are you lost?'

She had her back to me but at my voice turned swiftly to show me a face ravaged by tears, puffed up and red. Her hair was disarranged, her muslin frock much smeared and stained.

'You,' she spat out across the yards of thicket that separated us. 'What are you doing here? The one person I desire least to see.' She dissolved again into a paroxysm of weeping. I tried to get to her but the way was too choked up with undergrowth.

'I am lost,' I said, in answer to her question, 'but you are stuck. You must be. I cannot get to you. How did you get so far into that copse?'

'I *pushed* myself in,' she almost snarled at me. She held out her arms, which were covered in deep red weals and brutal scratches. 'I pushed my way in,' she said again, 'because I *wanted* to be lost. I didn't care how much it hurt me. Nothing *here,*' she lifted her mangled arms again, 'can begin to equal the pain I feel in *here.*' She pressed her hand to her breast. 'You have stolen him from me,' she cried out abjectly. 'My Barney, the one I love with all my *heart* …' Her voice broke on the words and she could not go on but only stood, imprisoned amongst the tightly woven withies of bramble and supple saplings.

'Oh Caroline,' I implored her, 'do not weep. Let me try and come to you.'

I tried again to push myself into the thicket, as she had done. My sympathy must not have been as strong as her agony of heart, for I could not do it, but only succeeded in getting my dress caught.

'No, *no,*' she shouted, manically as though I were some wild creature intent upon tearing her to pieces. 'Keep away. Keep *away* from me!'

'Very well,' I said, holding out my hands in surrender. 'Very well Caroline. Do not distress yourself further. I will go away.'

I wrenched my dress from the bushes, tearing it, but not caring, and ran back up the path to where it split off from the main route. I stopped to rip more material from my hem and tied it to an overhanging branch so that I could be sure to find the way again, before running back in the direction of the camp. The way was quite obvious to me now. I did not know how I could have gone astray before. I was half-panting from my exertion, half-crying from my encounter with Caroline Willow, hurrying with as much speed as I could when I heard the scream. It came, not from behind me, where Caroline was trapped, not from the waterfall and not from the direction of the rocks. It came from ahead of me.

29

I burst into the clearing. The servants must have taken advantage of our absence to wander off and rest under the shade of the trees. Of them, only Annie Orphan remained under the awning, tending a spirit stove that heated a kettle of water for our tea. She was not tending it now though. The kettle sang on its trivet sending a steady plume of steam into the air but she was too occupied by her sister to be able to reach out a hand to remove it. Sally wept on Annie's shoulder, clinging on to her dress and sobbing incoherently. It seemed odd to me that the bigger, stronger girl should be expecting so much in the way of comfort and protection from one who was so much smaller and slighter, but Annie appeared to be able to supply what Sally needed.

A moment later the other maid and one of the footmen arrived in the clearing from the other direction, evidently brought by the sound of the scream. Annie, seeing me, hustled Sally into their care and only when they had disappeared back towards where they had tethered the horses did she remove the kettle from the stove.

'Oh Miss Talbot,' she gasped out to me. 'Do not be alarmed, only ...'

she stopped abruptly and chewed her lip, evidently wondering how much she ought to tell me.

'Only what, Annie?' I prompted.

'His lordship startled Sally, ma'am. She has been unwell, you know, and his coming upon her suddenly …'

'His lordship? Do you mean Lord Petrel? What is *he* doing here?'

Annie's mouth flapped for a moment and I realised it was a ridiculous question to pose to a parlour maid. What did *she* know of a viscount's comings and goings?

'Never mind, Annie,' I said. 'Perhaps you can tell me where is he *now?*'

She gestured in the direction of the trees downstream, precisely, I realised, where Sally had been stationed ready to assist the ladies. An indistinct picture—I was such an innocent and fuzzy on detail—began to form in my mind. 'Did he take Sally into the trees with him?' I asked grimly.

Annie nodded. The corners of her mouth turned down and her expression was very frightened.

'He took her into the trees, she screamed and came out, and he is still there?' I put the sequence of events together.

Annie nodded again. I cast my gaze around the clearing. 'Where are Miss Binsley and Miss Brigstock?'

'They went walking together a little while ago. Before his lordship arrived,' Annie said. 'There was only Sally and me here, when he came.'

'How convenient,' I spat out, but not at Annie. 'Get the tea things ready, Annie,' I said. 'The ladies and gentlemen will be returning soon, I think.' I cast my eye up at the sky, trying to work out an approximate hour. I estimated it to be some time after four o'clock. 'Yes. It is time we had tea.'

I dithered. I had Caroline Willow to think of, distressed and entangled in the undergrowth. I ought to go back myself, or send someone else back to alert her mama and papa as to her plight. She was a silly girl and had got herself into her predicament. She was upset but she was not in any kind of danger beyond the ruination of her dress. But the idea of Lord Petrel encountering Miss Brigstock sent a spear of dread into my innards. I knew then what I think I had always suspected about him— that he was a rake and … what was the word Mr Brigstock had used? A *predator*. And Miss Brigstock, for some reason, was critically vulnerable, susceptible in a way that I did not quite understand and yet very much feared. Miss Binsley would be no protection from the viscount's machinations.

My dilemma was solved at that moment by the arrival of Mr Eagerly. I never did find out why he had cut off from the rest of the ramblers and returned to the camp; some premonition, perhaps, some ineffable instinct for the lost sheep.

'Mr Eagerly,' I said, 'I am so happy to see you. Miss Caroline has got herself trapped within the coppice. Her dress is snagged and she is distressed. *I* could not get to her to free her, but …'

Mr Eagerly straightened his shoulders. Suddenly he filled his clerical garb, which he had not put off despite the heat of the day or the exertion of his walk, and I knew that he was more than equal to rescuing Caroline. 'I will extract her,' he said with such calmness and confidence that I could have wept. 'Where is she?'

I described the place on the path, the shred of my hem I had left there, the way through the trees to where she was, and he turned on his heel and set off.

I crossed the clearing and followed the path along the river, in search of Lord Petrel.

I encountered them after about ten minutes of fast walking. It seemed that Lord Petrel had stumbled across Miss Brigstock and Miss Binsley mere moments before my arrival there. There was something about their demeanour—formal, mannered—that suggested acquaintance that had only just been formed. The three of them stood by the river, looking out over it, admiring the view and speaking in measured tones about the weather. Thank goodness, I thought. I had got to them before he could do any mischief.

'There you are,' I said, making them all start and turn towards me. 'I am come to say that tea is ready. Lord Petrel,' I turned a gaze on him that was full of contempt. 'I am *very* surprised to see you have decided to join us. You seemed so very decidedly against doing so.'

He gave a studied bow. 'I had no intention of joining your little jaunt, Jocelyn dear. I was out riding when something happened that made me feel I ought to come and find you. But now I *am* here I see how nearly I missed the opportunity of becoming acquainted with these delightful ladies.' He turned to Miss Brigstock and Miss Binsley and gave an elaborate bow. 'We have had to introduce ourselves. There is no impropriety in it, in these circumstances.'

Miss Binsley smiled—almost the first time that day she had done so. I could see her mind calculating that, beside a viscount, Mr Brigstock was no very great catch at all.

Miss Brigstock smiled too, but her lips were stiff and thin and her eyes glittered. 'I have walked much further than I intended,' she said. 'I shall go back. I would like some tea.'

'Let us all go back,' Lord Petrel cried. He held his arm out to Miss Brigstock. 'Please allow me the honour,' he said.

She shrank from him. 'Oh no,' she said, 'the path is too narrow and I shall do much better alone.'

She came towards me and I saw the expression of panic she bore. I turned to lead the way.

'I was just saying,' Lord Petrel said, raising his voice so that we could all hear him from where he walked, at the rear of our single file, 'that I am well known in town, intimate with all the families of rank and a member of some half dozen clubs, but I have not had the honour of encountering Mr Brigstock before his short visit to Ecklington some fortnight since, or even of hearing his name.'

'Indeed,' Miss Binsley simpered. 'But that is not surprising, for they are but lately come from the continent. Mr and Miss Brigstock have resided

Allie Cresswell

in Italy since their infancy.'

'The continent?' Lord Petrel almost crowed. 'How very interesting. And just lately come from there to take up tenancy at Upton? Well now, that *is* a coincidence.'

Behind me, Miss Brigstock almost stumbled. I turned just in time to reach out a hand to steady her. I was sure that she—like me—had connected Lord Petrel's interest in these particular circumstances with the rider on the road. *These* were the same details he had mentioned to me in the morning. And had not the viscount said something about having encountered someone on his ride?

She took my outstretched hand and squeezed it tightly. Her face was ashen and I thought she would swoon, but she gave me a little nod and we carried on our way.

Miss Binsley, with no notion of how excruciating Miss Brigstock was finding Lord Petrel's topic, trilled, 'What coincidence can you mean, my lord?'

'Oh,' he shrugged her question away, 'I do not quite know, *yet*. It is just a curious circumstance, that's all. There is not so much to recommend this part of the country that someone should come all the way from Italy to settle here.'

'No indeed,' Miss Binsley said. 'My brothers and sister and I have been heartily bored since we got here, if I own the truth to you Lord Petrel. We had no notion that there was such excellent company to be had at Ecklington. We were told the family was from home.'

'The Talbots were from home, and Jocelyn chose to desert me. But I was there, ill and alone,' he said with melodramatic emphasis.

'You were not ill,' I said over my shoulder. 'You slipped on a bar of soap and gashed your shin.'

'Oh, Jocelyn,' Lord Petrel chuckled—and the sound made my gorge rise—'how you do tease, dear.'

We returned to our emplacement to find the whole party had reassembled. The young men were wet and tousled from their swim but full of high spirits. Mr Brigstock took one look at his sister however, and went swiftly to her side. She whispered something to him and gestured towards the horses. He demurred and seemed to get her to agree to taking a cup of tea and a slice of cake. She took her seat again, but gingerly. Maud and Mr Gabriel showed their sketches to the rector and my parents; they had enjoyed a productive afternoon by the waterfall, producing many studies of rocks, falling water and each other. My mother, on seeing Lord Petrel, went rather pink, and I wondered if she minded him being here as much as I did. Lieutenant Willow had taken a cup of tea for himself and a second, which he held out to me. He beckoned me to follow him to some little distance from the others that we might have our first private conference of the day, but I shook my head, looking significantly towards Caroline. She sat apart on one of the boulders with Mr Eagerly and her mama. At their urging she drank some tea, but could not suppress the snivels and hiccoughs that continued to assail her from time to time. I knew that if I took a single step towards the lieutenant her distress would erupt again in unrestrained puissance.

Mrs Binsley fell upon Lord Petrel with a flurry of coquetry I would not have thought her capable of, uttering apostrophic cries of delight and fluttering her fan. Mama saw it too and turned away, disgusted. The viscount found himself the object of mother *and* daughter's flirtatious attention but he stood impassively beneath the awning, in the very epicentre of our gathering, and allowed his gaze to rove over the clearing. He took it all in, assimilating, penetrating, divining the network of relations that connected one with another, picking up on undercurrents and flows of subtext. He saw what I saw—that Caroline was upset, that Lieutenant Willow held two cups and wore a disappointed frown, that Miss Brigstock was pale and agitated, enveloped in her shawl and yet shivering so much that her tea slopped onto its saucer. I suppose he saw that Sally had disappeared, frightened away by his predation, and perhaps it made him feel very masterful and pleased with himself.

At last he spoke, and although others were involved in their own conversations the volume of his voice, his positioning himself there in our midst and the fact that he was, after all, a viscount, meant that all our peripheral occupations and separate exchanges ceased. He had our attention.

'You really must forgive my intrusion here amongst you,' he said with hollow self-deprecation. 'I had no intention of it although Miss Talbot did beg me very prettily to make one of her little party ...' His eyes flashed at me and I wanted to rake them from their sockets with my nails. 'I declined however,' he went on, 'and was out riding when I met a fellow ... I do not know his name ...'

Miss Brigstock stiffened and, in spite of herself, let out a little cry. Lord Petrel made a slow turn and bent his eye upon her. 'Excuse me madam, did you say something?'

She shook her head, barely able to meet his eyes.

'I think Miss Brigstock is unwell,' I cried. 'We have no time for speeches now, Lord Petrel. I really think she is not well.'

'Yes, you are right,' Mr Brigstock said. 'I think I must take her home.'

Victor Eagerly stepped forward. 'I hope you will allow me to attend you,' he said.

'Oh, but I beg you will wait just a few moments more,' Lord Petrel said, smooth as silk. 'You may be able to assist with my enquiries, or, I should say, this fellow's enquiries, for it is a matter of local interest.'

'The fellow is nothing to us,' Mr Brigstock growled, 'and I must take care of my sister.'

'Of course not,' I urged. 'Lord Petrel, your friend's enquiry must wait. The time is not propitious.'

'It is *most* propitious,' Lord Petrel objected. He was relentless. 'The first thing the man told me was this: there is war. It is declared. Declared this very day.'[xxii] He swivelled again and fixed his eyes on Lieutenant Willow.

'War?' the lieutenant cried out, and dropped both tea cups. They shattered into a thousand pieces, and something within me broke in concert. 'I must return to my regiment. Aunt, Uncle,' he turned to each, his hands held out to them, his face stricken. They ran to him and enfolded him in their embrace. Caroline Willow let out the most heart-rending cry—a curdled yell that came straight from her soul. She half stood but, before she could regain her feet, had fainted away into the curate's arms.

The rest of us sat on, immobile, as though impaled, while the lieutenant said his farewells and dashed to where the horses were tethered. He passed me as he went, stopping only the briefest instant to put his hand on mine and mouth 'farewell' before disappearing through the trees.

Lord Petrel had not done with us yet and those of us with an iota of sense, the merest shred of emotional intelligence, knew it. He turned and, very deliberately, placed his cup on the trestle behind him.

'The second thing?' my father said, angrily. Whatever the viscount's relationship had been with him in the past, whatever supremacy he had exerted of rank or manners or connexion, I do not think my father liked to have it so disgustingly displayed here amongst his neighbours and his daughter's friends. 'Spit it out, man, if you *must*. The day grows old and it is time we were gone from here. The ladies are tiring.'

'*I'm* not tired,' Miss Binsley declared, infuriatingly. 'Mama and I were just saying how splendid it would be if you all came home to dine with us at Binsley.'

'Well ...' her mother demurred, for of course the provisions at Binsley House could not be of the best at such short notice as this and Sir Diggory would certainly not relish being descended upon by such a crowd. 'We were saying, in point of fact, that it would be delightful to dine together *somewhere* ... Not necessarily at Binsley House.'

'Certainly *not* at Binsley House, if we wish for a decent dinner,' Mr Binsley put in. 'When I am baronet, it will be a different matter.'

It was stupefying to me that the Binsleys could be so crass, so spectacularly unaware of the currents of tension and anxiety that were so acutely apparent to me. Could they not *see* Miss Brigstock's anguish? Was not Mr Brigstock's utter fury patently obvious? Did they not know—as I did—that my father's temper was at its very frayed end?

Apparently not.

Lord Petrel held up a hand that might have been conciliatory but which was, in fact, commanding. 'Very well. I promised the fellow I met that I would make enquiry amongst my acquaintance. Let me fulfil my pledge and I am done. He seeks a family by the name of ...'

'Who would like some more tea?' I almost shrieked. 'Mrs Willow! I am sure *you* would ...'

'*Stockbridge*,' Lord Petrel roared, to drown me out, enunciating the word with great deliberation. 'It is not a name known to me but then I discover that I am not as thoroughly well acquainted with people of rank as I thought I was; I had not heard the name ...' he paused theatrically, '... *Brigstock*, until today ...' He dropped a look of acid significance at Mr Brigstock. I opened my mouth to speak again although I had no clue what I might say, anything to divert the viscount from his purpose, to protect the Brigstocks. Lord Petrel's hand shot out and grasped my arm. He would not be stopped. Miss Brigstock emitted another small cry and pushed her hand into the folds of her shawl. There was a bead of blood on her lip where she had been biting it. 'A lady and a gentleman by the name of Stockbridge,' Lord Petrel went inexorably on. 'They may appear as man and wife, or as siblings. He does not know.'

All eyes now were drawn towards the Brigstocks. Where, for the remainder of our time as friends, there had been the confidence of equals, the perfect assurance of mutual regard, now there was doubt, a palpable sense of shrinking back, the scent of scandal. Miss Brigstock sat on the very edge of her chair, her face pallid, her hands restless in the folds of her wrap. Mr Brigstock knelt beside her, trembling with wrath.

'He thinks they may have taken up residence hereabouts, renting a property, perhaps...' Lord Petrel raised his eyebrows and made a moue. 'I don't know. But there. My promise is fulfilled and I will leave you to your entertainments.' He released my arm, flashed me an evil smile, and strode away.

The atmosphere when he had gone was like those days when thunder has come nearer and nearer and now hovers overhead. There was dead silence. The hiss of the spirit stove and the careless tumble of water over rocks was the only sound in the clearing. Even the birds had fallen silent.

'Well,' Mrs Willow said at last, 'I am sure *I* do not know … I am sure I could not say … And yet, what a strange thing! Does it not seem strange? What a coincidence, indeed, the names so like … I am sure I do not know what to make of it at all.'

'Do you not?' Mrs Binsley crowed. 'I believe we have been taken in! Girls! Girls! We must gather our things without delay.' She turned a look of utter contempt on the Brigstocks.

Miss Brigstock gave another cry, louder this time, and doubled over. 'I am unwell, Frederick,' she gasped out.

'Dr Eagerly,' Mr Brigstock cried, motioning him near. 'My sister, she is … she must be …'

'I will run and speak to your groom,' I said, suddenly released from whatever frozen enchantment had held me. I hurried through the trees to where the carriages and the horses had been waiting. I was happy to see that Lord Petrel had departed, happier still to see that the grooms had put the horses to.

I beckoned the Upton barouche to come as close as possible. 'Your mistress is unwell,' I said breathlessly. 'You will have to travel quickly.' Some instinct caused me to add, 'but steadily.'

I turned to see Miss Brigstock being aided through the trees by her brother and Victor Eagerly. She stumbled and they had to hold her up. She was clearly in some corporeal pain and greater torment of mind. She seemed barely sensible.

They came near and I threw open the door of their carriage. As they helped her inside the folds of her shawl fell open and I saw, at last, what she had been at such pains to conceal.

Mr Brigstock saw my expression—shock and dawning understanding, but, I hope, no revulsion, no judgement.

As Mr Victor settled his patient in the carriage Mr Brigstock spoke to me. 'Miss Talbot,' he said, his voice laden with emotion, both fear and sorrow. 'I have wanted to tell you. I think you might see, now, how nearly I *have* told you. But the secret was not mine, and she is so ashamed, although she has no cause to be.' His voice cracked and I thought he might break down, but he mastered himself.

'We are ready, Brigstock,' said Mr Victor from within the carriage. 'We ought not to delay.'

Mr Brigstock took my hand and pressed it. 'May I write to you?' he asked.

I nodded. He climbed in beside his sister and their carriage drove away.

30

October 1813

The year is turning. All around our depression the leaves are taking on a greenish-golden hue, like the inside of a burnished copper bowl. Soon they will begin to fall and the gardener will rake them up and put them to the fire.

Since the rains in August our weather has been kind; gentle winds and warm days—we have hardly needed a fire in the evenings. But even so I see that there is an accumulation of deadwood building up in the kitchen yard behind the house. I suppose it has been brought down from the slopes and will be sawn and stacked, to supplement our coals when winter bites—which it will, with no warning, a sudden snap of ferocious jaws.

The orchard is heavy with fruit and once again they have set to picking and preserving, building up our stores for the winter. The other day I listened to them from my seat by the fountain. They were in the orchard.

Their talk was business-like, concerning ladders and loppers, preserving jars and sugar. I like to hear them. They are natural with one another; they speak, listen and laugh—or sometimes scold, or complain—with none of the stilted formality they use when they address me, especially indoors. Outdoors is different. They are used to seeing me on my knees in the borders now. There, they might speak to me before they are spoken to, remarking on the colour of a flower or the success of a shrub, the tenacious nature of a particular weed I am trying to get out. In the garden, with my hands dirty and an old apron wrapped over my dress, I am—not the *same* as them—but not so *very* different. Inside, things revert to normal. I am the mistress and they are the servants, there to clean the house and pour my tea and serve my supper. Indoors, if I want a window closed or a shawl fetched, I ring the bell. Outside, if I want a tool I get it myself from the shed. Recently I have begun to think it a very ridiculous, utterly artificial separation, this demarcation between 'house' and 'household', between upstairs and down. What can it matter, here, where the world does not see? This house and the grounds that surround it up to the lip of the broad-stretched moor is our own country, our own world. We are like the convicts who have been sent to Australia. There are no cells there, I do not think, no prison bars. The place is their penitentiary as this is mine. I should say 'as this is *ours*' for they are inmates as much as I am.

I listened in as they set about their day's work. There were things I could have busied myself with in the formal garden—cutting back perennials, dahlia tubers to lift—but none of it was very pressing. Thus far I had not ventured into what I had thought of as the servants' outdoor domain— the kitchen gardens and the orchards—but I decided that I would cross whatever invisible line exists between those and the decorative but useless precincts of the ornamental garden.

I went to the orchard and took up a basket. I looked for sliding eyes, for meaningful glances between them that might show their discomfort with my intrusion, but saw none. They made nothing of it.

Someone said, 'There are windfalls beneath the pear tree.' So I went and began to gather up the fruit.

Mrs Orphan brought elderflower cordial out after a while, and slices of seedcake. They did not bother with the niceties of plates or cake forks and neither did I. We ate where we stood, surveying the baskets of fruit, easing our aching backs, wiping the sweat from our foreheads with the backs of our arms and licking crumbs from our fingers. Mrs Orphan and Burleigh and Sally and her husband the gardener, whose name, I discovered—after all these years—is Tom. And me. What oddity of fate and circumstance has brought us together here, our disparate little company? What coalition of happenstance has marooned us on this island in the moor?

The children ran around us, through the long grass beneath the trees, holding up the hems of their pinafores to make slings for the apples and plums. They gorged themselves, the juices running down their chins. I don't look at any of them very closely; I find it easier to think of them as an amorphous group. My eye skims their heads as they run about, and if they address me I reply only briefly. If I am not forthcoming; if I do not supply their wants, they will learn to leave me alone.

One of the children picked up a windfall with a wasp in it and was stung. Her yells of pain and outrage echoed around our amphitheatre as she held out the wounded digit, and Mrs Orphan took her off to the stillroom.

Her cry reminded me of Caroline Willow's, that day when war took Barnaby Willow away—anguished and appalled, resentful that something could be so cruel and hurt so much. I found myself lost in memories again. While the others industriously gathered and sorted the fruit, I stared into the gloom beneath the trees, my empty cordial glass still in my hand.

31

Lieutenant Willow's departure was just the first in what turned out to be an exodus from our little circle. The Binsleys left Sir Diggory in peace two or three days later, the brothers returning to Oxford and the women going back to their house in town, taking Maud Willow with them.

My mother remarked that this was a good thing, that 'poor' Maud was too impossibly rustic as she stood to become the wife of Gabriel Binsley. 'She will need two years' tutelage,' Mama said, 'to make her anything like presentable.'

It seemed to me that Maud's artless simplicity was just what Mr Gabriel had fallen in love with, and that he would not be pleased to find his shy, sensitive fiancée ruined by fashion and empty affectation.

The Binsleys did not call to say goodbye. They sent no note. I was disappointed in Elinor, who I had begun to think of as a friend. I blamed Lord Petrel, who had wrought havoc at the picnic, so spectacularly ruining it and embarrassing the Brigstocks. I blamed the Binsleys too. What fickleness, to spend the spring trying to ensnare a man only to run away at the least hint of trouble. I hoped I would prove a truer friend.

I called upon Caroline Willow several times but was always told that she was from home or indisposed. I think she was indeed unwell with some mental indisposition attendant on the disappointment of a broken heart; she did not even make an appearance at church on Sundays. I had Mrs Butterwick send some delicacies down to the rectory but they were returned with a note from Mrs Willow. 'We send our most grateful thanks,' the note said, 'but Caroline has no appetite at present.' In the end it was Caroline who was sent to Basingstoke to stay with her grandmamma, the bishop's wife, where she might encounter no painful associations with her cousin and where there was no possibility of her meeting me.

The Brigstocks quit Upton but not immediately. Miss Brigstock's condition did not permit her to undertake any kind of journey for two or three weeks. In that period they were not seen outside the precincts of Upton Park except by Victor Eagerly. He attended on Miss Brigstock for a short period before his return to Cambridge became imperative. The evening before he left he called at Ecklington to bid us farewell. Thankfully I was able to receive him alone. Papa and Lord Petrel had gone to visit a stud with Mr Silver, and Mama had one of her headaches and was lying down.

I received Mr Victor in the conservatory. Against the bright flowers and immaculate chequerboard of the floor he did look very dusty and drab, his boots broken down and his coat all-but out at the elbows. He wore no hat—I suppose the footman had taken it from him at the door—and his jet-black hair stood up in tufts. I led him to my little arbour behind the screen of greenery and bid him sit down. He did so diffidently.

'And so you will return to Cambridge to take your degree,' I began.

'Yes, and thence to London. I am to complete my training under Dr Whitworth.'

'Yes, I recall,' I said. 'In Wimpole Street.'

'Do you ever go up to town, Miss Talbot?' he asked.

'I have not done,' I replied. 'However it is spoken of now as a certainty, but not until the autumn.'

It was my mother's intention that we should spend the summer at a seaside resort before going to town for the season.

'I hope that I will see you when you are in town,' Victor said. 'If you ever have need of me, you will know where to find me. Your father, you know … Oscar and I look upon him quite as an honorary brother, if I may be so presumptuous as to say so. He has been so good to us, Miss Talbot. If there is any small thing that we could ever do to repay his kindness …'

'Thank you,' I murmured.

'I am sorry that our agreeable circle of friends is to be so abruptly broken up,' he went on. 'It has been a pleasant time, has it not?'

I could not suppress a sigh. 'I have enjoyed it very much,' I said, 'and yet …'

I looked through the window down the slope of the lawn, lost for a moment in a reverie.

'And yet?' Victor called me back to myself.

'I have lived a very retired life, up till now,' I said. 'I have been solitary, sufficient unto myself, you might say. The advent of such company in our neighbourhood was welcome to me, and quite dizzying, at times. But it was not quite what I expected. I will own to you, Mr Eagerly, that I find people much more complicated than I expected. They have such hidden lives—such agendas and secrets, and such prejudices…'

He smiled and nodded his head, and the sun glinted off the glass of his spectacles. 'You are thinking of the Brigstocks?'

I nodded. It was useless to pretend with *him* that I was ignorant of the true situation. 'She will be harshly judged, I fear, but not by me.'

'Nor I,' he said.

'Your brother and the rector …' I began.

'Know nothing, from me, anyway,' he assured me. 'I adhere to patient confidentiality. As to my brother, even if he knew, *he* is a man who does not throw stones.'

'No,' I said. 'He is gentle and good.'

'He is. I am sorry that you, too, will be leaving the neighbourhood before too long. My brother will be bereft of all his friends.'

I shook my head. 'He has many friends in the parish,' I said. 'He is well liked. Where a house within a ten mile radius has a door, he will be welcome through it.'

'You are very kind,' Mr Eagerly said. He slipped his hand into his inner coat pocket and drew forth a packet. 'I am charged to deliver this to you,' he said, sliding it across the seat towards me. 'It seems that you, too, have friends, or—which is a better recommendation still—you are considered to *be* a friend.'

32

October 1813

This evening, following another day of helping to gather the orchard fruit, I feel very lonely. I sit in the library and have a small fire burning in the grate, for although the days are warm the evenings are chilly. The silence is deafening. The ponderous sound of the clock, the hiss and crackle from the grate, the scrape of a tendril of ivy against the casement do nothing to suppress it. I strain my ears, extending my hearing via the thick walls and dark passageways, allowing the house to subsume me into its fabric. My flight of fancy takes me up to the roof, where the crows hunker, their feathers fluffed against the cold. I wander in spirit through the empty, shrouded rooms of the east wing, the draughty attics, the grander, antique apartments of the original house. In the nether regions, I think I can hear the sudsy scrub of saucepans being washed, the click and clink of china being stacked on the dresser, the gloop and spit of boiling apple pulp.

I felt ridiculous in the dining room, earlier, having Burleigh serve my supper. His smart livery and buckled shoes seemed to mock me, the implacable expression on his face a pantomime after we had worked side by side all day. I know he has a sense of humour. I have seen him exchange jests with Mrs Orphan. Between *them* there seems to be an easy, equal, almost a familial connection. From below stairs I could smell vinegar and sugar as the blemished fruits were preserved. I imagined the peeling and cutting that would be necessary before this could begin, and wondered how *that* and my three-course dinner, had all materialised when Mrs Orphan had been out of doors before me and had stayed there after I had come in.

I tried to engage Burleigh in conversation, breaking our long, long habit of utter silence.

'We have gathered a goodly crop,' I said. 'I suppose that the whole fruit are stored, for the winter?'

If he was shocked, he did not show it. 'Yes, ma'am,' was all he replied.

'Perhaps,' I laboured on, 'you might show me, tomorrow?'

'Yes, ma'am,' he said again. He kept his eyes fixed on a portrait of what must be some Tudor Talbot ancestor, I suppose. He has spent so long in utterly rapt, unwavering contemplation of this subject that he must know every curl of hair, every gleam of eye, every detail of coat and earring and ruff as well as he knows his own face. I wanted to ask him, 'Have you had supper, Burleigh? Would you like some of this? Why don't you fetch a plate and sit down and dine with me?' Of course it was unthinkable, an aberration of the hierarchy. A footman dine with his mistress? What uproar there would be! Oh, but what would it matter? It would not reach us here, that cacophony of apoplectic outrage, that clamour of offended manners. I am conscious, more and more, that the hierarchy is, here, an aberration, in the same way that those stilted social niceties, in this place, are meaningless.

Overhead, above my little sitting room in the east wing, there is the patter of little feet. The child is being put to bed, her hands and face washed after her day outside with the other children, her stung finger thickly bandaged—much more thickly than necessary, but the quantity of gauze seemed to placate her.

I might argue that there, too, I have built a barricade that is meaningless, where none needs to be. But the truth is that I do need it. It is my heart's defence.

The way her dark curls frame her face—she reminds me so much of George.

Loneliness presses down on me and at last I reach for my writing desk and pull out the letter I received from Mr Brigstock. I have kept it all these years although I have not re-read it in a long time.

33

Upton Park
May 1803

Dear Miss Talbot

You were kind enough to agree to my request to write to you and so I set pen to paper, but without at all knowing as I do so how I might, with propriety, with honour and with honesty, proceed.

Generally one would assume that those three things—propriety, honour and honesty—would be so caught up in one another, so inextricably entwined, that no gentleman—or lady—would see a division, much less attempt to separate them. But this, I feel, is my task. I hope you will understand me when I say, Miss Talbot, that assumptions can be at best misleading and at worst deceitful things.

Propriety would dictate that I thank you most sincerely for your hospitality at the picnic and for your friendship during our stay here in the country. Propriety would suggest that we might meet again at some future—but unspecified—date, in town, perhaps. It would ask you to convey our respects to your parents and then would sign itself your most obedient servant and have done.

So you see immediately why mere propriety will not answer here. Your hospitality last Wednesday went so far beyond the ordinary. You provided for us, at the nadir of our troubles, so courageously, using every possible means at your disposal to shield us. And, at the last, you dispensed your care with such largesse—with alacrity, with discretion and with delicate understanding. Of all the things that assailed my sister as we drove home to Upton—and there were many—one of the things that made her feel most wretched was that she had stretched out no hand to you, had not thanked you or even acknowledged your great kindness. Propriety does not possess, in the word 'friendship', sufficient depth or breadth to encompass your goodness to us while we have been with you in the country. Do not think I have not seen it, Miss Talbot, in your many, discreet and successful attempts to protect me from the unwanted attentions of others. Your care allowed me to be in the company but apart. I think you saw how burdened my soul was, and provided the respite I needed. And how I have enjoyed, in the two or three tête-à-têtes you have been so kind as to vouchsafe me, the frank, unstudied discourse we have exchanged. All these things are so much more than the 'friendship' propriety defines.

Propriety would shrink from what I must, in honour, tell you. But I would have no one accuse me of deception beyond what I felt it politic for the safety of my sister, to practice. My name, as I am sure you will have divined, is not Frederick Brigstock but Frederick Stockbridge. I am the son of Henry Stockbridge, a gentleman descended from the illustrious Scottish family and associated with the town of that name. My mother was Caterina, Countess of Forlì, the daughter of an ancient and noble Italian family. I am honoured to claim these antecedents and lament most bitterly the necessity I have lately been under to forswear them.

Now I will tell you our story, honestly, as you deserve, though I fear there is no propriety in it and little honour either.

Our mother died young and our distraught father, seeking consolation in strong drink, soon followed her. We were brought up by our aunt, an avaricious, scheming woman without a shred of propriety, honour or honesty in her character. My father had been a wealthy man and had provided handsomely for both his children. Our aunt used our monetary worth to arrange for us both marriages that would advance her own standing in society by benefitting her friends and filling her own coffers. Our preferences were ignored. I was married when little more than a boy to a woman much older than myself. The marriage was short and, for me, cripplingly unhappy. The lady died and the callous truth is I was not sorry.

My sister's great beauty meant that there was much competition for her hand, not in the way of suitors coming to woo her and win her heart, but in the way of impecunious gentleman coming to proffer bribes and inducements to my aunt that their suit might be successful. Lydia was paraded day and night before men who flocked from every corner of Italy and beyond that they might possess her and lay hold of her fortune. Propriety would forbid me from using the word 'prostituted' but in honour and in honesty I must say that this is what poor Lydia was subjected to. At last my aunt chose Lydia's husband. I will sully neither my pen nor your eyes with his name. Suffice it to say he was the grossest, cruellest and most villainous man God ever set upon the earth. Lydia pleaded but was over-ruled. She was dragged to the altar and forced to marry.

At the earliest possible opportunity—but not, I fear, before he had tormented, tortured and brutalised her to a terrible degree—I got my sister away. We escaped through Italy and France to England. We did not know, when we began, that Lydia was with child. That was only confirmed to us once we set foot on English soil.

Our scheme was to hide Lydia—and also, once we knew of it, to hide the child, for otherwise I fear history will only repeat itself—from the pernicious interference of her husband. It still is. Thanks to the skill of Dr Eagerly the child is not lost and as soon as Lydia is strong enough we will travel to the north country where we have made provision for her confinement, and for the subsequent care of the baby.

No doubt society will judge us harshly, knowing nothing whatsoever of our circumstances. But I am not ashamed. Everything I have done, for the love and protection of my sister, I would do again. What pretence I have had to keep up, I have done for her sake. What brother would do less?

We will not be able to call on you before we depart, much as we would like to do. I am sure I am already branded as a liar and imposter, Lydia as a fallen woman. We do not care what other people think but we would have your good opinion, Miss Talbot.

In the assurance that you have mine, most unreservedly, I remain,

Your servant and friend,

Frederick Stockbridge

34

Annie Orphan 1803 - 4

Sally's bruises had faded to yellowish green by the day of Miss Talbot's picnic. Her eye had healed, although it would never lose a quirky pucker at its outer corner. Although physically she was healing, Sally's mental state gave cause for continuing concern. She languished in bed, day after day. Annie made infusions of camomile and valerian[xxiii] for her, and rubbed her wrists with lavender oil, but nothing seemed to lift her gloom.

It had been Mrs Butterwick's idea to send Sally to assist with the picnic—an outing, fresh air; it would do her good. Certainly Sally preferred that idea to being left at Ecklington Grange with her assailants, and with this inducement she had been persuaded to rise from her bed, wash and put on some clean clothes. She enjoyed the picnic; the finely dressed ladies and high-spirited gentlemen, the good humour of the grooms and the clement weather all served as a fillip to her frayed nerves. Mrs Butterwick had provided a vast spread of choice comestibles and the servants ate their fill of what the finer folk left behind. Sally helped the ladies in the confines of the tented enclosure and took the results to sluice away in the river, almost happy for the first time since that dreadful night. And then Lord Petrel had strolled into the encampment. Seeing her unprotected he had bundled her without even the pretence of ceremony into the thicket. He would without doubt have repeated his outrage upon her had she not raised the alarm.

The incident set Sally back considerably; she returned to Annie's room for a further week, and nothing would move her from it.

She *was* persuaded, in due course, when it became clear that she was not with child. But the absence of *that* consequence to her molestation in the stables did not mean the incident was by any means forgotten. The remembrance of it troubled her sleep. Even if she went to bed in her own room, in the night she would creep to where Annie slept and slip in beside her. She was subject to restlessness, clinging to Annie or sitting up start-eyed, hearing footsteps on the stairs when no one was there. Annie began to mix a sleeping draught for her; a weak concoction of crushed poppy-seed and plenty of honey to take away the bitterness. It was successful in making Sally sleep, but her slumber was troubled and, often she would mutter or cry out. For many months Sally was subdued, nervous of men's company. Her skin lost its bloom, her hair its lustre. She plodded through her work quietly, and did not engage in the other kitchen maids' ribald banter—which, in any case, since the attack, had lessened.

In truth, although it was never openly acknowledged to have occurred, the incident impacted everyone below stairs at Ecklington as well as the outdoor workers. The lewd, cider-fuelled shenanigans between stable lads and dairy maids came to an end. Hostilities between Marg and Edna over the desirable groom ceased as they became united in their hatred for Jackie Silver and Lord Petrel's valet Mr Goose, neither of whom, by the tacit understanding of all the servants, was ever to be allowed a moment's unsupervised company with a female. Mrs Brixie now never walked to the Grange from the village or back again without her son in attendance. Mrs Brixie was a middle aged woman of capacious girth, bandy-legged and hirsute. The idea of her being in much danger was not very great, but she took what she considered proper precaution for the protection of her person. Billy Brixie was a large-boned boy, perfectly amiable, not altogether bright but very strong. He would affably crush anyone his mama took exception to without questioning why. In spite of Sally's altered looks he took a shine to her. He sat for hours on an upturned barrel just inside the kitchen doorway where he could see both Sally, as she plucked fowl in the scullery, and his mother pounding laundry in the wash-house.

The entire household was relieved when, towards the end of May in 1803, the whole Talbot family quit Ecklington for the summer. The departure of the family meant the loss of Miss Nugent, Miss Peake and Mr Talbot's valet as well as two grooms who were to take care of the carriage and horses. This reduced the staff by a third, and the furlough for the duration of various maids of different degree and two of the four footmen reduced it still further. No one mourned the absence of Mr Goose, Lord Petrel's snooping, oily valet, for naturally the viscount accompanied the Talbots as a flea accompanies a dog. Jackie Silver was sent north, that he might commence negotiations for the purchase of blood stock. He, too, was seen off the premises without regret. It was a substantially reduced household—but a much happier one—that stood on the sweep as the Talbots' carriage disappeared down the long drive. It was known that they had taken a house in Brighton for the whole season and, from there, would go to their house in town.

Annie regretted the departure of Miss Talbot very much and did not like to think of her exposed to the nefarious machinations of the viscount. Miss Peake had left everything in Miss Talbot's chambers in order but Annie made it her practice to air the rooms and dust the dressing table weekly. She allowed herself the smallest possible day-dream of being Miss Talbot's maid one day and of having the care of all the young mistress's belongings.

In the principal living rooms everything was swathed in sheeting, the crystal chandeliers bagged and the turkey carpets rolled up. The shutters were firmly closed that sunlight might not fade the upholstery. The servants retreated below stairs. A period of scouring and scrubbing, reorganisation and indexing ensued as pantries were emptied, cleaned and painted with distemper. The stove was allowed to go out for the first time in twelve months, its enormous chimney swept by two small boys, its surface blacked and polished to a dull shine. Annie betook herself to the stillroom to assess her stocks of herbs and worked tirelessly in the medicinal garden, plucking leaves and picking off flower heads before crushing, boiling and distilling to boost her supplies. Then, with only a residual staff to cater for, the kitchen spotless and everything in order in the larder, Mrs Bray retreated to her room or to a sunny spot in the orchard to rest her bunions, leaving the kitchen maid to prepare the servants' fayre. Mrs Butterwick got out a skein of wool and began to knit socks for her nephew who was an enlisted man in the militia. Mr Swale retired to his sitting room with the newspapers he had been stockpiling against just this occasion. The rest of the household settled down to a period of comparative leisure, but not Annie Orphan.

The gardeners were the only staff members whose work did not let up at the Talbots' absence. When her work indoors was done Annie enjoyed joining the men who weeded the rows of vegetables in the kitchen garden. As often as possible she encouraged Sally to join in, but she was likely to rest from the work as soon as it was begun, and sit on a sunny bank staring vaguely into the distance. Annie learned to preserve legumes, to store root crops, to reserve seeds for the following year's sowing while Sally made daisies into chains that soon wilted and died. Annie watched as the gardeners pruned the fruit trees and soft fruit bushes to encourage good crops for the next year. Sally, wrapped in a warm shawl, was supposed to gather the lopped branches and build a bonfire, but the pile she made was too near the tool shed and had to be taken down and moved. Mrs Bray taught Annie to make jam and chutney and to seal stewed fruit beneath a wax seal in a tightly closed jar that it might be enjoyed when the trees were bare, while Sally lazed by the fire with her feet on the fender. Annie went into the smokehouse to see the sides of meat hanging in the dim, saw how much smoke would preserve and flavour the meat, and how much would make it tough and bitter. She begged the dairymaids to show her the method for making cheese and became competent in the task, and also in poultry management and pig husbandry. Sally moved around as though in a dream but Annie's thirst for knowledge was unabated as the months stretched on and the year turned.

Apart from their regular Sunday worship at the village church and their day at the picnic, neither Annie nor Sally had ventured beyond the boundaries of Ecklington since the day they had arrived. Now, with hours of comparative freedom to fill, they began to walk along the narrow lanes, finding woodlands and farmsteads and views over rolling hillsides. Sally was a reluctant companion on these sojourns but Annie gave her a basket and instructed her to help in the collection of sweetfern, to make poultices for the treatment of sores, and chamomile for digestive disorders. They encountered no one on these walks until one day, in the heart of an area of secluded woodland, where autumn leaves lay crisp and thick beneath their booted feet and birds chirruped overhead, they came upon Mr Talbot's game-keeper.

They had walked for longer than Annie had anticipated, around the periphery of several fields and thence into the woods. The day had been bright and crisp with clear skies overhead, but in the woods the light was filtered by the canopy of branches overhead and the sun's warmth did not penetrate. It was gloomy and a little eerie, the path indistinct. Sally, who had chattered on and off during the rest of their walk, had fallen silent, affected by the altered surroundings and Annie had already determined that they should retrace their steps and leave the wood.

Tom Harlish was a man known to both Annie and Sally. He came to the kitchen door with game for Mrs Bray several times a week. He assisted with lambing in spring and with the butchery of sheep, geese and pigs when that gruesome task was due. He was a tall man, broadly set, aged perhaps twenty five, always warmly dressed in thick tweeds with a hat pulled low over his brow. In character he was taciturn, a loner, which was fortunate since his occupation required many solitary hours. He was not a handsome man; some childhood pox had scarred his face. He had eyes of such a pale blue that in some lights they seemed to have no colour at all. His lashes were fair, his chin deeply cloven. There might have been something sinister about him—he tended to materialise, out of nowhere, so adapted was he to his natural surroundings, so soft his footfall—and his work of stalking, snaring and herding birds to their deaths certainly imbued him with a fearsome air. But in actuality he was gentle, softly spoken. The birds whose necks he wrung he had also tended and fed and protected from the fox. He might lie hour by hour and watch the hind and her fawn which, one day, he would kill, cleanly, with his musket.

His being there in the wood surprised Annie and Sally—not that he was there, it was his natural sphere—but that he had come upon them so suddenly. They both started and Sally went pale, clutching at Annie's sleeve and dropping her basket of willow bark. Mr Harlish, seeing their anxiety and perhaps knowing something of Sally's tribulations earlier in the year, removed his hat and said, 'Good day,' before laying his musket against a tree and easing himself onto a fallen log some distance across the clearing from where they stood.

'Good day to you, Mr Harlish,' Annie said. 'I hope we do not trespass on your work.'

The man shrugged, and rummaged in his pocket for a knife, with which he proceeded to whittle a piece of stick he carried. 'I've husbanded birds that no one will shoot this year,' he said dourly. 'It doesn't matter if you scatter them far and wide.' He nodded at their baskets. 'What are you collecting?'

'Willow bark.' Annie replied. 'And valerian and liquorice, if I can find any.'

'You don't have both in your herb garden?' Mr Harlish raised an inquisitive eyebrow.

Annie blushed, for she did have both, but had enticed Sally out of doors on the pretence of needing them for her stores. She took a few steps closer. 'I have brought a bottle of tea and some slices of cake,' she said. 'Will you share our feast?'

Mr Harlish nodded and Annie went to perch next to him on the fallen log. Sally followed and sat the other side of her, away from the gamekeeper.

'It must be a cause of some frustration to you,' Annie observed when she had poured their tea into the rough earthenware cups she had brought out with her, 'to do work that no one will benefit from.'

'The birds will benefit,' he said evenly, 'from not being shot from the sky by incompetent marksmen.'

Annie laughed. 'I suppose they will.'

'Are a great many of them wounded?' Sally ventured, taking the cup that she and Annie shared and wrapping her hands around it.

Mr Harlish nodded. 'I am afraid so, miss. For every one my dogs find dead they find another two winged. They must have their necks wrung, for if a bird cannot fly it cannot survive.'

'They will be killed by foxes, otherwise,' Sally mused sadly.

'As to those, Sir Diggory keeps their numbers in check,' he replied. '*There* is a gentleman who understands the responsibilities of land ownership. He is hunt-master, you know, over Binsley way, but horse and hound often come onto Talbot land.'

'And tear them limb from limb,' Sally muttered with a shiver.

'It's the way of it, miss,' Mr Harlish said with a sigh. 'Some men must chase things.' He waved his slice of cake. 'This is very good,' he said. 'Did one of you make it?'

In point of fact Sally had got so far as to cream the butter and sugar before she had lost interest in the task, and it had been left for Annie to complete. 'Yes,' said Annie, 'we both had a hand in it. Here.' She parcelled up the pieces that remained and handed them to him. 'Take what is left, for there is plenty more in the larder. Unless,' she hesitated, 'Mrs Harlish will take exception? I am sure she makes excellent cake.'

Mr Harlish gave a coy smile. 'There is no Mrs Harlish, miss. I live alone, apart from four dogs. Oh, and there's a badger cub I'm nursing back to health just now.'

Sally, with a new-found interest in the injured, asked, 'What's the matter with him?'

'Been bitten by one of his litter, I think. Wound has turned putrid. I'm treating it with a garlic poultice. Smells awful but seems to be doing the trick.'

'It would do,' Annie said. 'Honey works well, too. And smells better.'

'When he's better, will you keep him?' Sally wanted to know.

'No miss. Wild things belong in the wild.'

Mr Harlish had returned to his whittling. Annie collected the cups and the stone flask and put them back in her basket. The day was turning chill, and would soon grow dark. 'We had better be on our way, Sally,' she said.

Mr Harlish stood up and sniffed the air. 'There will be a frost tonight,' he said, returning his knife and the piece of wood to his pocket.

Sally shivered. 'It grows cold already. Annie, which way is the quickest home?'

Mr Harlish took off his coat and held it out to Sally. 'Put this around your shoulders, miss. I will show you the best way back to the lane if you will trust yourselves to me? There is not an inch of ground in these woods, not a tree or stone that I do not know as well as I know my own hands.'

The girls consented to follow him and he took them a route between trees already darkening as the afternoon turned to evening. They came out unexpectedly on the lane not far from Ecklington's home farm, from where they needed only to cross the farmyard to find themselves at the far side of their own kitchen garden.

Sally made to shrug off the gamekeeper's jacket, but he shook his head. 'Keep it, miss. I'll be up at the house tomorrow and can collect it then.'

'But you'll be cold,' Sally protested. 'Is your house far?'

'My cottage is down the lane yonder.' He indicated a narrow opening some small way along the hedge, which must have led around and behind the woodland. 'Five minutes and I'll be home and beside my own fire.'

'It sounds very cosy,' Sally said, with the smallest hint of her old coquetry. She looked up at him through her lashes. 'I'd like to see the badger cub,' she added.

'He is not a pet,' Mr Harlish replied gruffly, 'nor a curiosity.'

The light that had, so briefly, glimmered in Sally's eye, went out. She turned her face away.

'Thank you, Mr Harlish,' Annie said. 'And good evening.'

The year turned. Christmas came and went and there was no word that the Talbots would return. Annie presumed that Miss Talbot would be presented, would enter into the London season, might perhaps be engaged and never return to Ecklington at all. The thought formed a hard pebble of sorrow in her breast and shrivelled the remnant of her dream of being Miss Talbot's maid. Miss Peake would surely soon be pensioned off, if she had not been already, replaced by an experienced girl well versed in current fashion and hair-styling; even had Annie been trained, she could not possibly have trusted herself to pick the right gown or the most appropriate jewels for dinners and balls in London's most illustrious houses. She found herself staring through the stillroom window as beads of February hail peppered the glass. The light was poor; she could barely see the receipt book where Miss Nugent and generations before her of wise women had noted down the formulae for their unguents and tinctures. As she looked down upon the book a fat tear fell from her eye and landed with a splat, smudging the writing.

35

December 1813

The winter is come with a vengeance. What Yorkshire weather gives so graciously with one hand, it snatches back jealously with the other. We have had snow; many days of it, and vast quantities. The centre of our bowl, the part that is open to the sky, is easily two feet thick in deep, substantial snow. It has blurred all the edges; I cannot see where the parterre begins nor the edges of the borders, or the steps from the terrace. I stand and look out at it and try and make out one thing from another, but cannot. It seems an apt metaphor for my life, just now. The boundaries I thought existed seem not to; everything is merging, or is shrouded, covered by something else. There is no strict delineation and any that we impose—in society, in nature—will be transparent or temporary.

Snow lies up against the house on all sides, encroaching up towards the window sills. The house creaks as though it is being compressed, slowly, from without. From time to time heavy sheets of snow slide from the roofs and shatter below. It is dangerous to step outside; the weight of snow would crush bone to powder in an instant. Avalanches from the roof have formed quite a massif all along the terrace—a range of outlandish peaks and tortured outcrops separated by bluish crevasses and deep-scored valleys. The wind hones it like a sculptor, making a new continent every day. Fresh snow falls to shroud the sculptor's work, but just because a thing cannot be seen does not mean it is not there.

No one has bothered to clear the snow from the terrace, but around in the stable yard, where the door to the kitchen is, Burleigh and Tom shovel daily, making paths to the hen coops and the pig sty, the smoke house and the privy. I hear the rasp and scrape of their shovels, and the shrieks of the children as they cavort on the snow, all bundled so thickly in scarves and hats and layers of coverings that I can hardly tell which child is which when I watch them from my bedroom window.

The periphery of the hollow, even where it is sheltered by trees, is no less thickly covered by drifts flung out by the centrifugal wind. Burleigh tells me the drive is reasonably clear, protected by the canopy of branches above, but the moor beyond is impassable. The narrow lane from the gatehouse to the village is absolutely obscured; only a fool would attempt to navigate it, so we have not been to church.

The sky above us—what little we can see of it—is dark. Sometimes grey, sometimes purple, always angry. It is portentous, threatening Armageddon, the end of days. It makes you blind to look up into it. The snow stings and vision is distorted. The snow all around is searing, stealing colour. Even here, in our enclave, there is a sense of menace— the cold and penetrating damp, the unpredictable barrage of snow and weather. How much worse it must be on the moor, above the lip of our combe, where the wind is unchecked, a tirade, and where the snowfall disguises bog and rock. What is a storm here must be a blizzard there, terrifying in its power.

When I went back indoors after being out in the snow, everything was dim, my eyes blinded, but I never felt more comfort than in the solid thump as the door slid home. This house is a sanctuary, a refuge.

Our cove has been a cauldron of wind. Eddies of snow dance in the air like autumn leaves, swirling and circling and finding no place to rest. Anything not tied down has been picked up and thrown across the plot. Mrs Orphan tells me the bucket she uses for hen food has entirely disappeared. The log-pile has been repeatedly decimated, spread asunder as though by the hands of mischievous children. The noise of the wind, day and night, is terrifying—we are all pale and stricken with it—clamouring, rattling the casements, scrabbling at the windows and shrieking down the chimneys. The discordant tune of it is incessant; there is no relief. It makes the child cry in the night.

One night in particular it howled around the house like a demented dog, like a Fury, holding us suspended in the vortex of its power. The flue in every room moaned a different, off-key note like the warped pipes of a disparate organ. I was not asleep—nobody could sleep, with such a maelstrom outside—but sat up in bed, a thick shawl around my shoulders. Something in the attic flapped and crashed and then I heard breaking glass. My candle blew out. Then my bedroom door flew open and something I thought was an apparition appeared—it was white and miasmic in the gloom, and walked on feet that made no noise on the floor. It moaned and whimpered as it came towards me. I would have screamed had the sound not been absolutely choked in my throat from sheer terror.

Then Annie Orphan spoke. 'Miss Talbot,' she said, and she used that severe, no-nonsense tone that she keeps for when something must be done. 'You must take her. She will not be left, but I must go over the house and make sure things are secure.'

'Burleigh shall do it,' I cried, shrinking back against my pillows.

'He tends the outbuildings,' she almost snapped back. '*You* must take her.'

She did not even wait for an answer, let alone my agreement, but thrust her bundle into my arms. I flinched from it but she ignored my gasp of remonstrance and left the room.

The bundle was heavy, and surprisingly warm. It smelt a little damp. It lay on my lap and against my body. I could feel the dampness of her cheek on my neck, the softness of her hair on my face. The little sounds she had been making had stopped but every now and again her body shuddered with those hiccoughing, quick-panting sobs that go on after crying has exhausted itself. I supposed she was as shocked by the circumstance as I was. We were both rigid, shrinking, but she could not move—enveloped and rendered immobile as she was by a thick padding of quilt—and neither could I; she pinioned me to the bed. Very tentatively, as one might reach out to a stray dog that could prove rabid, I put an arm around her. She did not bite or scratch, or writhe. If anything she seemed, a little, to relax. I felt the weight of her increase. She made a little sighing noise.

I had kept my eyes firmly closed, a ridiculous attempt at self-deception— that what I could not see, would not exist, that I was not breaking every self-imposed prohibition I had set myself. But just because a thing cannot be seen does not mean it is not there. My eyes began to sting as they had done when the snowflakes fell into them, and at last my lids could not contain my unshed tears.

The only light in the room came from a chink between my curtains, an eerie glow that came from the snow outside, even though there was no moon. The night was thick with snow, the flakes carried on the restless wind. I could hear the hiss of them as they hit the window. The light seemed to come from the snow itself, luminous and bluish, as though generated by the ice crystals. It is strange how something so cold and sharp and inhospitable can contain such mysterious beauty, such visceral, illuminating warmth.

The weight of the child against my body began to melt the ice-shards I had packed around my heart.

'Now look,' I sobbed into the darkness. 'Now look what you have done.'

It is time to write about George.

36

George was a beautiful child, dark, with plentiful, curly hair, deep brown eyes and a healthy complexion. As a baby he was cherubic—plump and dimpled, his skin as velvety, his flesh as yielding as a ripe peach. He was strong, sturdy and determined, but not stubborn. He charmed his way through infancy with winning smiles and coy little pouts of his perfectly kissable lips. He suffered the usual childhood ailments but they scarcely seemed to touch him; he might be feverish one night but up and running about the following day. He shook off coughs and colds easily. I recall no occasion when his health was really feared for until that terrible period in 1804.

He was adventurous, always climbing trees and thrashing about in the lake. He learned to ride early; his exploits on a succession of ponies frightened Mama and me as we watched him in the paddock, our hearts in our mouths as he took higher and higher jumps. A few bumps and grazes were the only injuries he sustained in his exploits. When he first went to school he enjoyed sports, and was popular. I imagine he was the instigator of many an escapade of derring-do in the dormitory at night.

In one regard only did he appear to struggle. He was not good at his lessons. He lacked patience for study and had no interest in books. The principles of mathematics eluded him and he grasped only the most rudimentary Latin and Greek. When his school masters sent home reports of half-hearted effort and indifferent examination results my parents hired tutors, so that George might continue his studies during the holidays. George would have none of this however, escaping for the day with food purloined from the pantries to hide out in the stables, roam around the countryside or get under the gamekeeper's feet. When taken to task he was apologetic—very sorry to have disappointed the tutor—but cheerfully determined to pursue the same course on the following day.

My mother worried about George's lack of academic success more than my father did. She expected George to shine in everything, to attend university and gain his degree. She needed him to be in every way—personally, intellectually, in manners and taste—the equal of any young nobleman of his generation. He was to be unexceptionable, a paragon, the taint of his common blood utterly over-shadowed by the towering perfection of everything else. His faultlessness, when added to his fortune, would set him above any marriageable viscount, earl or marquis in England; George was to take his pick from amongst the daughters of the noblest families in the land. Once he had secured the hand of a suitable lady he could forget every Latin declension, every algebraic formula he had ever known, as far as Mama was concerned.

Papa took a different view. He wished to induct George into his business. An ability to identify opportunities in the markets, to command respect, to read in a fellow's eye whether he was likely to default on a loan, to deliver what he promised—these were the skills my father valued and looked to find in his son. Of course he would need to have a certain amount of intellectual capacity, but my father employed dozens of clerks and bookkeepers and lawyers to look after the minutiae of things. What the business needed was a figurehead, a leader, a man to think on his feet and make quick decisions, a man who was ready to take a risk, now and then. My father saw all these qualities in George and cared not at all when the school reports came back less than glowing.

George must be a gentleman. On that point Mama and Papa were both agreed. They would tolerate no coarseness of manner, no lack of courtesy, no cruelty or disrespect, and in this regard George gave no cause for concern. He was a kind boy, gentle with living creatures and careful of me, his sister. He had none of that aversion to bathing that so many boys evince. His table manners were good, his conversation polite. He endured my mother's scolding with great patience and charm; he was very sorry, he would try to do better, he wished he were cleverer, but there it was.

My mother determined that this defeatism should be swiftly and permanently eradicated; George *must* overcome his stubbornness at school. Therefore, when he was twelve years of age, she removed him from the school where he had been happily settled for a number of years and placed him at Stonybeck, renowned for its exacting teaching methods, harsh discipline and penal conditions. This was where he returned to that spring, just before the Binsleys and the Brigstocks came to the country. I had seen him go with some misgiving. He had seemed different to me during the Easter holiday; gloomy, moody and out of sorts. I knew that as boys grew into men they changed, just as girls did when they became women. I understood that some alteration in George's character was likely as he grew away from childish enthusiasms and the carefree life of boyhood. I had expected him to become more thoughtful, to keep to himself those ideas and dreams that he might formerly have shared with me, and so I did not press him when he showed reluctance to discuss his school fellows or his lessons. He behaved with Mama and Papa as he always had done, but when we were alone I found him uncommunicative, sometimes brooding to the point of sullenness.

He went back to school and my flurry of outings and social engagements began. I neglected to write to George for some three or four weeks. His letters home were brief, carefully written, enquiring after our health but saying nothing of himself.

'He will soon be home for the summer,' my father said one morning, when George's letter had been read and passed around the breakfast table. 'He will enjoy Brighton, I think. I shall arrange for him to come straight there to us, from Stonybeck.'

'I shall hire a sailing skiff or a small sloop,' Lord Petrel said from where he lounged at the far end of the room. 'I have not sailed since I was a boy. Do *you* sail, Talbot?'

My relationship with Lord Petrel had undergone a seismic shift since the picnic. Whereas, previously, he had been teasing and patronising, now there was about his manner a familiarity that I found uncomfortable. That he viewed me as a young woman rather than a child was clear from the slightly questionable banter he liked to bandy with me. It was suggestive, accompanied by eyebrow waggling and lewd winking. For my part I despised and distrusted him. I more than half suspected him of interfering with Sally Orphan. I lost no opportunity to make cutting remarks but, if anything, he seemed rather to relish these.

Now, I could not restrain myself from asking, with an exaggerated air of astonishment, 'You accompany us to Brighton then, do you?'

Lord Petrel gave me an arch smile. 'Should you rather I stayed here? It will be lonely, without you for company, my dear.'

His inference was quite clear to me; left to himself at Ecklington he would prey on the maids. 'We must not be selfish,' I said with acid insincerity. 'You have favoured us with your company for many more weeks than we deserve, I am sure. You must be inundated with invitations to illustrious houses up and down the land.'

'It's true,' he said with a sigh, 'and I ought, at some point, to see the earl. It is my earnest hope that you will accompany me, and be *my* guest. Unless you find some alternative role more convenient?' He gave me a look that was quite lascivious. I looked down the table at Papa, but he was hidden behind his newspaper. My mother seemed not to have heard. 'But,' his lordship went on, 'Flintshire is so far away, and unspeakably bleak. I fear I am unequal to the journey and, in any case, I find I am helplessly chained by my attachment to you all, my most *particular* attachment.' Again, that insolent gaze from beneath his beetling brows. 'There is no man in England I esteem more highly than your papa and your mother's graciousness is *sans pareil.* Then there is you, Miss Talbot. I find no equal to the pleasantness of *your* conversation anywhere.'

'Dear me,' I said, throwing him a withering look, 'other young ladies' conversation must be dull indeed.'

'Other young ladies are dull in general, compared with you my dear,' Lord Petrel replied.

We went to Brighton at the beginning of June and established ourselves in a lodging there, a tall, narrow house on East Street, only slightly removed from the sea front and the Steyne. The Steyne formed the centre of Brighton activity; the libraries were situated there, sports and games played, carriages driven and horses ridden. It also did service as the parade ground and temporary encampment for the Dragoons and numerous battalions of militia who were stationed in Brighton ready to repel Napoleon's invading forces. The multitudes of Brighton society promenaded on the Steyne, seeing and being seen; it was the liveliest, the most exciting and fashionable of Brighton's attractions. Games offered diversion. Acrobats and jugglers entertained, passing around their hats for pennies afterwards. Menageries with exotic birds, monkeys and performing animals vied for attention. I found the noise and activity there almost dizzying and I thought of the Miss Binsleys. *This* was just the kind of diversion they would enjoy.

Lord Petrel stayed at an inn, nominally, but took all his meals with us. He accompanied us to the Assembly, sea-bathed with my father and joined us on our excursions to various places of interest when the racing calendar allowed. He formed a permanent addendum to our family party; it was expected that we should go nowhere without him, or he without us. He was Lord Petrel, the son of the Earl of Flintshire[xxiv]. His rank gained us access to elegant soirées hosted by the Countess of Cumberland, dazzling dinners at Stein House[xxv] and even to the Royal Pavilion itself, although this was still undergoing some construction work. What Lord Petrel's rank could not achieve my father's deep pockets could, and between them both we had a delightful time of it.

I particularly enjoyed the assembly. I loved to dance and the music put me in mind of Binsley House. The Assemblies were crowded affairs with many people jostling together, chairs rarely to be found, over-heated rooms and a great cacophony of noise. Papa generally retired to the card room but Lord Petrel would stand sentinel behind Mama and me. He tipped a waiter to make sure we were supplied with punch or champagne, and to go on ahead and secure us seats at the supper table, so the viscount made himself useful. Conversation was not easy and I did not mind that I was not required to engage with him in that way. He and Mama kept each other amused by whispered exchanges concerning what they considered to be *faux pas* of dress committed by some of the older ladies, the state of inebriation of some of the gentlemen and likely *liaisons* between people who were not married to each other. It surprised me to hear Mama descend to gossip and unkind criticism. Occasionally his lordship would lead one or other of us to the set. For a large man Lord Petrel was surprisingly light of foot, but I did not like his manner, which was proprietorial.

I danced with innumerable officers at the Assembly, but, for a reason I did not know at the time but was later to discover, rarely with any more than once. All of them put me in mind of Lieutenant Willow. I scanned the crowd looking for his burnished curls, his arresting blue eyes. I had no absolute knowledge of his being in Brighton—troops were mustered all along the coast against invasion—but I looked for him all the same.

George joined us as my father had arranged and, against the bright, sparkling sea, the white and cheerful sprigs of the ladies' muslin dresses and the cherry red of the Dragoons to which my eyes had become accustomed, he looked pale and ill. I gasped at the sight of him. In truth, I think if he had not arrived in our carriage and been shown into our hallway I might not have recognised him. He was now thirteen years old. He had grown and was now almost as tall as me, but all his flesh had melted away; he was stick-thin, his clothes hung from his frame. His hair, usually thick and wavy, had been shorn from his head. He had a scab on his skull that he had picked at so that it wept and bled. The skin on his face was unhealthy and peppered with yellow pustules. His eyes were dull. His teeth looked too big for his mouth.

My mother looked taken aback at the sight of him, and I think she did have a moment of self-doubt, questioning the wisdom of having sent him to a school known for its austerity and rigour. It was plain that he had suffered.

I ran to him and wrapped my arms around him even though I knew my mother would frown on me for doing so. 'Oh George,' I cried, 'what has happened to you? Have you been ill? Have you been ill-used?'

For the briefest moment he sank against me, and I felt the weight of his head on my shoulder. I wondered if he might cry although I had rarely seen him weep, certainly not since he had been a very young boy. *I* felt like weeping. I was so appalled at the figure he cut, there, in the light, airy hallway of our lodgings. He looked small and frail, and I feared for him. I looked to where our mother stood, ready to accuse her, with my eyes if not with my voice, for having subjected him to such cruelty as he had obviously endured.

But then George straightened himself and stepped away from me. 'I am tired and very hungry,' he said, in a voice I did not recognise; it warbled between the fluting tone of his former speech and a deeper, manlier pitch. He crossed the hall and bowed to Mama. 'Good afternoon, Mother,' he said with great formality. 'I hope I find you well.'

'Yes, George dear,' she said, and it was one of the few times I heard her voice tremble, that I saw uncertainty in her eyes. 'And you ... well, how you have grown! You look in need of nourishment. And a bath!' She gave an artificial little laugh, as if those two things would bring back our old George to us. 'Your father is out, securing us tickets for the theatre. He will be very pleased to see you.'

George gave her a small, thin smile and then turned to one of the footmen who had brought his trunk into the house. 'I wonder if you might have that conveyed to my chamber,' he said, quite like a gentleman fully grown, 'and ask someone to draw me a bath.'

I did not accompany my parents and Lord Petrel to the theatre that night, but stayed behind with George. I watched him eat his supper from a tray in his room, which he did with an appetite that was almost desperate.

'Do they not feed you, at school?' I asked him, when every plate and bowl had been scraped clean, when I had sent down to the kitchen for more and when that, too, had been devoured. I did not ask in jest, for I feared it was too true.

'Fellows like me do not get a great deal,' he said, 'and what we do get is cold, by the time we are sent to the refectory.'

'What do you mean, 'fellows like you'?' I asked.

'The ones who do not retain their studies. We are kept back, in the classroom, where the stove has been allowed to go out. In the wintertime we are not permitted more candles, so even though we stare at our books we can barely see what is written there.'

'But George,' I cried, 'that is cruel!'

He gave a little shrug. He wore his night-shirt and a velvet dressing gown that belonged to my father. It was much too big for him. With his close-cropped hair and emaciated features he looked woefully young and vulnerable. 'It is my own fault,' he said, and I had the distinct impression he was repeating words that had been addressed to him. 'I do not apply myself. I am too easily distracted. I have no discipline. I am below par.' His voice cracked at he spoke these last two words and tears sprang to his eyes, which he quickly dashed away. 'But I will not think about that now,' he said, smiling up at me. 'Tell me about Brighton.'

I settled myself on the bed beside him and told him about the sports on the Steyne, the sea-bathing, the acrobats and exotic creatures. He relaxed against me as I spoke, and his head rested on my shoulder. I found his close proximity opened up a well in me; I felt flooded with emotion, with love and with an urge to protect that was almost visceral.

I tried to keep my voice level as I said, 'Lord Petrel has hired a small sailing boat.' In point of fact my father had paid the fee, but that went without saying. 'I was once persuaded into it, but found the rocking motion insupportable and the spray of the sea very cold.'

'I shall not mind it,' George murmured, with just a glimmer of his old confidence. He rested half against me and half against his pillow and his eyes were closed. 'I should like to go sailing.'

'His lordship pretends to know a good deal of the ropes and sails,' I said. 'He speaks with authority of currents and cross winds, but I think the skipper, who accompanies the vessel, has but a small opinion of Lord Petrel's nautical skills.'

George's mouth creased into a smile, but I could tell he was almost asleep. I spoke on, my voice a careful monotone. 'When the viscount balanced himself with a foot on the gunwales and put his telescope to his eye I believe his desire was to emulate Vice-admiral Nelson aboard the *Victory*, but the skipper and I shared a smile, for we were but a quarter mile from the shore.'

George's breathing was even. He was asleep. I rose from the bed and pulled the covers up to his chin, blew out the candle and crept from the room.

37

It took more than one nourishing meal and a hot bath to restore George to his former health. He threw himself into all that Brighton had to offer; riding, sea-bathing, fishing and accompanying Lord Petrel in his skiff, but he tired quickly and returned from these jaunts looking hollow-eyed with fatigue. He slept so deeply at night that he had sometimes to be roused in the mornings. He ate voraciously; it seemed no quantity of food could fill him up.

I spent a good deal of time with him. We often walked the cliff-path that rose up from the end of the beach. I liked to sit on the low wall that skirted the beach while George threw stone after stone into the sea. I cheered for him while he competed in the various races and tests of skill that were provided on the Steyne, and used my allowance to buy him fresh-cooked shrimps, pickled whelks, pies and buns from barrows trundled hither and thither by hawkers. I stopped going to the Assembly, preferring to stay at home with George. I would read to him, or we would play cards. My mother did not approve of this; I suppose her idea was that I would parade myself in the hopes of attracting a suitor; the idea disgusted me.

June passed, and gradually the flesh crept back onto George's frame, his hair grew and, tended by Nugent, his various sores healed. His features regained their former proportions but I never saw the shadow of suffering quite fade from his eye. Mama had suits of clothes made for him. New shoes and boots arrived from Hoby's in James's Street, London.[xxvi] He cut quite a dash as he strolled on the Steyne and I was proud to be on his arm. We explored the whole length of the beach. George became acquainted with the fishermen who drew their boats up onto the shingle and on several occasions was taken by them out to the fishing grounds. By unspoken consent we did not inform our mother of these excursions, knowing that the danger and the low company would both appal her. He would not speak to me of school, of the regime there, his lessons or his fellows. He did not study while we were in Brighton. Indeed, I never saw him with a book in his hand.

In time George made acquaintance with other young men about town and throughout July I saw less of him. He was bathing, fishing, sailing, riding—always hurrying off somewhere, with no time to talk. I was glad to see him so happily occupied. I found myself left to my own devices— Mother was much occupied by society; to her great satisfaction she had been absorbed into Lady Cumberland's circle. She urged me to accompany her that I might meet ladies of quality but I found their conversation—of court gossip, fashion and titillating novels—petty and boring. Papa and the viscount attended race meetings whenever they were held, which was often, and travelled into Sussex to visit stud farms, so were often away from home. Peake was supposed to chaperone me but she was happy to be left dozing in a chair on the Steyne while I strolled around beneath my parasol, or visited the circulating library. The weather was very kind to us—days of warm sunshine and cooling sea-breezes. It was pleasant to watch the boats on the water, the gulls wheeling above the little fishing wherries as they brought their catch back to shore.

In August my father and Lord Petrel went to Newmarket, in pursuance of their quest for blood-stock. The sailing sloop was put at George's disposal but only on the strict understanding that he must not take it out without the skipper. He took me out in it one day. I cannot say I enjoyed the experience any more than I had on the first occasion but it was joyous to see George looking so hale as he plied the tiller, his face in the wind, his bare feet nimble as he went fore and aft to adjust ropes and drop fishing lines from the gunwales. The skipper nodded from time to time as George tightened a line or loosened a sail, but on the whole he occupied himself with some little repair or other down in the cabin and did not interfere. George thrived on the man's tacit approbation. He seemed to me to be almost back to his old self.

Presently he settled beside me in the cockpit and we sailed for a while in companionable silence, admiring the view of the shore. His hair, newly grown into a cap of tight curls, was full of sea-spray. It shone as though beaded with jewels.

'You see how able I am, at steering the ship, Jocelyn,' he said to me after a while.

'Indeed,' I agreed, 'you are an able seaman. But then, you are good at so many things that require physical prowess. Look how well you ride and play sports.'

'Those are the things I most enjoy,' he admitted. 'I love to be outdoors. I do not care about the weather. I think I should be happy to be a ploughman or a coachman—anything of that sort. I should not mind the hardships.'

'I am sure you would not,' I said, 'but I fear that your destiny lies another way.'

He sighed, and his smile faded. 'I must return to school, soon,' he said. 'Oh Jocelyn, I do not wish to.'

'I know,' I said and, tentatively, took his hand. 'I do not wish you to return to *that* school. It is penal. I am sure you would do better with your studies with better encouragement than ... whatever they mete out *there.*'

'They seem to think that I am wilfully stupid,' George said, his voice rising. 'I do *try,* Jocelyn. I promise you, I *do. You* did not have such trouble with your schoolwork, did you?'

I shook my head. 'No, but then I am sure my lessons were not so hard as

241

yours. I am only a girl, after all, and we are not expected to know as much. And recall, my father was bookish. It is the only thing I know of him—that he was studious. You take after *your* father—he is active, with a head for business. I do not suppose he ever conjugated a French verb in his life!'

He smiled at that. 'I forget,' he said, 'that you are only half my sister. It must be a comfort to you, to know that, if you ever needed to, you could run to your father's people, and they would take you in.'

'I do not know who they are, beyond their name,' I said. 'I would not know where to run to.'

'I shall run away, if they send me back to Stonybeck,' George said gravely. 'I do not think I can endure it again.'

'I believe you,' I said, my voice gentle. 'I shall speak to Mama. It is she who is so very set on it. I do not think Papa cares so much.'

He squeezed my hand and we spoke no more of it.

I spoke to Mama a few days later. It was the middle of August and the evenings were growing chill. She had a little fire lit in her dressing room as Nugent prepared her for her evening out—she was to dine with Lady Cumberland and afterwards attend the theatre.

'I wish you would accompany me,' she said, adjusting her earrings. 'There is no substitute for really genteel connexions. Countess Castleton has two sons ...'

I could tell that she was about to enumerate to me the titular and pecuniary prospects of the countess's progeny, so I took advantage of Nugent's temporary absence in the adjacent chamber to say, 'Mama, I wish to speak to you of George,'

'Oh yes?' She turned slightly, to where I sat on a chaise longue on the other side of the fireplace. 'Arrangements must be made for his school things. Perhaps you might like to see to that, Jocelyn?'

'Not if he is to be returned to Stonybeck,' I said, summoning my courage. 'You must be aware how unhappy he is there, Mama. Look at how ill he was, when he arrived in June.'

'He was cold and hungry,' my mother said. 'Who would not be, after such a long journey?'

'He was thin and ill,' I cried. 'He had been ill-used. I think the regime is too cruel, Mama …'

'Your opinion is irrelevant,' my mother snapped. 'He must learn his lessons. He must excel …'

'He never will, academically,' I asserted, wondering how she could be so hard. 'But look at all his other excellent qualities. He is a superior horseman, very well-liked …'

'These things are nothing,' Mama said. 'A country hobbledehoy could claim as much. George must have a superior education.'

'Then let him be privately tutored,' I urged, 'by the best that can be found. With individual tutelage and kind encouragement I am sure he will flourish.'

'No,' my mother thundered, her mouth a hard line.

Nugent came into the room just then and began to adjust Mama's hair. We remained in silence while the maid tweaked at curls and tendrils and affixed a jewelled comb in place. I thought she tried, once or twice, to catch my eye, to offer a smile of encouragement.

At last she said, 'Will there be anything else, ma'am?' and my mother dismissed her from the room.

'Have you any notion,' I said, when the door had closed silently, 'of the conditions at the school? George does not get enough to eat,' I said. 'He is kept back in class, and when he gets to the refectory his food is cold or has been cleared away altogether.' This was more than George had actually told me, but I felt I could safely extemporise. I was sure no regime I could conjure, be it ever so callous or punitive, could equal the awfulness of reality. 'The dormitories are unheated and there is only cold water for washing. Each day begins with a run across country no matter what the weather conditions. Breakfast is frugal. And so, cold, exhausted and famished, the boys are sent to their lessons. Is it any wonder George does not thrive?'

'I am quite certain …' Mother began, but in a tone that suggested she was not quite certain at all.

'*Are* you quite certain?' I asked, emboldened. 'Did you view Stonybeck yourself?' I knew she had not; it was many miles from Ecklington, in the foothills of Wales. 'Did you interview any of the boys? Did they tell you of the beatings dispensed by the masters on the smallest pretext? Or the punishments meted out by the older boys onto the younger ones? George says nothing. Of course he says nothing; he is brave, he wishes to make you proud, but Mama he has been brutalised, I am certain of it … he has scars …' This much was true. I had seen them when George had removed his shirt to swim off the boat; a lacework of pink tracery on the skin of his back.

'Stop,' she shouted, covering her ears. I could see the diamonds and emeralds of her earrings glinting through her fingers. When she turned to face me there were tears in her eyes, which glinted too. I allowed myself a frisson of satisfaction, of pride. I had been successful.

'Do you think he has been beaten?' she asked me in a small voice.

I nodded solemnly. 'I am sure of it.'

'And… there is not enough to eat?'

I shook my head. 'Every one of George's ribs was visible, in June.'

She turned back to her dressing mirror. 'Teddy did not say,' she muttered.

'Teddy?'

'Theodore, I should say. Lord Petrel.'

'*He* recommended Stonybeck?' I was appalled, but then, not surprised. Only a regime as heartless as the one at Stonybeck could have created such a monster as Lord Petrel.

Mama nodded. 'It was his *alma mater*. He said it was the making of *him*.'

I snorted. 'That explains a great deal,' I cried.

Mama's head snapped around to me. 'What do you mean?'

'He is a bully,' I said. 'At the picnic he would have forced himself on one of the maids if I had not disturbed him. It would not surprise me if he had not already taken advantage of her. Sally Orphan was indisposed for several weeks after …' I stammered to a halt. Mama's face was so pale I thought she might faint. I reached for the bell by the fireplace but she waved me away from the pull.

'You are wrong,' she croaked out at last. 'I am sure you are wrong.'

I hesitated. I might have been wrong. I might have drawn an incorrect conclusion from what I had seen at the picnic, connecting it—wrongly— to Sally's illness. 'It is not really germane to the subject of George's schooling,' I said, knowing I had lost any advantage I might have gained.

She gathered herself, then. 'Not germane?' she repeated sneeringly. 'Not *germane?* The recommendation—the *personal* recommendation—of a peer of the realm, of a *viscount?* Lord Petrel made the arrangements *himself* for George's acceptance at Stonybeck. It would fly in the face of all he has done for us to withdraw George without even the courtesy of consulting him. No. No, George must return to Stonybeck at the end of the month. You will see to his things, Jocelyn.' She stood up and swept her tippet from the back of her chair.

'Mama,' I tried, one last time. 'If Papa were here, he would take George's part. He does not set such great store by academic success.'

'No, indeed,' my mother looked down at me, 'and look where *that* has left him. And in any case, your father is not here.'

The day before George was due to return to school I was obliged to accompany my mother on a day-long excursion in the countryside. We were to dine at the Rookery, a pleasure pavilion with private rooms for dining. Its extensive formal gardens were renowned for their beauty, and also for their discreet arbours, used for clandestine couplings after dark. Once a week, in the season, they held a fireworks display. I do not recall much of the day—it was pleasant enough, I suppose—or the dinner, except that the company seemed to me to be indecorous; much wine was drunk by ladies and gentlemen, the humour was ribald and I felt very uncomfortable to be part of it. To do my mother credit she behaved impeccably, as she always did, pretending not to understand the lewd quips and taking a turn about the room when the gentleman beside her became over-familiar. My father and Lord Petrel arrived as we finished eating. Having returned from Newmarket and upon making enquiry as to our whereabouts, they had followed in a hired chaise to be in time for the fireworks. I was very pleased to see Papa—I had not given up hope that I might yet save George from Stonybeck. It was time to go outside and I took his arm as we all moved out to the swathe of lawn beyond the pavilion. I lost sight of Mama and Lord Petrel, but assumed them to be together somewhere in the crowd.

'I am so happy to see you, Papa,' I began, but, amidst the crowds and with the noise of an orchestra that played somewhere within, it was hard to make myself heard.

He smiled down at me and patted my hand.

'I wish to speak to you about George,' I all but yelled into the fray.

'George?' My father looked about him. 'Where is he? Out exploring, I suppose.'

'Oh he is not here, Papa,' I clarified. 'He did not accompany the party today. He wished to have a final sail in the sloop, and to bid farewell to his friends. He goes back to school, you know, tomorrow ...'

'George is not here?' my father repeated. 'But where, then, is he?'

My heart began to beat a little faster. Someone pushed me roughly from behind and I cannoned into my father. He set me right with firm, strong hands. 'Was he not at home, when you called there?'

The gardens were illuminated by flares. They cast an eerie, flickering light over my father's features. 'No,' he said. 'The house was empty, but for the servants. We assumed he was with you.'

It was now past nine o'clock in the evening. George should have been at home and in bed.

'No. He didn't come, he wanted ...' my hand flew to my mouth. 'Oh Papa, you do not suppose he took the sloop out on his own, do you?'

Even in the ruddy light of the flares I could see my father had paled. He grasped my arm. 'Try and find your mother and Petrel,' he said. 'I will locate our groom and tell him to ready the carriage. Meet me at the front of the pavilion as soon as ever you can.'

He strode off into the crowd leaving me alone. Overhead, the incandescent arc of the first firework lit up the sky. It was followed by another, and another. Then the explosions began, the sky cracked asunder with bangs and pops as the firecrackers detonated.

I ran back into the room where we had dined but it was empty, the servants carrying away our dirty plates and discarded glasses. I returned to the garden, trying to identify my mother's dress, which was peacock blue, but the crowd was too large, too dense. I climbed upon a chair in an effort to see Lord Petrel, for he is taller than the average man and would normally have stood out above the heads of others. But there was no sign of him. I circled the crowd, but they all had their faces up-turned as they looked at the fountains of light that illuminated the sky. Their apostrophic cries of wonder, the endlessly sawing orchestra within and the percussive reports of the fireworks made calling out useless. At last, as satisfied as I could be that they were not within the crowd, I ran along one of the hedge-lined walks of the garden. Secluded arbours to either side of me were occupied by ladies and gentlemen. I could hear the odd giggle or sigh as I passed by. The way was poorly lit by a very few lanterns; the gloom, between the high hedges, was very pressing and intense. Then, a wayward firework cast a shower of iridescence over the scene and I made out, at the very far end of the walk, my mother's peacock blue gown. She and Lord Petrel strolled arm in arm toward me.

'Mama! Mama!' I cried out. 'You must come at once. George is missing.'

38

We all sat, very stiff and anxious, not speaking, as the carriage took us back to Brighton. Mama wrung her hands until Papa reached out and stilled them. Her face was ashen, as far as I could make it out in the dimness. I glowered at her. Her intransigence had brought George to this—whatever it was—because she had insisted that he return to his hated school.

'A jape,' Lord Petrel suggested at one point. 'He has gone on a jape of some sorts. I did the same, at his age, especially just before term began.'

'I am not surprised,' I spat out at him. 'From what I know, Stonybeck is a place of torture and starvation. There can't be a single boy who returns there happily.'

'What's this?' my father wanted to know.

'George does not apply himself,' Mama said, her voice wooden. 'You have seen his reports, Robert. The schoolmasters have been forced to bring all their experience to bear. Of course, they must be strict, sometimes.'

I leaned across the coach and touched my father's hand. 'George is unhappy at school,' I said. '*Very* unhappy. The privations are extreme.'

'Privations?' Lord Petrel half-hooted, 'Oh Jocelyn, my dear, is *that* what he has told you?'

'I have seen the scars,' I growled. 'Neither George nor I have made *those* up.'

'Scars?' Father turned to Mother.

'She says so,' Mother replied. 'I have not seen them. But what will it matter, if the boy is drowned,' she swallowed a sob. 'I wish you had never hired that boat, Robert.'

'He was not supposed to go out in it alone,' my father replied, tetchy, because he sensed that, whatever George had done, he would get the blame.

'We do not know that he *has* gone out in it alone,' Lord Petrel reasoned. 'For all we know he could be at home now, or in a tavern, or at a brothel. Those were *my* preferred haunts, as a youth.'

'I can easily believe it,' I said under my breath.

'I hope not *that* at least,' my father demurred, giving his friend a hard stare and sliding his glance significantly to me. 'Ladies present, Petrel,' he added, covering his words with an artificial cough.

'Oh *anything* will be better than that he is drowned,' my mother burst out.

The carriage brought us at last to Brighton. Papa had the coachman drive us to the place where the sloops were moored. 'I will investigate things here,' he said. 'You go on to East Street and see if he is not home by now.' He opened the door of the coach and jumped down, not waiting for the coachman to lower the step. 'Petrel,' he said, leaning back inside momentarily. 'If he is not at home you should go to every alehouse and … erm … other likely resort in the vicinity.'

'Certainly,' Lord Petrel agreed, by no means reluctant to tour every low tavern and bawdy-house in town.

We were driven to East Street where we quickly ascertained that George was not at home. He had not been home to dinner, nor anything seen of him since just after our own departure at noon that day. I ran up to his room. All was neat, his trunks packed, ready for the following day. A few items I would expect to see—his Bible, some silver-backed hair brushes Papa had given him for his birthday and his stout new boots—were missing. I scoured his room for a note, then my own, then Mama's sitting room and the drawing room mantelpiece. He had left no word.

When I got back to the hall Mama was perched on a chair. Nugent held a glass of brandy to her lips. Lord Petrel had already departed on his errand.

'This is because you would send him back to school,' I hissed in Mama's ear. It was nasty of me, I know, but I couldn't help it. She gave a little sob and pressed a handkerchief to her lips. Nugent threw me a reproachful look. She fished in her pocket and brought out her housewife. She unrolled it to find a vial, which she unstoppered and held beneath Mama's nose. Mama sniffed and then recoiled, but seemed restored.

We waited. The servants brought food and tea, both of which we waved away.

'The sloop must be gone,' Mama got out at one point. 'It must be, and your father is organising a search party. The fishermen will have to go out and find him. George could be in France by now, or captured by the enemy fleet ...'

'Papa will be searching the quayside places,' I said.

'I ... I had prepared a letter for George's headmaster,' Mother said after a while, 'asking him to ensure George's comfort. I intended to send him treats—cake and so forth—that he might enjoy himself and also use to placate the unkinder boys. That would have helped, would it not?'

I shrugged. From what little I knew of these things it seemed to me that a boy who ran complaining to his parents might well be more harshly treated than ever.

I paced the hallway, calling uncomfortably to mind my conversation with

George aboard the boat. He had threatened to run away. If I had taken more notice … I thought of him, out on the road, in the dark, overtaken perhaps by gypsies, or wet and cold in a ditch. Hadn't he lamented that he—unlike me—had no alternative family, no friendly place to which he could run for succour? Where would he go?

My thoughts were interrupted by a series of hard knocks on the door, Mother and I exchanged anguished glances. I clasped my hands very tightly together. The footman answered the door—with agonising slowness. He could not have moved with more stateliness and ceremony if he had been a hired mute as a funeral. At last the door was opened and there, on the doorstep, stood Lieutenant Willow.

Seeing us, he swept off his hat and executed a bow, but awkwardly. 'Good evening ladies,' he said with his usual wide, warm smile. He favoured me particularly with this. I read volumes in its intensity and particularity. His blue eyes sparkled. I read in his expression—oh!—ever so much more than his words could say. I wanted to weep with pleasure at seeing him. Of all the people who I thought could possibly comfort me in this dreadful hour of waiting and worry, it was him. 'I am sorry to call so late,' he said, looking from one of us to the other. My mother had remained seated. She looked bemused, slightly embarrassed, and I realised she did not recall the lieutenant.

'It is Lieutenant Willow,' I said, 'from Ecklington. He is the rector's nephew, you recall Mama.'

'Oh, yes,' she said vaguely. 'Yes.'

'It is unconscionably late, I know,' said the lieutenant, 'and I must admit to you, ma'am, that we had hoped to find you either still out, or already retired. My friend and I hoped to enter the property quite surreptitiously. But when we saw all the lights ablaze, we knew the game was up.'

'We?' I asked.

He carried with him some large encumbrance—I had thought at first it was a greatcoat draped over his arm, or a large kitbag. It drooped in the shadow that the hall lights cast behind him on the steps. Now he brought it forth. Very bedraggled it was, and the worse for drink. It muttered incoherently as he propped it against the door. It was my brother.

Mother shrieked. I thought she would swoon but that mistake just shows how I did not—then—know the extent of her essential steeliness, her utter resilience and will. Yes, she had grown pale. Yes, she had trembled. But these were instinctive, visceral responses to the disappearance of her child. Beyond these things, in the inner kernel of herself, she was as cold and hard as obsidian. She got to her feet and marched across the hallway where she delivered two sharp slaps, one to each of George's cheeks. That had the effect of rousing him somewhat, as well as expiating her angst. She had hit him quite hard. Only the support of Lieutenant Willow's arm stopped him from falling. She turned to the lieutenant and at first I thought she would deliver the same treatment to him, but she thought better of it and only unleashed on him the full measure of her torment and her scorn.

'How *dare* you,' she yelled, and I thought she sounded like nothing so much as a fishwife. 'How dare you lead my son astray, get him inebriated, keep him from home. Do you know how old he is?'

'Yes, ma'am,' the lieutenant answered levelly. He looked past my mother at me, his good humour and pleasure at seeing me not one bit eroded by her vitriol.

'All the more shame on you,' Mother cried. 'You are a disgrace to your regiment.'

A small group of passers-by, people going home late from Brighton's places of entertainment, had gathered on the pavement.

'As to that madam, I fear I must contradict you,' Lieutenant Willow said, mildly reproachful but still very respectful.

'Mama,' George said blearily, 'you're making a mistake.'

'Let the lieutenant come in and explain matters,' I suggested. 'Let George be taken up to bed and someone be sent to tell my father and Lord Petrel that he is found safe.'

Mama, seeing the on-lookers, saw the propriety in this, and it was done as I had directed. Lieutenant Willow was shown into the drawing room where Mama and I joined him. There she renewed her rant but with less vehemence. She had regained control of herself. Now she simply assaulted him with questions—*where* had he come upon George? *How* had he become so intoxicated? What kind of *exhibition* had he made of himself? Why had it taken until *now* for George to be restored to safety? She gave Lieutenant Willow no opportunity to answer any of her enquiries. He took all she had to say bravely however, squaring his shoulders to it as she threw her accusations and indictments like a volley of musket fire.

She was almost done when my father burst into the house. 'He is found?' he panted.

'Yes, sir,' Lieutenant Willow replied, turning utterly unscathed from my mother's tirade. 'Apart from a very sore head, he will have no lasting hurts from his escapade.'

'Where did you find him?' I asked.

'Not in a tavern,' he was quick to point out. 'Personally, I seldom frequent them. As to his inebriation, that was all his own doing. He was intoxicated when he came to us, very determined to enlist.'

'Enlist?' I had thought my mother's chagrin all exhausted but she had a little left.

'Indeed ma'am. It seems he has spent a good deal of time around the barracks of late and had used his time in discovering the procedure for enlistment and in particular which sergeants were more likely to overlook any question of age or fitness. He is astute, your boy. He equipped himself with a little pecuniary inducement, should one be necessary.' At this the lieutenant drew forth a purse of money, which he handed to my father.

'He sold his silver brushes and his boots,' I murmured.

Lieutenant Willow nodded, confirming my speculation.

'Thankfully I overheard the exchange, and when I heard the lad's name, naturally I took particular interest, since I have the honour to be acquainted with the family.'

'You persuaded him against,' my mother said faintly, and I hope she felt a modicum of remorse for her earlier outburst.

'Thank God,' my father said.

'I do not think I can claim as much as that,' the honest lieutenant demurred. 'He was—he still is—very determined. But I intervened. I know he is not of age.'

'He is not yet fourteen,' I said.

'I recalled as much.'

My father held out his hand. 'My very sincere thanks to you Lieutenant,' he said. The men shook hands and my father held out the purse of money. 'For your inconvenience,' he said.

Mother and I both stood aghast at the gesture. Lieutenant Willow gave a tight smile and took a step backwards. 'There was no inconvenience sir. It was my pleasure. I knew how worried Miss Talbot would be. I would save her any disquiet, if it were within my power to do so.'

My father turned to Mother and said, 'After this, the boy must not return to school.'

'He is most reluctant,' the lieutenant remarked, but lightly, for of course it had nothing to do with him.

'He certainly shall not go tomorrow,' my mother acknowledged. 'He will be ill for days, I should think, after such dissipation. As to the future, we will see.' She set her mouth in a hard line and my heart fell, for I knew my mother. She would not be dissuaded, once she had made up her mind.

I showed Lieutenant Willow into the hallway and offered him my hand. 'My eternal thanks,' I said. 'I have not sufficient words to voice my gratitude.'

He pressed my hand and I looked at his face. I saw no diminution of passion, no lessening in regard from what had been there in the spring. 'To think you have been in Brighton these many weeks,' he said, 'and I not know of it. What opportunities we have squandered.'

'I looked out for you,' I said, and then bit my lip, for it was not ladylike to admit as much, 'but without hope. I had no notion where in the world you might be.'

'Right here,' he said, and pressed my hand to his heart. 'May I call on you tomorrow?'

I nodded.

39

George was ill for three days after his misadventure. Once sober and recovered from his sickness he was contrite—very sorry for having put Mama through such anxiety, and Lieutenant Willow to such trouble—but he was extremely loathe to return to Stonybeck. He stood before us in the drawing room, his feet planted firmly apart on the hearthrug, but I could see one of his knees was trembling. He had dressed himself with care, his hair neatly combed, but his face was pale and drawn, all the good his weeks by the sea had done him eradicated in the unease of the hour. He swallowed repeatedly, some clot of apprehension that would not go down.

I think my father would have given in, but Lord Petrel was vociferous on the necessity for George to go back to school; for some reason I could not fathom he had been invited to join the family conference. 'No enemy,' he said, 'is ever overcome by running away from it. Will Napoleon be beaten if we lay down our arms? These are lessons in manhood that George simply must learn. It may be unpleasant at times, but it is character-forming. The boys unite against the masters and the bonds they make endure for years afterwards. Why, look at my own circle of acquaintance. Viscount Vauxhall and the Marquis of Penge are both fellows I knew at school. They are the best of men, like brothers to me!'

'Do *you* have friends at school, George?' I asked. I was surprised to have been allowed to be present, but I was not going to waste the opportunity; I would help George all I could.

He shook his head. 'Not really. They are all …' he paused, looking warily at Mama and Papa.

I knew what he was going to say: of noble family, titled, aristocratic. I knew too that for him to say as much would be to play on all our parents' insecurities.

'They don't seem to like me much,' George finished, 'unless it is in sports. *Then* they like me well enough.'

'There you are then,' Lord Petrel cried. 'And who would not wish to have such a fleet-foot as you on their team?'

'We do not send George to school to play games,' my mother said with a vinegarish tone. 'He must learn. He must out-perform all his peers, if he is to overcome the disadvantage of his birth.'

That antagonised my father. 'There is no shame in being a Talbot,' he roared. 'The Talbots have been a notable family for a hundred years.' The lure which Lord Petrel had dangled though, was too much for him to resist. He liked the idea of his son having dukes and earls as his friends.

'Notorious, rather than notable,' my mother demurred. She turned to George and I knew that his fate was sealed. 'You will go back to Stonybeck,' she said, very cold, very determined. 'I am sure you can endure whatever occurs *there*, if you were prepared to subject yourself to the field of battle. Whatever deprivations there are at Stonybeck you will not be blown asunder by cannon, nor bayonetted, nor trampled by fifty charging cavalry horses. You will not be infested with lice nor forced to feed on rats. You will not be asked to march until your boots disintegrate. The very fact that you were willing to face these things shows me, George, that you *can* survive school. And so you will return there next week.'

George's bottom lip wobbled and he threw me a haunted look.

'Oh Mama,' I pleaded, 'have a heart. Do not be cruel!'

'Cruel?' she turned her insufferably aristocratic face towards me. 'I am not cruel, Jocelyn, I am kind. In time George will thank me, for I have prevailed upon Lord Petrel to take George back to Stonybeck, to speak to the headmaster and to show the other boys that George has friends in high places.' She gave George a beatific smile, clearly delighted with her solution to the problem. 'Shall that not make things easier, George? Are you not indebted to Lord Petrel for his patronage?'

George's expression became if possible more wretched, but he said, 'Yes. Thank you Mama. Thank you sir,' and ran from the room.

I gathered that Papa had not been apprised of this arrangement, for he looked extremely surprised at it and not altogether pleased. I suppose it was not flattering to hear that another man could influence things more powerfully for George than he could himself. That he—the man who paid the school fees, and provided the uniform and books and had made, to boot, a large donation to the school's reserves—was as nothing compared to a titled alumni, especially one who was no relation whatsoever to the boy and certainly no benefactor to the school. 'It is good of you, to take the trouble, Petrel,' my father mumbled.

'Well,' Lord Petrel said, crossing to the fireplace and ringing the bell, 'Mrs Talbot asked me most particularly, and, I must say, very prettily, and someone must see the boy gets safely to school, for I suspect he would do a bunk as soon as he was five miles from Brighton if someone were not there to prevent him. Ha! The boy has spirit! You should be proud of him, Talbot. I'd be proud of him, were he *my* son. Ah!' A footman appeared in response to the bell. 'A decanter of sherry, if you please. I think we could all do with a little tonic, don't you?'

George remained at home for the remainder of his reprieve even though I tried to entice him outside with offers of treats and our favourite walk along the cliffs. I had seen Lieutenant Willow almost every day since the night of George's disappearance, his duties allowing. The lieutenant also kindly urged George outdoors, securing for him the use of a horse, and inviting him to watch the men at musket practice. Nothing could tempt George from the doldrums of his chambers however. He sat with his school books out before him, but I fear he took in nothing from their pages. When the morning of his departure came he clung to me, very briefly, in the dawn light of the hallway. Lord Petrel was present, of course, and had seen George's trunk, and his own portmanteau, loaded onto the carriage. George looked as woebegone as possible, drooping and defeated in a way I had never seen him before.

'I am so sorry, George,' I whispered to him. 'I tried my best to save you from this.'

He nodded glumly. 'I know. I shall have to endure it, for I know I cannot mend things. I will never be the prodigy Mama desires.'

'It may not be so bad, having Lord Petrel speak for you,' I suggested, but doubtfully.

It was obvious that George shared my reservations. 'It will make no difference,' he said. 'The masters are very fawning towards the parents but the moment they are gone …'

'He says the boys …'

'The boys are worse than the masters. They call me Georgie Dalit. Do you know what a Dalit is?'

I shook my head.

'No, neither did I. It is the lowest caste of Indian. It is because Papa made his money there. It means his wealth—and I—are untouchable. Do not let Mama send food. It will only be put down the latrine.'

'Oh George,' I cried, 'are they really so cruel?'

Sounds on the road outside indicated that the carriage was ready. George took my hand. 'Jocelyn,' he said most earnestly, 'do not trust Lord Petrel. I doubt his sincerity. I fear his intentions. I would rather travel with the devil himself to Wales, than with him. There is something about him …

like a wolf.'

'Now then, young master,' Lord Petrel said, bounding up the steps and taking hold of George's arm. 'Let us get you settled in the coach. I see you take a fond farewell of your sister. I will follow your lead.' He took my hand from George and raised it to his lips. When I tried to snatch it away he only tightened his grip. My resistance seemed to please him; his eyes shone with a cold fire. 'Ah,' he said, smiling, 'feisty. Yes. I like that.'

'I am no defenceless kitchen maid,' I spat at him, wrenching my hand from his grip and wiping his kiss away on my skirts.

'No indeed,' he said, not even pretending to misunderstand me. 'Much more desirable.'

I saw them go, down the deserted streets of Brighton, and when the carriage was out of sight I went back upstairs with a heavy heart.

To my shame I must admit that it did not stay heavy for long. I was engaged to walk with Lieutenant Willow that morning, and the prospect of his company, his merry blue eyes and his warm, winning smile soon put George out of my head.

I had seen Lieutenant Willow several times since the night of George's escapade. He had called the following morning as he had promised, and Mama received him in the drawing room. The following day she invited him to join us in our carriage as we took the air in the direction of Shoreham, the gentlemen being again engaged to attend the races. He had made himself agreeable and useful, and she had made no objection when he asked permission, as the rector's nephew and a family acquaintance, to escort me about the town. Thereafter we had been unchaperoned but of course had confined ourselves to the populated areas of Brighton.

On George's final evening at home we had attended the assembly. Although I had prevaricated about remaining at home with George, he had encouraged me to go. 'I will not run away again,' he had assured me. And so I went to the assembly with Mama, Papa and Lord Petrel, and Lieutenant Willow waited for me in the foyer. How handsome he looked in his dress uniform, with his golden braid and brass buttons, his boots highly polished, his hair still damp from his bath. His face, on seeing me, lit up with pleasure, and I was glad of Peake's excellent skills with my hair and dress. For the first time in my life I felt pretty. He stepped forward and offered me his arm with every evidence of pride and delight, nodding respectfully to my parents before leading me to the dance. We danced two sets before propriety dictated that I should have other partners, but when it was time for supper he was there to escort me, with places reserved. He ordered champagne, which I would have declined, as I know that a lieutenant's pay cannot be much. We sat together, exclaiming at how unlucky we had been not to encounter one another in Brighton all summer long. The coffeehouse I preferred was only two doors along from the one he frequented. He had attended some of the same concerts as me, and walked on the Steyne most afternoons, as I did, if he was not engaged with his men.

'I have heard from Caroline,' he said. 'She writes very frequently, but she said nothing of your being in Brighton.'

'It's possible she did not know,' I replied charitably—I thought it impossible she was ignorant of the fact. 'Is she not in Basingstoke now?'

'Yes, with our grandparents. And Maud is in London with the Binsleys.'

'How quiet the rectory must be,' I said with a sigh, recalling the happy fortnight I had spent there.

'It will not have been, all summer,' the lieutenant said. 'The little girls have been home from school, you know.'

'Ah yes,' I said. 'I had forgotten about them. I do not know when I shall return to Ecklington. We are to go to London from here.'

'My plans are not even as fixed as that,' he said, helping me to syllabub. 'At any moment, we may be mobilised.'

I leaned a little closer towards him. 'Do you keep your bouquet of memories fresh, against that day?' I asked.

He touched his glass to mine. 'Very fresh,' he said, 'and added to, every day.'

Lord Petrel was some little distance from us. He sat and glowered at us throughout supper. Unusually, Papa had eschewed the card room that evening and had himself escorted Mama to supper, leaving Lord Petrel to hand in a dowager of Lady Cumberland's party, very cumbersome and slightly moustached, but very grand.

'Your father's friend, Lord Petrel,' Lieutenant Willow said to me, throwing a glance down the table. 'He is a surly fellow, is he not?'

I smiled, happy to think of the viscount as put out in any way. 'Does he give you dark looks?'

'*Very* dark,' the lieutenant admitted. 'His eyes throw daggers and knives. I take it he has no prior claim?'

'*I* did not promise to take supper with him,' I said.

'I did not mean quite that, exactly.'

I blushed. I thought about what Mama had said on my return to Ecklington from the rectory. The recollection was sobering. 'To own the truth,' I said slowly, 'Mama did hint that there is some partiality on his part. He has been told there is no prospect of such a thing though. The idea disgusts *me*.'

'I have no right to an opinion on the subject,' Lieutenant Willow began, 'but I own I am happy to hear of your disinterest towards the man. Now, let us return to the dance.'

On the morning of George's departure I was glad to have the malevolent presence of Lord Petrel removed, even if George must bear the brunt of it for the next three days. I disapproved of my parents' decision to return George to Stonybeck. I disliked the influence that Lord Petrel seemed to have over them both. I failed to see why he must be our constant companion wherever we went. For all he was a viscount, and would be an earl, it did not seem to me that he was particularly well liked by his noble acquaintance. The previous night, at supper, the dowager had looked as displeased with her escort as he had. But now he was gone, and we were to have some respite. I rang my bell and asked Peake to bring me some chocolate and a pastry for my breakfast, and to look out my walking costume.

Lieutenant Willow called as we had arranged and we walked to the shore before bending our steps to the cliff path. We passed the area where the ladies bathed. Brightly coloured bathing huts stood on the beach ready to be drawn into the surf. I had bathed with Mama, and found it exhilarating, but she had disliked having her hair disarranged and the clinging coldness of her bathing habit to her body, so we had not made another attempt at it. She preferred the baths, where the water was warmed and there were no waves and where she could change in more comfort. The ladies there were elderly or infirm, needing much assistance. I found their crooked bodies and withered limbs pitiful. I think Mama liked being the most hale, most beautiful lady present. She enjoyed the envious eyes.

Further along the beach—beyond the scope of all but the keenest eyes— was the gentlemen's bathing area. Here there were no huts and no bathing clothes. Naturally I interested myself minutely in the wild flowers that carpeted the grass on either side of the path.

The lieutenant and I talked as we walked—of the previous evening's Assembly, of my fears for George, of the new play to be shown at the theatre—but I thought him less lively than usual, more reticent. The path climbed quite sharply and was wide enough for only one. We did not speak at all as we trudged up its steepest places. At last the way levelled out and we could walk side by side again. The vista of the sea before us was very splendid, blue and silvered with foam. A fresh breeze blew inland and I redoubled the ties on my bonnet lest it be blown away. The air carried scents of the sea, a salty tang that stayed on my lips. Seabirds wheeled overhead. Far away, where the sea merged into the sky, a smudge of grey might have been France.

'Do you think Napoleon will invade?' I asked.

Lieutenant Willow nodded, and I knew that he had been wondering the same thing. 'The King seeks to make another alliance,' he said. 'Meanwhile France's coffers are newly filled[xxvii] and Napoleon has invaded Hanover.[xxviii] If he does invade England, it will not be until the spring. For myself, I think there are easier pickings for him in Europe.

Nevertheless, we must stand ready.'

We lapsed again into silence. I perched on a boulder. The lieutenant paced to and fro across the grass. Presently he came and sat beside me. 'Jocelyn,' he said, and I turned to face him. His expression was solemn and I wondered what was coming, but his using my name suggested it was of some import. 'Do you recall, last evening, I asked you if there was an understanding between yourself and Lord Petrel?'

I nodded. I remembered our conversation perfectly.

'Do you think it is possible that there might be some arrangement that you know nothing of?'

I frowned. 'What kind of arrangement?'

'Between your parents and the viscount. An arrangement that pertains to you but of which you have not been apprised.'

I cast my mind back. 'Mama said that … that is, she implied that he had said something of the matter, but that he had been told I am too young, and that there is no question of matrimony at present.'

'At present,' he repeated thoughtfully. 'But they have not dismissed the idea out of hand?'

'If they have,' I said stoutly, 'they have not informed me. But why do you raise this topic again?'

The lieutenant wavered, toying with the cuff of his coat, clearly considering how much it would be politic for him to say.

'You must tell me,' I pressed. 'What has occurred?'

'Last evening,' he said at last, 'when I returned to my lodgings, he was waiting for me.'

'Lord Petrel?'

He nodded. 'The same.'

'I am astonished,' I said. 'What was his business?'

'He implied to me—very forcefully implied—that you are all-but engaged to him. That it is an understanding, long held, between your parents and himself, that he will make you the Countess of Flintshire when it is within his power to do so. I take it the earl still lives?'

I nodded. 'Beyond all expectation, he does. But that is immaterial. I will never marry Lord Petrel. He is impertinent. He assumes far too much. As for Mama and Papa, well …' but here I faltered, for I could not say certainly that it was not within Mama's scheme that I should become a countess. Indeed, it was just what she *would* wish. I thought of the cold ambition with which she had overruled George's pleas to be withdrawn from Stonybeck. I had no doubt that she would, with the same, icy determination, force me to the altar with Lord Petrel if it suited her. On the other hand, had she not warned me to stay away from him? 'I must speak to Mama,' I concluded. 'I must make my feelings clear.'

Gently, he took my hand. 'Do you know your own feelings?' he asked, and his voice was so low I had to bend my head to catch it.

'Regarding Lord Petrel, I certainly do,' I said.

'And, in respect of … anything else?'

I searched my heart. I certainly liked Lieutenant Willow very much. I felt comfortable in his presence. I trusted him, and I could think of no situation in which he would not be a boon. Indeed, his appearance on the night of George's adventure had been no less momentous than the manifestation of the archangel Michael of whom, it now occurred to me, Lieutenant Willow reminded me very strongly.[xxix] He was very handsome. But did I love him? I could not say. I was too young, too inexperienced to know.

'I do not know,' I said at last, very lamely.

He squeezed my hand. 'That is quite all right,' he said in his habitual voice. 'And now, let us return.'

40

Lord Petrel returned to Brighton a week later, and reported having delivered George safely to the custody of his school masters. He said there could be no doubt of their understanding, now, in what manner their pupil was to be supervised. His school fellows had been treated to more buns than it was good for any boy to consume and would likewise hold George in better regard in future. All in all we were not to worry. We were to put George from our minds.

I continued to see Lieutenant Willow, but my unchaperoned promenades with him were at an end. I felt sure Lord Petrel had vetoed the permission my mother had given. I was not permitted to dance more than one set with him. When supper was served Lord Petrel was unfailingly at my elbow to lead me to the dining room. If we arranged to walk it always transpired that Lord Petrel was going in the same direction. I ought to have spoken to Mama about it, but her behaviour towards George gave me pause. What if my raising the matter were to result in her insisting, *forcing* me to allow Lord Petrel's attentions? I might precipitate, rather than quash, the question. I behaved coldly towards the viscount but he didn't seem to care. Indeed, the more haughty and disdainful I was towards him, the better he seemed to like it.

We had taken our lodgings for six months, and were not due to quit until November, by which time the Brighton season would all but have ceased in any case. To my surprise, at the end of September, I was told to pack my things; we were leaving Brighton for London. To be honest I was tired of the Steyne by then, the pretentious posing, the affectation of it all. There were few new plays and the attractions of the circulating library had gone stale. I did not mind going to London, where I hoped a wider circle of acquaintance would reduce the malign influence of Lord Petrel on my parents.

But I did not wish to say farewell to Lieutenant Willow; leaving him behind would be a wrench I was not sure I could bear.

I did bear it however, giving him my hand and wishing him well, with Lord Petrel standing proprietorially over me.

My parents' house in London was centrally located in Grosvenor Square, a fashionable district although not as exclusive as Piccadilly, Park Lane or Arlington Street. It was close to the shops of Bond Street and Mama immediately made it her business to equip me with gowns and accessories suitable for the London season for, she said, what would do very well in Brighton would not pass muster in town.

The Binsleys called upon me. Edward Binsley was now a gentleman-about-town, enrolled in several clubs, given to much lounging and aimless strolling, also gaming. He was an avid and fearless rider, reckless in the hunt. Miss Binsley had evidently forgotten there was any such person as Mr Brigstock; she made no enquiries about him, anyway, or his sister, quite as though they had never existed. She had now set her sights upon a Mr Ridgeworth who had been introduced into the family circle by her brother. Mr Ridgeworth was a young gentleman with a property in Dorset and ten thousand pounds a year but nothing else whatsoever to recommend him that I could discern. Like Mr Binsley, he idled between one place and another, paid calls, rode his horse in the park and seemed generally bored. Elinor Binsley was her former friendly self, and we picked up our close acquaintance pretty much where we had left it off at Ecklington the previous May, over-leaping the hiatus of awkwardness caused by the Brigstocks by simply not mentioning it. Maud Willow accompanied them, of course. She was not so different from the girl I remembered as I had feared. I was happy to tell her that I had seen her cousin and that he was well and she said she would inform the family at home.

I asked after Caroline's health but Maud shook her head. 'She has been very low in spirits,' she said. 'She finds solace in religion, but not much else.'

I was absorbed into the tier of London society that my parents inhabited. We attended balls and dinners, the play and the entertainments at Vauxhall Gardens. Everywhere we went Lord Petrel came too and it was inevitable that I would take his arm as Papa took Mama's. I was desperate to stifle any misapprehension that this might provoke. I was sure there was whispering behind fans but it was a topic impossible for me to raise. These things—like so much in that hidebound, infinitesimally regulated society—are ever present but never spoken of. I found it all—the elegant, prescribed manners, the lightweight, scripted conversation—to be artificial and specious; a thin veneer that covered scrabbling ambition, flirtation and adultery, pride, vanity and spite.

In early December we heard from George that he had decided to remain at school for the Christmas vacation. The headmaster had invited him to stay, and promised him some intense tutelage in an attempt to fill the gaps in his learning. That being the case Mama and Papa decided not to return to Ecklington for Christmas. I was very sorry about this, for Christmas at Ecklington was always a special, happy time. Instead we were to travel with Lord Petrel to the earl's seat and spend Christmas there. Once again, the marked particularity of this sent out messages about the nature of my relationship to the viscount that were wholly without substance: it was rumoured that I was to be taken to Flintshire and presented to the earl for his approval. It was too much, and I told Mama so, but she waved my objections away.

'No one will entertain such a notion,' she said. 'You are only seventeen years old. But even if it is true, would it be so bad? To have your name mentioned in the same breath as Lord Petrel's will only enhance your reputation.'

'You are all contradiction,' I cried. 'One moment I am too young to be engaged, but the next my marital worth is being weighed as so much barley on the Exchange!'

'One day you will marry,' she said, 'and it is never too soon to lay the foundations for such a matter. You should be grateful for Lord Petrel's patience with you, for I am sure he would not endure such surliness from anyone else.'

We went to Flintshire, to the earl's seat, aptly close to the town of Mold. The journey was tedious, the accommodations draughty and the food greasy and unrefined. The mood of our host was curmudgeonly. Apart from all of those things, we had an agreeable enough time. No mention was made of any future betrothal although the old earl did look me up and down very narrowly. He was a very elderly man, stooped, always swathed in wraps and coverings. His conversation was monosyllabic. He reminded me a great deal of Sir Diggory. I was not sorry to come away.

We had been back in town some weeks, when the messenger came from Ecklington.

41

March 1814

The snowstorm went on into the New Year, and then, in January, the snow stopped but temperatures plummeted, gripping us in an icy fist. Ice rimed the insides of our casements every morning. Mr Burleigh had to hack at the trough with an axe, to access the water some two or three inches below a thick, transparent plate, and this some twice or three times in a day, for the trough stands in an elbow between the kitchen and the stable, where the sun never reaches. He carried the ice diligently to the icehouse, supplementing it with blocks from the fountain and from the tops of the rain barrels, for, one day, summer will come and where now we struggle to keep things warm, then we will crave all things cool.

We kept fires burning day and night, to stave off the cold and to keep the flues warm, for once they cooled it was impossible to get the fires to draw again. To retain heat and to make domestic arrangements easier I directed that the household be shrunk down to its essentials. This small sitting room is now my dining room also; there is a folding table which does quite well. We bank the fire up each evening and place a guard before it, so that it is warm in the morning. My bedroom fire is likewise kept alight, and the one in the child's room, where Mrs Orphan sleeps. The kitchen fire, of course, must be continually stoked. Mrs Orphan tells me, with a heavy significance that is lost on me, that 'she believes' Mr Burleigh sleeps in an apartment somewhere beyond the kitchen, which 'she understands' is warm enough. Sally and Tom tell me they are snug in the gatehouse, and I suppose there are sufficient bodies there to make things cosy; she delivered her fourth child at Christmas.

We have seen nothing of the outside world for many weeks, and I do not lament its absence. I am thankful to Mrs Orphan and the others for their careful husbanding of our resources last summer and autumn; we have survived beautifully on the smoked and dried meats, the preserved fruits and vegetables, the jams and chutneys and cordials that they made from the produce of the garden. I do not miss church. Mr Foley's dry, scholarly sermons are never very edifying, even to me. What the farmers and dairymaids make of them I cannot imagine. I am happy to forgo the veiled antipathy of Mrs Foley's visits; the exquisite parry and thrust we indulge in, over tea and seedcake. The lane between our gatehouse and the village remains impassable, indistinguishable from the undulating topography of moor either side of it. It is dense, hard-packed snow and ice. Snow has drifted against the drystone walls that surround our bowl and even overtopped them in places. Nature has provided a barricade, a clear delineation between them and us. We are protected, contained, exclusive.

Within our curtilage—*because* we are separated and hidden, *because* eyes cannot pry nor fingers wag in judgement—things are more blurred. The divisions that used to exist are becoming nebulous. Since I helped in the orchard, and especially since Mrs Orphan placed the child in my arms on the night of the blizzard, I have sought to infiltrate the walls of the servants' deference. I do not wish to be their mistress—a useless, cosseted creature who is a drain on resources but makes no contribution. After a lifetime of following orders they do look to me for guidance, for permission, and I understand that within any society there must be degree. But I do not wish to be so widely separated from them. I would have us work together, for our common good. Accordingly, now, I get up from my chair when Mr Burleigh or Mrs Orphan bring my coals, and take the bucket from them. Numerous times I have fetched fuel in myself. I get myself dressed now; Mrs Orphan has enough to do about the place, and in tending the child. The formal dining room is abandoned, and I no longer require Mr Burleigh to wait on me. My dinner arrives on a tray, and that is quite acceptable to me. Every so often I have Mrs Orphan dine with me here, and, with her, the child, who is now two years of age.

She babbles merrily. Mrs Orphan is less communicative. I sense that she finds the new arrangement awkward, that she is much more conscious of her origins than I am. There is much I would ask her for I still yearn to have the tangled web of my being here unravelled. I want to know who sent her. What is her understanding of my situation as regards my family and the wider world? How are we funded: is she sent money? What are her instructions, if any, and how are they received? Is there a term to our sentence? If she would give me the least chink of an opening I would prise the rest from her, but she resolutely keeps to neutral topics—the weather, the garden, the book I am reading. Sometimes I feel a smile curl my lips and I have to dab with my napkin lest she see. It strikes me as amusing: the wide disparity in our beginnings, the paucity of her prospects then, the great potential of mine. She has profited by the advice I gave her—she has made the best of her opportunities, that's certain, and I do not think anyone could force her where she did not wish to go. I, on the other hand, have squandered all my advantages, been used and downtrodden to dust.

On Christmas day I insisted upon joining them for dinner. I descended the servants' stair and took my place at the long table. At first it was awkward. The children stared at me, goggle-eyed, as though, indoors, I was different to the creature who had gathered apples and pears with them in the autumn. Mr Burleigh did not know where to place himself. He hovered at my elbow, ready to ladle soup and pass condiments until I sent him into the cellar to bring up a few bottles of the best we had. That move eased things considerably. Tom and Sally were soon merry. I suppose they are not used to drinking fine wine. Sally, who has never lacked gall, became inquisitive: did I receive news from "home," by which she meant Ecklington? Did I have news of Mrs Bray—was she still cook there? Was it my intention to remain in Yorkshire "for always"?

'I am sorry Sally,' I said, 'but I cannot enlighten you on any of these questions. I receive no word from Ecklington so I know nothing of Mrs Bray. As to my own situation, I can only say what I am sure you know already. I am sent here to be out of view, myself and the child. For all I know I will remain here until my dotage.'

'But not the little one.' Sally had her elbows on the table and laid her chin upon her upturned palms. 'She must have her chance. Out in the world.'

I could only shrug, and say that I did not know.

'She'll go to school, I suppose,' Sally conjectured.

I gave a little shiver at that suggestion, and had to swallow a ball of bitter revulsion before I could reply. 'Not if I can help it,' I said.

Now it is March and at last the snow is melted. The last accumulation of it, in a shadowed angle behind the fountain, was gone when I walked out this morning. The snowdrops show bright green beneath the trees, their buds already open. I presume they did not mind competing with the snow. They seem to have been unaffected by the pressing weight that has been on them all winter. I see other signs of spring—daffodils break the surface of the soil, there are fat buds on the magnolia and the hellebore is in bloom. This morning we had fresh cows' milk instead of the goats' milk that has sustained us recently. A churn was delivered to us; the lane must be open. I feel conflicted by this development. I am not sure I want the outside world to invade our enclave. What we are building here is so fragile—so new—that I am not sure it can survive the carping criticism of the Caroline Foleys of this world.

The day closes in and I have drawn the curtains across the window. The child plays on the rug before the fire with some wooden animals Tom has made for her. I stop writing and watch her. She looks up, alerted by the stillness of my pen. She is lit from behind by the fire. Her hair is a halo of ebony fire. Her eyes regard me. She is George. She is all George.

42

Annie Orphan 1804

As the afternoon light faded and a thin, cold, mizzling rain fell, a figure appeared on the long, winding carriageway that led up to Ecklington. The young man's coat was mud-spattered and torn, soaked through with rain. His hat, very woebegone, dripped water down his face and over his shoulders. His steps stumbled and wove across the drive. Once he fell and lay on the gravel, his arms and legs spread out anyhow, gangling and awkward, but at last he gathered them together and got back to his feet. He staggered onwards, leaving one shoe behind, but it was so broken, flapping at the sole, that he seemed to get on better without it. At last he came to the wide sweep before the door and half crawled up the smooth steps to the doorway. He raised his fist and smote the door, but with so little strength that the sound barely resonated within. The family had been so long from home that no one, now, stood duty in Ecklington's hallway and it was some time before the youth's hammering was heard in the servants' hall.

Mr Swale mounted the stairs, a candlestick in his hand, for it was by this time quite dark, and in any case all the shutters in the house were tightly closed. The butler pulled back the bolts and turned the weighty key in the lock. At last he opened the door and the young man fell through. He was horribly dirty and very emaciated, his clothes hung like rags on his body. Filthy water ran from his coat and made a brown puddle on the immaculate tiles of the hall.

Mr Swale stepped back, partly in fear and partly in revulsion, for the boy smelt very bad; feral and foul.

The boy raised his head from the floor and looked up at Mr Swale. Through the grime that caked his face, he smiled, but his face was so ravaged that it seemed to the butler more like a grimace.

'I am George Talbot,' rasped the young man, 'and I am come home.'

The sudden return of Master George Talbot to Ecklington—and in such a pitiable state—precipitated a time of great activity and industry for, naturally, it was expected that where Master George arrived the rest of the family would soon follow. The furloughed staff were brought swiftly back and put to work. Rooms were opened and aired, coverings removed, beds prepared, windows cleaned. Mrs Bray put in a large order for staples.

Added to Annie's duties about the house were her ministrations to the young man. The physician, who had been immediately summoned, prescribed poultices for the treatment of the chest, which was congested, and various unguents for sores to the feet and wounds to the back, all of which oozed yellow matter. There was fever to be brought down. The patient was declared to be starved and dehydrated and altogether in a most prodigiously run-down state. His life was not absolutely feared for, but there were multiple causes for concern.

At his request Annie took the doctor to her stillroom, where he expressed approbation and showed her how to concoct his various treatments.

The patient—stripped of his threadbare, travel-stained clothes, bathed and put into a clean, warmed bed—slept. Annie sat in vigil at his bedside. He sweated, soaking the sheets, which were stained anyway by the salves she had smeared onto the lacerations on his back and by the green mess of poultice she had applied to his chest. The room smelt noxious, from the bitter herbs and rancid goose fat that had been used to make the poultice, from infection and from the boy himself, who exuded the scent of illness. He fretted and muttered in the bed, turning his head this way and that. From time to time he opened his eyes but his pupils were enormous, vacant, the portal to suffering too profound for her to comprehend.

Sally visited daily. She was not really permitted above stairs and came stealthily, in the very early morning, to rouse Annie from where she slumbered in a chair with a cup of tea and a slice of bread.

Sally's own suffering had awakened in her a light of intense compassion that had not been there before. She looked down on the young man with pitying eyes.

'Poor boy,' she said. 'Poor boy. He has been badly-used. They treated us better at the orphanage, didn't they Annie?'

This kind-heartedness was not the only change in Sally Orphan. Her recent, troubled demeanour seemed reduced. She was less liable to jump at shadows, less timorous. Something of her old boldness had returned; she did not now need a sleeping draught and she did not come to Annie's room in the night. Her distraction however, her inattentiveness to the task in hand, had increased over the past few months—she day-dreamed, much occupied with her own thoughts—but it seemed as though her thoughts were pleasant ones, that she did not relive, as she had at first, the night of her molestation. She hummed under her breath, and a small smile could be seen about her lips. She had taken again to going missing for hours on end. Billie Brixie, the laundry-woman's son, had continued to look out for Sally even though Mr Silver had not been seen back at Ecklington since his departure the previous spring. But there were times when even Billie could not find Sally. He would shamble from the laundry room to the kitchen garden, from the sluice to the scullery via the stables and the dairy but Sally was not to be found.

While the house had been in stasis her absences were not of much moment, but once the young master arrived and matters galvanised, it was different. Sally was needed in the kitchen and was never to be found there.

With this in mind Annie said, 'Sally, you must mind your duty, you know. Mrs Bray notices that you are often not where you should be.' She spoke quietly, so as not to disturb her patient.

'Oh?' Sally's mouth bent in a smile that was secretive and smug. 'I am just about the grounds. I never go very far.'

'But there is work to be done, and the other girls resent you doing less than your share,' Annie urged.

Sally shrugged, and twitched unnecessarily at Master George's counterpane. 'I might not be a kitchen maid for much longer, so I shall not care about *them*,' she said at last. Her eyes flashed, some of their old, mischievous fire.

'What do you mean Sally? Are you going to leave Ecklington?' The idea stupefied Annie. Ecklington was home. She understood their being brought to work there by Mrs Talbot as a kind of adoption; once sealed it could not be broken.

'I shall not leave Ecklington,' Sally said, 'but I shall not be a kitchen maid. That is all I mean.'

'What will you do then? How will you earn your keep?'

Sally smiled again, an expression that suggested she would say much, but could not. 'It is a secret,' she said at last. 'I may not say, but, mark my words Annie, it will certainly be so. Before Michaelmas.'[xxx]

Annie did not know whether to be amazed that Sally had mysterious plans afoot, or dismayed that she was not to be party to them. She had known Sally all her life. Sally was the closest thing she had to family and as ashamed she had been, at times, of Sally's waywardness, her sassy attitude and her idleness when it came to work, she did not wish to think that, at any point, their paths might diverge. 'I hope you will not do anything rash,' she said. 'I hope you will not throw away your good opportunity here.'

'Oh no,' Sally threw off, reaching for the door handle, for it was time for her to begin work in the kitchen. 'No, I shall improve upon it.'

Master George had been home four days before his mama and papa and sister returned to Ecklington. Lord Petrel, of course, was of the party. The ladies had been easily located in their London house. The gentlemen had been less easy to find; messengers had sought them at various country estates where they were thought to be shooting deer but they had eventually been run to ground at the race course in Shropshire. Be that as it may, some quick packing and hard riding converged them on Ecklington more or less together.

Mrs Talbot was very shocked at the consequences to her son—again— of being at Stonybeck school but if she had any self-doubt over her decision to send him back there she did not display it. Mr Talbot was extremely angry, striding around his study. He scattered an accumulation of correspondence that awaited his attention there but found no word from the school that his son had run away.

'Irresponsible!' he fulminated. 'A dereliction of duty! I shall sue the shirts from their backs, Petrel. There must certainly be an investigation. How many other boys have been cruelly used, as George clearly has?'

Lord Petrel denied absolutely that the Stonybeck regime was the cause of Master George's broken health. 'I spoke to the headmaster personally,' he said. 'It was quite understood that he was to be let alone.'

'I have sent cakes by the dozen,' Mrs Talbot said.

'Exactly,' Lord Petrel agreed, laying a sympathetic hand on Mrs Talbot's arm. 'You have done more than any mother in England would do. No, I conjecture that his journey here, on foot, contending with the elements, is to blame for his sorry state of health. It was a foolish adventure to embark upon, very foolish.'

They gathered around George's bed. Mr Talbot knelt beside it and took hold of his son's clammy hand. 'When the boy is well I will speak to him,' he said, his voice soft now and full of remorse. 'I will hear, from him, all that has occurred, and why he has run away from Stonybeck.' He looked up at his friend and his wife, his emotions barely kept in check—sadness at the state of his son vied with anger at the circumstances that had brought the boy to this pass. 'He was sent back there very much against my better judgement, you recall,' he added darkly.

'As to that, Talbot,' Lord Petrel said archly, 'I would not press him too hard. You will recall from your own school days… well, perhaps *you* will not, but *I* certainly do… that there is a code of honour. What happens at school stays at school, you know.'

'We can assume,' said Miss Talbot, who was also in the room, 'that the conditions must have been extreme for George to contemplate such a journey. He must have walked for weeks, slept beneath hedges, gone hungry…'

'Yes. Yes my dear,' Mr Talbot said very sorrowfully. 'I feel… mortified,' and truly he had tears in his eyes as he looked upon his boy. 'You, Jocelyn, were more stalwart in his defence than I was. I upbraid myself most severely, that I was… *persuaded*,' he threw a look replete with bitterness over his shoulder.

'Poor George,' Miss Talbot cried. 'He tried to tell us. He did!' She looked accusingly from her Mama to Lord Petrel, but neither of them would meet her eye.

She knelt at the other side of the bed and took George's other hand. 'I think it will be good if you encourage him to speak of it, Papa,' she urged in a confidential voice before saying more generally, 'In the meantime we should thank Annie.' She turned to where the maid hovered in the corner of the room. 'Annie has obviously devoted herself to George's care. We are indebted to her.'

'Yes, Annie,' said Mrs Talbot, who had not noticed the girl before this, 'you have done extremely well. But Nugent will take over Master George's care now.'

Annie curtseyed, and left the room. She returned to her usual duties, which included preparing the salves and tinctures that Miss Nugent administered to the patient. Annie was happy to have Miss Nugent's company once again, and to hear the tales of Brighton and of London she had to tell. In her turn she confided her concerns about Sally. 'She has some scheme afoot,' she said, 'but I cannot fathom it. She says it will come to fruition by Michaelmas.'

'She seems altered to me,' Miss Nugent observed, 'and for the better. Oh, do not mistake me. She applies herself no better to her work—she is still slip-shod and careless—but she has learned to guard her tongue and her personal hygiene is improved. I hope she makes something of herself, I really do.'

Annie did not have to set herself to watching Sally for very long to discern the change that came over her when Mr Harlish, the gamekeeper, brought game to the kitchen door. It appeared to Annie that Sally was in expectation of these visits—she would smooth her apron and tease a tendril or two of hair from beneath her cap. She made it her business to greet the gamekeeper and take hold of whatever he brought—a brace of hare or pheasant. She never failed to offer him a cup of ale from the barrel or a slice of pie from the larder. She detained him with enquiries about his work. Sally was not coquettish as she had once—thoughtlessly—been, and in any case such overtly flirtatious behaviour would not have served with Mr Harlish, who was not the kind of man to be swayed by a kittenish manner.

Annie made it her business to be in the stillroom when Mr Harlish was expected. If she kept the door open she could hear their murmured conversation, and she found excuses to pass in and out so that she could observe the gamekeeper's behaviour to Sally. It was respectful, but tender. He was gentle with Sally as he would have been to a wounded bird. He kept his eyes fixed on her face—which was, after all, very comely to look at—rather than on her bodice, which was arguably comelier still. Annie observed the passing of little gifts; an iridescent feather, a posy of anemones, a squirrel carved from wood. It was easy to see that Sally's affection was reciprocated, and Annie felt at ease. Wherever Jackie Silver was, he was not at Ecklington, but Lord Petrel was back and so was Mr Goose. Their return might have upset Sally but she seemed unperturbed, too caught up in her romance to be pulled back into her chasm of fear.

Master George's health continued to give cause for concern. He was weak, his constitution undermined by who knew what privations suffered at school or during the arduous, lonely journey home again. Eventually he was well enough to be carried downstairs by one of the footmen and placed in the conservatory for some portion of every day. It was warm there, and bright, with no suspicion of draught. It was hoped that the bright display of tropical plants would cheer his spirits. The boy's face was extremely haggard, his colour sallow. He languished on a wicker settee beneath a heavy blanket. The energetic child they had all known was quite gone. Now he sat hour by hour in repose, lost in his thoughts. Miss Talbot was his constant companion. She read to him, played upon the pianoforte and showed him folders of engravings. If he preferred quiet she sat nearby with her embroidery. He seemed to enjoy his papa's company, was eager and doting when Mr Talbot was near. George listened avidly as his father told stories of India whereas he had not much of warmth to show for his mama and would not interest himself in the conversation she offered. If Lord Petrel approached him he would ring the bell and say that he was tired; he wished to return to his room.

All through April and half of May George Talbot ailed, but towards the end of May he rallied. One day he said he would enjoy a ride in the carriage, and it was immediately summoned.

'I wish to see Pocklington Abbey,' he said. 'I was sorry to have missed your expedition there last year. And to see the waterfalls also. Did you not have a merry time of it, at your picnic Jocelyn?'

His sister gave a wry smile. 'It was an eventful day. Not altogether a successful one.'

Mrs Talbot decided that her son needed distraction, and invited a number of acquaintances to stay at Ecklington. Annie's workload expanded exponentially as there were bedrooms to be opened and aired, beds to be made, the larger entertaining rooms cleaned and made ready for an influx of guests. Mrs Bray looked to her larder and called for a wholesale culling of geese, sheep and pigs that she might be in readiness to feed the Talbots' guests. Mr Harlish, as usual, was called to assist in the grisly business, which went on late into the night, a fact not calculated upon by Lord Petrel.

Ecklington's home farm was the site of the slaughter, but the carcasses of the animals were then brought around by the kitchen garden to the yard behind the kitchens, where there were facilities for plucking and drawing and where the meat could be hung in preparation for butchery. This task fell to the scullery maids and kitchen wenches. One evening, well past ten of the clock, Sally alone remained at work, scrubbing the large, rough-hewn table that had been the site of her industry for most of the day using hot water she had decanted from a tub heated for the purpose. At the back of the shed, hanging high in the rafters, beasts' carcasses dangled from large iron meat hooks. Their blood dripped onto the cobbles and ran down a drain towards the door.

The evening was hot and Sally—for once, perhaps motivated by the proximity of Mr Harlish—had worked hard. She felt sticky and smelly. Her dress was damp with sweat, her apron much larded with blood and offal from the day's business. Her hair had escaped from her cap and hung in lank hanks down her back. Noises from the kitchens had ceased and she assumed that Mrs Bray and the others had retired for the night. No light shone from the precincts of home farm. She was alone.

Her work done, she was on the point of extinguishing the lamp and making her own way to bed when the tub of hot water caught her eye. It was still more than half full, clean and inviting. An idea came to her. She knew it was risky; she could not be certain that everyone else had gone to bed. But she had gone to all the trouble of heating the water in Mrs Brixie's copper, had transferred it with a bucket to the tub and dragged the tub down the alley to the shed. All this had been a labour in itself, notwithstanding the scrubbing and sluicing she had then embarked upon. Here she was hot and sweaty and there was the water. And tomorrow Mr Harlish would find some excuse to visit and wouldn't it be nice to have clean hair? The idea of Mr Harlish in conjunction with her thick, wavy hair was especially thrilling. She had a fleeting notion of his strong hands stroking its soft tresses.

That did it. She pulled the door of the shed closed, removed her cap and apron and undid the buttons of her dress. She peeled it from her shoulders, pulling free her arms so that the dress hung from a drawstring at her waist. She plunged her hands and bare arms into the delicious, warm water and splashed it over her face and neck, sluicing away the grime of the day. She so rarely had the luxury of warm water; it made her skin tingle. She wet her hair, lathering it with soap and rinsing it again until it squeaked. Now the water in the tub was foamy and soft. Beneath her dress she wore a chemise, a simple undergarment fastened at the neck with a cord. She pulled the ribbon and let the chemise fall to her waist, releasing her full, peachy breasts from their containment before using a rag to cleanse her armpits, throat, bosom and belly. She let out a little giggle. It was almost like having a bath, as Mrs Talbot and the young mistress did. Wouldn't *she* like to try it, just once! The tub was large and she speculated about stripping off entirely and climbing into it. The naughtiness of the idea was intoxicating. But she decided that it was not quite large enough, that she would dry her hair and upper body and pull her dress back on before tackling her lower half. Then the door behind her squeaked, and a draught made the hairs on her arms stand up and her nipples pucker.

Behind her, in the doorway, stood Lord Petrel, and, just behind him, lurking and sniggering, his valet, Goose.

All Sally's innocent—and not so innocent—pleasure in the hot soapy water evaporated in an instant. She went pale, her mouth opened in a terrified maw.

Lord Petrel smiled—an unctuous, sinister expression. He gestured Mr Goose into the shed and closed the door. 'My dear girl,' he said, eyeing Sally's soft, curvaceous body, 'I do believe you're more beautiful now than you were before. Would you like to earn yourself another guinea?'

Sally tried in vain to thrust her arms back into the sleeves of her chemise and her dress, but her arms were wet and the sleeves were inside out. She gathered up the material to cover her nakedness.

'No,' she said. She tried to shout, to scream. That had worked in the woods, after all. But her voice came out as little more than a croak. The valet moved around the shed, passing behind the large work table and approaching Sally from behind. Lord Petrel made no move towards her, enjoying her distress, savouring the anticipation of what was to come.

Sally cast about her wildly. There were meat hooks and knives on a shelf, but too far away for her to reach. Apart from the table and the tub and the dangling beasts the room was bare. In desperation she grasped the edge of the tub and yanked it over, sending water flowing over the cobbled floor. It mixed with the blood in the drain and soaked the viscount's boots with pinkish scum. The clatter of the tub on the stones of the floor was loud.

She felt the firm grip of Mr Goose's hands on her upper arms. 'No, no!' she shouted again, and this time her voice did not fail her.

'Oh good,' drawled Lord Petrel, stepping out of the ooze of water and putting a hand down to the fastening of his breeches. 'I like a fighter. The more you buck and struggle the better I shall like it, but then, you know that already, don't you?'

The valet hauled Sally onto the worktable. He was surprisingly strong, for such a string-bean of a man. He pinioned her there while his master forced Sally's legs apart and clambered onto the table between them. He undid the fastening of his breeches with one hand, rummaging under Sally's skirts with the other. Sally writhed and struggled, but to no avail. Goose let go of one of Sally's arms long enough to place his bony hand onto one of her full breasts. He squeezed it hard and she let out a cry. Then he bent his mouth to Sally's and probed it with a furred, yellow tongue.

'You shall get your turn, Goose,' Lord Petrel said, 'just hold her still for me first.'

Then the door of the shed was thrust open. Mr Harlish and Billie Brixie burst inside. With a roar, Mr Harlish threw himself onto the viscount, seizing him by the collar, hauling him off the table and throwing him to the floor. The cobbles were wet from Sally's bath, and slick from the charnel of the day's work. Lord Petrel floundered for a few moments, unable to find his footing. Billie Brixie lumbered across the shed and landed a punch on Mr Goose's bony face with his meaty fist. The valet went down immediately, out cold.

Sally scrambled off the table and cowered in a corner of the shed, her voice released; she screamed and screamed until Billie crossed the shed to her, and placed his body before her, a defensive wall.

Mr Harlish reached to the shelf and laid hold of a meat hook. By the time Lord Petrel had righted himself the gamekeeper was standing over him, the meat hook held menacingly aloft. The viscount raised himself to his full height but with his breeches around his knees and smeared as he was with gore, he did not look very dignified.

'You'll answer for this,' he snarled, grappling to set his costume to rights.

'Yes sir,' Mr Harlish replied, his expression implacable.

'Very well then,' Lord Petrel growled, shouldering past Mr Harlish to the door of the shed. 'Have the wench yourselves, if you like. I won't fight you for her.'

The noise of Sally's screams had brought people running; a footman and Mr Swale and Annie, and the man from the home farm who had been up late tending a difficult calving. Neither Mr Harlish nor Billie Brixie spoke. The unconscious Mr Goose and Sally's state of undress pointed sufficiently to what had transpired. Sally was taken to bed. Mr Swale locked up the shed with the valet inside.

Naturally there were repercussions. The next morning Mr Goose found himself hauled from the shed and dragged before his master and Mr Talbot. Mr Harlish and Billie Brixie were also summoned. None of the servants were disposed to say much about what had occurred until it became obvious that Lord Petrel's intention was to entirely obfuscate his own role in the proceedings. He spoke of having followed his valet to the kitchens, curious as to his intent. He claimed to have been on the point of restraining the manservant from interfering with the maid when the two Ecklington men had burst in and misunderstood the situation.

Mr Goose's eyes opened as wide as his shiner allowed. His mouth flapped but a severe look from his master kept him silent.

Mr Talbot turned to Mr Harlish to ask, 'Is what his lordship says correct?'

'You would take a gamekeeper's word over mine?' Lord Petrel thundered.

But perhaps Mr Talbot had been overruled by his friend once too often. 'I will hear what he has to say,' he replied, his voice equally loud and booming.

Mr Harlish considered. 'I would say,' he said at last, 'that it could be as his lordship says. But, to my mind, a man with his breeks around his knees is not best placed to *save* a maid from assault.'

'That's slanderous,' Lord Petrel shouted, but his blush belied his words.

Mr Talbot turned to the window and tried to master his temper, which boiled very hotly within him. Then he turned to his friend. 'I take it you'll dismiss your man?' he demanded vehemently.

'Oh, instantly,' Lord Petrel flung out, but then he narrowed his eyes, 'if you'll dismiss the gamekeeper. He laid hands on me, Talbot. He threatened me with a meat hook.'

'*Did* he, by God,' shouted Mr Talbot, his tone and angry, suffused face suggesting powerfully that he would have done as much himself, and more. He strode to the console table and poured himself a glass of spirits, which he threw back in one swallow. At last he said, 'Your man will be dismissed without references. Mine will be redeployed. I will not dismiss a man for defending a woman. He will go to one of the properties in the North Country; you will not encounter him again. Billie Brixie is not an employee of mine, so I have no ability to sanction him, even if I wished to do so. Frankly, I am not minded to do anything other than praise him for his courage. You may all go.'

The servants left the room. When they had gone Mr Talbot remained agitated and vexed. He paced the room, fulminating. At last he said, 'Leave my maid servants alone from now on, Petrel. Find your pleasure elsewhere, do you hear?'

'If you like,' Lord Petrel said, pouring himself a glass of Madeira. He did not meet his host's eyes. 'She was only a kitchen wench,' he muttered. 'It isn't as though she mattered.'

'She *does* matter,' Mr Talbot said. 'She was brought from the workhouse as a child. She belongs at Ecklington. I have a responsibility towards her.'

'You are sentimental, Talbot,' Lord Petrel said, 'but it shall be as you say.'

'It *shall* be as I say,' Mr Talbot repeated emphatically. 'By God, Petrel, you have been a good friend to me and I owe you a great deal but, lately, you have pushed my patience.' No doubt the master of Ecklington had in his mind Lord Petrel's interference in the matter of George's schooling but he could add to that the business of bloodstock, for Mr Talbot had paid out a great deal of money on his friend's advice and, so far, seen no return. Now here was a further gross abuse of hospitality.

'Would you like me to make myself scarce for a few weeks?' Lord Petrel said.

Mr Talbot hesitated. His wife would not like him to go as far as that, he thought.

The viscount read his pause. 'I am not sure that Vauxhall and Penge will quite like to come here, if I am away,' he observed. 'Mrs Talbot did ask me most particularly to urge them to accept her invitation.'

'You must find a new man,' Mr Talbot said with ill grace—for he knew he had been out manoeuvred again—'In the meantime, Swale will attend you.'

Mrs Talbot's guests began to arrive over the next few days and the servants of Ecklington were busy. The house bulged with company. Dinners were lavish. The bells in the servants' hall rang constantly for hot water in the bedrooms, for tea in the drawing room and out on the lawn, for Madeira and sack, brandy and port in prodigious quantities.

Mr Goose departed Ecklington under a cloud, not at all lamented by anyone he left behind. He trudged down the driveway with his portmanteau, very wrathful against his former master but with a letter of introduction in his pocket that would secure him a new place without much difficulty. Mr Harlish went quietly, with his dogs and chattels piled into an old dog cart and an address in the North Country in his pocket. One morning the gamekeeper's cottage was simply empty, its occupant absorbed by the countryside's byways.

Sally Orphan cried without ceasing for two weeks.

Mr Talbot was a genial and a generous host. His guests, once come to Ecklington, were loath to depart; they stayed all summer long. He enjoyed seeing his wife so much in her element, surrounded by ladies who had rank and wealth—sometimes both. He liked seeing Jocelyn befriended by the daughters of illustrious houses. He took particular pleasure in seeing his son restored to the full vigour of health, riding his horse, swimming in the lake, eating voraciously and sleeping sound and unmolested in his bed at night. All in all he felt he had achieved his aim. His status as a gentleman could not be questioned when he had people of rank beneath his roof and at his table. His business thrived; indeed, he had information that Napoleon intended an embargo of goods from Britain within his territories[xxxi], which was sure to increase demand for them exponentially; Talbot was in the throes of putting in place a route to supply France's black market. Two things prevented him from being wholly at ease. One was his own sense of restlessness. He was beginning to feel stout and out of condition. He was rather bored—he missed the cut and thrust of negotiation, the satisfaction of active mercantile involvement. He thirsted for one last adventure before his age would preclude it. The other source of disquiet was his son. There was no possibility of the boy being returned to Stonybeck. Other schools existed, schools with gentler regimes and kinder masters, but he felt on the whole that his son would never shine at his lessons. He was an active boy, courageous. He seemed very interested in India.

And so it occurred to Mr Talbot that the solution to his two problems might be one and the same. He proposed to take George to India. His own education had been completed in like manner and he had not been the loser by it. Indeed George had the advantage, for he was already a gentleman in taste and manners and by connection. George would go to

India as a boy but return as a man. He would be competent in the business. The Talbot wealth, by Mr Talbot's personal oversight in Bengal, could only increase. George would step ashore in five or ten years' time and take up immediately all the laurels it had taken his father twenty years to accrue.

Such a scheme would not be without its dangers. The French fleet would have to be reckoned with, as well as numerous privateers. But his clippers were used to avoiding these foes. They were fast. Their captains were wily. He believed there was not a fleeter, more agile flotilla of vessels anywhere.

He mentioned the idea to his son, whose eyes widened in delight and expectation. Mrs Talbot was less enthusiastic, but not as thoroughly against the idea as he had feared. She expected, in his absence, to do as she wished; she stipulated that as an absolute condition of her husband's going abroad. She would take Jocelyn to Lyme and Bath. They might return to Brighton. Since their successful house party they had invitations to various noble houses. Jocelyn was now eighteen, eminently marriageable; it was time a suitable match was sought.

Mr Talbot half expected his friend Lord Petrel to join the jaunt to India, but the viscount vetoed the idea. 'Oh no,' he said with a yawn. 'That's not my thing at all. I'll remain here, Talbot, and keep my eye on the ladies.'

With all impediments swept away Mr Talbot began to make his plans for a departure as early in September as could be arranged, so as to be around the Cape of Good Hope well before the worst storms.

In late August Sally came very tearfully to Annie. She had been down-hearted since the departure of Mr Harlish, and had actually been quite sick in June and July. Now she was physically restored, but very troubled. In halting sentences and with eyes downcast she sobbed out her story.

'I went to Tommy's cottage the night before he was to go,' she whispered.

Annie's heart sank, 'Oh Sally, you didn't.'

Sally nodded. 'I couldn't bear for him to go away without saying farewell. We were sweethearts, Annie, and he had spoken to me of marriage.'

'He should have said as much to Mr Talbot,' Annie said.

'He said he thought about it, but with not knowing where he was to be sent, he thought it better not.'

'I see,' Annie sighed, 'and so you went to his cottage.'

Sally nodded again. 'Yes, and... oh Annie, we could not help ourselves.' She allowed herself a small smile. 'It was lovely. Not at all like... not at all like before. He was so gentle with me, Annie. But now... now...'

'You're with child?'

Sally's woeful expression answered for her. 'Can you make me a potion, Annie, to bring it away?'

The idea appalled Annie. 'Certainly not,' she said. She calculated on her fingers. 'It's too late. Even if such a thing was possible before, it is not now. And in any case, it's wrong, Sally, especially for a child conceived in love, as this one was.'

Sally stroked the mound of her stomach. 'But what shall I do then?' she wailed. 'I will be dismissed. I will be sent to the workhouse! Oh Annie, do not desert me!'

She threw herself into Annie's arms. Annie stroked her back until the paroxysm of tears had passed. 'I will think of something,' she said.

Annie spoke to Miss Nugent and the two of them brought Mrs Butterwick into their confidence.

'The girl certainly must be dismissed,' the housekeeper said. 'She must be made an example of. We cannot have all the maids thinking they can do what Sally has done and suffer no inconvenience. Oh Annie!' Mrs Butterwick lamented. 'If only Mrs Talbot had chosen another girl to come with you; a girl more like you. Sally has been trouble from the start—workshy, impertinent and wayward. I knew she would come to the bad.'

'It was not her fault that she was forced,' Annie said. 'That was none of her doing.'

'It *was,*' Mrs Butterwick replied. 'What was she doing in the stables in the first place but looking for trouble? But no,' she allowed, 'what occurred to her was more than she deserved.'

'So you will really send her away?' Annie asked, her eyes swimming with tears.

Mrs Butterwick considered. 'I shall have to speak to the master. It will be awkward, but I had rather him deal with it than the mistress. *She* would give no quarter.'

Accordingly Mrs Butterwick approached Mr Talbot and matters were arranged.

Three weeks later, the day before Mr Talbot and George were due to travel to Liverpool, Sally departed Ecklington. She endured a severe dressing down from Mrs Butterwick and Mr Swale in full view of all the other servants, standing before the hearth where, four years before, she had warmed her bare feet as a child just come from the orphanage. She bore their chastisement bravely, crying only a very little as they expressed their disappointment and disgust at her conduct, called her ungrateful, and prophesied disgrace for her future. Then she left the house, carrying a pitiful bundle of clothes and her shame with her. She went out past the kitchen gardens, her steps dragging and her shoulders drooped. She passed through the yard of home farm where the dairy maids were assembled to witness her humiliation. They tittered behind their hands and sneered as she went slowly down the farm track to the lane. Once out of view her head lifted and her shoulders squared. Her steps quickened. Before long she was running between the hedgerows and on her face she bore a broad, bright smile. A mile down the lane a trap waited for her. She climbed into the seat and threw herself into the arms of the driver, Mr Harlish.

43

Yorkshire

September 1814

We hear that the war is over and that Napoleon is imprisoned in Elba. For all that I know him to be an evil man I cannot help feeling some sympathy for his situation. I know what it is to feel banished and friendless, to be separated from every familiar creature and comfort, to have one's expectations of the future snatched away.

I hope that he makes peace with his fate, as I have done. I hope he even begins to discover, within his imprisonment, a kind of freedom. I do not compare our sins. He has been ambitious. God knows, I was never that! If I had been, my destiny would have been different. He has been careless of life, sending countless thousands to their deaths in his name. My hands are clean of blood, indeed, my name has been cast into the dirt to save one little soul. Somebody did die, but it was none of my doing. I absolve myself of the guilt, but I am not sorry for it.

I am come to the part in my story where the memory is raw and painful to look upon. The relating of it will cost me dear. The impossibility of the predicament they placed me in still feels like a snare; the more I struggled, the more it tightened, the more completely I was trapped. I looked to George to save me, as Mr Brigstock saved his sister. But no.

I have not written in my journal for many months. I have been busy in the garden and about the house. Work is an excellent antidote to brooding resentment, to anger and pride. I have been guilty of all those sins but this strange, sequestered place has released me from their power. I am content.

I have found fellowship here; Tom and Sally Harlish, Annie and Mr Burleigh. We work side by side in a common cause. Some of us work harder than others. Sally does not pull her weight, but what she lacks in application she makes up for in happiness. Her joy is infectious; her laughter is refreshing to all who hear it. Tom Harlish is a man of the land, of trees and moor and water. I should think, to him, this place is a kind of heaven. He lies on the moor for hours waiting for grouse. One day I actually stumbled over him, concealed in the woods so effectively he had disappeared from view. Like him, Mr Burleigh seems content. Sally's oldest boy is almost ten and has taken a great interest in the horses. Mr Burleigh likes to teach him horse husbandry; the two of them are often to be found in the stable yard, soaping tails or picking hooves. I watch the way he engages the lad, showing him the way of things in a manner that has nothing didactic about it. I wonder if I could engage the child in the same way.

I think Annie still labours under some kind of cloud. She carries a burden whose nature I do not understand; some restraint, some lingering threads of regret that anchor her to the past. Perhaps she left something behind at Ecklington that cannot be compensated for here. I wish she would confide in me. I wish we could be friends. How strange that I should wish it, but this house throws everything into such different perspectives. Through its prism I see myself—and Annie —so much more clearly. How angry Mama would be. She condemned me to this imprisonment in deference to society's code; but I am of the mind that society's code is meaningless and in my imprisonment I am set free.

44

George and my father sailed for India in September of 1804. I was sorry to see them go. I knew I would miss them and I was afraid for what might befall them out there in the world but I had no qualms about their journey. In the circumstances it seemed to me a proper course of action.

In the months of George's recuperation we had grown as close as when we were children. Little by little he confided in me some of the appalling practices of Stonybeck school, the cruelty of masters and pupils alike, the deprivations he had endured and the cloud of despair that had engulfed him, all-but snuffing out his desire for life. It was this, finally, that had motivated his desperate escape. My father was privy to these revelations and I saw tears stand in his eyes as the details spilled from George's faltering lips. I saw also pride in his son's courage and resilience. Our shared appreciation for George's mettle drew us closer together; I felt closer to Papa than I had ever done before. It was the first I had seen of his true feelings. I had known him to be conflicted—sometimes tortured by a sense of inferiority and sometimes inflated by hubris—and angry that all he had achieved counted for nothing against ancient acres or the stamp of a heraldic crest. These two aspects together had formed a dark maelstrom at the heart of his nature that had frightened me. Now I saw a softer layer in his character, and when he had gone I found I missed the affectionate disposition I had found in him. I comforted myself by thinking of my father on board his clipper and then in India, undisputed master, respected as a man of business and of integrity. I liked to think of George with the wind in his hair and a healthful glow to his skin, scampering along the decks and scaling the ropes. I tried to see through his eyes all the exotic shores he would visit, all the things he would learn that really mattered. I was happy for him.

For the first year of Papa's absence I was busy and relatively happy. It was novel to me to travel, to see new places, to stay in the houses of illustrious families. When I could I saw Elinor Binsley and indeed late in 1804 she and I were bridesmaids to her brother Gabriel and Miss Maud Willow. Tragic circumstances had precipitated their marriage; his brother Edward had been killed in a hunting accident making Gabriel Sir Diggory's heir. Very soon after this Sir Diggory also died, and Sir Gabriel and Lady Binsley moved in to Binsley House. Of course Caroline Willow also attended her sister down the aisle and she and I were thrown into one another's company as we prepared the bride for her nuptials. I found Caroline very much changed from the giggling, romantic girl I had known. She was stout but with none of the softness that usually characterises the fuller figure. I found her stiff to the point of severity, both in her person and in her manner. She was superlatively religious, attending services twice daily. She officiated on the wedding day as though her sister were to be presented at the altar for sacrifice, rather than for matrimony. I observed to her that it was a day for happiness and she appeared very shocked, telling me that marriage was a solemn sacrament before God, not an excuse for romantic flummery. I thought her opinion sad, and rather ironic. I did enjoy seeing the rector and his wife once more. They, of course, were happy to know that Maud would be settled so close to them.

Lieutenant Willow did not attend the celebration, being at that time awaiting deployment to Hanover. I pressed upon Mrs Willow my very kind wishes for him, and requested her to mention when she next wrote that I had asked after him.

For the next six years my life was as elegant as it was empty, as pampered as it was pointless. I recall few specific details of it; it is a blur of candlelight on gilt, the hypnotic thud of hooves on the road as we went from one place to another. We stayed at a succession of noble houses, whiling away our time over tea and cards and pieces of embroidery that had neither beauty nor function. We walked on manicured lawns and around interminable shrubberies. We dined, the courses increasingly pretentious, rich and cloying but not so as to outdo my fellow diners, whom I found stultifying and dull; trivial, vacuous and pompous. We danced, the elaborate figures of the set as unvarying as the day's routine. I grew sick to death of changing my clothes. Peake retired and I had a new maid, very *au fait* on the subject of accessories and hair arrangement. I did not like her. She had cold, bony hands and a pursed mouth that always seemed to be bristling with pins. I dreaded her swift, impersonal ministrations.

We went from baronial mansions to places of popular resort—Bath, Cheltenham, Brighton, Weymouth—where we took houses for the duration. The scene may have varied but the routines and the company stayed the same. *Still* we must saunter beneath parasols, dine and dance. *Still* I must endure the gossip and platitudes of Mama's circle of acquaintance. *Still* I must be dressed and re-dressed for morning calls, for afternoons at home, for rides, for walks, for dinners, card parties, concerts and balls. I was paraded—displayed—before marriageable young men and their pernickety mamas, my manners scrutinised, my looks assessed, my tastes and opinions interrogated. It sickened me, if I am honest. Not one of those titled—but I presume impecunious— young men ever smiled at me as Lieutenant Willow had done. None of them made any attempt to know me, Jocelyn Talbot. To them I was a brood mare, a quantity of money. The more I met of them the more I realised what a gem Lieutenant Willow was, how personable, how sincere, how honourable. In comparison these men were arrogant, cold-blooded and sneering. I despised them all. They had not a uniform between them, their blood too thick and blue to be wasted in battle. My utter indifference to them made me question my feelings for the lieutenant, feelings I had been too young and green to fully recognise, let alone to fully comprehend. That thrill of delight I had felt just at the sight of him, my sense of easy companionship in his company, the flutter in my innards that the press of his hand had produced. Were these things signs of love?

Throughout our peregrinations from castle to manor, between countryside and coast, from spa town to metropolis Lord Petrel was our constant companion; his life seemed as inextricably entwined in ours as ivy in a tree; constricting and parasitical. His being there helped me settle my feelings for Lieutenant Willow: opposite in every way. I loathed the viscount. I detested his drawling, superior manner, his person, which was becoming more florid and bloated with every passing year. Beneath the thin veneer of his manner I discerned a littleness, a meanness of spirit, even a malevolence that made me flinch whenever he was near. The constancy of his attendance only strengthened the impression of a closer relation than actually existed. While I was exhibited in all my many gowns, and my accomplishments demonstrated as a horse is put through its paces, his proprietorial demeanour gave every impression that the prize had already been claimed. No one spoke of our engagement—certainly not to me—but it was every day attested. Why else must he always be included in every invitation to dine or to dance? There seemed to be some implicit understanding that where the Talbots were, there must he be also. I could not fathom it. I disliked the misapprehension that our betrothal was a settled—if unacknowledged—thing. I found it objectionable and confusing that this was implicit but not spoken of, especially to me. Did people think I was in some way in his power? Or that I was so much my mother's vassal—so helpless and pliable—that it had been settled over my head?

The easiest way of putting an end to the mistaken assumption I felt was rife in our circle would have been to encourage one of my would-be suitors, but that was impossible. There wasn't one amongst them I could tolerate for more than five minutes and in any case I would not feign admiration where I felt none. Without giving encouragement to any of those chinless inbreeds I was resolute in showing by every gesture and expression at my disposal that Lord Petrel disgusted me. He took this in his usual imperturbable manner, laughing off my insults, praising me for my spirit and declaring himself so far from injured that he would have no other dinner companion, no other dance partner, than me. Lord Petrel's possessive conduct kept those vapid young men at bay—I received no proposals of marriage. He may even have gone so far as to warn them off, as he had Lieutenant Willow. This advantage was somewhat pyrrhic however, for it reinforced still further the impression that there was an understanding between us. Whatever his intentions or his actions, I was glad that Mama did nothing to affirm them even if she did not deny them, which I would have preferred. She was assiduous as a chaperone, constantly in attendance. She never allowed Lord Petrel to compromise me. Whatever people might *infer* from Lord Petrel's intimacy with our family, no impropriety could ever be proved.

What a fool I was! What an utter fool!

Those years were wearisome to me, like walking a great distance in a flat, unvarying landscape. Lord Petrel was a stone in my shoe that could not be got rid of.

45

In the spring of 1811 we found ourselves back at Ecklington. It had been many months since we had been there. In our absence the staff had been reduced to a minimum. Mrs Butterwick had been unwell and Mama had given her permission to travel to her sister's house where she might convalesce. To my surprise and pleasure Annie Orphan had become de facto housekeeper, although while we were at home, with the staff reduced, she still performed all her old duties. Annie was by this time perhaps two and twenty years old. She would always be slight but she had an elegant bearing that gave her presence, and from what I saw she handled the maids with quiet authority. I gathered that she was respected. I wondered if she still had that plant I had given her—if it thrived as she had thrived. I hoped so.

We were at Ecklington without company. What a delightful respite! Lord Petrel was put up at the Rose and Crown for the sake of propriety but, like everything he did, the propriety was a façade for his own darker purposes. We had long passed the pretence that the viscount was a guest who must be entertained and I made no allowances for him as I planned calls at the rectory and at Binsley House, long walks in my beloved woods and time in the conservatory where the plants had become overgrown.

Binsley House was unrecognisable from the drear mausoleum I recalled. Maud Binsley had made wholesale improvements to the décor, purchased new furniture, replaced window hangings and banished the dogs. She had two small children, who added cheer and levity to a house that had been in the doldrums for so many years. I could see that she and Sir Gabriel were very happy together.

We sat on the lawn and drank tea as the children played around us. Sir Gabriel had set his easel up at a distance and was painting and so she and I were able to talk confidentially.

'My sister is to be married. Perhaps you have heard?' Lady Binsley told me.

'No indeed,' I said. 'That is happy news. I wish her felicitations.'

Maud made a moue. 'Caroline views the matter in a somewhat sombre light,' she said. 'She speaks of duty, of service, not of happiness.'

'And which gentleman has been so fortunate as to win her hand?' I asked.

'His name is Foley. He has been grandfather's chaplain these many years. Of course there is some disparity as to age, but Caroline does not seem to see it as an obstacle.'

I sipped my tea. 'She has quite given up her dreams of her cousin, then?'

'I fear she will never relinquish those, but she has had to accept they will never be reciprocated.'

'Ah, yes,' I sighed, and with some sadness, for I had never let the lieutenant know that his feelings for me were reciprocated. I had not known it myself. 'To have one's feelings reciprocated is a wonderful thing.'

'It is,' Maud agreed, and she looked fondly across the lawn at her husband. 'You know, Jocelyn, when I accepted Gabriel's proposal Mama and Papa were doubtful. They said we had known each other such a short time, and indeed we had. But I had no misgivings. I *knew* with a certainty I could neither explain nor describe, that Gabriel was the only man I would ever love; that I had been waiting for him. I was, you recall, already three and twenty when he came to Binsley. Mama feared I was already past my bloom …' She faltered, perhaps bringing to mind that I was older than she had been, and still unmarried. She recovered herself to say, 'Gabriel will hear no talk of that kind. He says I grow more beautiful in his eyes with every day that passes. Beauty is in the eye of the beholder, they say.'

I must say I agreed with Sir Gabriel. Maud, when I had first met her, had been somewhat graceless, tall and thin, with a sour expression. Her countenance now was much softer, and had about it a beauty that radiated from a contented heart. 'Would we could all be as happy as you,' I said, my own heart full. 'To recognise our soul mate from the first! To know our own heart! And then to have a path that is without impediment—no objections as to birth or fortune.'

One of the children came just then and clambered onto his mama's lap, and I was glad of the excuse to rein in my feelings for I was overwhelmed with the idea that I had let my own chance of happiness slip away.

'I encountered Mr Brigstock when I was last in town,' Maud said when the child had run away again. 'Or, I should say Mr Stockbridge, for that is his name. Indeed, to be entirely accurate, I should call him Lieutenant Stockbridge, for he is commissioned in the Marines.'[xxxii]

'I can imagine he would take to a life of danger and adventure,' I said, for it was well known that the marines were instrumental in naval action both in defence and attack. 'He is gallant in adversity, and will sacrifice himself in a cause he considers right. Did he mention his sister?'

Maud frowned. 'I am sorry to say that she died, not long after they left Upton Park.'

We looked at each other, both knowing but not wishing to speak of the child. 'He did not mention …' I murmured.

'No,' she said. 'He did not. An unhappy situation for all concerned.'

'For her, especially,' I said emphatically. Of course I could not divulge the information that had been vouchsafed to me in confidence, but I went so far as to add, '*She* was not to blame, however things appeared. We should not judge what we do not fully know.'

'No,' Maud agreed, but reservedly. 'On the other hand, we must call a spade a spade, as Plutarch advises, must we not?'

'Not if it is *not* a spade,' I replied. Lydia Stockbridge was dead and, for all I knew, her child with her. What harm could it possibly do to speak of her tragic story now? And yet I refrained. I am sorry now. Perhaps if I had suggested to Maud an alternative explanation for what seemed so obvious to her, she—and through her, her sister—might have looked more kindly on me, when the time came.

We spoke of other things and as the day grew late I was invited to remain at Binsley to dine. I sent a message with one of Sir Gabriel's men to inform Mama that I would be back at Ecklington in the evening. I had a pleasant time. It was late in May, quite warm, and the sun did not sink until after eight of the clock. We returned to the garden after dinner and sauntered in the lengthening shadows. Maud at last volunteered the information I had been eager to know but hesitant to ask; her cousin was in Spain with Sir Arthur Wellesley. He was safe and in good spirits. I expressed great pleasure at the news. I thought Maud observed me narrowly as I spoke, and would perhaps have made further enquiry as to the nature of my interest in him, but she desisted.

When I returned home I enquired for Mama as Swale greeted me in the hall. The manner of his reply struck me as unusual. Swale was consummate master of everything that occurred at Ecklington. I had sometimes thought he had some cunning system of listening and seeing that extended into every room. Wherever you might be in the vast house, in whatever far, sequestered drawing room, if you wanted more coals for the fire they would unfailingly appear before the thought had fully formed itself in your mind, carried by a footman but undoubtedly conjured by Swale. He could put his hand unerringly on any book, cushion, map or rug you required. He was like a puppet-master, each maid and footman connected to him, able to be summoned by him—or dismissed—by the slightest twitch of his brow. He always knew where every member of the household was to be found. It was unthinkable to me that he would not know where in Ecklington my mother was, but in answer to my question he said that he did not know. Did not know?! I looked at him in astonishment and he could not meet my eye. He handed me my candle. This, too, I thought odd, a subliminal indication that I should retire to my room, rather than seek out Mama. I took the candle, and mounted the stair without quite knowing what had propelled me. It was quite late, and I concluded that Swale was simply ready for his bed. I went to my room smiling. Perhaps we are all Swale's puppets, I thought.

In spite of the fact that I had enjoyed a delightful time at Binsley and was tired, I could not sleep. Thoughts of all Maud and I had spoken of chased themselves around my head. My room was hot and at one point I got up and wrestled with the casement, to admit some air. Just as sunset comes late at that time of year, sunrise comes early. I must have slept a little but a cool breeze from the open window and the slightest possible lightening of the dimness in my room woke me. I got up and pulled on a dressing gown. The fire was out, which told me it was very early indeed, for the maid usually came at five o'clock to kindle the bedrooms fires and remove the night soil. I pulled aside the curtain. The dawn was a blue-grey gloaming. The trees in the park were charcoal spectres against a steely sky. The lawn was a sea of ink. No bird stirred. I shivered and pulled my casement closed. Where was the maid? I wished to have my fire lit. I knew there was no point in ringing the bell; nobody would be awake at this hour but Annie.

I opened my door and went out onto the landing. My room is on the main landing that travels from the front of the house to the back. There is a window at each end, one giving onto the sweep and driveway, the other onto the stable yards. Close to this rear window is the servants' staircase, and I walked towards it with the idea of listening to see if I could hear Annie on her way up. I would ask her to light my fire first. I was barefoot and my footsteps made no noise on the polished wood of the landing floor as I made my way through the gloom. I came to the door of the stair head. It is panelled, cleverly concealed, with a recessed handle. I opened it and listened. I thought I could hear something—a voice, low and gruff. Then a murmured reply. A softly closing door, and then the unmistakable tread of feet on the stairs.

The day outside had lightened to a pearly grey. I could make out the roofs of the stables below, the dark mass of the pump, the square trough, but no light shone. The landing, too, was unlit, the stairwell a black chasm before me. I knew Annie was there before I could see her. She wore a grey habit with a black apron. She carried two buckets but she came absolutely noiselessly. I believe I heard her breath—slightly laboured from her climb—before I could make her out. I felt no fear as she materialised from the shadowed stair like a little billow of smoke separating itself from a plume. She started very much upon seeing me however, only just having the presence of mind to hold on to her buckets. I suppose I must have looked like a ghost, the white of my dressing gown glowing and miasmic in the dim. Neither of us spoke. We regarded each other. Her eyes were wide with shock and something else that I could not immediately read—apprehension, I thought, and perhaps subterfuge. They would not quite meet mine. Her lips were parted and she swept her tongue nervously across them, as though preparatory to speech, but no words came. Slowly, inexorably, her gaze slid to the window. My own followed it and we both looked down on the stable yard.

Even in the few seconds that had passed since I had last looked out there the sky had brightened. Everything remained monotone, leached of colour, but there could be no mistaking what we saw. From the murk of one of the stables a figure stepped forward. At first I thought it a shadow, a dark silhouette against the grey of the stable, but then I made out his livery. It was crumpled—his coat unbuttoned, his stock untied and loose about his neck—but unmistakable, and I recognised the man as Lord Petrel's valet, the mulatto who had replaced the oily and unpleasant Goose. What was he doing here, at this time? I looked my question at Annie. For all I had spoken to Maud Binsley about not judging, not making assumptions, now all manner of speculation about Annie and the valet crowded my mind. She met my eye however, unwaveringly, and closed her mouth into a hard line. Then, perhaps in answer to my implicit accusation, she turned her head once more, telling me without any words that I should look again.

Below me, from the door that leads from the ancillary areas of the kitchens, another man stepped into view. He covered the space between the kitchen door and the stable and clapped his hand on the valet's shoulder. I recognised this man too. His hair was dark, thick and wavy, his shoulders broad. I knew his swaggering walk. It was Lord Petrel.

The valet led forth two horses. The men mounted and rode away.

The truth hit me with the force of a gale. It assaulted me. It must have blown me back down the landing and into my bedroom. I remember nothing but the raw, open wound of knowing I had been a fool, a pawn. I trembled with it, deluged by shock and anger and revulsion. Annie must have lit the fire, for my body thawed even while my mind continued to be stabbed with a thousand icy shards of times, places, circumstances. She put brandy to my lips, and I drank. I recalled—and reinterpreted—incidents from the years of my father's absence: Lord Petrel's unquestioned assimilation into all our plans; the sliding eyes of our hostesses as they requested him to hand my mother into dinner, as they placed him beside her in carriages and at concerts. I had been glad of it! Glad of Mama's readiness to place herself between us. All these years I had thought that she had been chaperoning *me*; that she had been protecting *my* reputation, when in fact, I had been protecting hers.

Her hypocrisy astounded me. My mother—always so correct, such a stickler for etiquette and manners and form. So ambitious to be assimilated into the most superior circles and, all the time, a cuckold— and with such a man! A man who trounced kitchen maids. The penniless heir to a crumbling pile of masonry on some godforsaken Welsh promontory!

Annie pressed another cup to my lips and I drank. The liquid was sweet with a bitter aftertaste.

'You are in shock,' she said into my ear. 'You must sleep.'

I think I recall her putting me to bed. My limbs grew heavy and the blizzard in my mind became a white-out.

I slept the clock round, and when I woke Annie Orphan was in the chair by my bed. I was glad my maid had been sent away. I did not care to explain my indisposition to her. I did not wish her to see me broken and confused.

Annie brought me chocolate and sweet pastries and watched me consume them. Then she laid out my clothes for the day and helped me wash and dress. We did not speak of the revelation, but the room was thick with it. Annie was anxious. She feared she had broken some unwritten code, but I sensed, beneath her anxiety, a clear but naive idea that the truth could never be wrong.

I went downstairs and greeted my mother with a kiss, but it was perfunctory. After that we continued with our day, quite as though nothing had happened.

46

We remained at Ecklington for the remainder of May, through June and into July. There was no talk of going to the seaside that year and I was glad of it. It was hard enough playing our charade with only the three of us present; I could not have kept it up—I could not even have stood by and watched it, much less participated in it—should we have been staying somewhere with Lady Cumberland and her coven. I observed my mother and Lord Petrel very closely but saw no hint of the affair that I knew must be going on. They were discreet. They were practiced at it, I suppose.

It is impossible that my mother did not discern my coldness towards her, but she did not ask me about it. I wonder if she guessed that I had divined her secret. If so she showed not one iota of shame. She behaved towards her lover as she always had done—ineffably polite, elegantly cool with just a trifle of indulgence because he was, after all, a viscount. We drove out in the carriage. We entertained the rector and the Binsleys to dinner. We attended church. We did everything as we had always done it, apparently in perfect fellowship with one another. The atmosphere within Ecklington was as cold and brittle as glass. It hummed, sometimes, with the quivering reverberation of pretence and lies.

The church services were conducted by Mr Eagerly in those days, the rector having retired from the work if not from the rectory, the income or the kudos of his profession. Lord Petrel took his place in the Talbot pew as he had always done, and bent his rapt attention to the sermon, and sang out the hymns like a saint. My mother read her prayer book in a low murmur. I don't know how I endured watching the poor, unsuspecting curate dispense the communion bread into their lying, adulterous mouths. I shut my own firmly and would not take it from his hand. He looked at me quizzically, but then passed on. I considered confiding in him. He was, after all, a long-standing friend of my father's and had stood, throughout my growing up, almost as an uncle to me. He was my spiritual advisor, my mother's also. Who better, who more discreet, who more qualified in morality to untangle the web of deceit she had woven? But I could not do it.

From time to time I excused myself from the calls and excursions that made up our days. Mother and Lord Petrel went off alone, often without a groom to attend them, with no sign of the unseemly eagerness they must have felt at finding themselves alone. It sickened me to think of them tethering the horse to some tree while they hurried into the woods to rut like animals. I pictured my mother on her back in some glade, his fat, white thighs between her thin, fleshless ones. There was no degeneracy, no obscenity I could not believe them capable of.

At the end of July Lord Petrel received word of his father's death. He showed no grief, only relief and a grudging admiration that 'the old codger had lived so damnably long.' Naturally there were affairs to settle and the funeral to arrange. Following a night celebrating his new status and title, and the thorough pillaging of my father's wine cellar for toast after toast to the new Lord Flintshire, he departed Ecklington. My mother and I were left alone. We looked at each other as the carriage disappeared down the driveway, our eyes speaking much but our mouths silent. It seemed that so much was permitted, in that prescribed, straitlaced society we inhabited, as long as it was not spoken of.

We avoided each other as much as possible. She slept late in the mornings and lounged the remainder of the days away on a *chaise longue* in the shade of some trees, or in the house. I walked in the grounds or read, but always somewhere away from her. We took our meals together but eschewed the dining room in favour of the breakfast room, which was smaller and where there was no possibility of any conversation out of earshot of the footmen. We spoke of nothing—new drapery for the library, the splendour of the roses, new trimmings for an old gown. I had always been studiously polite with my mother—with superlative irony she had always demanded excellent manners, a stiff adherence to the social code—but now I was wooden, perfunctory to the point of rudeness. She did not question it. As they say, people in glass houses should not throw stones.

In late August my mother's laziness turned into a malaise. She was sick, could face no food. The weather was clement and we had every window in the house open but she looked pale and sallow. I witnessed whispered conferences between Nugent and Annie—Mrs Orphan, as she was now called by the whole household—and I knew that they concocted tinctures and tonics in an effort to restore Mama's health. I supposed that she missed her lover; that she languished for want of him. It made me bitter. She had not been so downcast when my father had gone away.

By the end of September Mama's health was considerably worse. In addition to the sickness she was enervated and snappish, her nerves frayed. I suggested the physician be summoned but she absolutely refused. 'Nugent is treating me,' she said, through lips that were ulcerated from where she had repeatedly bitten them. 'I am tired, that is all. Nugent's tonic and plenty of rest are all I need.'

As October came in however, with squally storms that ripped the leaves from the trees, it was clear that Mama's condition had not improved. 'I will go to town,' she told me. 'There are specialists there.'

'I will come with you,' I offered. I did not wish to be left at Ecklington alone in case Lord Petrel—Lord Flintshire, as he must now be called—should return. For all I knew him to be my mother's lover, I did not trust myself to him alone. There was no atrocity of which I would not believe him capable.

'No,' she said vehemently, 'I will go alone.'

'Not at all,' I cried, with assumed carelessness. 'There is Elinor Binsley's wedding, you know. I must get wedding clothes, for I am to be bridesmaid.' This much was true. Elinor was betrothed to the heir to a baronetcy. The wedding was to take place at Christmas. 'The season is beginning,' I pressed. 'I long for society.'

'Very well,' she said. 'You may come.'

We had been in London but two nights when a quiet tap at my door woke me and I found Nugent by my side. She was flustered and hurried. Her hand shook as she attempted to light the candle. 'Miss Talbot,' she said, her face drawn and eerily illuminated by the guttering candle. 'Your mother is indisposed. She is very ill. A doctor must be summoned but …'

I got out of bed and reached for my dressing gown. 'Let it be done.' I said, naming our usual man. 'Why have you delayed? Let Dr Bleak be sent for.'

'It cannot be him,' Nugent hissed. 'Mrs Talbot will not have him and the nature of her indisposition … It is delicate, Miss Talbot. We must have someone discreet …'

I wrenched open the door of my room and went down the hall to my mother's chamber. Many candles were alight inside, and the fire was lit. It was stiflingly hot but my mother lay on the floor before the hearth shivering uncontrollably. Her face was ashen. I knelt beside her and called her name but she did not respond. When I turned her face to me I could see only the whites of her eyes.

'She is insensible,' I said, panicky and anxious. But then she groaned and curled into a ball, her hands clawing at her stomach. I lifted the blanket that covered her. The swell of her belly was unmistakable. Her nightgown was bloody at her groin—not much, a few smears—but enough to make me recoil.

'She is with child,' I gasped out.

Nugent nodded and wrung her hands. 'I have tried everything I know, but to no avail. And today we went to a woman ... a practitioner ...'

'A doxy with filthy hands and rusty instruments,' I cried.

'No. No. It was a draught. She took a draught. I advised against it. I have been most unwilling, but your mother...'

'Oh, I know,' I said, getting up. 'She is stubborn.'

I crossed the room to Mama's writing desk and took a piece of paper and a pen. I wrote down a name and an address. 'Send for this man,' I said.

Dr Eagerly was in Grosvenor Square within the hour. He had altered quite considerably since I had last seen him, but eight years will do that to a person. Indeed, the past six months had aged me ten or twenty years. His strikingly dark hair was as glossy as ever although it had receded at the temple. He wore a neatly trimmed beard which was quite unusual for the time. The coffee-brown of his complexion was dull, from living and working indoors. His eyes had lost their humorous light; I suppose he had seen tragedy and suffering enough to extinguish it. His clothes however, were very fine. Gone were the threadbare coat and broken boots. It looked as though his practice thrived.

He smiled at me as he put down his bag. 'I am glad you remembered me, Miss Talbot,' he said. 'I am happy to be of service to you.'

He knelt beside my mother and examined her, lifting her eyelids and peering at her eyes, smelling her breath and then running his hands over her body. At the mound of her stomach he paused, palpating it gently. He lifted her gown and probed between her legs. Then he turned to Nugent. 'What has she taken?'

Nugent, shaking and stricken, produced a vial of murky, brown liquid. Dr Eagerly unstopped it and sniffed the contents. He shook his head. 'When did she take this?'

'This afternoon, about four o'clock,' Nugent replied. 'I begged her not to. I had tried every remedy I thought safe, that I have heard to be efficacious without harming the mother, but to no avail. I did not trust *this*,' she indicated the ampoule. 'I did not trust the woman she got it from.'

'We must administer an emetic,' he said. 'It will not be pleasant. Bring sheets and a large bowl, some warm water and some salt. A good quantity of salt.'

Nugent hurried from the room. The doctor laid my mother out straight on the rug and lifted her chin so that her head was tipped back and her throat stretched. 'You may wish to leave the room,' he said to me, busy about his preparations.

'No,' I said grimly, 'I'll stay. What are you going to do?'

'I'm going to make her vomit. She must bring up what is left of the quackery she swallowed. But I fear we may be too late. Much has already been absorbed. It accounts for her catatonic state.'

In spite of all my anger and disgust at my mother, I found I was crying. 'Will she die?' I asked in a small voice.

Dr Eagerly looked over his shoulder at me. 'I will not deceive you, Miss Talbot. She may do. I am not hopeful. Where is your father?'

'He is in India. He has been for six years.'

'I see. So this child is not ...?'

'No. Not a Talbot. That's why ...'

'Yes,' he said. 'I understand. There is no need to explain. Come,' he said, gesturing me closer, 'if you wish to remain you can make yourself useful. Hold her hand, talk to her, see if you can rouse her.'

I did as he asked. Mama's hand was lifeless in mine, cold in spite of the roaring fire at my back. 'Mama,' I said, tears spilling down my face. I shook her arm and stroked her face. 'Mama,' I begged. 'Wake up!'

She groaned and drew her knees up to her stomach. Her brow was furrowed, her face a rictus of pain.

'She is cramping,' Dr Eagerly said. 'We might try an enema in addition to the emetic.' He reached for his bag and withdrew a long rubbery tube and a metal funnel.

I wiped my eyes with the sleeve of my dressing gown. 'Will it work?' I asked him, half ashamed of the question. 'Will it bring the baby away?'

He looked me squarely in the eye. His eye-glasses glimmered in the firelight and I could see myself reflected in them, white-faced, my eyes dark hollows. 'If she dies then naturally so will the child. It is too soon to deliver it. If she lives then the child will be safe, I think. Her cervix is tightly closed. She is not contracting.'

'And you will not …?

'Absolutely not.' His forehead creased, and I knew he was disappointed in me.

I looked down at my mother, so white and troubled. I wondered how it could be possible to hate someone and love them at the same time. I despised her but I also admired her—her foolish bravery, her attempt to put right what she had done wrong. But when I thought of the child all I could feel was loathing. It was the manifestation of my mother's adultery, of Lord Petrel's goatish propensities. It embodied their joint betrayal of my father's trust and generosity. 'I hope it dies,' I spat out, but then clapped my hand to my mouth, for hadn't the doctor as good as told me that the child's death would follow my mother's?

47

My mother lay at death's door for three days. Dr Eagerly scarcely left her side and neither did I. His treatment of her had seemed barbaric but it had been efficacious in that she lived. On the third day she opened her eyes. She looked neither at him not at me, but lifted the coverlet to observe her stomach. Then she began to cry.

'No, no,' she sobbed, and rolled away from us so that we could not see her face.

She remained in bed for several days, almost sulking because she had been foiled in her plan. She seemed not to regret the danger in which she had placed herself, or the doctor's trouble, or any disquiet she had caused me. Her stubbornness appalled and annoyed me. Her pride was astonishing.

'Mama,' I said to her one day, 'it is ridiculous that we do not speak of what has occurred. I cannot pretend not to know that you carry Lord Flintshire's child. You must tell me what you intend.'

She turned to look at me, her eyes very cold. 'I *intended* to rid myself of it,' she said nastily. 'Only you interfered.'

'You would have destroyed yourself,' I cried out. 'You took poison.'

'Better that, than this,' she replied. She turned her head away, and would say nothing more.

A few days later we received a message from Lord Flintshire to say he was in town, staying at his club. The note was addressed to Mama but I opened it and replied immediately, summoning him without delay. I received him in my father's study, so that Papa might be as present as possible at the interview I was determined to have with his so-called friend. Papa's books were on the shelves, his cigar box on the desk, his smoking jacket on the hook behind the door. I pulled out the chair and sat behind the desk, my hands steepled before me. I had seen Papa sit thus when receiving men of business.

Lord Flintshire was in excellent spirits, puffed up with his new status. He came quickly into the room bringing with him the smell of horses and brandy, though it was but eleven in the morning.

'Your Grace,' I said, but I did not stand up. 'Please to take a seat. May I offer you refreshment?'

He laughed, a loud bellow, throwing his head back. 'Oh good!' he said, his face alight with pleasure. 'We are to play one of our games. You are going to pretend to be very cross with me, and I must be contrite. Shall you whip me?' He looked around the room for a cane. 'You are not well prepared. I left my riding crop with the footman. Will that suffice?'

'This is no game,' I said. 'But you are right, I am very angry. I am very disappointed in you, my lord, and so would my father be.'

I do not know if it was my tone, the seriousness of my expression or my reference to my father, but Lord Flintshire's face stiffened. All hint of mischief left it. He narrowed one eye. 'Oh yes?' I could see him calculating what his offence might be and how to handle it. It spoke much to me that he did not know. Were there many ways, then, that he might have disappointed my father? His eye strayed to the drinks tray on the console.

'Help yourself,' I said. 'You will need a drink when you have heard what I am going to tell you.'

He poured himself a glass of sherry and drank the whole of it, before pouring another for himself and one for me. He placed it on the desk before me. 'You look as though you need one too,' he said. He remained standing. Curious, a little apprehensive, ready to bluster, deny, laugh. At last he burst out, 'By heavens, Jocelyn, speak. I cannot bear the suspense.'

'Very well,' I said, but took a sip of my sherry. I found I quite enjoyed having him, for once, at a disadvantage. I took a deep breath. 'I will speak plainly, sir. There can be nothing whatsoever gained by polite euphemism. The time for propriety is past, *long* past.' I looked at him frankly. 'My mother carries your child.'

I do not know what he had expected but he had not expected that. He went as pale as his florid complexion would allow, and then so red I thought he might have an apoplexy. For once he had no words; no joke, no rebuttal, no sniping sally. He did not so much sit as fall into the nearest chair. I watched his discomfort. I will not pretend I did not enjoy it.

'A child?' he got out at last.

I nodded.

He stared, blindly unseeing, around my father's study.

At last his gaze returned to me. 'Can it not be ..?'

'No,' I interrupted. 'Everything has been tried. Her last attempt was almost fatal to herself. We have feared for her life, sir, these past days. However, she is recovered and the problem remains.'

He said something then that surprised me, but curdled my stomach. 'I calculated on her being too old,' he said. My mother was then two and forty years of age, rather old for child-bearing but, clearly, not too old. What stupefied me was that he had considered the risk, rather than the morality of it. There were so many things he could have said that might have moved me, a little: 'I knew it was wrong,'; 'I felt badly, on your father's account,'; 'I loved her too distractedly to help myself.' Some remorse, some sense of having done an injury, some evidence of real attachment. But no. Just this—a gamble that had not paid off.

I stood up quickly. I could not abide to be in the same room as him a moment longer. 'She is in her private sitting room.' I said. 'You may go up to her. I assume you know where it is and will not need to be shown the way. You must decide what is to be done together. After all, this is as much your problem as it is hers.'

I left the room, leaving the door open.

I realise, now, that I made a mistake. I should not have allowed him access to my mother. Her wretched desperation and his superlatively scheming character could only have resulted in the outrageous plan they hatched together. Of course, *she* was never going to allow the least taint to her stainless reputation! *She* would endure no ignominy! She was stiff-necked, her eyes fixed on some distant point while her feet trampled anyone who got in her way.

As for him, well, naturally, he would get what he had always got—his own way.

48

My mother and Lord Flintshire remained closeted in her sitting room for the rest of the day. They called for food and wine at periodic intervals. I cannot imagine what the servants thought of his being received with so little appearance of decorum—she was not properly dressed, her hair not arranged. Nugent was sent away. Their flagrancy would have been astonishing, but I was past being astonished by them and I suppose the servants were too.

I took my dinner alone and retired to bed very early. In truth I was exhausted from my nights sitting vigil at Mama's bedside and the ordeal of facing my nemesis.

In the morning I found my mother up and dressed in the breakfast room, her hair swept up in its habitual style, a string of exquisite pearls at her throat. I had never seen them before.

'A gift from his lordship?' I asked acidly, spooning honey onto my toast.

She gave a small smile. All trace of her illness was gone. I could hardly relate the poised, collected woman before me with the one who had retched and voided uncontrollably just a few nights before. I found my eyes drawn to her body. Beneath the skirts of her dress I could see the swell of her stomach. She followed my gaze, and deliberately drew the fringe of her shawl across her lap. 'His lordship will be here shortly,' she said, motioning for the footman to refresh her coffee. 'There is a matter of import we must discuss.'

'There certainly is,' I replied dryly. 'He went back to his club, did he, last night?' I added with specious sweetness.

'Naturally,' she replied.

Lord Flintshire arrived just before noon. He was handsomely dressed; indeed it seemed to me that he had taken more than usual care of his appearance. He had regained his usual swaggering manner; I saw no evidence of his discomfiture from the day before. We all repaired to the library where a fire was lit, a pot of coffee and a tray of cakes laid ready.

'I had these brought in,' my mother explained, 'so that we will not be disturbed for the next hour or so. Jocelyn, would you mind?' she motioned me towards the coffee pot and I found myself dispensing refreshments as though we were at a garden party.

'Very thoughtful, my dear,' said Lord Flintshire, helping himself to some cake.

My mother sat on a settee which was placed at right angles to the fireplace. Lord Flintshire sat beside her, but not so close as to be touching her. They seemed perfectly relaxed, at ease, as though the matter in hand were a trifle. My heart raced very fast. I sensed a plot. I might have been mistress of the situation the day before but now I felt out of step.

'We will speak plainly,' my mother said, placing her cup down with infinite care upon its saucer.

'We are beyond anything else,' I agreed.

'Indeed,' she said thinly. 'Lord Flintshire and I…'

'Why can you not call him by his name,' I interjected. 'I am sure, in private, in your *bed*, you do not call him 'Lord Flintshire.''

'Only for fun,' the earl quipped lewdly, but was silenced at a frown from Mama.

'Very well. Theodore and I have discussed what must be done. The situation is regrettable, of course …'

'Regrettable?' I shouted.

'Yes, Jocelyn, it is regrettable,' my mother snapped. 'I hope I have given sufficient demonstration of how much I regret it. Would you wish me to bleed, to vomit, to be humiliated *more*? What further torture would you have me endure? I was ready for it, I do assure you.'

'No,' I allowed. 'I know you suffered a great deal.'

'Unfortunately,' Lord Flintshire put in, 'this matter is beyond your mother's ability to resolve by herself. We must come to her aid.'

'We?'

'Yes, Jocelyn, you and I.' He put his plate down and stood up. He took two or three steps across the hearth rug to where I sat on a low chair. He stood over me, one hand on the mantelpiece, the other behind his back.

I looked blankly from one to the other of them. 'I do not understand.'

'Do you not, Jocelyn?' the earl said, and his voice was soft, coaxing. In the next moment he was on his knee before me. He took my hand. I gave it up to him in a sort of stupor. 'We will marry,' he said, 'and raise the child as our own.'

'What?' I snatched my hand from his and pressed myself backwards into my chair, as far from him as I could get. 'That is a diabolical idea.'

Lord Flintshire's demeanour did not alter. I gathered he had anticipated my response. 'Why is it?' he asked, in a voice that I think was supposed to be winning. 'We will go away for a while, for a few years. To the Americas, perhaps. And when we return we will have a child. No one will make enquiry as to its age. Children are never seen until they are three or four anyway. Who is to say how old *exactly* ours will be? Do you not see how easy it will be?'

'No,' I said vehemently. 'I do not see. To begin with, in this tangled web of lies and pretence, how is the child to be got to us, in the Americas? You cannot send an infant alone …'

'Oh no,' my mother chimed in, chuckling at the absurdity of the notion. 'Of course not. I will come with you.'

I looked again from one to the other, barely able to believe my ears, to encompass, in my mind, the scheme they suggested. 'Come *with* us?' I repeated. 'Do you mean …' I was aghast at the idea. I had never dreamed … 'Do you mean to propose,' I got out at last, 'some kind of *ménage à trois?*' The idea made me feel ill.

Lord Flintshire, still on his knee, waggled an eyebrow and the corner of his mouth twitched, 'Well my dear,' he said, 'if you like.'

'The notion is disgusting,' I said. 'The whole plan revolts me. I will not be drawn into your subterfuge. I suppose you would have me tell Papa that the child is his grandchild, rather than your *bastard,* which is what it will be. We must pretend that George is an uncle, and not a half-brother.'

'As to that …' the earl began, but Mama cut him off.

'We will not need to say anything. They will assume,' she said. 'Think what we will be saving them from. It will be a noble sacrifice, on our part.'

'A noble sacrifice? *You* will sacrifice nothing. Your reputation will be intact; you will even keep your lover. His lordship will be the gainer in every way. Only I am expected to pay the ransom. No,' I said. 'No.' I pushed my chair backwards and got up, leaving Lord Flintshire stranded on the rug. He got up and dusted off his knee.

'I told you she would not co-operate,' he said. 'I do not know who else she thinks will have her, at her age.'

'Charming!' I flung out.

'Oh, Theodore,' Mama replied, so archly, with such assurance. 'We are not done with her yet.'

I paced about the room, my hands clasped tightly before me. They watched me dispassionately. Lord Flintshire ate another slice of cake.

At last I stopped and turned to face them. 'Let me make this very clear,' I said. 'I will not marry the earl. I would rather marry the chimney sweep. I will not pay the price for your sin.'

My mother threw me a look I knew well from my childhood, a look that told me I would reap what I had sown.

She arranged her face into a picture of disappointment. 'You will break your father's heart,' she said bitterly. 'You will ruin your brother's prospects. Our family will be shunned; people will decline to know us.'

'*I* will not do these things,' I cried. 'You, *you* have done them.' I pointed at her stomach. 'There it is: the proof. It isn't here,' I turned my finger towards myself. 'I am innocent of this crime.'

My mother lowered her gaze. The earl said, quite conversationally, 'I never met a girl who didn't wish to be a countess. Would you not like to be a countess, Jocelyn?' He came towards me again, his face all specious allure. He leaned in very close, so as to whisper words my mother would not hear. 'I will be gentle with you, you know. I can be gentle. And it will be pleasurable, I do assure you.'

Mama's expression, as her lover romanced me, was a sight to behold. She looked as though she had sucked a lemon and choked on a pip.

'You disgust me,' I replied.

'You are being very selfish, Jocelyn,' my mother said, her patience gone. She got up and, like me, moved around the room. 'After all that has been done for you. After all *I* did for you. Do you think I wanted to marry Robert Talbot? Of course I did not. But I had you to consider, and my family. I did my duty, Jocelyn, as you must. It is a woman's role. We must do our duty. And,' she concluded witheringly, 'there are worse things than being a countess.'

'I should think so,' the earl observed. 'With Talbot's money—for he will give you a generous dowry, Jocelyn—and my title, why, you will want for nothing.'

'I shall want for love,' I whimpered, and, in spite of my resolve, I began to cry.

Mother took me by the hand and pulled me on to a sofa beside her. She gave me her handkerchief and I dried my eyes. 'It will be easy,' she said, her voice more conciliatory, but I was not deceived by it. 'You and Theodore will marry, very quietly, at Ecklington. The three of us will go on a wedding tour. No one will think it odd; naturally you would not leave me alone, with your father and brother away. We will go somewhere very retired. I know of a place; indeed the arrangements are in hand. Once the child is born we will go abroad. Everyone will assume the child is yours and it *will* be yours, Jocelyn. I shall give it up entirely to you. As to Theodore and myself, that shall be at an end. I give you my solemn word. Think how delighted your papa will be when we write to him with the news. Think of what you can do for George. With a countess for a sister he will have the daughters of marquises and dukes scratching each other's eyes out for his hand.'

I grasped my mother's hand. Surely, somewhere, she had a heart I could move. 'I wish to do all the good I can for George,' I said.

'Of course you do. You're a good girl.'

'And I would not injure Papa for all the world. But Mama, why must I do a thing that my mind, my heart, my entire being utterly revolts against? There must be another way.' The Brigstocks came into my mind. They had arranged a private adoption. 'Cannot you make discreet arrangements for the child? Some respectable family ..?'

'Impossible!' Mother waved her arm, dismissing the idea. 'It could not be done for no money, and any money that is spent, your father knows of. It could be taken to the workhouse, like the Orphan girls, but I doubt its fate will be as good as theirs. It would end up in a mill or down a mine.'

'Or on the streets,' Lord Flintshire put in. 'A common prostitute. Is that what you want for it?'

'Of course not,' I sobbed. 'I would save any child from such a fate.'

'Then save this one,' Mother said smoothly. 'It is in your power to do so.'

The earl came and sat at the other side of me. 'Would it really be so terrible?' he asked.

This close to him I could see the broken veins on his cheeks, the threads of grey in his hair. His eyes were bloodshot, his teeth slimy and yellow. All in all he exuded an air of carnal dissipation, greed and fleshly appetites. He made my skin crawl. My innards clenched and I thought I might be sick.

'Yes,' I croaked, scrambling from where they had me wedged between them. 'Yes. It would be unbearable.'

Mother sighed. She and Lord Flintshire exchanged looks. This too, I realised, they had anticipated. We had not plumbed the full depths of their machinations yet. 'So be it,' Mother said. 'Remember, this was your choice, Jocelyn.' She paused for a moment and gathered herself, and I had the strong impression that the next words she would speak were prepared, rehearsed. 'I will have none of this child; I have sacrificed enough. One way or another you will raise it. You may do it honourably, as the countess of Flintshire or you may do it dishonourably, in obscurity, where no polite house will admit you, where no genteel eye will even look upon you.'

'Or you can consign it to a life of drudgery,' his lordship threw off, as though this were a small detail.

'Mother,' I cried. 'Mother! You will not do this to me! You cannot!'

'Indeed I can, if you force me to it.' Mama nibbled at a morsel of cake. I could not believe her heartlessness. 'There will be rumours that you have disobliged me. Your reputation will be put in doubt. It is very easy to cast a slur; the merest hint will do it. Then you will be sent away and nobody will hear of you again.'

'P ... papa will not allow it,' I stammered, but I felt my life slipping away from me. Indeed I felt as though reason had departed. It was a nightmare. A joke. A hallucination.

'Papa will be glad to have you out of the way, such a disgrace as he will believe you to be. He will be glad, for the first time in his life, that you are no flesh of his. And it is of your father that I particularly wish you to think, Jocelyn. Would you rather he heard of the joyous union of his dear daughter with his best friend? Or that his daughter is brought to bed with a bastard child? Think of your brother. His happiness rests in your hands.'

49

I did think of George, and I thought also of the brother and sister I had known as Brigstock, and of all Mr Brigstock had sacrificed to save his sister from a marriage that was insupportable to her.

I wrote to George, a long epistle that explained all that had occurred and the impossible choice I was presented with. I vilified our mother and Lord Flintshire and poured out my sorrow for poor Papa who had been so badly used by both. In doing so I thought it possible that Papa might not return from India at all, ever. Why would he come home to such a wife? Such a friend? My letter would mean his effectual banishment as thoroughly as my refusal to marry Lord Flintshire would mean mine. I did not know if I could bear to have his unhappiness on my conscience. I worried about George. His ordeal at school had already undermined his self-belief and it was no doubt true that the scandal of my apparent fall from grace would jeopardise his future. Would he care? Would he defy convention and put me first? It was a lot to ask, especially when, in refusing the earl's proposal I would be putting my interests over my brother's. Would I not be asking him to make a sacrifice at which I had balked?

My letter lay on my desk for some days. I copied it over, adding detail here, expanding argument there, appealing to his brotherly support and reminding him of his own dislike of the earl. But I did not send it. I knew it was hopeless. A letter would take six months to reach George in Madras by which time, one way or another, my fate would be sealed.

We were not at home to callers and we accepted no invitations while we were in Grosvenor Square. Lord Flintshire came daily and was closeted with Mama. Every day he came to me also, even in my chamber. He brought me gifts of trinkets and ribbons, all gallantry and charm, his person fresh-groomed and his breath sweetened by cachous.[xxxiii] His love-making nauseated me even though he made no physical attempt upon me—did not so much as take my hand—and when he had gone I had my maid throw open the windows though the weather outside was wet and cold. I was assailed at night by thoughts of his pawing hands on my body—kneading my breasts, his thick fingers probing my intimate parts, his sour breath on my face as he grunted and thrusted. This nightmare was made more acute by visits from Mama, who also came just as I had blown out my candle, to whisper her threats into my ear. Did I wish to be spurned by the likes of the Binsleys? Did I know that sexually immoral girls were often sent to asylums and put in chains? But perhaps that was preferable to being walled up and left to die like Clara de Clare.[xxxiv] What did I think?

'You are cruel,' I sobbed into my pillow.

'I am a woman,' she replied. 'A mother, doing my duty. Do you not think I cried when my mother came to me with your father's proposal, and then with Robert Talbot's? Of course I did. I did not wish to be a chattel to be bargained over. Unfortunately that is simply the way of it, Jocelyn. We are not allowed to marry for love. What love we are allowed we are born to. It comes from our parents and our siblings and, in time, from our children. Do you think you can be happy without it? For who will love you, Jocelyn, if we, your family, do not?'

Sleepless, in the small hours of the mornings, I thought deeply about what she had said. In refusing the earl I would save myself from his mauling hands, the outrage of his body in intrusive connection with mine. Though we would be sanctified by marriage I could not think of the deed as other than an assault, a violent trespass. I would be spared that, but I would leave myself without love of any kind. My parents would disown me in pursuance of the lie that I was unchaste. Such friends as I had would likewise cast me away. What was the point of such sacrifice? I recalled the words of St Paul: I could give up everything, but if I have not love, what do I gain?[xxxv]

A week or so passed in this manner. My sleep was disturbed and my appetite gone. I was wretched, tortured—by indecision, by doubt and a caustic sense of injustice. My letter remained in my desk unposted. Then, one morning I was woken not by my own maid but by Mama's. Nugent slipped into my room with a distinct air of subterfuge and handed me a letter that she said had been delivered the previous day but not sent up to Mama with the rest of the mail.

'It is from your brother,' she whispered, passing me the packet from where she had secreted it in her pocket.'

I looked at it blearily. 'It is addressed to me,' I observed.

'Yes,' she said, 'but of late Mrs Talbot has opened all your correspondence in advance of you receiving it. I do not think it is right. I kept this back for you, though I might lose my position for it.'

'Thank you,' I said. 'I am grateful to you.'

The letter was a long one, crossed, the paper stained with ink blots and wine spills and curled from exposure to sea-spray. George's spelling was atrocious, but I was used to that. He described his adventures, his long journey and hinted at some momentous event to occur in the near future. He announced himself to be then in Spain, just come to port at Santander. He was coming home! I wept with happiness! Oh! The relief as my dreadful dilemma fell from my shoulders. I searched for the date of the letter. It had taken some weeks to get to me. George could not be far behind.

I pinned all my hopes on him, on his being home before anything irreversible could be done, on him saving me from the devious plotting of our mother and the earl. I longed to have the comfort of his counsel, the support of his protection. George would be a man, now, one and twenty, hardened by travel, made confident and autonomous by our father's encouragement and tutelage. He would not allow me to be sacrificed.

I knew I must prevaricate, draw matters out, to give George time.

I dressed myself carefully and went down to breakfast. My mother was there, as I had expected, elegantly dressed for callers she would not receive and visits she would not make. I said nothing to her of my resolution, but asked for chocolate to drink and fresh eggs to be brought to me. Presently, as was his wont, Lord Flintshire joined us. I motioned to the footman that he should serve his lordship and then waved the man from the room.

I addressed the earl only. This was to be between he and I; my mother was irrelevant. 'Your Grace,' I began, 'I have decided to accept your offer.'

He smiled, and it seemed to be genuine; more than just the satisfaction of a point gained. My mother nodded sagely but showed no flicker of emotion, either triumph at having gained her object, or jealousy at the loss of her lover.

'My dear girl,' Lord Flintshire said, 'I am so glad. You have made me the happiest …'

I cut him off. 'Let us not pretend that this is a match of love,' I said. 'I sacrifice myself to my mother's reputation and my father's continued ignorance. I have two stipulations.'

The guilty couple exchanged a glance loaded with meaning but the earl nodded and said, 'I am eager to hear them.'

'Firstly,' I said, 'your liaison with my mother will end. When the child is born Mama will go away. Far away. I do not care where. Ecklington, here—anywhere that is not near us. She will never be given the opportunity to endanger the Talbot name again. I cannot die twice, on the scaffold of her infidelity.'

Mother flinched at my words, and the colour drained from her face, but she made no remonstrance. Lord Flintshire did not look overly concerned, as if he had tired of her anyway. He gave a small nod. 'Secondly?'

'Secondly, I will have nothing to do with the bastard spawn she carries. In name only will it be ours. It shall have wet nurses, nannies, governesses, whatever care it needs but I will never love it. Indeed I shall hate it, for what it has brought me to.'

From the corner of my eye I saw my mother recoil and her hands fly to the fullness of her dress. She made a small whimpering sound and I knew I had wounded her. It gave me satisfaction to think that she had not got all she wanted from the devilish scheme she had devised. She swallowed. I hoped her bile was bitter. She reached for her cup but her hand shook so much she could not grasp its handle.

'It shall be as you wish, Jocelyn dear,' Lord Flintshire said, and I turned to look at him. Just for a moment, in my fascination at my mother's discomposure, I had forgotten about him. He stood up and walked towards me, and bent and kissed me on the cheek.

Behind him, blocked from view by his bulk, my mother gave a strangled cry, pushed her chair back and hurried from the room.

We returned to Ecklington, my mother back in full control of her icy tranquillity. She gave instruction that the furloughed staff should not be recalled. 'We will manage,' she said. 'We will not be staying long.'

Mr Eagerly was summoned that he might prepare matters for the nuptials. He seemed very surprised to learn that I was to marry Lord Flintshire; his usually genial and open countenance puckered with concern and doubt. He looked at me narrowly as my mother spoke of the arrangements she wished him to make—a quiet ceremony, very simple. No, there would be no bridesmaids, no guests. The rector, she hoped, would consent to give the bride away, if someone must. He and she herself would stand as witnesses. There would be no breakfast. The wedding tour would begin immediately after the ceremony. It all smacked of haste, unseemly haste. She named a day the following week—would that be too soon? I suggested a day some two weeks later. I had my clothes to see to, I said, and Lord Flintshire would have matters pertaining to his estate to attend to before a trip that could last many months. Surely Papa's man of business would have to be consulted? There would be papers to be drawn up ... I went on in this vein, plucking postponements and deferrals from the air, bringing forth impediments, anything that would allow George to come home before the deed could be done.

'My dear,' Mama said with artificial sweetness, 'you cannot hold poor Lord Flintshire off *now*, you know. Your engagement has been interminable.' She turned to Mr Eagerly to add, 'You are perhaps unaware, but there has been an understanding for some time. Mr Talbot agreed before he went to India that once his lordship attained his title the marriage should take place.' I listened open-mouthed as the lies dripped from her tongue like honey from the comb. What could I say? Everyone who had seen the intimate standing of the earl within our family would believe her.

Mr Eagerly looked as though his misgivings were hardly assuaged. At the conclusion of his visit he asked me to show him the plants in the conservatory. I was sure it was a ruse, an attempt to secure some few moments' private discourse with me, but my mother pretended to need me for something in her private sitting room and he deferred to her.

'I do hope, however,' he said as he made his departure, giving me a very significant look, 'that you will feel able to call on me at any time. My cottage door is always ajar.'

Mother was much occupied with arrangements which she did not share with me. My maid was dismissed. Nugent attended me, which I did not mind. She began packing for my journey—warm clothes, thick underwear, plentiful wraps and shawls.

'I am not to come with you,' she said to me one day. 'Others will attend you. Mrs Talbot has arranged everything.'

'Where are we going?' I asked her, but dully for, if George came, it would not matter. If George did not come, I did not care where we went.

'North,' was all she could tell me.

My wedding gown arrived. It was pretty, but not what I would have chosen. Nugent set about altering it to fit me. She spoke of trimmings and flowers and satin slippers but with tears in her eyes. She behaved as though she stitched my shroud. She was assisted in her work by Annie Orphan. Mrs Butterwick had returned to Ecklington at last, fully restored in health and ready to take up her duties. I wondered how Annie felt about having the keys taken from her. I observed her as she went about her work, passing pins and basting the hem as I stood on a box in the middle of my room, the layers of tulle and gauze falling around me like foam. She was pale, as usual, her grey eyes soft, and somehow, speaking. She kept looking at me; a questioning, quizzical light in her eye. All three of us knew what Lord Flintshire was in relation to my mother but I had the idea that she knew more, and I remembered her sister Sally. I wished I could tell her not to worry—that I had no real intention of marrying the earl, that I merely bided my time until my brother should come. I did not know what would happen after that, what disgrace would come when my mother's philandering was laid bare. Of course there would be consequences. We might well be ostracised; the family, the household all broken up. All the humiliation that Mama had predicted might well come to be but I would have George and he would have me. I clung to that: George and I would be all right.

Ecklington was in a kind of stasis. There was a palpable sense of waiting in the air, in the walls. The servants walked on softer than usual feet. They whispered, and none of them would meet my eye. Many of the rooms had stayed closed up, their furniture sheeted and shutters closed. In the gloom the shrouded shapes looked like clumsy, overweight ghosts.

The days passed and George did not come.

Then, on the morning of the eve of my wedding day, Lord Flintshire rode up from the inn with a companion. 'Look,' he said, ushering his friend into the breakfast room where he had come upon us, 'who I met on the road.'

Mama and I both looked up from our breakfast perplexed. The man was tall, heavily bearded, his skin very brown, his hair cropped short. His clothes were travel stained and of a peculiar style. His coat was long, made of silk and asymmetrically cut. It was beautifully embroidered. He wore loose breeches tucked into high boots. His fingers were thick with gold rings. I looked him over curiously. Then he smiled, and I was out of my chair and in his arms. 'George,' I sighed, 'you have come.'

'George?' Mother rose to her feet. She wore a loose morning wrap and it fell open as she got up, revealing the swell of her pregnancy. George's eyes travelled down to it and then back to her face. I regarded him very closely but he did not start or recoil. I looked at Lord Flintshire and saw that his eyes were upon me, observing my response to my brother's arrival, and my spirits fell.

He knew I was expecting him, I thought to myself and, what's more, he knows I hope George will put an end to this travesty.

In confirmation of my thought, the earl raised a knowing eyebrow—smug and triumphant—and I knew I was doomed.

'You are not surprised to see George?' my mother asked when George had kissed her and we were all seated around the table.

'No.' I said. 'I had a letter before we left London.'

'Yet you did not mention it,' she mused.

'No,' I replied, sugaring my tone with oozing sarcasm, 'I did not. I thought it would be a lovely surprise for you.'

'I went to the house in Grosvenor Square first,' George said, wolfing pastries. 'I couldn't get the man there to admit me. He would not believe I was George Talbot.'

'You have changed a great deal,' Mama said.

'Indeed I have,' George agreed.

'You are well?' Mama enquired.

'Quite well,' George told her.

'How was your crossing?' Lord Flintshire wanted to know.

'Oh, a little rough. Nothing remarkable.'

I looked on in amazement. Were we really going to discuss such trivialities? What next? The weather? The success of the harvest? The progress of the war, perhaps? Why did George not ask about my mother's condition? Was he not appalled at her? Why would he not meet my eye?

'I will have your room made ready,' my mother said. 'I am afraid you find Ecklington in a poor state to receive the prodigal son. No fatted calves.'

'George is not a prodigal,' I put in fiercely. '*He* did not leave under any kind of cloud. *He* has nothing to be ashamed of.'

'A figure of speech,' Mama murmured.

George held up his hands. 'I have a sufficiency of rings, already,' he said with a smile that did not reach his eyes.

'One might say a superfluity,' the earl remarked.

'Oh, it is the fashion in Madras,' George said. 'Do not go to any trouble about my room, Mother. I shall not be staying above a day. I left my trunks in London.'

'How is Papa?' I asked. 'I trust you left him in good health?' I sighed theatrically. 'Dear Papa. How we have all missed him.'

Mother gave a delicate cough. George looked down at his plate. 'Indeed yes. He was in excellent health when I left him. He sends his fondest love.'

'You left him in Madras?' the earl enquired. 'What propelled you to come home without him, I wonder.'

George reddened. 'I had good reason, your Grace,' he said.

The footman came and refreshed the coffee pot and our conversation faltered. Then I dismissed him and he closed the door behind him.

'I am so happy to see you, George,' I said. 'I have been hoping against hope that you would come in time.'

'In time to walk you down the aisle?' Lord Flintshire suggested. 'What a splendid idea.'

'In time to save me from it,' I spat out. I turned to my brother. 'You cannot be ignorant of the way things are here, George. You see my mother,' I waved in her direction, 'and you surely guess the rest.' My other arm extended towards the earl.

'Well, yes,' George said, shifting uncomfortably in his seat. 'Yes, I gather what has transpired.'

'And are you not outraged?' I cried. 'Are you not disgusted? You yourself described this creature as wolfish! How right you were!'

I got up and stood at his elbow. He studiously avoided my gaze but fiddled with a crust of bread that remained on his plate.

'George!' I almost shouted his name.

'Yes,' he said at last. 'I am disappointed. I see what has happened, but what did my father expect?'

I stared at him, incredulous. 'You are not surprised?'

He shook his head. 'No. I am not surprised. I suspected something, and indeed, his lordship hinted as much when he was *so good* as to escort me back to Stonybeck from Brighton.' There was some resentment there, some latent fire of bitterness that gave me a flicker of hope.

Mother remained on the other side of the table, her face a stone effigy of indifference. She knew no shame, no particle of remorse.

'All these years …' I gasped out.

'Oh, and more,' George added darkly.

Lord Flintshire made a little moue, grudgingly proud of the deceit he had so consummately practiced on my father for so long.

I sat heavily back on my chair, struggling to absorb this new revelation. George stirred his coffee but did not drink any. Lord Flintshire swept an invisible crumb from his sleeve. Mother sat utterly immobile, her hands in her lap. I felt my hope—that bright star of salvation I had pinned on George—begin to crumble.

When I spoke I found my voice was hoarse, my throat constricted with dread. 'George,' I said slowly. 'Do you know what is proposed, as a remedy for this situation?'

Still he would not look at me. The crust was a pile of crumbs on the plate before him. 'Indeed,' he said. 'His lordship was so good as to apprise me as we rode up the drive. I understand congratulations are in order.'

I wondered what else Lord Flintshire had told George on the long driveway from the village to the house. Had all the advantages of their deplorable scheme been laid before him, as well as the dire consequences of not pursuing it to its execrable conclusion? Could my brother possibly have been swayed by such spurious arguments? Surely *surely* he would not stand for it?

'But George,' I said, as calmly, as reasonably as I could, 'you will not allow it, will you? You will not consign me to such a fate? George? George!' My voice rose, hysteria forcing it into a whine, almost a shriek. 'I have always loved you, George,' I sobbed out. 'I tried to save you from school—you know I did. I nursed you back to health *twice*. You know I would do anything for *you*, George.'

'I know. I know you would,' my brother said, his voice so low it was all but lost in his beard. At last his head turned to me, so slowly it was as though time had put a brake on the world. Indeed the earth seemed to shudder beneath me as though impeded in its orbit. I gripped the table as if it would tilt. I expected the cups and plates to slide to the floor. George's eyes were downcast but gradually, inexorably they rose to meet mine. Tears swam in them and trembled on his lashes. 'I know,' he said again, or, at least, his lips formed the words but no sound came. He licked them and swallowed. 'I know you would. That's why,' he croaked, 'that's why I need you to do this.'

50

November 1814

Mrs Orphan found me earlier, crying over my book. Something I had written—some words of George's—had struck me with such force they were like a dousing of cold water.

Suddenly, I think I understand.

Rain beaded the casement but I had not been conscious of it, so wrapped up as I had been in my memories. My shawl had slipped from my shoulders but I felt no cold, even though the fire had burned low. She brought lights, for the dusk had long since fallen and my single candle was barely sufficient to keep the gloom at bay. She brought the child also, who was washed and ready for bed. It was time for me to read her story, which I do every day now at about that time, when Sally and Tom Harlish have taken their children home to the gatehouse.

I roused myself and dried my eyes. I did not want her to see me crying. Mrs Orphan stoked the fire and set the lamps around the room, fussing, to distract the little girl's attention. I brought out our book from where we keep it on a low shelf, and we settled ourselves down in the comfort and warmth of the room. The drone of my voice must have been particularly soporific; she was asleep beside me before Mrs Orphan brought her cup of warm milk. She looked down at the recumbent, peaceful form and made as though to gather her up.

'Oh do not,' I cried out. 'Let her stay here for a few moments. You stay too, and let us talk.'

Annie's face is always pale but even in the glow of the candles and the firelight I could see that she went a shade or two paler. Annie has a very fine countenance; there is nothing the least coarse or common about it. I wonder if she ever thinks about her parents—what manner of people they were? What exigencies brought her mother to the workhouse? It is easy to assume low conduct—a service rendered for money paid over—but it could equally have been a case of doomed romance; a girl of good family seduced and then abandoned. Annie—and Sally too, I suppose—could have birth and breeding, as this child does. I half suspect it of Annie. She has a natural refinement of manner, an elegance of person that is quite inherent.

'What would you speak of, ma'am?' she asked at last, drawing me from the distraction of my thoughts. 'Is there something ... have I offended?' She spoke low, so that the child would not be disturbed, and the whole of our ensuing conversation was conducted in the same murmuring, confidential tone.

'Of course not,' I said mildly. 'It is just that, in my book, I have been writing my history, and I came to a recollection that has shocked me and yet has clarified for me a matter I have struggled to understand.'

'Oh?'

'Do you recall my mother's maid, Nugent?'

She nodded. 'Yes indeed. She taught me a great deal in the matter of ... in many things.'

'She was with my mother for many years I believe, from the time of my parents' marriage. If anyone could confirm my suspicion, it would be she. Do you correspond with her?'

Annie toyed with her hands in her lap. 'I did write, many years ago, but I received no response. She did give me to understand, at the time of your … your last stay at Ecklington, that she intended seeking an alternative situation.'

'That is disappointing,' I said with a sigh. 'It will be impossible to find her now. Do you receive news from anyone at Ecklington? Mrs Butterwick, for example?'

Annie shook her head. 'I think she, too, will have left. I hear from no one. I wrote to Mrs Butterwick once or twice but received no answer. Before your mother left she gave me the address of a man of business in London. I write to him when we have need of things we cannot supply ourselves. It is strange,' Annie mused, 'for Miss Nugent took particular interest in me. But,' and here she faltered and the tangent of her gaze slid to a far corner of the room, 'there were things I left behind me at Ecklington that may have changed Miss Nugent's good opinion of me.'

'I find that hard to believe,' I said. 'If it comforts you, I will tell you that my letters receive no reply either. We have been quite cast away.' I spoke lightly, and indeed I do feel, these days, that my injury does not pain me, certainly not as it once did. I spoke lightly but my words hit some nerve in Annie. She threw at me a look of such guilt and agony of soul that I could hardly believe I had read it right. Her eyes had that expression I have seen before in her; speaking, willing me to understand, but using a language that is foreign to my ear. She opened her mouth and I expected a torrent to surge forth but instead she said, 'What did you wish to know, of Miss Nugent?'

I looked down at the child, who slept in the crook of my arm. Her dark curls framed her heart-shaped face. Thick lashes lay on her cheek. I recollected the glimpses I had caught of her throughout the day, labouring up the long, steep staircase, running after the other children with stout determination to be a part of their games, begging Mr Burleigh to lift her up to sit astride one of the horses.

'You will not remember my brother George, when he was this child's age,' I observed.

She shook her head. 'No ma'am, he was already at school when I came, eight or nine at least.'

'The resemblance of this child to him is uncanny,' I said. 'Not just her looks, but her character.'

'That might not be so very surprising,' Annie suggested.

'Because they have the same mother? No,' I agreed. 'But look at me. I am my mother's daughter but I have none of the features that George and this child share. This girl has her father's dark colouring and so, it occurs to me, did George.'

Annie puzzled—for my step-father, Robert Talbot, was fair. Then her expression cleared.

'Yes,' I said, nodding. 'You see it, now.'

'You think that master George ...' she began.

'Yes. I believe that he was Lord Petrel's child, as much as this one is. George was passed off as my father's—there would be no reason to suspect his provenance. Indeed, after a year of marriage, *no* issue would have been more suspicious. But this girl could not possibly have been a Talbot, and so ... And so my mother concocted her scheme.'

A coal fell from the grate. Annie rose and picked it up with the tongs, tucking it back amongst its fellows.

'I did not know ... about the child,' Annie said, her back still turned to me. Her voice was stiff. It was almost as though she spoke against her will, the words struggling out through recalcitrant lips. 'I had no inkling of what you have just told me. I had no notion that she could be so dishonest. I thought it was all him.'

'Lord Flintshire?'

'Yes, as he was by that time,' Still, her back was turned to me. She spoke to the chimneypiece. 'I did not understand it, but it seemed to me he had in some way duped you, or driven you. I knew what he was capable of.'

Her hand reached out and grasped the mantle, which was high, on a level with her shoulder. She bent, slowly, as though intolerably burdened, and rested her head beside it. It was the oddest gesture, for her, who was always so strong and capable, so sure.

'Yes,' I said. 'Your sister Sally. I recall.' She stood thus for a few moments, weighed down, until I said, 'Annie, your dress. You are too near the fire.'

She straightened, slowly, but I could see it was difficult for her. Presently she sat down again, but this time on another chair, one pushed back from the fire and the circle of lamp light. I could not make out her face very clearly and she avoided my eye.

I looked instead at the child. I had been determined to hate her for what she threatened to force me to and for what she represented—my mother's adultery, and determination to sacrifice two of her children to her own good name. As the baby had grown, the more she reminded me of George the more I had feared her because I did not think I could bear to be betrayed again as he had betrayed me. I had loved George above any other creature. His willingness to sacrifice me had hurt more than all the rest. Now I understood George's treachery, for, of course, Lord Flintshire had told my brother the truth of his birth that day, as they rode up together from the inn. Probably even before, on their journey to Stonybeck, he had hinted at it. The awful truth had been held over George as a weapon that would wound him irrevocably, and likely kill Robert Talbot. George had just spent seven years in constant company with my father. Papa had restored George's confidence and his health, had escorted him into manhood and dazzled him with all the world could offer by way of adventure and thrill and joy. Of course George's allegiance would be to Papa. It was for Robert Talbot's sake, not his own, that he had required me to marry the earl.

Forgiveness for George washed over me. I felt it rise like a spring from my heart and flood my soul. The purity of it sluiced away my angst and resentment, the gnawing pain of my confusion. I hoped and prayed that one day, when Papa could no longer be hurt by his wife's lies and machinations, he and I would meet again.

I pressed the child to me. She stirred in her sleep, and drew a hand across her sleepy eyes, but did not wake.

I lifted my eyes to where Annie Orphan sat, her face in shadow but her grey eyes large and round. 'Does this child have a name?' I asked. 'What do you call her, downstairs? What do the other children call her?'

Annie squirmed in her seat. 'We did not know … It was not our place. But we call her Rose, on account of her mouth—like a rosebud.'

I nodded. 'Good. I like Rose, but I have a name we will add. She shall be Georgina Rose.'

'Very good, ma'am,' Annie said. I thought she was mistress of herself once more, that whatever shade had passed before was now gone.

'Oh, Annie,' I said, 'can you not call me Jocelyn? Are we not beyond the world's formality, here?'

She shook her head, and, to my surprise and alarm, she began to cry. 'I cannot,' she stammered out. 'I do not deserve such kindness.'

'What do you mean?' I asked, disentangling myself from the child and going to her side. I took her hand as she had, years before, taken mine. 'You deserve all my thanks,' I said, looking earnestly up into her face. 'Where would I be without you? Where would I have been, these years, without you to watch over me?'

I intended my words as a balm but they seemed to distress her further. Her thin shoulders shook. Her hand lay limply in mine as her tears fell.

'Oh ma'am,' she sobbed out, 'if you only knew. If not for me, you would have been … your life would have been very different. But I did not know. Oh ma'am, I did not know.'

51

Annie Orphan 1804 - 11

Lord Petrel was not long in replacing his valet and it was soon agreed amongst the servants at Ecklington that the new man was of a completely different—and better—ilk. Mr Burleigh caused quite a stir when he first came amongst them in the servants' hall, for he was a Mulatto, his skin the colour of cocoa, his hair—beneath his powdered wig—a close-cropped mass of tight, dark curls. Edna gasped at the sight of him. Madge was so rude as to reach out and touch his skin, as though she believed its colour might come off on her hand. He was personable however, and used to being stared at. He laughed off Madge's rudeness and Edna's astonishment with a bright flash of his wide, white smile. He proved himself very ready to converse with the others around the long refectory table, happy to assist the reduced cohort of footmen with their tasks when his master did not require him. He was well-built. He laughed when Mrs Bray remarked on it, that he was 'burly' as well as 'Burleigh', tall, with broad shoulders and long, strong legs. He cut a dash in his livery. He showed an interest in everything.

'Since coming to England I have worked at only one great house,' he told them. 'My mother was brought from Antigua to be cook to the Marquis of Penge. His family has plantations there, you know. The marquis' butler, a Mr Foxham, taught me my trade from boot-boy and up, and my schooling too comes from him. My new master and the marquis are old school fellows, I believe, and it is due to that connexion that I have been so fortunate as to secure this great opportunity.'

'And how do you like your new master?' Annie Orphan asked from where she sat at the bottom of the servants' table.

Mr Burleigh shrugged. 'I barely know him, as yet. He seems, for a man of his age, he seems ...' the valet struggled for some polite, diplomatic euphemism for his master's propensities. 'He seems still very energetic,' he concluded.

Annie smiled and nodded knowingly. 'I comprehend you,' she replied.

'I will be forthright with you, young man,' said Mr Swale. 'We did not like your predecessor. He colluded in your master's ... energy, as you put it. We will have none of that here. I hope I make myself very clear.'

Mr Burleigh met his look. 'Very clear sir,' he said. 'But I assure you, you need have no fear of it, from me.'

Mr Swale nodded, satisfied, and got up from the table.

'I will show you around, if you like,' Annie said. 'I was lost for the first few weeks of my being here. I was only a child then. But I will not see you flounder.'

After Mr Talbot and George had left for India the rest of the family did not very often return to Ecklington. Annie received regular correspondence from Miss Nugent as the ladies and their faithful attendant travelled from castle to manor, from watering place to seaside resort. While Annie was glad of the opportunity this lightening of her duties afforded her to learn the business of housekeeping from Mrs Butterwick and to develop her skills in the stillroom, she found that she enjoyed the periods when the Talbots were in residence for the sake of the chances it gave her to become better acquainted with Mr Burleigh.

Annie had never troubled with the young men on the estate. Of the footmen, one was old and crotchety, another somewhat fey, the rest aloof and unfriendly. Mr Burleigh was the first man of about her age with whom she felt she might make friends. He was handsome. She thought his figure very comely and well-muscled. His face was kind; his eyes soft and seductive, his mouth full and very sensual. She liked his smile. But all this would have been nothing without the distinct sense she had that their minds were in accord. He was decent, upright, honourable. As much as she had liked Tom Harlish she had always been disappointed at his fall to temptation. She did not think Mr Burleigh would be so weak. Even so, she did find herself lured into the imagining of it; herself and Mr Burleigh alone in a warm, cosy cottage, and her pulse quickened at the idea.

In 1809 Mrs Butterwick sickened. Annie used all her skill to restore the housekeeper's health but the physician prescribed a period of complete rest and she was sent to her sister's cottage on the coast to recuperate. To her surprise, and her great pride, Annie was handed the housekeeper's keys. Mrs Butterwick pressed them into her hand as she took a last look at the servants' hall and the kitchens.

'You have done very well,' she said. 'I am proud of you. No mother could have been prouder.'

Annie swallowed back a lump of emotion and dashed a tear from her eye. 'Get well,' she said earnestly. 'Get well, and come back.'

With her new status came new responsibilities. It was Annie's job to ensure that all the maids were accounted for, indoors and in their beds before the kitchen door was locked. Mr Swale attended to security upstairs, touring each shrouded, shuttered room, checking the fastenings of French windows, before pulling the bolts across the front door. They would communicate with each other in the silence of the servants' hall— a soot-fall in the drawing room that would require the attention of the parlour maid, tarnished silver that a footman should be set to polish. When the family was at home these late evening tasks were more burdensome. There might be dirty glasses to collect, candles to replace, fires to damp down and decanters to replenish. Annie and Mr Swale would mention these things in murmurs, tired and ready for their beds. Even so, Annie liked to be the last below stairs, briefly mistress of her subterranean domain. She liked to admire the cleanliness of the kitchens, the swept flagstones of the floor, to ensure all was in order before she retired to her little garret room to sleep.

It was thus, during one of the Talbots' sojourns at Ecklington, that she found Mr Burleigh alone in the dim light of the kitchen fire. He sat on one of the chairs, leaning forward, his elbows on his knees and his eyes looking intently into the embers.

'Oh! Mr Burleigh, you gave me a start,' Annie said. 'Is his lordship still upstairs?'

Mr Burleigh nodded. 'I usually wait in the stable, Mrs Orphan, but it was rather cold out there this evening.'

Annie took a seat opposite him. 'Usually?'

'Yes. It is often very late when the viscount comes away.' His eyes shifted uneasily.

'Are you sure he has not already returned to the Rose and Crown? Mr Swale made no mention of the family remaining up.'

Indeed, Mr Swale had completed his rounds and gone to bed some half an hour ago. If anyone had remained in the drawing room, he would have mentioned it, and left a footman to attend them.

'I am quite sure. Our horses are in the stable. I am afraid to tell you, ma'am, but it is frequently so.'

Annie's mind pondered the import of the valet's intelligence. 'You mean,' she ventured, 'that Lord Petrel keeps late company with ...'

'With Mrs Talbot,' Mr Burleigh finished. 'Yes. When we are at Lady Cumberland's residence, or one of the other houses, I await his return in his chamber so it is no real inconvenience. But here, or at the spa towns, of course Lord Petrel takes his own lodgings and I must wait until he is ready to go back there. Sometimes, I will own to you ma'am, it is so late as to be ... almost morning.'

Annie put her hand to her mouth. She doubted that her mistress could be guilty of such conduct—such a refined, haughty lady as she was—but she did not disbelieve Mr Burleigh. She had a sense that he was incapable of telling an untruth, particularly one as incriminating as this.

Mr Burleigh waited for Annie to collect and organise her thoughts. Then the trajectory of his gaze lifted from the fire and came to meet her own. 'You are shocked and disappointed,' he said.

'I am.'

'You have not … your experience of the world is not wide, I take it,' he suggested delicately.

'No. I came here as a child and I have been nowhere else, ever. Are things—out in the world, as you describe it—are they like … *this?*'

Mr Burleigh gave an awkward smile. 'It is not unknown. Of course it is all done discreetly. It is like that lake you have here—all gleam and glister on the surface, all sludge and slime below.'

Annie gave a little shudder. She had no reason to think well of Lord Petrel. In truth she harboured against him a bitterness that sometimes burned her throat. He was no gentleman. What he had done to Sally, and what he had allowed to be done to her—a dog would have shown more kindness. He provoked in her feelings of revulsion and loathing that were alien to her usual character. She despised him.

The following day she took the opportunity to speak to Miss Nugent on the subject.

'I am sorry to say that your information is correct,' Miss Nugent said. 'I do not commend Mr Burleigh for telling you. I am disappointed in him.'

'He did not really tell me,' Annie said, quick to defend the valet. 'What other conclusion could I reach, with him still in the kitchen at gone midnight? I am not worldly but neither am I stupid.'

'Of course not,' Miss Nugent allowed. 'You must keep this matter secret though, Annie.'

Annie sat on the window seat of the sewing room and watched Miss

Nugent repair a rent in a camisole for a few moments. 'Does the viscount ...' she began, 'does he have her in his power? We know him to be a bully. Is she perhaps forced to submit to him? If that is the case, surely it is our duty to ...'

'No,' Miss Nugent interrupted. 'There is nothing of that in it. They ...' She looked for a moment as though she would say more, but closed her lips firmly.

Annie wrestled with her disappointment in Mrs Talbot—a feeling she had never expected to entertain for the woman who had rescued her from the workhouse and set her on her current successful course. Concerning the viscount her feelings were less conflicted—there was no baseness she would not believe him capable of, and here was just one more. Foremost in her concern however, was Miss Talbot. It did not seem right to associate that innocent young lady with such shameful behaviour. She would not like to think that Lord Petrel might, in the future, ensnare Miss Talbot into his power.

It was not quite accidental, then, that early morning in the spring of 1811, when Annie, encountering Miss Talbot at the top of the servants' stair, allowed her gaze to travel to the stable yard. Annie had encountered the viscount in the kitchen as he made his departure. He had been jaunty from his illicit tumble in Mrs Talbot's bed, gnawing on a chicken leg he had purloined from the pantry. He was careless of his valet, who had patiently waited virtually the whole night through. His brazenness had appalled Annie—he had actually winked at her as he passed. It wasn't right. It irked her that Sally had been sent away in disgrace for doing once what Mrs Talbot and her lover did night after night. She grasped the handles of her buckets as she mounted the back stairs, consumed with anger and a sense of injustice.

Miss Talbot's being there to greet her had seemed like a sign. Here, Annie thought, was her friend of old, and if anyone could interfere on the side of righteousness and decorum, surely it was Miss Talbot!

Afterwards, seeing Miss Talbot's distress at the revelation, Annie regretted it, but it was too late then.

The summer had worn on, Miss Talbot pale and withdrawn, the atmosphere at Ecklington leaden. The adultery went on unabated; now that Annie saw the signs—the marital stains on Mrs Talbot's sheets, the tincture of Queen Anne's Lace[xxxvi] that Miss Nugent concocted in the stillroom, the jar of sponges soaked in vinegar[xxxvii] pushed to the back of the shelf—she wondered how she had remained ignorant for so long. Annie found herself bridling with hatred against the viscount, and when word came that he was to be earl she was defiant. All the servants were invited to toast his lordship's health but she refused, pushing away the tiny glass of wine and keeping her lips firmly closed as the hurrahs rang out.

Miss Nugent saw the incandescence of Annie's fury. She neither condemned nor condoned. 'It is not our place,' she said.

Mr Burleigh saw it too. Often he and Annie were thrown together, the last to remain awake while the earl and Mrs Talbot cavorted in the privacy of her chamber. 'I am not happy to be party to it,' he said, 'nor to what goes on at the inn, for, believe me, his lordship's appetites are by no means satiated by your mistress.'

Annie shuddered.

'Forgive me,' he said. 'I should not have said as much.'

'You only speak what is true,' Annie told him. 'If the truth is dreadful, it is not your fault.'

Annie was untouched—unkissed. Her experiences of the sexual act were all vicarious, and all adverse. It was no wonder she looked upon the thing with biased, bruised eyes. Sally had been torn and ravaged, her body and her spirits altered permanently by brutal men. For all Annie knew her own mother had suffered similar treatment, or been forced to sell herself to men who could not inspire sufficient love or tenderness in a woman to gain him a marital bed. Now here was the Earl of Flintshire, casually taking for himself what belonged to another—purportedly his friend—turning, by his devilry, a good woman bad. The quiver of sexual awakening she had begun to feel in relation to Mr Burleigh turned into a tremor of fear. She shrank from her dreams.

Annie was not sorry when, in September, the Talbots left Ecklington to return to London. The earl had already departed, taking his valet with him. She had not even that reason to wish the family to stay, when it threatened to pull her into sin.

In October Mrs Butterwick returned, and Annie was heartily glad to see her even though it meant her demotion back to parlour maid. 'It will not be for long,' Mrs Butterwick assured her. 'I have decided that I will serve the Talbots for only five more years, then I shall retire. My sister will be happy to accommodate me. When I am gone it is certain that you will be given my place.'

Annie could not see so far into the future. She had a strong premonition that something was afoot. Before her departure to London Miss Nugent had been solemn, uncommunicative, busy in the stillroom with elixirs whose nature she kept from Annie. She felt that Lord Petrel's elevation to earl could bode only ill although she did not know what the nature of that ill might be. It stood to reason with her that an evil man, given increased status and power, would likely use it for more mischief. Then there was her little mistress, Miss Talbot, now twenty five years of age and still unwed. What hope had she of escaping the sordid company of her mother and the earl? How was it possible that she would not be tainted by it?

A few days after her return Mrs Butterwick summoned Annie to her sitting room and bade her sit down. 'I have had a letter from Mrs Talbot,' she said. 'It is most curious. She asks me to make certain arrangements pertaining to a property in the north. You know the place I mean.'

'Where Sally is?' Annie mouthed.

Mrs Butterwick nodded. It had been solemnly agreed that Sally's whereabouts should never be mentioned at Ecklington. It would not do to allow the maids to think that, after all, there was nothing to be lost by giving in to a young man's desires. 'Yes. It is to be equipped, furnished—here is a list.' She brandished the paper. 'It is all ordered and will be delivered in the next few weeks.'

'That is very curious,' Annie agreed. 'I wonder why.'

'So do I,' Mrs Butterwick said, 'yet it is not our place to enquire. But that is not what I wished to tell you. You are to go, Annie. She says so quite clearly here. You are to go and be housekeeper there.' Mrs Butterwick scanned the letter. 'She speaks of loyalty, a debt of gratitude, the need for discretion. Well, I must say, as far as that goes, she could not have chosen better.'

'And … when am I to go?' Annie asked, her chin trembling. 'And … how long am I to stay?'

'That she does not say,' Mrs Butterwick concluded. 'You are to make yourself ready to go at short notice, by post[xxxviii]. An inside seat! That is handsome of her, I must say.'

Annie's mind whirled. A new situation, somewhere far from Ecklington, her little mistress and—she swallowed a ball of regret—from Mr Burleigh. How could she agree to such a thing? How could she refuse?

'I shall be happy to see Sally again,' she stammered.

How conflicted were Annie's feelings as she assimilated the change that was, so unexpectedly, to come upon her. It was impossible not to feel flattered by the confidence being placed in her by Mrs Talbot, and yet the trust of a woman such as Mrs Talbot—deceitful, lascivious—felt to Annie like a doubtful boon. She found herself swamped by all her old sensations of fear and bewilderment as she imagined herself in a new place, so far away as to be almost a new country. Sally's being there was a reassurance, but then Sally was not known for her domestic skills. Home comforts would probably be few. Marks of order and cleanliness would likely be fewer still.

Mrs Talbot, her daughter and her lover returned to Ecklington in late October with the news that Miss Talbot and the Earl of Flintshire were engaged and to be married within the fortnight. Annie's dismay knew no bounds—her worst fears realised, and just as she was to be sent too far away to offer her little mistress any aid in what surely must be her abject distress! She encountered Miss Talbot rarely but used every opportunity that was vouchsafed her to communicate her sympathy, her concern and her aid. It seemed impossible to Annie that Miss Talbot had entered the engagement willingly yet she saw no tears or remonstrance even if she saw no happiness either. She set herself to watch and to wait, to be called upon. She thought there was nothing she would not do to save Miss Talbot from such a fate. It appalled her that she was asked to assist in the preparation of Miss Talbot's wedding clothes. She would rather stab herself in the eye with her darning needle than add a stitch to that false trousseau! But yet the prospect of being near the bride was too precious to give up. She pinned and tacked, and let her eyes send what messages they could.

The wedding day was named but no instructions came down to the kitchen that a breakfast should be prepared, that rooms should be made ready for guests.

'It is to be a hole-in-corner affair,' Annie said to Miss Nugent as they worked together making up the lace for Miss Talbot's veil.

Miss Nugent pressed her lips together and made no rejoinder on that matter, offering instead, 'I am to be left behind when they go on their wedding tour. Other than that the climate is cold, I am to know nothing of their itinerary. Lately I have felt less inclined to serve Mrs Talbot. I think perhaps I shall seek alternative employment.'

Disapproval of Mrs Talbot—of the whole murky affair—was implicit in her remark.

'Mrs Butterwick says she will stay but five years more,' Annie observed. 'I wonder if she will remain as long as that. She cannot approve of what goes on here in the master's absence. Personally, I feel for the young mistress,' she concluded. 'She will stand no chance, against Mrs Talbot and the earl.'

'Perhaps Miss Talbot hopes for reprieve,' Miss Nugent suggested.

But of reprieve came there none, for Miss Talbot. Annie's reprieve came in the form of a hurried word from Mrs Butterwick. Annie was to be ready to depart to her new posting on the morning of the wedding day, very early. 'The trap is to convey you to the mail coach,' she said. 'The coach departs at six. You must be ready with your things at five of the clock.'

'I shall not see Miss Talbot in her bridal clothes?' Annie asked, struggling to hold back tears. 'I shall not be able to offer her aid or comfort before—'

'Now, now,' Mrs Butterwick said, matter of fact. 'She is to be married, not sent to the scaffold.'

During this time at Ecklington the earl had refrained from his late-night conferences in the chamber of Mrs Talbot. It was, Annie supposed, the bare minimum of respect he could show his prospective bride, to hold off from his prospective mother-in-law. Lord Flintshire's artificial decorum however, had the consequence of limiting Annie's opportunities to speak with Mr Burleigh. It was not until the wedding eve, when speculation at Mr George's return had run its course below stairs, that she had the chance of a few minutes' conference with him.

He found her in the medicinal garden, gathering such herbs as she thought might be useful to her in her new situation. 'Here you are,' he said, smiling, but without his usual broadness. 'I am happy to see you, but my happiness is heavy, for I fear we must say goodbye.'

Annie bent low over the last, ragged stalks of St John's Wort, pretending to select the choicest leaves but actually concealing her face that he might not see her tears.

'You are to accompany the bridal couple—or, perhaps I should say, the bridal trinity?' she said, her face still averted. And then, before he could answer, added, 'I am glad, for Miss Nugent is not to go. Miss Talbot will have nobody to protect her.' Now she could not prevent the tears from falling or the sobs that shook her body. She could see no leaves, no plant, no soil before her through the veil that cascaded from her eyes. 'And I ...' she stumbled on, wishing to have just one person in whom she could confide her secret, 'I am to be ...' But the prospect of it was too stark, too terrifying to say out loud.

She felt his hands gently upon her shoulders, felt herself raised up and turned towards him, felt her body pressed to his. She grasped the lapels of his coat and buried her face in his chest.

'I will do what I can,' he said at last, his voice so low as almost to be snatched away in the gusty October wind. 'And I will pray that one day we will meet again.'

'I pray so too,' Annie muttered, afraid to admit as much.

He put his hand beneath her chin and raised her face to his. She regretted her tears, the blotched face and swollen eyes, but he seemed to see none of it. He lowered his face and put his lips on hers. The gesture was so far from brutish—as she had imagined all such things between a man and a woman must be—that she gasped in surprise. It was gentle, reverent. The upsurge in passion it provoked in her belly was a barely unfurled thing, an organ she'd had scant use or understanding of before, but now awakened.

She stepped away from him, astonished and rather shocked. Did he know? Did he feel it too? He smiled at her and gave the slightest of nods. He did.

She gathered her shawl around her and walked away, her herbs left scattered on the ground.

The servants' supper that day was solemn, for all the old Ecklington retainers knew by some instinct that things were not as they should be. Speculation was rife. Some believed that Mr Talbot was bankrupt or dead in India. They brought Mr George's reappearance in England forth as their evidence. Others thought that Mrs Talbot was likely dying. That she was ill was beyond dispute and although no inducement could drag a word on the subject from Miss Nugent, her lack of absolute denial spoke as much as any hint of confirmation. The uneasiness below stairs was so strong and widespread that when wine was sent down from the dining room, that the servants might toast the couple, nobody had any appetite for it.

That evening—her last at Ecklington—Annie did not intend to sleep. Her bundle was tied, her cloak laid ready. The trap would come so early for her that she would in all likelihood have laid her head on the pillow only two or three hours before she must raise it up again. She would bid no adieus, for no one was to know that she was leaving, or where she was bound. It felt insidious to keep a secret whose nature she did not clearly know, to be creeping away as though she had something to be ashamed of. She knew, by long association with the household, what connotation would be put on her going—without a word—into the night. Her unstained character would count for nothing. She burned with ire against her mistress, by whose decree she would unknit all the painstakingly wrought fabric of her reputation. Most of all she feared disappointing Mr Burleigh; next to Miss Talbot's good opinion, his mattered more to her than anything else. One by one the servants took themselves to their beds. Annie watched them go with a heavy heart.

The doldrums of the servants' spirits had been more than made up for that day by Lord Flintshire. He had called for champagne, for hock, for claret and for brandy at intervals throughout the day, and Mr Burleigh rolled his eyes at Annie as their paths crossed near the stillroom. He knew—they both did—that the earl's inebriation would mean a late return to the inn.

Annie made her way to her attic room. All was neat, her bed stripped, the blankets folded on the ticking[xxxix] mattress. The only anachronism in her room was the plant that Miss Talbot had given her so many years before. It had flourished, growing to be as tall as Annie was herself, with frondy leaves of glossy green. She picked it up—with difficulty, for it was heavy and awkward—and made her way down the servants' stairs with it. The landing was deserted; a single lamp at the far end burned low. Miss Talbot's room was in darkness, the occupant hidden behind the drawn curtains of her bed. Her bridal gown hung on the press, a spume of lace and silk, its beading refracting the lamplight that seeped in with Annie's wraithlike figure. She placed the plant down in the corner of the room, silent as a ghost, the practice of years making her no more than a slight draught in the sleeper's dreams.

When she returned to the servants' hall it was silent and empty. A single lamp burned on a side table. Occasionally a coal fell in the grate. Annie had it in mind to occupy her last hours at Ecklington in making up a draught for Miss Talbot, a sedative of poppy seed and some other ingredients that might dull her nerves as the nuptials approached and assuage the pain of the consummation when that awful business was done. She would creep into the bride's chamber before she departed, she thought, and leave it where Miss Talbot would see it as she dressed. Miss Nugent would attend to the bride's dress and the arrangement of her hair and she would recognise the distillation and discern its intent and use.

Annie worked in her stillroom, grinding poppy seeds, adding valerian, chamomile and magnolia to a concentrate that could be carefully measured into a tea or stirred into sweet wine. Her thoughts strayed back to the night of Sally's deflowering, her mangled flesh and black bruising, her broken spirit. Her pestle mashed the seeds and herbs to a pulp as she recalled it all. As her arousal earlier in the garden, so now the savagery of her fury took her by surprise. Men like the earl, she snarled to herself, deserved to be crushed.

So great had been Annie's concentration, and so consuming her wrath that she had no exact idea of the time. She assumed everyone was in bed, that the earl and Mr Burleigh had departed. The final hour or two of her life at Ecklington ticked inexorably by and still she worked on. Her concoction was ready and sealed into a jar. It only remained to spoon out tiny, careful doses into small ampules to be mixed into medicine, and carry them upstairs.

She went to the bottom of the stair that led up to the hall, to see if she could hear the chime of the longcase clock that stood in that room. Suddenly a figure loomed into the dimness of the stairway. It was large, bulky. It stumbled down a stair or two, grabbed the banister and half slid down a dozen more.

'Who's there,' called a voice, and Annie froze, her heart beating high in her chest, her hands suddenly wet with sweat.

'I can see you,' the earl called out. His voice was thick and his words slurred. 'Answer me, for I am as good as master here now.'

With a trip and a stagger that was almost a fall he descended the final portion of the staircase and arrived in the servants' hallway, coming up short against a dresser that effectively saved him from sprawling on the floor. 'Oh, it's you,' he said blearily, 'miss fast-shut fanny Annie.' His words were slurred, all but incomprehensible. 'I am come in search of wine, for the damned footman has abandoned me and the decanter is empty.' He held it up—one of Mr Talbot's heaviest, most beautifully wrought crystal decanters. 'See?' His arm wavered as he proffered the vessel forth, partly because of its weight and partly because of his inebriation. His legs could hardly hold him up. They bent and buckled as though he were on board a ship. As Annie watched he swayed alarmingly and she reached out and took hold of the decanter lest he let it fall. 'You fetch me some,' the earl mumbled. He cast his eye around the room. 'Why is everything moving?' he grumbled. Suddenly he lurched across the flagstones, plaiting his legs. He grabbed for a chair-back, missed it and ended up prone across the refectory table.

'You are drunk, sir,' Annie spat out.

'Oh yes,' the earl agreed. 'But not drunk enough.' He turned his bleary gaze on Annie. 'Why are you still standing there? Fetch me wine, girl.'

Annie had not much experience of drunkenness but she thought it likely that the earl was on the point of passing out. His eyes, always protuberant, were staring and mazy, the whites an unhealthy yellow and shot through with capillaries. His face was bloated and suffused with blood to such a degree that it was almost purple. His stock seemed too tight for his thick neck and indeed from time to time the earl did run a restless finger between it and his throat as though it irked him.

She watched him grope for a chair without offering to assist him, as she would normally have done. She found herself to be coldly tranquil on his account. She did not care if he fell and hurt himself. She rather enjoyed his degraded helplessness. At last he managed to seat himself at the table and look about. He seemed already to have forgotten where he was. His regard travelled slowly over the accommodations of the servants' hall, taking in the dresser, the console table, the fireplace and coming to rest at last upon Annie who remained where she stood, the decanter clasped in her hand.

'Bring me some wine,' the earl said, 'Talbot's good wine, for I am to wed his prim little daughter. And then I shall break her.'

'Like you broke Sally?' Annie asked, her voice an icy shard in the warm room.

'Sally?' The earl's face was an animation of slow-motion recollection. All his expressions were exaggerated, ponderous. He shook his head.

'You do not even remember her,' Annie threw out acidly. 'She is my sister. You molested her in the stables.'

The man's eyes widened. Memory flared in the dullness of his addled brain. A slow grin spread across his face. 'Oh yes,' he said pleased to have the incident called to his mind, and with no shred of shame. 'Yes indeed. *Just* like that. But I only had one attempt at that. With this one I shall have unlimited access.' His expression crumpled into what he might have meant for a naughty grin.

A cold fire ignited itself in Annie's breast. She felt its flames envelop her body. The hairs on her arms stood up, her scalp prickled with hiss and fizz of deadly combustion. 'I will fetch your wine, sir,' she said.

She spooned her concoction into the decanter; two, three, four doses. Too much, *much* too much. More than enough. She added honey, to assuage the bitterness, and some of the wine that had been sent down from the dining room earlier and left untouched. She agitated the decanter, watching the particles swirl and dissolve with a clinical eye.

'Here you are,' she said, pouring the brew into a glass and pushing it towards the earl. He lifted his head from where he had laid it on his arms. He was almost asleep, or unconscious. His eyelids were heavy, his eyes mere slits between their crusty lids.

'That is not very much,' he objected. He reached for the glass clumsily, almost sending it skidding across the table.

'Careful,' she said, bringing it close to him again. 'It is Mr Talbot's very finest vintage. I have brought it up from the cellar for you. Mr Swale will be angry with me. He said it is too good for the likes of you.'

'Did he, by God?' The earl summoned a ragged, incoherent bluster. 'I'll show him!' He threw back the contents of the glass and swallowed them.

He pulled a face, 'Ugh!' he shuddered, gasping at the sweet top notes and underlying bitterness.

'I knew you'd appreciate it,' Annie said, pouring a second, the final glass. 'This is the last of the bottle. Mr Swale will drink it, if you do not.'

'I shall have it all,' the earl declared, swallowing down the poison. Annie tipped the glass for him, that he might drink even the dregs.

His head sank back onto his arms.

'I do not think so,' said Annie.

Upstairs the clock in the hall struck four. Behind her, in the passageway from the stable yard, came the soft tread of a step.

Annie turned to find Mr Burleigh standing in the halo of light from the lamp. 'I have killed him,' she said, lifting her arm to where the earl lay slumped on the table.

'He breathes,' the valet said, quite conversationally.

'Just now, he does. But soon—very soon—he will not. I have given him poison.'

Mr Burleigh's face stiffened but he made no move towards his master. He considered for a moment. 'Good,' he said at last.

'You had better call someone,' Annie said dully. The cold fire had gone now, replaced by a sick dread.

'Will they know that he was poisoned?'

Annie held up the glass and the decanter that she held in her hands.

'If we wash them?' Mr Burleigh suggested lightly.

'Oh, then no. Probably not. They will think his heart has failed. Miss Nugent might guess, when she sees what I have made in the stillroom. But I do not think she will say anything.'

Behind her the man on the table made a number of soft, choking sounds, his breath very shallow and wheezing. Then he exhaled, a long, rattling breath.

'There,' Annie said.

Mr Burleigh crossed the space between them and took the glass and decanter from her hands. 'There is a trap in the stable yard,' he said, casually, carefully. 'The driver says he is to collect a young woman and take her to the mail coach.'

'Yes,' Annie said. 'That is me. I was to have gone to a property in the north at Mrs Talbot's behest.'

'I think I know where you were going. You will still do so,' Mr Burleigh said. 'Collect your things. I will arrange matters here. Wait for me outside.'

Annie nodded and moved across the servants' hall woodenly. She stopped and turned back. 'You don't think ...? We had not better ...?'

Mr Burleigh shook his head. 'Collect your things,' he said again.

The stable yard was dark, full of shadows. A restless wind blew autumn leaves around in maddening circles. The horse, put to between the shafts of the trap, stamped its hooves on the cobbles.

'You are early,' Annie said to the driver. She could not make out his features. He wore a hat pulled down low, a scarf wrapped around his mouth and nose. He was some ostler or other from a livery. Not anyone associated with Ecklington. Mrs Talbot had been very careful.

Presently Mr Burleigh joined her and handed her into the trap. Then he climbed in beside her.

'What are you doing?' Annie asked wonderingly.

'I am coming with you,' he said, motioning to the driver to start. 'This morning my master gave me the address of a house in the north country. I was to make my way there today with all haste and secrecy.' He patted his coat pocket. Coins clashed within. 'He gave me ten guineas for my trouble. We will stop at the inn and collect my valise.'

The trap travelled away from Ecklington. Annie sat very close to Mr Burleigh and when he reached and took her hand, she did not refuse.

52

December 1814

My tale is done but for a very few pages. It has been cathartic to me to write it down. I am glad to know Annie's part in it. We have absolved one another and now we must both look to the future.

In regard to which she and I have had an interesting conversation about her relationship with Mr Burleigh. I had half suspected some attachment between them; they are easy in one another's company. He is gallant towards her, a *real* gentleman, whose chivalry goes much deeper than his waistcoat. She tells me—falteringly—that they would like to be married. Customarily servants are not permitted to marry and stay in post. This, she tells me, has caused a difficulty they have been unable to conquer. 'For neither of us is skilled in anything else that might support us,' she said. 'And, in any case, we do not wish to leave … here. Or you.'

'Oh, Annie,' I said, amused by her strict propriety, 'what is custom to us here? I am surprised you did not leave Ecklington a maid and arrive here a wife. I am sure that is what Sally did.'

'What suited Sally does not suit me,' she replied, a little hoity-toity. 'I wish to be respectable.'

'The world's respectability is a very moot point, as far as I am concerned,' I said. 'But do you not think that here, where we are, we can do as we wish? We are literally beyond the pale. We cannot offend society any more than its hypocrisy can touch us. This is what I have come to understand. We are free.'

She looked at me doubtfully.

'I think we should do what we feel is right, what we can answer for, honestly, on the day of judgement,' I said. 'If you wish to be married, I will not oppose it, and you will not lose your place. I wish you had spoken to me of this a long time ago, Annie.'

'You know why I could not,' she muttered. 'How could I ask it, when I had taken from you—'

'You took a life of misery from me,' I interrupted. 'I am glad of what you did.'

'But I did not know…' she waved her hand in the air, to indicate the house, the scar in the moor, the life I have come to.

'I know,' I said. 'You did not know about the child; that provision would still have to be made for it. But it does not matter, Annie. I am content. All that is behind us. I will speak to Mr Foley.'

It is Christmas. Beyond the window of my sitting room snow falls, but it is gentle, benign and cleansing. It blankets the harsh edges of the escarpment in softness.

In the village, above our hollow and across the broad-swept moor, the church bell tolls, calling us to worship. Mrs Orphan and Mr Burleigh have gone. I am supposed to help Sally keep an eye on the goose. I fear neither of us is to be trusted with such responsibility.

The shrieks and laughter of the children drown out the chimes; how much more pleasing to heaven those hosannas must be! They are playing in the garden, throwing snow at one another, leaping into the drifts, rolling on what, in summer, will be the lawn. Georgina is amongst them. I cannot tell just now, through the snow-peppered window, which warmly wrapped little body is hers. They all waddle like skittles, their pink faces glowing with health. Sally is with them, roiling in the snow, her face as rosy as the rest.

The Christmas feast is doomed. I should go and inspect it, but I cannot tear my eyes away from the children in the garden. What do they know of degree? What does it matter that one is the daughter of a gardener, another the daughter of an earl? It only matters that the one who is strong aids the one who is weak. That he who is quick and bright assists his brother who is slow. I might be the child of a rich man while their father is poor, but what does that count for? These past few years I would have been nothing—I would not have survived—without them. Mrs Orphan's manners are better than Lady Cumberland's; Mrs Orphan is naturally superior, with an inherent elegance that owes nothing to silk or pearls but is just the poise of her character. Mr Burleigh has more honour in his little finger than the Earl of Flintshire ever had. Sally's heart is generous, Mr Harlish is wise. I rate these things far above income or birth.

We will eat our goose in the grand dining room—all of us; we have no artificial divisions, no pretence, no hypocrisy.

I ought to go and set the table.

I wrote those words yesterday, and closed my book intent on my task when, through the leaded casement I saw a figure emerge from the shadowed tunnel of the drive. A stranger, here, is a relatively unusual thing. We occasionally get tinkers or gypsy women, sometimes a man with some game he has poached. Ironically he has probably poached it from us, for if the land surrounding us is not Talbot land I don't know who else it can belong to! We always buy it anyway, or exchange it for eggs or preserves, and send him on his way in good fellowship. Recently we have had soldiers returned from war looking for work. It disturbs me to see them. They bear scars—lack an arm or an eye. They have about them a look of inner trauma, their eyes in some way crazed and dull. They retain an air of astonished horror, as though they simply cannot get over the dreadful things they have seen. The children look upon these visitors as phantoms of nightmare, and it is all we can do to help them see the wounded soul beyond the disfigured skin and truncated limbs.

'Everyone you will ever meet is hurt in some way,' we tell them. 'Some hurts you can plainly see, others you cannot.'

This man—the man who appeared yesterday—had a distinctive limp, and leant heavily on a stout stick. Something about him was familiar to me. He wore a long, black coat and black boots. His hat was pulled over his hair. He stood quite still in the shadow of the trees, watching the children play as snow fell and coated his shoulders and the brim of his hat.

I wiped the inside of the glass, but of course the snow was on the outside and I only succeeded in smearing the condensation, making marks that would later have to be polished clean. I pressed my face to the glass. It was the man on the moor.

I left the room and walked along the hallway to the front door, snatching up my shawl from the back of the settle that sits by the wide fireplace.

I wrenched open the heavy door and stepped out beneath the portico.

Everything in the garden was monotone. The snow, white as sugar, matt and anything but flat, made a layer of unkindled brightness against which the trees were starkly black, or grey in shifting tessellations of twig and branch. The sky above our hollow was a miasmic lid, dense with snowflakes with an inner luminescence, like an opal. It seemed like a magic portal, a vortex that might lift me up to heaven. I put a hand out to the house. It was solid, its stones every shade of grey from pearl to pewter, its lichen coat the colour of grey sage. My dress was green and my shawl was one that Papa sent me from India a long time ago—gold, rich with embroidery depicting exotic flowers and birds I am sure could only exist in the imagination. I must have stood out like a beacon, and yet I felt barely solid, transparent, an ancient shade manifested by a trick of the light, a premonition from the future stepped back through a veil of years.

The man on the drive seemed transfixed, as though he, too, had crossed some divide and stumbled into a world of make-believe. We looked at each other across the snowy gardens, the hoary shrubs, the frozen fountain. The children played on, oblivious to the stream of questioning wonderment that added its colour and texture to the scene.

Then, slowly, so as not to break the spell I suppose, the man raised his hand and lifted his hat. A tumble of burnished curls fell forth, like tongues of fire against the deeply shadowed wood, and seemed to conjure from each snowflake its latent light of iridescent fire.

I did not even have my boots on, but I ran down the shallow steps of the house and out across the lawn.

Captain Willow stayed for a long time on Christmas Day, and ate his goose with us. He seemed not to mind the presence of the others in the grand dining room—not to find it in the least odd which, of course, it is. I presume his time abroad in military encampments has made him, like me, see the artificiality of class division. He seemed not to mind the charred nature of the fowl either. Annie Orphan, on the other hand, minded it very much, and I could see that but for our guest, Sally and I would have been roundly chastised for our negligence.

There was no time, that day, for the long narrative of our separate stories. As much as we might have wished to detail every day of the ten years that have passed since we last met, the festivities precluded it; the high spirits of the children drowned out all conversation. In any case, the effort of chewing the stringy bird kept our jaws busy enough. Over the table though, mazed by wine and candlelight, the captain and I exchanged sufficient glances for us both to know that the feelings we had harboured *then* were with us still. The only intelligence I managed to glean from him was he was staying with his cousin Caroline having arrived the previous day, and that it had been from her only that very morning that he had finally prised the fact of my being in residence at the house in the hollow.

He left as the twilight came on, disappearing into the shadowed driveway as he had appeared—suddenly, almost mysteriously—as though passing between enchanted realms. Tom and Sally Harlish were gathering their children together and would soon follow up the steep and twisting driveway but I could not help thinking that they would not overtake him, even as slowly as he walked, leaning on his stick. My heart was heavy as I closed the door. He had been a phantom, a dream, a visitor from the land of disappointed hopes.

I need not have worried. The next day he came again, on horseback this time. The snow had stopped falling although it lay thickly. The day was crisp and bright. He assured me that the moor was safe for riding so I asked Mr Burleigh to please saddle my horse while I changed into my riding habit, and Captain Willow and I rode together up the driveway and onto the moor.

For all the intervening years, all the events that had occurred, for all we had to say to each other, we rode in relative silence. The driveway was a tunnel of hush, the thin sunlight dappled on its surface, the birds within the plantation strangely subdued. As we rode I mused to myself how we might open the Pandora's box we carried between us; how much he might say of his experiences of war, his wounding and illness, how much I could reveal of the circumstances of my coming to Yorkshire. I felt that if there were one person in the whole world in whom I could confide the truth of my family's perfidy, it would be him. On the other hand, my pride told me that if I discerned the least shrinking in him, the smallest tendency to condemn, I would stay silent. That Caroline Foley had kept my residency at the house in the hollow from him did not surprise me, but once he had forced the information from her I was certain that my character had received the blackest, most critical indictment possible. What must he think of me? If I told him the truth would he even believe it? And yet I discerned no reproach in his eye, no shade of disappointment. I hoped he would broach the topic for I was sure that I could not.

It was a relief to come out between the gate posts, past the gatehouse and into the fresh, wide openness of the moor. The ground was a pristine carpet of snow, the sky above the palest blue. The air that came across to us was sharp and clean. It made my face tingle and my eyes water. The snow lay thick but a line of boulders I had not noticed before marked a pathway and I realised that we were making our way towards the milestone.

'I thought I saw you here once,' the captain said. 'I thought you were a ghost.'

'You *did* see me,' I countered. 'But my bonnet blew off and when I had caught it again you were walking away. I did not know it was you and yet, somehow, I recognised you.'

'I had been very ill,' he explained. 'My wound, and then a fever. I had come to recuperate here. My aunt, you know, is unwell these days, and Maud has sufficient claims on her time.'

'I know nothing of your aunt,' I said. 'I am very sorry to hear that she is indisposed. I do not know if I can explain to you with sufficient clarity the extent of my utter isolation. I hear nothing, from anyone. These past years I have lived in absolute retirement.'

The captain gave an odd half smile—shame and sorrow mingled—and looked away.

He thinks I deserve no better, I thought.

But to my surprise he said, 'I am very angry with Caroline. She kept me cooped up those weeks I was here, the April before last. I was not permitted even to attend church. Of course, *now* I know why. She wished to prevent us from meeting.'

'She sought to save you from the taint of my acquaintance,' I said cynically. 'I am certain that was her rationale, when you confronted her yesterday.'

'Yes indeed,' he replied warmly, 'and I called her a hypocrite, for if it does not blemish *her,* why should it disgrace *me?*'

I let the import of his words sink in. He believed the lie, then.

'She has been assiduous in her visits,' I admitted, a bitter note to my voice, 'most charitable and earnest in her desire to see me shriven.'

He turned to look at me again. 'You doubt her sincerity?'

'I don't know,' I threw out. 'Sometimes I have suspected her of wishing to turn the screw, to gloat. She has been very desirous of seeing … what she thinks of as the proof of my infamy. But I have not obliged her.'

Captain Willow narrowed one eye. 'Perhaps she just likes children,' he suggested mildly, 'having none of her own.'

That gave me pause. I had not considered it. 'I may have been wrong in my reading of her motivations,' I said in a low voice, 'but she has been very stiff-necked, apart from once … but that was in relation to another matter. I saw no gentleness in her demeanour, only judgement and disdain.' It did not escape me, even as the words came out of my mouth, that for a long time my own attitude towards Georgina had been one of harshness and blame. I am sure I blushed. Captain Willow, who watched me closely, could not have helped but see it.

'I blame myself,' he said presently. 'Caroline *has* turned into a very hard and self-righteous woman. If things could have been otherwise, if I could have loved her, as she loved me—'

'You cannot *make* yourself love a person,' I put in, 'even as you cannot stop yourself from hating one.' I considered before continuing, 'And yet both may happen of their own volition, in time. I hated Georgina for a long time. I could not help it. But now I love her very much.'

Captain Willow gave a little cough. 'She is …?'

'Yes,' I said.

I determined that I should allow him to go no longer in his misapprehension. I opened my mouth to tell him the truth about

Georgina, but before I could speak he said, 'I could never have loved Caroline as she wished me to love her. Even if I had married her, we should have been more like brother and sister than husband and wife. Neither of us would have been happy, and so I would not yield to the pressure to offer her my hand. And then I met you. She sees only *that*—your interference in what she sees as our romance. She does not believe in my own resolution. I am sorry to say that it has caused her to act in ways that were very wrong. I can hardly tell you how has she has injured *you*. When I discovered it, yesterday morning, I was angrier than I can express. There was a scene …' He shook his head. 'Afterwards she was unequal to attending church. I went with Mr Foley, for of course he had to officiate and I hoped to encounter you. But when you were not there I came in search of you.'

'I was never more surprised to see anyone in my life,' I said. 'You materialised as though from another realm.'

'I felt I had entered some strange, other-worldly place,' he said. 'All day, at table, with your … friends. That odd, sequestered house—so ancient. The trees crowding around … And seeing you there, in the flesh, when I have only been able to conjure you in dreams, and believed you utterly lost to me. It all seemed like an enchantment. I forgot all about Caroline and our terrible altercation in the morning. When I got back, she had gone. Mr Foley has had her removed to a sanatorium. He would not say much, but the maid gave me to understand that she spent the day raging as one who has lost her wits …' He turned a stricken face to me. 'What have I done?'

We had come by now to the milestone, and we both dismounted. The wind blew strongly, cold but not biting. I imagined Caroline's fit of jealous rage. I had seen her indulge in it before, at the picnic, when she had deliberately impaled herself in a thicket of thorns.

'She has always been highly strung,' I said. 'I am sure Mr Foley will ensure she gets proper care. You cannot be held responsible, for you have only revealed what she has kept hidden.'

'Hidden, indeed,' said Captain Willow, his voice heavy and low. He put his hand on the dark, moss-covered stone of the mile post, leaning heavily upon it, the knee of his injured leg bent, bearing no weight. I realised that he had not brought his walking stick with him.

'Does your injury still trouble you a great deal?' I asked.

He nodded. 'My leg will never be whole again; the muscle is wasted and there is much stiffness in the joint. The pain sometimes is … That day, the day I walked here having by some chance escaped Caroline's clutches, it pained me very much. I had walked much further than I ought, and was in some doubt of being able to return to the vicarage without assistance. My head was mazy with the pain. I was weak anyway from the aftermath of fever and,' he pressed his eyes with his thumb and index finger, as though to press away a painful recollection, 'it assaulted me as I stood here, leaning against this pillar, that the man I had been had gone, that I would ever afterwards be lame, incomplete. And then I saw you, or, a vision of you, as I believed, and it seemed to me that some cruel hand had drawn back a veil to mock me. When I had known you, at Ecklington and afterwards at Brighton, *then* I had been a man—whole and strong—a man who had found the completeness of himself in loving you.' His voice broke as he uttered these last words. As he spoke his head had sunk, his eyes shielded behind his hand, and in my compassion and, yes, in my love for him I stepped towards him. I reached up and put my hand behind his head, and pulled it onto my shoulder. He let it rest there for a few moments. I could feel the rise and fall of his shoulders, the raggedness of his breathing. When he spoke again his voice was raw, suffused with emotion. 'I am not the man I used to be, Jocelyn,' he said, and his use of my name set a flame alight in my heart. 'I am haunted by my experiences of war. When you lie in some terrible, rat-infested drain, and listen to men and horses screaming, the blast of cannon, the smack of musket shot into your comrades … These are things that torment a man …' He lifted his head from my shoulder and looked into my eyes. His eyes, as blue as ever, had lost their humour. I could see the pain in them, and in the creases at their corners. His golden hair was threaded with silver. The flame in my heart spread outward, its heat seeping through me like fine wine. Love and compassion coursed through my veins, an empathy so strong it made me breathless.

'Your bouquet of memories ...' I began, but stopped, for it was ridiculous to think that such a naive, romantic idea could have sustained him through the horrors he had described.

'Wilted quickly,' he confirmed, with a glimmer of his old humour.

'I too have had my troubles,' I said. 'I am not the green girl you used to know.'

His eyes held mine. They did not look away. 'I know,' he said. The power of his assurance kindled sparks of helpless gratitude. I needed no one's forgiveness but to know that it was mine anyway made my limbs tremble as with a holy drenching.

'It doesn't matter to you?' I asked wonderingly.

'Nothing matters,' he said. His arms had crept around me and now they pressed me to him. 'Nothing matters. I don't care about what has gone before.' He leaned down to kiss me.

Everything within me yearned towards him. I thought I would combust if I did not pull his lips to mine but I held back. 'She is not mine,' I croaked out. 'She is my mother's child. I am ...' My cheeks were on fire, my whole body a blazing torch of desire that belied my mumbled claim. 'I am pure.'

'I don't care, I tell you. It doesn't matter,' he said fiercely.

Then I kissed him, wantonly, with the passion of a woman with anything but purity on her mind. We made love in the snow, against the ancient milestone, surrounded by the endless moor and the impassive stones. Above our heads curlews wheeled and cried.

'I love you, I love you, I love you, my Jocelyn,' he gasped at the last, and we mingled our tears.

'Ohhh,' was all I could reply.

'Now I am what the world believes me to be,' I said later, as we rode slowly back towards the gatehouse. I did not care.

The day was fading. The sky above was greenish, rippling with iridescence. Purple shadows stretched themselves across our path, making the snow around them shine with amethyst fire.

Through the thickly leaded casements of the gatehouse I could see the heads of Mrs Orphan and Mr Burleigh. There were sounds of merry-making, the children's squeals of delight. I could hear Georgina's fluting voice in song. 'They have left the house to us,' I said.

Captain Willow—Barnaby—put out his hand and smiled. 'Come then,' he said.

Barnaby saw to the horses while I went inside and stoked up the fire that had been left burning in my sitting room. Food and drink had been left there for us; a plate of cold-cuts, bread and butter, the spirit stove so that I could brew tea, also a decanter of wine. I drew the curtains on the darkening day, smiling to think of Annie Orphan's preparations for my deflowering. Too late, I thought.

When he came into the room Barnaby looked hesitant, and I feared for a moment he regretted our abandon on the moor. He reached into his coat pocket and pulled something out. In the firelight I could not make it out.

'I did not get to explain to you how Caroline has injured you,' he said.

'I think I have forgiven her,' I said dreamily, turning to look into the fire.

'You mentioned that you receive no word from Ecklington, or elsewhere?' He perched on a footstool opposite to where I knelt.

I shook my head. 'Not a syllable,' I said.

'But you write?'

'I did do, at first. But receiving no reply, I stopped. Mrs Orphan says that she writes to a man of business if she needs anything, and he supplies funds. I know nothing of that. But she gets no news from Ecklington either.'

'And here is why,' said Barnaby, proffering two packets of letters. They showed signs of age but as they fell from his hands I could see that their seals were unbroken. One packet contained all the letters I had written to George, variously addressed to Ecklington, to the house in Grosvenor Square, to Papa's club and to the bank—I had tried every avenue to communicate with him. Also in the bundle were the letters I had sent to my father in Madras. There were some directed to Mrs Butterwick at Ecklington. I presumed these were the ones Annie had sent. So they had heard nothing from me! What must they have thought? That I was proud? That I was stubborn? That I luxuriated in what they believed to be my sin and degradation? The other contained but three letters. One letter bore my brother's execrable handwriting, another my mother's flowing script. A last was in a hand I did not recognise. I picked them up in wonderment.

'How came you by these?'

Barnaby creased his brow. 'They were in my cousin Caroline's possession. I am sorry to say that she has been stealing your correspondence.'

It took a moment or two for the information to register itself in my understanding. While I waited I set about the brewing of tea. 'She always offered to take our mail,' I said. 'She never posted it?'

Barnaby shook his head. 'It seems not. And no doubt she took charge of the letters directed to you, promising to bring them to you. Mr Foley gave me these at breakfast. It seems he has been looking through Caroline's things. He is as dismayed as possible, you must believe me. He had no notion of her subterfuge.'

'I do believe you,' I replied, but my mind was not on Mr Foley or even on the injury Caroline Foley had done me. I fingered the letters, aching to open them but fearing the contents.

'Open your letters,' Barnaby said, getting up and taking over the tea preparations. 'You have waited long enough for news.'

I opened George's letter first. It was dated some two or three weeks after Georgina's birth, and had been written from the house in Grosvenor Square. His script was, as always, difficult to make out, but I will precis the contents here.

My dear sister Jocelyn

Our mother has returned to Ecklington. She came directly here from wherever she has left you but I can by no means discover where that is. Her lips are utterly sealed on the subject of what has occurred. If I mention your name she assumes a look of vague bewilderment, as though she does not recall anyone called Jocelyn. I see now that this is how she has maintained her composure all these years; she can convince herself into believing whatever version of reality is convenient to her. I am appalled by her icy lies, and to all intents and purposes I have broken with her. I have sent her to the country. By mutual agreement she will reside there on a permanent basis unless she is a guest elsewhere or takes a house by the coast or at a watering place. In any event she will come no more here. *This house shall be my residence, and when I marry my wife and I will make this our home for the time being.*

I am to marry, Jocelyn. This news I could not communicate to you at our last, sorry meeting, for I did not wish to arm Lord Flintshire with further ways to impose himself upon our family. Bibi is an heiress of Anglo-Indian pedigree with whom I became acquainted in Madras. Her mama, an English gentlewoman long resident in India and married to an Indian Nawab, was bringing her home with a view to her coming out into English society and making an advantageous match. I could not allow her to slip away from me and so I sought Papa's permission to take ship in pursuit. I caught up with them at Cape Town and had happily staked my claim before we docked at Liverpool. Dear Jocelyn, this was one of the reasons why I could not take your part against our mother and her lover. The scandal that would certainly have emerged would have precluded my own suit with Bibi's father, the Nawab Bahadur.[xl] As well as being a respected plantation owner he has influence within his government and with the East India Company. My marriage to Bibi will be for love, but it will also carry enormous benefits to us in terms of business. Bibi is gentle and kind, and very beautiful, well-educated—she runs rings around me! But that is no great feat—as modest and charming as it is possible to imagine. If you could have met her, as I wished, I know you would have loved her, and embraced her as a sister. Mama, because she is proud and embittered and wished me to ally myself with an English noblewoman, has turned her face from the match and will have nothing to do with Bibi or her mother. But I do not care, for I have our father's blessing and very soon now I hope to have her father's permission also.

When I wrote to Papa to inform him of my happiness I agonised over how to present to him the matter of your current situation. As you know from the evidence before your eyes, letter-writing comes hard to me, and you can imagine how blotted and scratched the missive I drafted to Papa was. I did not think he could endure to know of our mother's betrayal but neither would I be complicit in her lies by perpetuating them. I would not malign you. In the end I intimated some strong difference of opinion between yourself and Mama, and stated that, so far as I knew, you were to enjoy a stay of some duration with friends in the country until matters might resolve. Whatever the truth of his actual relation to us, no one could have been a better father than Robert Talbot has been. I do not think he will ever return to England. India suits him; he is himself there. Nevertheless, it is to him that we owe our loyalty and our duty. Whatever we owed to our mother, she has forfeited.

Naturally I informed Papa of Lord Flintshire's death. It pleases and relieves me that he, who would have made much mischief, is put beyond the ability to injure either of us. He has cast a long shadow over my childhood since that woeful journey we took together from Brighton to Wales. He threatened to destroy everything our father had created, to ruin our mother's reputation and to take from me my rightful inheritance in favour of the Eagerly brothers who, as I am sure you have divined, are our father's half-brothers and could inherit the Talbot fortune if my own legitimacy were to be called into question. This, anyway, was Lord Flintshire's threat should he have been thwarted in his plans to marry you. He made it abundantly clear to me as we rode together that morning from the Inn to Ecklington. As well as the delicacy of my betrothal to Bibi, this influenced me in my inability to take your side. I saw that you, however reluctantly, had come to the same decision, and although your determination faltered slightly at the last I am sure you would have pursued the matter to its ugly end for our father's sake. Thank goodness the necessity was removed from you! Perhaps it is wrong for me to thank God for the demise of a man who was (much too) intimate with our family for so many years, but I do not scruple to do it. I am sure that you do too. As for the other matter, in time we will set things right. Mama's despicable web of intrigue shall be unravelled. Bear with me, Jocelyn, until I put my own situation onto a surer footing, and then all shall be well.

I await your reply with much eagerness and some trepidation, for I fear that you will feel that I have abandoned you to our mother's devilish scheme. I send this via Papa's man of business here in town. He resists all my efforts to reveal your whereabouts but he undertakes to ensure that my letter reaches you.

Your loving brother

George Talbot.

I looked up from the pages in my hand to find that Barnaby had brewed the tea and placed a cup on a small table by my side. I picked it up with a faltering hand and took a sip. Of course Barnaby had not read the letter but in some way that was a part of my sense of being inseparably connected to him, I spoke as though Barnaby had assimilated its contents just as I had.

'George will think I do not forgive him,' I murmured, reaching out to the packet of letters from me that George had never received. 'Because, as far as he knew, I did not reply.'

Barnaby spoke no word but his eyes filled with unutterable sadness tinged with a species of impotent rage that filled me with foreboding. 'It is worse than that,' I whispered, translating his expression. 'Is George *dead?* Did he die, believing me to hate him?'

Barnaby got up from his chair and knelt on the rug at my side. He took my hand in his but I snatched it away and put it to my mouth. 'Oh, my God,' I gasped. 'George is dead!'

'No, he is not dead,' Barnaby said quickly, reaching out and capturing my fluttering hands. 'No. He is well. He thrives. His business is successful. He is happy. He is content, with his wife and his children. No, Jocelyn, do not fear *that*. But he believes *you* are dead. Your mother told him you had died of a fever, and the child also.'

Rage overwhelmed me. I leapt from my seat and flung myself across the room. How *could* she have been so callous, so cruel? To have wiped me out of existence with a lie! How could such baseness exist? My fury had no object since my mother was not within reach, but I snatched up instead the letter that was in her hand and tore it open with such force that the paper ripped half across.

The letter was short, written in a firm hand and dated February of 1813. It began without preamble. *I am dying. I have an incurable tumour on the spine that will likely carry me off slowly and with a great deal of suffering. If it spreads towards the brain I shall go mad. If it progresses the other way I shall be paralysed. I do not complain, but thought to write to you while I still can, before the laudanum to which I increasingly have recourse, or addled wits, prevent me from forming a coherent sentence.*

Jocelyn I regret the disservice I did you. Disservice! Is *that* what she calls it? *It gained me nothing but lost you much. I have made you the best reparation I can by letting it be known that you and the child have both died. I have not seen your brother but I understand he was inconsolable at the news. I hope this comforts you.* Comforts me? To think of my brother distraught, and without proper cause? How skewed her idea of comfort is!

So, Jocelyn Talbot and her illegitimate daughter are no more and you are free to reinvent yourselves as whomsoever you wish, to go wheresoever you wish so long as you do not rise from the grave to embarrass your brother, your father or yourself. No one, you know, will believe the truth. I do not advise you to attempt to restore your reputation; you will be laughed out of town.

The late Earl's notion of the Americas had merit and I suggest you consider it carefully. You shall not lack for funds. The lawyer who has overseen your maintenance so far has been paid to manage matters for you for as long as necessary. He will supply any documentation you need for travel and a generous sufficiency of money for your future. He will be the sole living creature who knows your true identity apart from Caroline Foley, who has also been well-recompensed to watch over you but who has her own reasons for wishing you cold in the grave. I am confident that neither will betray us.

The Eagerly brothers attend me. The irony of this is not lost on me. One doctors my body, the other ministers to my soul but both, alas, are lost beyond redemption. You are not, however. It pleases me to pass to you the words of comfort Reverend Eagerly brought me today. "Therefore if any man be in Christ, he is a new creature: old things are passed away; behold, all things are become new."[xli] You, now, Jocelyn, have an opportunity that is given to no one in the corporal realm. You can make yourself anew.

Hester Talbot.

I let the letter fall from my hand and it drifted onto the hearth. 'She is dead, then?' I asked.

Our tea had grown cold and Barnaby had poured us both a glass of brandy. He handed me mine and nodded. 'A year or more.'

'Did she suffer?'

'Yes,' he said. 'My uncle intimated as much.'

I searched my feelings. Was I sorry? I found I was—not that she was dead, particularly, but that she had died in pain. Perhaps, after all, I had not paid all the price for her sin. The brandy burned my throat but restored me. My anger had dissipated in its fumes and I sat down heavily in a chair.

'The world believes me dead,' I remarked.

'It does. *I* believed it, and when I saw you on the moor that April day, as I said before, I thought I had seen a ghost. But then, something my aunt said when I saw her just a few days ago … I think I mentioned that she is unwell. Her mind is confused and she speaks nonsense much of the time … but something she said about Caroline having you under her eye made me reconsider. What if I had seen, that April day, not a ghost but you? It would explain why Caroline kept me confined throughout my recuperation, why she would not even allow me to attend church. I determined not to remain with my aunt and uncle for Christmas but to come here without delay and get the truth from Caroline. I hardly dared hope … but if there was even a possibility of you being here I had to find you.' He looked as though he would say more. He hovered on the rug before me, his glass held awkwardly in his hands. I regarded him expectantly but he only said, 'You had better open the third letter.' He handed it to me and I broke the seal. It was dated November 1813

Dear Madam

I have the honour to be lawyer to the late Mrs Talbot of whose demise it is my sad duty to inform you. In accordance with Mrs Talbot's direction I write to confirm the arrangements she had put in place for you. I hope it is some comfort to you, delicately placed as you are, that your mother had your care and welfare uppermost in her mind even as she faced her own mortality. She was a splendid, honourable lady and I extend my condolences on your loss.

With regard to your peculiar situation: I understand that you adopted Robert Talbot's name but that your father was Mrs Talbot's first husband. My advice would be that you revert to your original name, since parish records will be in existence for that.[xlii] I can arrange corroborating documentation, references and letters of introduction for yourself and your daughter as required. Your mother intimated to me that you would probably travel to the Americas. I await your instructions.

I remain your servant

William Burrows.

'So I *am* free,' I said wonderingly. The idea made me smile because, for the past several months I had felt entirely free. I had felt happy. I was not sure how this revelation would impact me—what I would do, where I would go. Did I wish to leave Yorkshire? Would it not be a fine thing to remain here, hidden in the hollow, free of society's restraints, for the rest of my days? On the other hand, as my mother had stated, a fresh beginning was something vouchsafed to few. 'It is suggested that I re-invent myself as Jocelyn Gilchrist—that was my father's name—and leave Jocelyn Talbot at peace in the grave. What is your opinion of that idea?'

Barnaby knelt again at my side. 'I have no opinion of it, since, if I have my wish, you will soon become Jocelyn Willow. But you *are* free,' he assured me. 'I will not curtail your liberty to remain here in anonymity or to go out into the world new-made. What I can promise you is that in becoming my wife you will forfeit neither your security nor your independence.'

I looked at him in wonderment. 'Do you wish to marry me, Barnaby? In spite of everything?' I had in mind the woeful behaviour of my family and the legacy of deceit that must necessarily always accompany me; the existence of a fatherless child for which the snooping world would always require some explanation. But also the oddness of the life I have carved out for myself here in the hollow. And this was not to mention my wanton behaviour of a few hours before. Given all these things, was I not a liability?

He smiled. 'Oh yes,' he said. 'I care nothing for the world. I have my property in Wiltshire, tucked away amid the Marlborough downs, and am content to farm my pastures and breed my livestock there. I dislike the noise and bustle of town, so I never go there. I see Maud occasionally, but I think she will harbour no prejudices even if we do not tell her the truth.'

'For George's sake we cannot tell anyone the truth,' I said. 'Maud must make of me what she will. It is possible she will refuse to know me. Would you lose her favour, for me?'

Barnaby said, 'It will not come to that, I am certain. The Binsley family is not without its skeletons. Wiltshire is nothing like Yorkshire. Have you been? It is not so wild or desolate as here, nor so pretty as Oxfordshire, but it is beautiful in its own way. Will you not come and live there with me? You and Georgina and … any of your friends here who wish to join us? I have a number of cottages and a lodge-house. Accommodation and work shall be found for all.'

I grasped his hands. 'You are so kind,' I said, my eyes filling with tears. 'They are become my family. I should not like to leave them if they chose to come.'

'But *you* will come?' he urged, lifting his hand to my face and sweeping a stray tear away with his thumb. 'You and Georgina will come?'

I looked searchingly into his eyes and saw there all the frankness and honesty and a glimmer of the old humour I had loved without knowing it when I was a girl.

But even as I gazed at him some deep frisson gave me pause. A thread of hesitation twanged in my soul, setting up a resonance that hummed in an off key note. High above our heads the crows on the roof set up a clamour and it echoed down the chimney in a ghostly remonstrance. I felt the house around me like a jealous lover, its stones closing in, the roofs lowering into a frown of discontent. Would I really leave it, now, after it had restored and sheltered me for so long? Would I abandon it to the encroaching trees, the damp and the mournful wind over the lonely moor? I could feel it waiting to see if I would spurn it.

'I have come to love this house,' I said quietly.

'I understand,' Barnaby said, 'but a house cannot love you as I do.'

I nodded; it was true.

As he kissed me, a billow of sooty smoke erupted from the fireplace and engulfed us.

AFTERWORD & ACKNOWLEDGEMENTS

I wrote this novel during 'lockdown' in the UK, which—for me—lasted from 16th March to 15th June 2020. We had been due to move house on 19th March and our household chattels were all packed into boxes, our kitchen equipment reduced to the minimum and the only clothes not in vac-packs were three tops, a pair of jeans and the requisite quantity of underwear.

I hadn't planned to begin a new book until at least September, when, I reasoned, we would be settled into our new place, have it decorated and at least a plan for the new (large) garden sketched out. As it was, on 16th March we cancelled the removal company, the alteration in insurances, the change of address notices and all our plans for the foreseeable future. I went up to my study, which was bare of everything but my desk and chair, unpacked my laptop and began to write.

I wrote every day, seven days a week. For those thirteen weeks my husband did all our shopping (properly masked and gloved) and I did not go out at all apart from for exercise and, to be honest, that was rarer than it perhaps should have been. *The House in the Hollow* is the result. It is a prequel to *Tall Chimneys*. I found that the odd sequestered hollow in the Yorkshire moors would not let me go, the solid grey house that hid there had more secrets to yield. Both had bewitched me, as they had Evelyn and now also Jocelyn Talbot.

Since writing the book what has occurred to me is the link between its story and the lock-down. Jocelyn Talbot is as effectively locked down in her Yorkshire house as we all were in ours. She is separated—as we were—from family and friends. Her life shrinks to its essentials, as ours did. What she finds, in that reduced, inner-space, is freedom. She finds herself. She finds acceptance and forgiveness. She finds what's *really* important and, at last, she finds love.

If you were one of those heroes who spent lock-down working in essential services, I thank you from the bottom of my heart. If you were someone for whom lock-down was a nightmare of stress, balancing work and home-schooling and money worries, if you were trapped indoors with no recourse to a garden or a park, if you were lonely and afraid, my heart goes out to you and I am in awe of your fortitude and endurance. But if, like me, you found, amidst the strangeness and chaos, a nugget of pleasure in the quiet, the joy of seeing a bird on your window ledge, the thrill of a friendly voice on the phone or over the wall, I think you'll understand what this book is really about.

My thanks are due to my friend Becky (B Fleetwood), who always encourages me. Carole Henderson (Carole Henderson Therapies) was a fund of information concerning the healing properties of plants and how ailments might have been treated in the period. Sallianne Hines of Quinn Editing Services handled my story and my—sometimes shaky—grammar with gentleness, and explained the difference between an en dash and an em dash with patient erudition. Sarah Reid (Red Raw Studios) came up with the perfect cover and Rebecca Watson (Rebecca Watson Brand Designer) did the graphic design with her usual speed and efficiency. Thank you all.

Thanks—as always—to Tim. You can never know what you mean to me.

YOUR REVIEW MATTERS

Thank you for reading this book. As a self-published author I don't have the support of a marketing department behind me to promote my books. I rely on you, the reader, to spread the word.

A short review provides great feedback and encouragement to the writer, and is a helpful way for others to know if they might enjoy the book. Please write a few words along with your star rating.

BIBLIOGRAPHY

Victorious Century by David Cannadine, Penguin Random House, 2017

The Anarchy: The Relentless Rise of the East India Company by William Dalrymple, Bloomsbury Publishing 2019

ABOUT THE AUTHOR

Allie Cresswell was born in Stockport, UK and began writing fiction as soon as she could hold a pencil.

She did a BA in English Literature at Birmingham University and an MA at Queen Mary College, London.

She has been a print-buyer, a pub landlady, a book-keeper, run a B & B and a group of boutique holiday cottages. Nowadays Allie writes full time having retired from teaching literature to lifelong learners.

She has two grown-up children, two granddaughters, two grandsons and two cockapoos but just one husband – Tim. They live in Cumbria, NW England.

The House in the Hollow is her eleventh novel.

ALSO BY ALLIE CRESSWELL

Game Show

Relative Strangers

Crossings

Tiger in a Cage

The Cottage on Winter Moss

The Hoarder's Widow

The Widow's Mite

(Coming soon) The Widow's Weeds

(Continuing the Talbots' story)

The Lady in the Veil

Tall Chimneys

The Highbury Trilogy inspired by Jane Austen's *Emma*,
comprising:

Mrs Bates of Highbury

The Other Miss Bates

Dear Jane

[i] A combe is a small, steep-sided, dry valley or naturally occurring hollow in a hill.
[ii] 1780 - 1784
[iii] 1775 - 1783 The American Revolutionary War
[iv] Sir Arthur Wellesley (later Duke of Wellington) led the British and allied campaign in Portugal for five years from April 1809
[v] Deal is a cheap, soft wood.
[vi] Out in society, meaning they had been presented at court or were formally marriageable.
[vii] 1 Corinthians 13:11
[viii] A small fabric roll or bundle in which ladies kept sewing materials and other items for emergency repairs to their dress like ribbon, bootlaces etc.
[ix] Maratha Wars 1802 - 1805
[x] By Henry Boyd, published in 1802
[xi] Queen Charlotte's Ball was an annual event at which young ladies were presented to the King. After this they were 'out' or marriageable. Proceeds from the ball were given to Queen Charlotte's Hospital.
[xii] Marigold has anti-inflammatory properties and is effective in treating sores, ulcers etc.
[xiii] Similar uses to Marigold
[xiv] Willow Bark has analgesic properties
[xv] Witch Hazel works as an antiseptic
[xvi] As a kitchen maid Sally would have earned about 14 guineas a year, so this would have been a substantial amount but not a fortune. However it is much more than they would have paid a common prostitute.
[xvii] A town which Wellesley's troops besieged, unsuccessfully at first.
[xviii] Euphemism for lavatory
[xix] An open-topped equipage seating four.
[xx] A closed carriage.
[xxi] The privy.
[xxii] War was declared on France on 18th May 1803
[xxiii] Soothing herbs, famed for the treatment of anxiety and depression.
[xxiv] There is no Earl of Flintshire although Flintshire does form part of the lands of the Earl of Chester. No affiliation or relationship is implied here.
[xxv] The home of Mrs Fitzherbert, mistress of the Prince Regent
[xxvi] The maker of the iconic boots worn by Wellington
[xxvii] France sold a great tract of its territory in America to the US in a deal known as the Louisiana Purchase. The price was 50 million francs.
[xxviii] A German State that later became a Kingdom in its own right
[xxix] The Archangel Michael is the defender in battle against wickedness and the snares of the devil. He is generally pictured as blond haired.
[xxx] 29th September. Michaelmas traditionally marked the time of year when servants and farming labourers renewed their contracts.
[xxxi] Something that did not actually occur until 1806
[xxxii] Elite fighting force of the Royal Navy
[xxxiii] A breath-freshening sweet made from essence of rose or violet, cardamom,

liquorice or cinnamon.

[xxxiv] Sir Walter Scott's 1808 poem Marmion has as one of its motifs the immurement of the fictional nun, Clara de Clare, on grounds of unchastity. The stanza XXV reads: And now the blind old abbot rose, To speak the chapter's doom. On those the wall was to enclose, Alive, within the tomb.

[xxxv] 1 Corinthians 13:3 And though I bestow all my goods to feed the poor, and though I give my body to be burned, but have not love, it profits me nothing.
[xxxvi] An ingredient, along with ginger and neem oil, believed to prevent pregnancy by precipitating menstruation.
[xxxvii] Another method of contraception practiced at the time.
[xxxviii] The mail coach was the fastest way to travel but was not always very comfortable. However, an inside seat was much preferable to an outside one.
[xxxix] Canvas woven from hemp, also called hurden or tow, was the material used for mattresses. It prevented feathers or straw stuffing from escaping or poking through.
[xl] Literally means Illustrious Viceroy, a title of Indian nobility.
[xli] 2 Corinthians 5:17
[xlii] The government's registry of births, deaths and marriages did not begin until 1837, so a birth certificate as such would not have existed. However baptisms, marriages and funerals were registered in the parish records.

Printed in Great Britain
by Amazon

83706822R00222